REVIN'S HEART

STEVEN D. BREWER

Published by Water Dragon Publishing
waterdragonpublishing.com

ISBN 978-1-962538-52-7 (Trade Paperback)

10 9 8 7 6 5 4 3 2 1

FIRST EDITION

ACKNOWLEDGMENTS

THE SERIALIZATION OF *Revin's Heart* was my debut work as a new author. When I first wrote "The Third Time's the Charm", I had a sense for the larger world in which it was set, but I had not fully plotted out where the story would go. Having the opportunity to tell the rest of the story has been immensely gratifying. But I could not have done it without support of many people.

I'm grateful to my editor Steven Radecki who gave me enough to rope to ... No, who trusted me enough to commit to publishing the rest of the series having seen only the first two parts. I have learned a vast amount — and have had a huge amount of fun — writing the rest of the series with the support and partnership of him and Water Dragon Publishing.

I need to also acknowledge the enthusiastic cheerleading of my review team, in particular Francesca Forrest and Martha Allard, who've read the episodes as they've come out and provided unflagging support and encouragement.

I would be remiss to not also mention my brother Philip and my son Daniel who are my trusted beta readers. They read my earliest manuscripts, while they're still sketchy, to help me identify problems with story structure and pacing. And to offer both helpful comments and unfailing mockery.

And there's my mom, Lucy, who reads everything I write if only to tell me how everything I do is perfect. Though even she admits that some things are more perfect than others.

And my wife Alisa. She won't read anything I write, but is always supportive and helps manage my life so that I have the time and attention to devote to my new career as an author.

Finally, thank you to you — all my devoted readers and fans — for coming with me on this adventure!

REVIN'S HEART

CONTENTS

1

THE THIRD TIME'S THE CHARM

"DO NOT NEGLECT YOUR READING, young Revin!" Professor Dirge said.

Revin, startled out of daydreams, looked away from the tiny, half-translucent window, back toward the heavy leather-bound book of 3rd century property laws on the tiny cabin table. He blew on his fingers, trying to warm them, before turning the page. Professor Dirge peered with watery eyes for several minutes while Revin pretended to read, but eventually he began to write again, scratching on the parchment, and glancing periodically at Revin whenever he dipped his quill. Revin stared at the letters on the page until they started to run together and swirl around with his thoughts. His mind's eye returned to the captivating vision outside the airship window: the boundless ocean dotted with tiny islands; white clouds forming on the lee side of volcanic peaks in the afternoon sun;

and the glowing blue tow lines of remmers, drawing them inexorably forward, toward an unfamiliar land and unfamiliar people. And a new life, however circumscribed by Professor Dirge and his dusty books, but which promised an escape from his past. A knock at the cabin door brought welcome relief.

"The Captain invites you to dine with him this evening," the attendant said. "Please present yourself at the Captain's quarters in thirty minutes."

Revin began to close the book, but Professor Dirge rebuked him with a glance.

"I'm sure another fifteen minutes of reading will give you great benefit, Revin," he said. "You may find an interesting anecdote to relate during dinner."

Revin didn't think that was likely. He was currently reading about the origins of laws that governed stripping the coats of arms from men convicted of inappropriate relations with other men. He had been working for a year as the Professor's apprentice, and tried to educate himself in the law — whenever he could get out from under the Professor's mania for having him research ancient history.

Finally, Professor Dirge finished his paragraph and Revin gratefully closed his book.

Before they headed to dinner, Revin made his excuses to stop in the lavatory. After using the facilities, he checked his chest bindings to make sure they were tight and didn't show through his shirt. And the pad, which was still spotting, but thankfully the worst of the flow was done. Then he stepped out and rejoined the Professor to head to the gondola.

Their cabin was the last of the 10 poorest cabins on the *Madeline*, located at the very end, under the aft gasbag. It was dark and cramped ... and bitter cold. They had to walk the length of the airship, along the narrow gangway, through the cargo stowage, and past the midsection team of remmers — one of the two teams of remmers which kept the airship stable and drew it forward. By tying into lines of ethereal flow moving at various speeds, the craft was pulled through the air, but remained under control.

Remmers had originally been used on ocean vessels because they could draw the ship when there was no wind, or even against the wind. But they had come into their own when lighter-than-air vessels, capable of moving three or four times the speed of ocean vessels, had been constructed. Gasbags containing lighter-than-air gasses lifted the airship, but it was the remmers that provided the motive force.

At the midsection, a craft always carried a team of apprentice remmers whose job it was to maintain attachments to slower moving ethereal streams to keep the craft stable and under control. Remmers were always in short supply because there were so few people who showed aptitude. And most who did could still only maintain a single attachment — and that inconsistently, at first. Maintaining an attachment required constant attention. The two master remmers worked in shifts in the gondola and were responsible for the key attachments that provided the motive force. Occasionally key attachments slipped or ethereal streams changed speed or direction, which could take the craft in unexpected directions, so maintaining multiple attachments was critical for the stability of the vessel. Each remmer stood at a station that had a floor-to-ceiling pole to which was attached a sliding metal frame that held a lens as big as the span of Revin's fingers. The lenses allowed the remmers to see the ethereal streams and bind an attachment —which appeared as a glowing, blue towline — to the pole.

After passing through a hatch, Revin and Professor Dirge entered a heated section of the *Madeline* with increasingly luxurious cabins until they reached the ladder which led to the captain's cabin in the forward gondola. Looking ahead, before climbing down the ladder, Revin could peer into First Class — the fanciest sections of the airship — where the wealthiest passengers were feted and treated and dined.

Entering the gondola, Revin found himself nearly blinded by the light coming through huge windows on both sides of the airship. The vision, so tantalizingly indistinct through their tiny cabin window, lay out before him in staggering clarity. The steward had to direct Revin twice before he shook his head and allowed himself to be guided into the captain's dining room at the aft end of the gondola.

They were seated near the foot of a long table with a number of other passengers and several of the officers. People introduced themselves to one another and exchanged pleasantries. Revin was seated next to an aristocratic young man who took one look at Revin and did not deign to look at him again. Revin heard him introduce himself as "Lance" to one of the other passengers who was of a suitably high class.

After everyone was seated, the captain strode in and greeted everyone formally. One of the officers stood and proposed a formulaic toast, and then the meal was served.

Revin savored the wine and ate gratefully, even though the food was strange and not to his taste. He would have preferred simple bread, eggs, and cheese to crackers, fish eggs, and spiced eels. But, when you are hungry enough, almost anything tastes good.

"I hear they've captured the Queen of Belleriand," Lance said to the officer seated next to him.

Revin's ears perked up, wondering if this represented a titanic shift in the war.

The main topic of conversation among the officers and aristocrats involved the never-ending war with Belleriand. The island nations were evenly matched, and neither could hope to overwhelm the other, so the battles generally tended towards raids and skirmishes ... and attacks on shipping.

"She's the fastest airship in their armada," the officer said.

Revin realized with disappointment that it was not some actual queen.

"She was on the ground when our boys took the aerodrome. But she's ours now."

After dinner, some of the passengers stayed to chat. The sun had set, but there was still a redness in the clouds that Revin's eyes greedily devoured. He dreaded the moment he would have to return to their tiny, freezing cabin and be shut in the dark all night.

As he savored those last few moments, he was startled when he heard the captain hurry past him, attended by a younger officer. The captain was speaking quietly, but Revin distinctly heard the words "evasive action" as he strode by.

Professor Dirge seemed to have had a bit too much to drink. Normally rather meek, he was declaiming to a small audience of wealthy passengers — several of whom tried more than once to make polite excuses, before turning tail and fleeing. The conversation finally petered out, and the Professor led Revin back toward their cabin.

As they climbed the ladder, the airship suddenly took a violent turn. The Professor lost his footing and swung precariously by his hands alone. Revin closed his eyes and held on, hoping that the Professor's stomach was stronger than his felt — he didn't want to end up wearing the Professor's dinner of fish eggs and spiced eels. They both succeeded in regaining their footing as the airship leveled out. As they reached the top of the ladder, the ship turned violently again, throwing them onto the floor. Revin could hear screams from cabins up and down the length of the airship.

The Professor had taken several steps aft and, tumbling back, managed to catch hold of the ladder. Revin had just reached the top, but lost his grip and began to slide forward along the gangway. Professor Dirge still clung to the top of the ladder when several sharp explosions shook the airship. The ladder suddenly plunged down, taking the Professor with it. As Revin fetched up against a bulkhead, he could smell clear, fresh air flooding the hallway. Revin lay, stunned, as the enormity of what had just happened sank in. The Professor was gone. And he was alone.

Men ran along the gangway.

They must be marines from Belleriand, Revin thought. *But they aren't wearing uniforms. So pirates, then.*

One pointed a crossbow at him for a moment, but then ran on. They began to call out to one another as they secured locations throughout the ship. Revin heard cries of anger and some clash of steel.

One man didn't run, but walked purposefully toward Revin, expressionless, nodding as the men called out, "All secure, Cap'n".

He stopped where Revin was still lying on the floor. "Get up, boy!" he said, extending a hand.

The captain of the pirates was short, but compact and lithe, with powerful muscles like a gymnast or acrobat. His complexion was fair, with a close-cropped beard and long hair pulled back in a ponytail. His loose-fitting clothes looked like silk and seemingly concealed no weapons.

Revin shook himself out of his shock, reached out cautiously, and allowed himself be pulled to his feet.

The captain looked him up and down and then winked, in defiance of his grim mien. "Do you work on this here ship?"

"No, sir," Revin said, finding his voice. "Passenger."

"Well, you're not a rich one, by the look of you. Tell you what, boy. Go back to your berth and no harm will come to you."

They locked eyes for a moment and the man gave him the slightest of nods.

Revin moved carefully along the wall and edged past where the ladder down to the gondola had been. He could hear the movement of air and see light glimmering on waves far below. A large, thin-faced man with dark hair pushed past him and caught the captain's attention.

"The wind's changed, Will. Storm coming up," he said. "Be here in two or three hours."

"See to the remmers, Grip," Will replied. "Make sure they don't try to pull us apart."

Grip turned and followed Revin aft.

Beginning at the front of the ship, Revin could hear yells and screams as the armed men began to ransack and loot the first class cabins. Revin saw men shifting cargo from the hold. They had cut a hole in the side of the craft, and were now loading boxes and crates on pallets to be run down along a line that led at a gentle angle down into the dark — presumably to another airship. There was another hole in the airship at the very end of the gangway, just past the last of the cabins.

Revin reached his cabin and shut himself inside. He collapsed into his seat and began shaking with tension and fear. Seeing the professor's unfinished manuscript on the table, he closed his eyes, leaned back, and tried to take deep breaths. What was going to happen? Of one thing, Revin was certain: the pirates did not mean the *Madeline* to be airworthy when they were done.

Revin fumbled through one pocket after another, but found nothing but a few coins and the key to the trunk. He thought of what he might have in it, but couldn't think of a thing that might be useful. He pulled out the Professor's trunk and began rummaging through its contents. He shoved clothes aside one way, and books and papers another, hunting for something useful. Near the bottom, he found a small bag of coins; he pocketed those. He also found a small, sharp knife that the Professor had used to erase letters from manuscripts — it was terribly sharp, but was insignificant as a weapon.

Revin had begun to hatch a plan. In the more luxurious parts of the airship, there were real walls; in this part, the walls were lacquer-stiffened, stretched canvas. If he could go through the back wall, he would be behind the guard. He was terrified at the thought of trying to attack the guard, but maybe he could get past him and onto the other airship. His plan didn't really extend farther than that. But, since he had become convinced that the Madeline was doomed, he couldn't shake the feeling that the ship was already plunging toward the ocean.

Behind the seatback, Revin listened and, hearing nothing, tried to cut a small hole. The noise seemed incredibly loud in the cabin. The whole wall seemed to bow out as he pressed the knife blade against it. He began to worry he would snap the blade. He paused for a moment, deterred, then felt along the edge of the wall and, tearing the cushions away, along the floor. He found stitching there that held the fabric to the frame. It was hard to get the point into the stitches, but, as he cut them, they parted almost silently and soon he had a gap that he could hold apart and peer through.

He could see into what had been an interior space inside the *Madeline,* between the exterior of the airship and the walls that enclosed the gangway. There, he saw the breach the pirates had made coming through the skin. He couldn't see much, though, due to the poor lighting — there was no light in his cabin and only a little light from the gangway that filtered into the interior space.

Revin cut more stitches, more eagerly now, and quickly produced an opening he could crawl through. As he began to squeeze through, he belatedly realized that there was no flooring in the interior spaces of the airship. For a moment, he overbalanced and almost fell in, but, scrabbling for a handhold, he caught hold of a rope, used by workmen to move along the interior, stretched between the ribs along the exterior wall. He dragged himself onto the rope and edged along the wall until he reached the entrance to the pirate ship.

Revin found the ships winched together with a gangplank and rope bridge. He peeked into the *Madeline* and spied the back of the guard not more than 3 feet away.

Looking into the pirate ship, he could see nothing. Steeling himself, he set foot on the gangplank and walked over without looking back, as quickly and as smoothly as he could.

The pirate aircraft seemed nearly abandoned. Revin heard some activity to his right as plunder from the *Madeline* was shifted across a second rope bridge near the midsection. Even in the dark, he could tell the craft was much more open than the *Madeline*. Lanterns strung along the middle illuminated the walkway, but left the sides and upper reaches of the craft in shadow. The craft was stripped down to the bare essentials for speed. Revin felt his way along the wall, trying to keep out of the light, and looking for a place to hide. He found cargo netting securing some boxes to the wall where there was a narrow space that he could just squeeze past a rib to get into. Beyond, between the ribs, there was ample space. He sat down, wiping the sweat from his face, and began to wait.

Waiting was torture. In the darkness and silence, he could hear sounds from the doomed *Madeline*, people crying and sobbing. Revin rocked back and forth. He stood. He knotted his fingers together. He racked his brain for what he could do. Then an idea struck him and he was flooded with resolve.

He squeezed back out and ran to one of the lanterns. After pulling it from its hanger, he carried it over to the wall of the aircraft. The lantern was a strange design, but suddenly Revin realized he that had seen its like before: miners carried such lanterns where gas might explode. Sweating, he got it open, and, tearing a piece from his shirt, he fed a bit of cloth into the flame, until it began burning. Then, he worked on transferring the fire to the cargo netting. He got a spark and began blowing on it, until a flame appeared.

He had been lucky: the movement of the lamp had gone unremarked, but the appearance of light near the edge of the aircraft caught the eye of the men working forward. They came running back with a shout, which suddenly turned to a cry of horror as the flame raced up the netting and began to lick at the side of the aircraft.

Revin felt his hair singe and he began to scrabble backwards. The fire was spreading with unbelievable speed. He gained his feet and sprinted for the gangplank, jostling with the four or five men who, but a moment before, had been running to catch him.

The flames burst through the skin of the craft. It began to collapse in the middle, dragging the *Madeline* toward the flames. Will suddenly appeared and, taking a sword from a dumbfounded guard, began hacking at the ropes holding the two craft together. The two ships separated and, with a tremendous roar, the burning aircraft fell away. The *Madeline* was thrown violently to one side and everyone ended up in a tangle on the deck.

Revin realized that his arms were being held. Will turned towards him, his face purple with rage.

"You've cost me my ship, boy," he shouted, gesturing at him with the sword. "And you've done for us all."

"It's no worse than you were going to do to me," Revin shouted back into his face, too angry to be afraid. "To all of us."

Will mastered himself and gestured to his men. "Bring him along." He walked back along the gangway to the hold, and clapped Grip on the shoulder. "Well done, Grip. You cut the one and I cut the other. But if there was ever a time we needed your skill, it's now."

"Aye, Will. The wind is picking up already."

Will turned to Revin, indicating him with his sword. "You there. Take me to your cabin. I want a word with you."

Revin led him back to the cramped cabin and took his seat. The cabin was a wreck: the professor's trunk sat open and the seat torn apart. Will glanced in the trunk and noted where Revin had cut through the back of the cabin, then he closed the professor's trunk and sat down on it.

"You're resourceful, lad. And bold. And you're a man of learning?"

"I can read. I was apprenticed to Professor Dirge, who'd been hired by the Duke of Havelock to teach law at the new University."

"Professor Dirge, eh? A lawyer? A fate worse than death for a man like yourself," Will replied with a wink.

Revin didn't laugh.

"Or a woman, eh?"

Will's revelation felt like a knife through Revin's guts. Will stood up and turned away. A flash of lightning illuminated the room, followed by a rumble of thunder.

"Aye, you're not the first I've seen. The professor's eyesight was none too good, I'll wager."

"What gave me away?" Revin whispered.

"When I gave you a hand up, earlier I could see your chest bindings through your shirt. Once I knew what to look for, it wasn't too hard to tell."

"You can't imagine what it's like growing up in the duchies for a woman," Revin said bitterly. "No choices, no opportunities, no chance to go anywhere or do anything. Or be anyone."

"You're talking to a pirate. Every mother's son of us has a story just like that, though I'll admit that what you say goes double for a woman," Will said. "But the real question is: are you a woman pretending to be a man? Or are you a man in a woman's body?"

"I ... I don't know."

"It matters not to me," Will said. "Boy you are and boy you shall remain.

"But I saw right off that you were going to be trouble. I says to myself, 'Let's pitch this one through the hatch before he does you a turn.' But I didn't." He turned and looked Revin in the eye. "I can always use one such as yourself on my side. We'll all have to work together now, just to stay alive. But when we reach the end, you'll think about what I said."

The wind was picking up and the back wall of the cabin began to flap. Will went out to supervise the men trying to tack up some fabric over the hole where they'd cut into the *Madeline*. Rain was beginning to fall — a light pattering at first and then heavier drops. Revin sat, and then stood, and then paced. Lightning flashed again. Then the storm hit.

The *Madeline* heeled over as one of her attachments failed. The wind caught her and she tumbled sideways throwing Revin against the wall. He heard a scream and then realized it was the sound of tearing fabric. The wind had gotten behind the hole cut in the side, peeling the skin forward, tearing the outer wall of his cabin away. A long strip had torn loose and was running forward. Over the wail of the storm, Revin heard a shout from outside: Will was dangling from the end of the fabric.

Hail began to hammer the *Madeline*. Will dangled eight feet down as the strip continued to tear inexorably forward. Revin caught hold of it with his hands and braced his feet against the rib. The tearing slowed, but he felt himself being dragged forward; he wasn't strong enough. Grip suddenly appeared in the cabin and caught hold of the fabric. Together, they stopped the tearing, but did not have the strength to pull Will back.

Revin saw a blue flash and thought they'd been struck by lightning, but then he realized that there was a remmer towline pointing nearly straight up into the sky. The weight on the fabric grew less. Arm over arm, Grip pulled Will up. The towline flickered out once Grip had a hold of Will's hand and pulled him in.

As soon as Will was in the cabin, he and Grip began working frantically to tie off the end to the table support. Gusts of rain and hail filled the cabin. Revin crawled for the door as the *Madeline* bucked and heaved at the whim of the storm's touch.

In the hallway, Revin sank shuddering with exhaustion against the wall, panting to catch his breath. He looked back into the cabin in time to see Will embrace Grip.

"Get some rest, love," he said to Grip. "I'll see to the remmers for a bit."

Will ran back toward the remmers while Grip helped the men stitch the patch more securely. After a few moments, Revin felt the *Madeline* swerve wildly against the wind. Suddenly, the noise and vibration decreased.

Grip stepped back and settled onto the floor next to Revin. "There's none better than Will in a pinch," Grip said. "He's got us turned into the wind again."

"Is Will a remmer?" Revin asked.

"Aye. Once a remmer, always a remmer, as they say."

Revin closed his eyes and leaned his head back. He realized that he was absolutely exhausted and couldn't keep his eyes open any longer. The roar of the storm and bumps from the wind gusts reminded him of swimming in the ocean as a child — the roar of the waves lifting him up and setting him down.

Revin fell asleep.

Revin and Grip awoke when Will nudged them.

"It looks like we're losing gas."

"Damn!" Grip said. "We'll never be able to fix that in the dark."

"Aye. It's near dawn, but not near enough by half. We'll need to dump ballast." Will turned, then looked back at Revin. "Are you coming, boy?"

"What? Why me?"

"It'll be fun, boy! It's too tight down there for most men," Will said, "Grip and the others won't fit. But you and I might be able to make it."

He reached a hand down. Revin grabbed on and let himself be pulled to his feet. Will grabbed a lantern and all three walked forward to the remmer's stations.

The remmers were exhausted after a night of constant effort to keep the *Madeline* from being tumbled by the storm. Half of the remmers lay asleep on the floor or in the corners. Grip jumped to work, keeping the others focused, moving from station to station, keeping them on task. The storm had passed, but strong winds, coupled with the lack of the key gondola remmer stations, meant that the *Madeline* still required constant attention. At the front of the remmer's cabin stood a hatch with a ladder leading down into the crawlspace.

The crawlspace was dark and cramped — less than the height of a man. The compartment was dominated by a large tank filled with water, used both as fresh water supply and as ballast for the aircraft.

"Don't trust your foot on the hull — like as not, it'll go right through. Keep your feet on these ribs and supports. It's a wonder she's holding together at all."

Will edged into the space along the side of the tank carrying the lantern. "I can see the valve, but I can't reach that far."

He backed out and handed Revin the lantern. Revin edged into the space, like he'd seen Will do. Laying down in the narrow space and reaching his hand under the tank, he could just get his fingers on the valve. The valve was normally operated by a long shaft that came up from the gondola, but the shaft had snapped off. He could feel the lever that the shaft connected to, pulled it, and was rewarded with the sound of water rushing out of the ballast tank. He was afraid he would have to keep holding it, but it had been damaged and bent when the shaft pulled away and now seemed stuck in the open position, so he struggled up and worked his way back to the end of the tank.

"Well done!" Will said, clapping him on the back. "Now we need to do the forward tank before we become unbalanced."

They checked with Grip once they'd climbed out of the crawlspace, who confirmed that, although they were still heavier than air, their rate of descent was slowing as the ballast was dumping, but already Revin thought he could feel the floor tilting forward as they ran along the gangway.

To get to the forward ballast tank, they had to pass through First Class again. Guards stood posted at both ends of the corridor. Anger radiated from each of the cabins they passed. They went through an elegant dining room, far surpassing what Revin had seen in the gondola, and then into a kitchen. Will seemed to know right where a panel in the floor would reveal a ladder leading down into the crawlspace. This time he was able to reach the valve control shaft himself and tie it off, releasing the ballast.

Will was rubbing his hands together and stepping back to the ladder when they heard horns and cries and the clash of steel. Revin, reaching the top of the ladder, saw one of the pirates fall back with a quarrel standing out from his chest. For just a moment, Revin's mind teetered between worlds and then he made his decision.

Revin threw the panel upon the top of the ladder and stood on it. Will began pushing against the panel and tried to throw him off, yelling, "Let me out, boy! Let me get to my men."

"I have the captain of them in here!" Revin yelled.

Will shouted imprecations and threw himself against the panel, but couldn't lift it enough to throw Revin off.

Two uniformed men charged into the kitchen and Revin saw a third standing by the entrance, aiming a crossbow at him. He raised his hands cautiously.

They motioned him away and opened the panel, weapons ready. Nothing happened. They motioned again to Revin, who came over and looked down into the space. Light was flooding in through a hole in the floor. Between wisps of fog, he could see the first rays of sunlight reflecting off the ocean below. Will was gone.

The guards set up a search for the pirate captain throughout the ship, but were unable to find him. It was presumed he had leapt to the ocean. The guards had come up in the early morning fog and boarded the ship in the same way that the pirates had, and half of the pirates had been killed. The other half would be taken to Havelock to face hanging. Revin hadn't been able to meet Grip's eyes when he saw him kneeling with the prisoners. He found he was glad that Grip hadn't been killed outright, but didn't see how he could hope for the man's situation to improve.

•　　•　　•

For the next three days, the *Madeline* sat tied up at a guard aerodrome on the coast. Revin and the rest of the passengers were questioned. Revin was questioned endlessly because they couldn't decide whether he was telling the truth or not.

Eventually, in the afternoon of the third day, he was released with the remains of his and Professor Dirge's belongings. Suddenly faced with liberty, he felt overwhelmed with the decisions confronting him. What to do next?

The coins he had taken from the professor's trunk left him with some means — at least enough to travel to the city and manage a few days of lodging — if he was careful. He found a wagon that was going that way and, for a few copper coins, was able to bounce along in the wagon with the two trunks to the University. He figured he should go there at least to tell them what had happened to Professor Dirge.

The University was housed in what had been the Duke's ancestral home. Built in a generation when fortresses rather than palaces were the order of the day, it had been extended with more luxurious buildings, but still presented a low and stolid exterior. The Duke, having built a much more luxurious palace, had left the old fortress to start the University after his mother had died.

At an arched gateway in the outer wall, Revin jumped off the wagon and pulled down the two trunks. Before he could speak, one of the guards called out, "Hey! Are you Revin? Where have you been, boy! Professor Dirge will have your hide!"

"The Professor?" Revin said with confusion. "He's here?"

"To be sure! And I've been told to send you up immediately and have a porter take the trunks to your lodgings. Now run! The Professor has taken up residence in the West Wing."

Revin's head was swimming while he ran through the dark corridors. Following signs, he found his way, first left, then left again. Arriving in the West Wing, he was stunned by the light of a glorious sunset flooding through huge floor-to-ceiling windows. Revin's mouth fell open. Thick rugs lay across the floor and rich tapestries hung on the walls. A fire crackled in a great hearth. Silhouetted against the window stood a figure in long dark robes.

"What kept you, boy?" Will called out.

He turned and Revin found himself speechless. Will had shaved his beard and head. Will looked at him gravely, and then gave him a big grin, showing his teeth. "You've done for me twice, but the third time's the charm, I've always said."

"Oh, no." Revin said. "No! This will *never* work!"

"Sure it will," Will said, comfortingly. "This here berth is going to be easy, compared to where we've been. But now to work — we've got to get my men out. Aye, we've got to get Grip out."

"How do you propose to do that?"

"First, we need to buy ourselves some time. They're due to be hanged in the morning. Is there anything we can do to slow things down legal-wise?"

"Um ... What if you had a letter of marque?" Revin asked.

"Oh, aye. Things would be different then."

"Sorry — let me restate. What if you *claimed* to have a letter of marque?"

"Why, that's nearer to the mark! They'd have to check and that would give us some time."

"Let me draw up a brief and I'll file it for you," Revin said.

"Good lad," said Will. "While you're so engaged, I will conduct a bit of research."

Six hours later, Revin found himself asking his way to the Admiralty to deliver the stay of execution. The brief had been accepted by the court and, in response, a stay was issued until the question of the letter of marque could be resolved.

"But they've already received their last meal," the bailiff complained. "They're to be hanged at dawn. They've already erected the scaffold."

"I'm just the messenger," Revin lied. "It probably won't take long to sort this out."

Having assured himself that the prisoners would not be immediately executed, Revin headed back. It was well after midnight as he passed the line of bars and restaurants just outside the University gates.

"Hey! Boy!" Will called.

Revin looked over and saw Will staggering out of a bar with several other inebriated patrons.

"Give us a hand, boy!"

Against his better judgment, Revin went over and let Will throw an arm over his shoulder as he said goodbye to the others. Will leaned on him heavily as they made their way through the University gates.

"This was your research? Getting drunk?" he said, more bitterly than he really meant to.

"Now, now, boy!" Will said with a sly grin. "I may have had a sip or three, but it sometimes pays to look more drunk than you really are."

Once they were out of view of the street, Will straightened up and walked briskly back to their rooms. He led Revin into their living quarters and directed him to sit at the table while he busied himself in the kitchen.

"You must be exhausted, but you've had nothing to eat, I'll wager. Let me fix you something to keep your strength up."

In just a few minutes, he'd prepared two bowls of a fresh soup served with some thick, crusty bread to go with it. Revin tasted the soup somewhat suspiciously, but found it light and flavorful.

"How did you learn to cook?" he asked.

"Hmm. Ah, that takes me back. When I was just a sprat, I worked odd jobs in the kitchens of a seaside inn. There was an old man there who'd been a remmer until he lost a leg. Balthezar, they called him. Well, he took a shine to me and taught me how to cook. But also, how to tie and bind the streams. He was a real virtuoso, he was. The best there ever was. He could tie twelve streams simultaneously and that's the record. And he wrote me the letter of introduction that got me onto my first airship."

With a full belly, Revin began yawning uncontrollably.

"You'll hurt my feelings if my stories just put you to sleep," Will said. "Shall we go to bed?"

Suddenly Revin snapped awake with panic, realizing he was alone with a strange man he barely knew. He struggled to collect his wits, but Will raised his hand.

"Steady on, lad. Steady on. I just meant that we should get some shut-eye; neither more nor less."

Revin let himself be led to an austere little room. It was sparsely furnished, but had a narrow sturdy bed with a good mattress of bedstraw. Also inside was a wardrobe and a small wooden table and chair. And a chamber pot. His trunk was already here at the foot of his bed.

"Good night, boy," Will said with a smile, slipped out, and shut the door.

•   •   •

Revin awoke to the sound of shouting. He threw water on his face, ran fingers through his hair, and headed out to the public rooms of their quarters where Will, in the guise of Professor Dirge, engaged in a shouting match with another man who was dressed in some kind of fancy, official uniform.

"The Duke was expecting a hanging this morning," the stranger yelled. "But thanks to you, I find out — from the Duke! — that the men were given a stay of execution! Now we have to wait until tomorrow!"

"You know what would've happened if those men were executed while holding a letter of marque," Will thundered. "You'd have given the bastards in Belleriand fair license to slaughter our good airmen left and right."

"You jumped-up academic from the duchies!" the stranger shouted back inches from Will's face. "You need to remember your place here!"

"Ah, let me introduce young Revin," Will said with a smile, noticing him peeking around the corner. "This here's the seneschal from the Duke."

"Pardon me, sir," Revin said, taking his cue and bowing deeply. "It was my fault. We clearly should have run our request through your office. But time was short, and we're still finding our way here. Please accept my humblest apologies."

"That's more like it," the man said gruffly, somewhat mollified. "You should take some lessons from your clerk, Dirge. Or your stay here will be a short one.

"In fact ... Revin, is it? If you ever want to leave your master's employ, I'm sure we could find a place for a promising young man like yourself in our offices."

After he left, Will directed Revin to sit at the table and seemed deep in thought while he pulled together a ploughman's breakfast of bread, cheese, and sliced apple. He set it before them and took a seat.

"I'm going to tell it to you straight, boy," he said as Revin began to eat. "I have a plan, but it's by no means a sure thing. Tonight, I'm going to wager it all on one long throw of the dice. But, see, you've got a choice. Think it over and decide. Be true to yourself.

"If you're coming, pack a satchel — something small that won't weigh you down. And be ready at midnight."

After breakfast, Revin went out and walked through Havelock. It was a sunny day and school children were headed to classes. He went to a park and watched gulls wheeling overhead. Suddenly his eyes were filled with tears, mourning the future that he'd worked so hard to secure. His throat closed on the rage he felt at everything going wrong. Was he prepared to become a pirate? And now the seneschal had offered him a post! How was he to decide? It was impossible. Everything was unthinkable.

He tried to imagine himself as a pirate. What could he offer to pirates? He had an easier time imagining himself working for the seneschal. But when he remembered the officious little man, dressed up like a peacock, so eager for flattery, his blood ran cold. He could imagine that future only too well.

He spent the rest of the day just wandering through the town. As the sun began to set, he headed back to the University. When he returned, their rooms were dark and quiet. He found some bread and butter and ate it as he watched the sun set through the grand western windows. When the last glow of the sun was extinguished, and the stars were filling the sky, he struck a light, carried a lantern into his room, and packed a small satchel.

At the stroke of midnight, Will returned. He was still wearing his university garb, but Revin could see that under it he wore the loose, silk clothes he'd been wearing when they met. A satchel hung slung crosswise over his shoulder and he carried a tall, slim staff. In his other hand, he held a small bag.

"Boy! Are you there? Are you ready?"

"I'm ready," Revin said.

"Good lad!" Will said. "Let's go."

They followed back streets and approached the Admiralty from the side. Will led them down a narrow alley that opened up to a blank wall of the compound — two-stories high of smooth, fitted stone.

"Here, we'll wait for a few minutes. The shift changes at the second bell and we should go just shortly after 1."

"How are we going to get over the wall?" Revin asked.

"Never you mind about that," Will said with a wink. "Here's what I need you to do." And he handed him the bag he was carrying.

Revin looked inside and recoiled as though the bag was full of snakes.

"No, Will," he said. "No. Anything but that."

"It's just a disguise, lad," Will said. "I'd wear it myself and let you bop the people on the head if you thought you could do it."

Much to his dismay, Revin allowed himself to be persuaded to put on the white ruffled dress and pink wig. Without the chest binding, he filled out the dress surprisingly well. He looked down, his face red with shame.

"You know you asked before if I was a woman pretending to be a man or a man in a woman's body?" Revin whispered.

"Yeah?"

"I think I know the answer now."

"Good for you, lad. Be true to yourself! Now here's the plan: We'll go to the top of the wall and take the stairs down that lead to the lower level. Then we'll spring Grip and the others."

"But ... How will we scale the wall? How are we getting out? Why am I wearing a dress?"

"You'll see, lad. You'll see. Let's go!"

Will led Revin up to the wall, then slipped a monocle over one eye and planted his staff.

"Put your arm 'round my shoulder, boy!" he said.

A thin blue towline snapped into existence between Will and the sky. Revin suddenly felt an inexorable force pulling them forward and up. Will put out his feet and began to run up the wall, dragging Revin along with him. When they reached the top, the line winked out, and the force vanished as suddenly as it had appeared.

"What just happened?" Revin said.

"If you know what you're doing, you can use the streams for more than pulling an airship. Balthezar was the real master, but I know a thing or two."

Revin looked around from their vantage point atop the wall. The Admiralty compound contained a large parade ground with a long scaffold erected for the gallows. But dominating the landscape was a sleek airship moored close to ground level.

"Yes, that's the *Queen of Belleriand*. The Duke is coming to observe the executions and to tour the airship. That's our way out. Now here are the stairs — lead us down!

Revin took the lead as they trotted down the stairs. The stairs took frequent turns going down, with murder holes at every landing. Gas lighting cast unreal stark illumination, and would have left them easy targets had anyone been about.

"The guards I was drinking with told me more than they probably realized about the workings of this place," Will chuckled.

At the bottom, they came out into a corridor and, with Will's guidance, turned right and went down a long, windowless corridor that ran the length of the wall. Eventually, they emerged into a guardroom.

A guard drowsed behind a counter. He started when he saw Revin, but then rolled his eyes.

"Hey, you hussy! If somebody snuck you in for a little late-night fun, they'd better sneak you out again right quick before the shift changes."

Will set his staff and suddenly a thick blue line winked into existence. The guard was whipped up out of his chair and smashed against the roof of the chamber. He dropped bonelessly to the floor, his neck at an odd angle.

"Get his keys! C'mon!"

Revin knelt by the body and found a large key ring on the man's belt. He also grabbed the man's knife out of its sheath.

Will let out a low, penetrating whistle. Suddenly, the corridors that led from the guardroom came alive with responding calls. Revin ran with the heavy key ring and began trying keys until he found the right one and started opening doors.

One of the pirates tried to grab and kiss Revin, but a quick rap on the head from Will's staff put an end to that.

"Hands off our brother pirate," he growled to the chastened man.

When he opened Grip's cell, Will embraced him tenderly, kissed him on the mouth, and said, "Wait 'til ye see the birthday present I brung ye."

Grip led the pirates around two turns and then up a flight of stairs to the parade grounds. Revin and Will brought up the rear. As they reached the top of the stairs, they ran directly into a small group of guards that had been ambling back a little early for the shift change. A shout went up and someone began ringing a bell.

The pirates overwhelmed the party of guards by sheer numbers and began sprinting for the airship. Crossbow bolts flew from guard posts atop the walls but, in the dark, with people running, most went astray. One pirate went down with a bolt through his calf. Two other pirates seized him up and dragged him to the airship.

"Run to the tail and cut the mooring line," Will cried, giving Revin a push.

Revin ran as hard as he could. As crossbow bolts began to fall around him, he started zigzagging, hoping to throw off their aim. He reached the rope and pulled out the knife he'd taken and began sawing at it. He saw Will doing the same at the front. One big cord was severed, then another and another, and, finally, the rope parted with a snap and the aft end of the airship began to rise. Revin looked forward and saw Will complete his cut as well. The *Queen of Belleriand* was free, rising majestically into the night sky.

Revin looked around, trying to decide what to do next. The gangplank to board the airship had already fallen away.

He watched as Will planted his staff as crossbow bolts continued to fall around him.

Revin ran toward him as guardsmen began to stream onto the parade ground. Revin watched with horror as they converged on Will. But then, one by one, they were whisked up into the sky on shining blue cords. Revin counted *one, two, three* ... as they sailed off. More and more were skyhooked out of the parade ground as they charged. He kept count of each one as he ran. ... *ten, eleven, twelve,* until they were right on top of him.

One drew back a shortsword to strike Will in the back, but Revin put on a burst of speed and sank his knife into the man's kidney. The man screamed, falling against Will. Will spun toward Revin, winked with a grin, and suddenly Revin found himself sailing up and through the air along a thin blue cord with Will's arm around tight around his waist. They spooled up until they reached the open hatch of the gondola where strong hands grabbed them and pulled them aboard.

"Status!" called Will, and once again he was the stern captain of pirates.

Grip came at a run and they began a rapid-fire exchange of questions and answers — the weather, winds, crew, injuries — as they walked forward.

The guards on the ground and walls continued to shoot crossbow bolts, but they all fell short. The men, milling around below, already looked like mere insects.

The pirate crew, after their losses and imprisonment, were short-handed and weak. But, even in the unfamiliar airship, they all knew their stations. The remmers aboard established towlines, and the ship began moving forward, headed toward the sea.

Revin stood alone, feeling somewhat forgotten. He turned this way and that, wondering what to do next. Then Will broke off for a moment and came back.

"Revin, my lad," he said warmly. "Welcome aboard the *Queen of Belleriand.*"

"Thank you, Will — I mean, Cap'n," Revin replied.

"Now why are you just standing around in that dress! Get changed and get to work, cabin boy!"

"Aye, aye, Cap'n!" Revin said, snapping to attention and beaming with pride.

With a light heart, he turned to find a lavatory to change in and to throw the hated dress away, never to be seen again.

"Oh!" Will said, calling after him. "And just you hang onto that dress, mind you! You never know when we might need that thing again."

"Aye, aye, Cap'n," Revin said, somewhat less cheerfully.

INTERLUDE

R EVIN'S FIRST DAY ABOARD the *Queen of Belleriand* was a blur. He was constantly being asked to fetch and carry. He quickly learned that being Cabin Boy meant that he was asked to do anything and everything that needed being done. He brought water to the remmers. He carried food to the Captain in the cockpit and to the First Mate who was manning the observation deck. He was sent from one end of the airship to the other and was constantly on the run. By 10 bells, he was dead on his feet. Will spotted him staggering and told him to get some sleep.

"Where?" he asked.

"Oh, right," Will said. "Yeah. The men generally have hammocks in a common space. But I think we should have a cabin for the Cabin Boy. Let's get you bedded down."

Will advised Grip he was leaving the cockpit and then led Revin back down the main gangway in the *Queen* and they found a small cabin, practically just a closet, but with a bunk.

"There are only three cabins," he said. "One was for the captain. One is a VIP cabin. And I think this one was for the VIP's attendant. Let's have you use this one."

"What will the men say?" Revin said, worried he might be perceived as receiving special favors. "Shouldn't I just bed down with them?"

"Are you going to want to change your clothes with all of them?" Will asked, gently.

Revin suddenly realized what bedding down with the others meant and grew pale. Will smiled. "I'm Captain and what I say goes. And I'm telling you to sleep here. That's an order, Cabin Boy!"

"Aye, aye, Cap'n!" Revin said.

Revin entered the cabin, blindly collapsed onto the tiny bunk, and was asleep in moments.

•   •   •

"Wake up, Cabin Boy!" Grip said, shaking Revin's shoulder.

Revin opened his eyes, cautiously.

"We've arrived," Grip said, cryptically. "All hands to unload!"

Revin heard feet hammering on the gangway. He rubbed his eyes, then turned out of the bunk.

Since they were only just arriving, there was functionally nothing to be carried off the airship. But Revin learned that this was an important ritual: Everyone, but everyone, turned out to help unload and no-one left until released by the Captain.

Revin collected his satchel and joined with the others as everyone ran down the gangplank, stood in formation, and waited to be dismissed.

Will and Grip came last off the *Queen*.

Will surveyed the hands, standing before them as a stern captain of pirates. Everyone held their breath for a moment.

"All hands dismissed," Will said.

"Dismissed!" bellowed Grip.

The men set up a huge cheer and the ground crew that had been left behind embraced the returning men who had been long overdue. They could see that the hands were still ragged from their mistreatment on Havelock. They helped the injured make their way to the camp.

Revin turned around and around trying to figure out where he was and what he ought to do next. He was still exhausted, half asleep, and totally out of his element.

"Come with me, lad," Will said kindly, took his elbow, and steered him toward a tent.

"The mate who used this tent previously, Master's Mate Robert Carpenter, didn't make it back," Will said. "You can use the tent from now on. But collect the man's belongings and pack them up. Grip will take them and return them to his next of kin with my letter."

Revin opened the flap of the tent and stepped inside. Inside, he found a cot, an old trunk, a satchel, a small table, and a chair.

Revin, picked up the satchel, intending to put it into the trunk, but it spilled its contents out onto the ground. There was a quill, a bottle of ink, a small journal, several letters, a small jar of some kind of unguent, a knife, an earring, and a handful of coins — mostly copper bits, but a few silver miners as well. Revin gathered them up and transferred them to the trunk.

Under the cot, Revin found some soiled clothes. And a book with drawings of people engaged in various graphic amorous couplings. Revin picked it up curiously, not sure what to do with it.

"Let's not send that back with the other things," Grip said.

Revin spun, surprised, as he hadn't heard Grip enter.

"Is everything else in here?" he continued. Revin nodded. Grip hoisted the trunk on his shoulder and carried it out.

"But what should I do with this?" Revin asked, holding out the book.

"Use it!" Grip laughed.

Revin blushed all the way to the floor. He looked around the tent as if he might find someplace to conceal the embarrassing book. In the end, he tossed it back under his bunk. And then took one of his shirts and carefully placed it on top, so it wouldn't be in view.

Then the stress of the past couple of days caught up with him and he collapsed onto the cot and slept for a long time.

• • •

When Revin awoke, he came out of the tent, rubbing his eyes, and followed the sounds of people laughing to the mess tent. He fell into line and was handed a cup of coffee and a plate with a hearty breakfast of … Well … Revin wasn't sure what you'd call it. There was some stuff with other stuff on it and some stuff melted on that. But it smelled good and when he dipped a spoon into it, he found it surprisingly toothsome. He promptly cleaned his plate.

"Hey, new guy!" someone said. He was a grizzled old-timer. Revin hadn't seen him on the *Queen* and supposed he must be part of the ground crew.

Revin looked up. "Hmm?"

"Have you done the Wild Animal check yet?"

"Wild Animal check?" Revin asked.

"Yeah!" he said. "It's the first thing you have to do! Come with me!"

He led Revin out and handed him a sack.

"There are wild animals that are always trying to get into camp. And we need to keep track of them, see?"

"Yeah?" Revin said.

"So *you* need to walk all around the camp and when you find animal scat," he said pointing at a pile of animal droppings, "you need to collect it in the sack and then take it to the Captain straight away!"

"The Captain?"

"Yeah! This is how he knows what wild animals are trying to get into the camp! So he can take …"

"Protective countermeasures," finished one of the other pirates.

"Yeah! Yeah! Protective countermeasures!" echoed the first.

"Well ... Okay," Revin said, dubiously.

With disgust, Revin picked up the feces and put them in the bag. Then, according to the directions of his fellow pirates, he carefully circumnavigated the pirate camp and, under their watchful eye, found four more piles of animal dung that he scooped up and added to the bag. When he had finished his circuit, the other pirates directed him toward the Captain's tent.

He arrived at the entrance to the tent and looked for some way to alert the inhabitants that he was there. Seeing nothing to knock on, he cleared his throat and entered the tent. Will and Grip were asleep, entwined, naked on a large mattress lying on the ground. Revin turned red and averted his eyes.

"Begging your pardon Cap'n. But I've completed the Wild Animal check," he held out the sack.

"Oh! Oh, those ... Animals!" Will bellowed.

Howling laughter could be heard outside the tent. Revin blanched.

"Did they ...? Did I ...?" Revin asked, mortified.

"Revin," Will said, gently. "You can just take ... that ... those ... back out and dispose of them. There is no such thing as a Wild Animal check."

Revin, pale, backed out of the Captain's tent where the other pirates met him with a cheer, slapped him on the back, and led him back to the mess tent. Revin, initially abashed, felt the comradeship of the other pirates seep in as they welcomed him cheerfully into their company. And, in degrees, Revin gradually began to realize that, if he was not yet fully one of them, he was well on his apprenticeship.

2

FOR THE FAVOR OF A LADY

"**A**IRSHIP, HO!" Revin called out.

Still barely a speck on a horizon, Revin — who had the sharpest eyes among the pirates — spotted it the moment it emerged from behind the clouds.

"Call all hands," Will, the captain of the pirates, said. He stood short and compact, like an acrobat, his hair still growing back after their previous adventure.

"All hands to quarters!" Grip, the first mate, cried. He was a big man, well-proportioned, with broad shoulders and dark hair.

Echoing thumps and footsteps answered him as men rolled out of hammocks and raced to their positions.

The *Queen of Belleriand* leapt forward among the high clouds over the ocean, poised and ready for action. Revin's heart raced with excitement as they flew among the towering cloud tops. The *Queen*, a sleek rigid-hulled dirigible, was the pride of Belleriand. Captured by Havelock during a skirmish between the two island nations, she had been "liberated" by the pirates when they escaped. She appeared menacing with painted countershading: dark silver above and light silver below.

Revin had seen enough of these engagements now to know how things would likely play out. He watched as the airship they were pursuing, the packet ship *Martha's Pride*, turned and tried to flee, but she was no match for the *Queen*. Once within range, a blue remmer line sparked out, grabbed hold of their quarry, and pulled her back. Revin heard the crew's consternation as the *Queen* drew alongside in moments. Once close enough, grappling hooks pulled them right together and the pirates charged aboard.

The airmen in the packet ship offered only token resistance once boarded. In just moments, the *Pride's* airmen were sitting sullenly on the deck with their hands on top of their heads. Will supervised the operation while Grip ran from place to place encouraging the men to hurry or to lend a hand when needed. The pirates were well-organized and ransacked the ship thoroughly. Anything of value was brought back over to the *Queen* and, in just shy of an hour, the lines were cut and the *Queen of Belleriand* pulled away from the despoiled packet ship.

Revin had stayed back while the *Pride* was being boarded. He was learning to fight and to master arms, but was still little better than a novice. And Will had told him that it was his brains rather than his brawn that they needed.

"At least he didn't say, 'beauty'," Revin thought.

So Revin stayed behind and helped direct the stowage of the plunder as it was brought across and the *Queen* began to make way.

He was quick to notice, however, that Grip was upset about something. Will noticed too and put his hand on Grip's shoulder.

"Is something wrong, love?" he asked, quietly.

"I found this among the mail," Grip said, handing him an embossed note on cardstock: a wedding invitation.

"Someone we know?" he asked.

"It's my little sister."

The next morning, the *Queen* descended toward Kapper Island, the secret base of the pirates. The small, uninhabited island was little more than a mountain peak with steep sides that ran down straight into the ocean. The *Queen* turned and approached a side of the mountain that appeared rugged and inaccessible. Revin stood by watching and, when he saw the flicker of light, he used his own signaling mirror to quickly flash the countersign — lest the men on the ground mistakenly attack their own airship.

"We're good to go, Cap'n!" he called to Will.

The remmers brought the *Queen* down and under the broad camouflage netting that extended over a narrow ledge where the airship could be moored. Airmen at the bow and aft ends threw down ropes to groundsmen who winched the *Queen* into her berth. Once she was secure, Revin and the entire crew were engaged with offloading the plunder to be sorted and repackaged for use or sale or trade. With many hands, the work went quickly and, in minutes, a cheer went up as Grip dismissed most of the hands from work.

That night, the pirates built a bonfire to celebrate their recent successes. Several men brought out musical instruments and began to play familiar folk tunes. The delicious smell of roasting meat wafted through the air. Someone tapped a barrel of ale and a true party atmosphere began to take hold.

Revin, as both rescuer and cabin boy, had quickly become a favorite among the men, and went from group to group, soaking up the adulation. Eventually, he got some skewers of meat and found a quiet place to sit off to the side.

Will and Grip sat nearby at the periphery drinking wine, nodding and smiling as men walked by.

"I need to go to my sister," Grip said to Will. "She's just too young."

"You must do as you think is right, of course," Will said. "But you shouldn't go alone. Take Revin with you."

Revin choked on his skewer.

"What?" he finally asked.

Grip handed him the wedding invitation. "This says my little sister is getting married," he said. "But I think she's too young. She's just a kid! So I'm going to go check on her to find out who arranged this marriage and why. And Will says I should take you."

"Why?" Revin asked. "What could I do?"

"I would go myself, but I can't," Will said. "Don't sell yourself short! If there's anyone that can think their way through something, it's you. Sleep on it."

But Revin lay awake late into the night.

•   •   •

Revin was on watch early the next morning. The pirate base had observation posts to provide 360-degree coverage for the island to watch for approaching airships. The consequences of being caught on the ground were too severe to ignore for any airship. The standing orders, if any airship was sighted, was to wake the captain to decide whether to call general quarters. But in the weeks Revin had been observing, airships were few and far between.

This morning was no exception.

Revin stood at the southern observation post for nearly his full two hour shift, watching the horizon. Then he saw something pass between clouds and he ran to the captain's quarters.

He found Will and Grip lying naked, asleep, in a tangle of limbs after the previous night's debauchery.

"Cap'n," he said, rapping at the cabin and averting his eyes. "You asked me to wake you if any airships were spotted."

Will kissed Grip, pulled on some clothes, then returned to the observation post with Revin, and looked where he indicated.

"You've got good eyes, boy. I can still barely see it," Will said, putting on his monocle. "Let me check what etheric flows they're attaching."

"Is it coming this way?"

"I don't think so," Will replied after a few moments. "It looks to me like it will pass well to the west of us. Still — pass the word to stay under wraps."

Revin made the circuit of the base quietly alerting everyone to the airship and the need to stay under cover. All of the cooking fires were extinguished, and the men stayed to the shadows until the airship vanished to the west by midafternoon, and everyone started to breathe again. The cooking fires were restarted and preparations for dinner were put underway.

Revin just happened to be looking up when he thought he saw something move up high on the mountain. It was just a dot, but he watched for a moment and realized that it was, in fact, moving. Approaching! Fast!

He shouted and others had time to react and look up as it began to take shape. Its form was unfamiliar and reminded him a bit of the way kites look at a great distance. Its trajectory flattened out and it passed over above the treetops almost silently before turning in lazy circles down to the narrow strip of sand that passed for a beach on the island's southern coast. It skidded to a stop, and then flipped over. Revin, with his sharp eyes, could see someone strapped into the device with a harness.

Revin sprinted down the switchbacks of the trail to the sea. A few of the most athletic pirates got ahead of him by running straight down, bypassing the switchbacks. But five or six of them arrived at more or less the same time to see the man — for they could see now it was a man — with wild white hair and a gray beard scramble out of the harness. But Revin could see something was terribly wrong. The front half of him was crawling out of the harness, but he was leaving his legs behind.

"Aaaa! What's happened to your legs?" Revin asked in shock.

"Those aren't my legs," the man growled. "Those are just for balance."

"But you don't have any legs! What happened to your legs?" Revin persisted.

"Airshark got 'em," the man replied, gravely. "Have you ever seen an airshark? Terrible creatures."

Revin was dubious. He started to open his mouth, then realized that all of the pirates were standing in a circle, watching his facial expressions, and trying not to laugh. He turned bright, bright red and they exploded with laughter, rolling on the ground. Gently hazing the new cabin boy was a popular pastime among the pirates. And now the strenuous efforts of the pirates to get there ahead of him were explained.

Will and Grip strolled up.

"Didn't I tell you not to do crazy things like this?" Will said to the old, bearded half-man.

"Now, there you go again," he replied, animatedly. "I told you it was going to work, didn't I? And if I was a remmer, I could probably stay up there all day."

"Okay, okay," Will said. "You've made your point. We'll take it with us from now on."

"Hmph!" the man grumbled, still peeved.

"Oh, Revin!" Will said. "Let me introduce you. This is the Professor. He's our scientist and engineer. He helps us keep the airships flying."

"Ah! So you're the famous Revin!" said the Professor. "I've heard the men speak of you in glowing terms. I think I was off island when you were here before."

"You lot," he continued, looking at the other pirates. "Don't just stand around! Grab that and carry it back to camp. Carefully, now!"

The Professor, now extricated from the harness, grabbed two arm braces and started handwalking with them back across the sand. Revin noticed that his arms and shoulders were unbelievably muscular.

"How did you even get that thing up there?" asked Revin, walking alongside.

"Winched it," he said. "It took me most of the day and night. Couldn't ask for any help because his nibs would have gotten wind of it and stopped me!"

They reached the camp and, walking below the belly of the *Queen*, the Professor suddenly let loose with a tirade of cursing and swearing at the men.

"What have you useless lot been up to? Get to work, you lazy slugs! I left strict instructions about what needed to be done and it's like you haven't even gotten started!"

The men, who obviously loved the Professor, seemed accustomed to his style of badgering and accepted his lecture in the spirit in which it was intended.

•　　　•　　　•

By midnight, the *Queen* was made ready to depart.

"Next stop, Belleriand," Will said.

"Really?" Revin asked in wonder.

"Oh, you didn't know that Grip is from Belleriand?"

"I hardly know anything about Grip," Revin replied.

Will, as the grave captain of pirates, merely cleared his throat. But then he leaned in close and whispered, "Please keep him safe for me in that snake pit."

After several hours, Will brought the *Queen* in as close as he dared to the capital of Belleriand. They touched down just before sunrise in a small field sheltered on three sides by woods. Revin and Grip ran down the gangplank and made for the forest while the *Queen* lifted off and beat a hasty retreat for the sea, before patrols could give chase. Provided the patrols were not alerted, Will had said he was confident the *Queen* would be able to quietly return and stand off and on near the capitol until they signaled. But they still had a two-day hike to get there.

It was chilly in the pre-dawn twilight. The birds made a cheerful racket from the treetops. They warmed up as they headed east and, when they reached a trail, they turned south.

Grip set a brutal pace with his long legs. Revin struggled to keep up, but finally began to fall behind. After a few minutes, Grip noticed and turned back, his face full of concern.

"I'm sorry, Revin," he said. "I'm so wrapped up with my worries about my sister, I wasn't thinking about you."

"It's okay," Revin said. "Let me rest for a moment to catch my breath and I'll be ready to go again."

The forest had given way to a huge field of tall grass. They were following an overgrown trail that had not been used recently, but Grip seemed to know just where they were.

"What's next?" Revin asked.

"We're entering the salt marsh that borders the estuary," Grip replied. "Before long, it's going to get muddy and then we'll have to wade across the estuary at low tide. This trail leads to the best place to cross."

After a few minutes of silence, they pressed on.

"You don't talk all the time, like Will does," Revin said after a bit. "He's always 'boy this' and 'lad that'."

"He sure does talk a lot," Grip said, with a grin. "When he's not capting." Revin smiled to hear the depth of the love in Grip's voice.

By noon, they reached the place where Grip aimed for them to ford the estuary. The solar tide was near its peak, so they found some shade under some willows where they could wait and munched on sandwiches Revin had packed for them.

"It doesn't get really deep here, because it's so wide."

"Won't we be all muddy by the other side?" Revin asked. Grip smiled.

"I know a place where we can get cleaned up. Just wait and see."

After the ebb tide had peaked, the water levels were lower, and they began to cross the estuary. Holding their bags overhead, they floundered through sticky, waist-deep mud. Revin let Grip lead and his eyes were drawn to Grip's muscular physique. The sweat made his shirt stick to his back and the harsh, overhead light emphasized each muscle.

Revin felt his face color and he looked down, not solely to keep his footing.

When they reached the other side, Grip guided them along a trail that headed up toward a line of rocky cliffs that overlooked this side of the river. He seemed to be watching for something and, after a while, he turned right and followed a stream that issued from a narrow canyon rich with ferns and mosses.

After a half an hour of climbing and scrambling over wet, slippery rocks, they entered a small grotto. Here, the stream ran over a ledge into a small pool cut in the stone, making a small waterfall. Behind the waterfall lay a sheltered area that looked dry and sandy. Revin could see a fire circle and logs, suggesting that this site had been used many, many times in the past.

"It's cold, but you can shower here and get cleaned off," Grip said. "You go first. I'll gather some wood and get a fire started."

Revin put his things down and stepped cautiously into the pool of water. It was cold. It was really cold. He took off his clothes and washed them, as best he could, in the rocky pool. The water was so cold his feet began to cramp and it took everything he could muster to force himself under the waterfall. The cold chilled and burned, but refreshed him too. He lathered up with a bit of bar soap he'd brought along and then rinsed off. He heard a sudden gasp and tried to shake the water out of his eyes.

Grip had returned and was staring at his naked breasts with shock. They both mumbled, "Sorry."

Revin finished rinsing off, then went over to the fire to dry off and warm up while Grip bathed.

Later, the silence grew awkward at the campfire. The two stole glances at each other across the flames, but neither knew how to break the silence.

"I knew," Grip said. "I mean, Will told me. But I didn't know-know, you know. That you were … Um … Like that.

Maybe I'm not expressing myself well. I don't even know what I'm saying."

"Yeah," Revin replied, uncomfortably. "Since you're with *him*, I didn't think about how you might ... Uh ..."

They suddenly locked eyes, anguished. But that broke the spell and they both started to chuckle, then laugh.

"Just how long have you and Will been together?" Revin asked.

"It will be two years next week. On Thursday." Grip said.

"You know it to the day. That's very sweet," Revin said.

Grip looked down, blushing. But he looked happy.

"They've been the best two years of my life."

"How did you meet?" Revin asked.

"Oh, that's a long story for another time," Grip replied. "But I should tell you why I left home, since we're headed that way."

Grip added another log to the fire then leaned back.

"Two years ago," he continued. "A man tried to force himself on my little sister." He clenched and unclenched his fists at the memory.

"I stopped him and challenged him to a duel," Grip continued. "And we fought. But when I touched him, he stopped and tried to declare honor satisfied."

"And then did you kill him?" Revin asked, with horror.

"No," Grip replied, with a wry smile. "No, that would have been too easy. No, I slit his nostril, so he can wear his shame for the rest of his life. But the scandal of cutting a man who'd declared himself conquered compelled me to leave for a time. I haven't been back since. And I wouldn't go now, but for my sister."

•　　•　　•

The next morning, they started walking again. They followed small trails, some barely noticeable as such, until they reached a road, and then began to follow it toward the city. Revin noticed increasing signs of habitation: farmers' fields, barns, and then the occasional small house.

They encountered some wagons heading the other way, but eventually a wagon overtook them, traveling in the direction that they were headed, and they traded a copper bit each to sit in the wagon and bounce along for an hour or two. Revin enjoyed the break in the tedium to look around. They had reached an area with large agricultural fields growing both familiar crops, and some Revin had never seen before, with large leaves. Houses appeared more frequently now.

Eventually, the wagon reached its destination. They hopped off and started trudging along the road again. As they approached the city, Revin noticed Grip had put his hood up and was watching everyone very carefully as they approached.

"Are you worried we're going to be attacked?" Revin asked.

"I'm worried that I will be recognized," he said. "In fact, we should probably walk separately so that, if I'm recognized, you won't be caught up in it."

"That bad, huh?"

"It could be pretty bad."

So they started walking single file with Revin trailing Grip about ten feet behind him.

They reached the outskirts of the city at dusk. Houses became closer and closer together until they reached the walls of the old city. The gates weren't manned anymore, so they were able to enter without difficulty.

Inside the walls, the city became a warren of narrow twisting streets and alleyways.

Grip led Revin through a maze of dark alleys to the back door of a tailor's shop. The door opened in prompt obedience to his knock. A tall, thin man with elaborately coiffed and powdered hair looked out.

"Lord Belthingstone!" the man gasped.

Revin looked at Grip, stupefied. Grip had drawn himself up and thrown back his hood. His carriage and expression had changed: he stood tall with a look of authority about him. It was almost as though he had become a different person.

"Well met, Cedric," Lord Belthingstone replied.

"How may I serve Milord and ..." Cedric said, peering at Revin.

"My squire," said Lord Belthingstone.

"Squire?" said Cedric.

"Squire?" said Revin.

"Squire," repeated Lord Belthingstone with finality. "We require suitable clothing after our arduous travels, plus appropriate vestments for the upcoming ceremony."

The man paled. "The ceremony is so soon, Milord. I'm not sure ..."

"I'm confident you will rise to the occasion, as you always do." Cedric looked pained.

"Well, let me get your measurements," he said, studying Grip and leading him around a screen. "Ooh! You've lost some weight, I see. Oh! But you've also put on some muscle. Oh, my. Yes!"

While this was going on, Revin looked at the clothes in the shop, his eyes goggling at the brilliant colors and rich fabrics. He looked surreptitiously for a price tag, but there were no prices. It was evident that for the patrons of this establishment, price was no object.

After a few moments, he brought Grip back around and then led Revin back behind the screen. When they were out of sight, he leaned close to Revin and began to whisper in his ear.

"Does Lord Belthingstone know what you are?" Cedric hissed.

"What I am?" Revin said, nervously.

Cedric rolled his eyes dramatically.

"Look, honey," he said. "I can tell the difference, okay?"

"Yes," Revin whispered, thinking back to the night before when Grip was staring at his bared breasts. "Yes, he knows."

Cedric breathed a sigh of relief and rolled his eyes skyward.

"Thank the stars! I would do anything for him, you know. And I could never lie to him! But I wasn't going to just out you either, honey," he said, then he spoke louder. "We will need to make a few alterations for something that will fit your, ahem, measurements. And I think we also have something that might work better than those chest bindings you've been using."

Two hours later, Revin and Grip were appropriately attired. For what, Revin had no idea. He felt utterly ludicrous wearing a brightly colored doublet, half blue and half white, topped off with a huge blue and white hat. He wanted to crawl under a rock. But underneath the brightly colored exterior, it was all fine: a comfortable buff-colored shirt with dark breeches — all cleverly adjusted to conceal his narrow shoulders, broad hips, and ... other characteristics. And in place of the chest bindings was a kind of halter that was both more comfortable and did a better job of concealing his breasts.

Lord Belthingstone, on the other hand, just wore black — and wore it well: a black shirt, black pants, and a long black cloak. Cedric had even sent next door and acquired suitable footwear: leather shoes for Revin, tall black boots for Grip.

"Somehow we'll have your vestments ready in time for the ceremony," Cedric promised.

Lord Belthingstone nodded regally.

"Now," said Grip as they departed. "It is time to go home."

"Whee," said Revin, with growing apprehension about what lay ahead.

They stepped out into the evening street, through the front door this time. Lord Belthingstone now strode down the middle of the street, nodding benignly to the people that bowed or curtsied as he passed. Revin followed in his wake, his head spinning. *Just who was Lord Belthingstone, anyway? Was Grip just worried about being recognized out of costume?*

They reached the middle of the city, and came to a long boulevard that was lined with palatial homes. Grip led them directly to the grandest house of all — one that was, quite literally, a palace, with walls, and spires, and turrets.

"This is Ravensbelth, my family's ancestral home," he told Revin. "Are you ready?"

"Hell, no," Revin said. "I'm totally out of my depth here."

"Don't worry," said Grip. "Just calm down! Here's all you have to do. First, don't say anything. If you open your mouth, people will instantly know you're not a nobleman. Second, only pay attention to me. Don't pay attention to anyone else, no matter what they do. Finally, do everything I tell you to. You don't have to do it right. So even if you don't understand, just do something."

"Got it," Revin said.

"Ssh!" Grip hissed.

"Oh, right. This is hard."

Lord Belthingstone walked up to the door. Guards, standing at each side of the door snapped to attention. The door opened and an aged, white-haired butler bowed respectfully. That is, he looked perpetually bowed, but he imperceptibly bowed just a tiny bit more.

"Welcome home, Milord," he said.

They stepped into an antechamber that was larger than the entire house where Revin grew up. His eyes goggled. The room had marble floors and pillars, four stained-glass windows, luxurious rugs, doors leading off in all directions, plus a huge, grand staircase that led to the upper floors.

"Thank you, Youngman," Lord Belthingstone observed.

Revin bit his tongue to prevent himself from laughing at the idea of this ancient creature being called 'Youngman'.

"Is the Baron in?"

Revin suddenly realized that Grip's father was the Butcher Baron of Belleriand! The implacable enemy of Havelock! His blood chilled.

"No, sir," Youngman replied. "The Baron and your mother had tickets to the opera."

"Is my sister here?" Grip asked.

Before Youngman could reply, there came a squeal and all eyes turned to see a willowy young woman, elegantly attired in a long, yellow dress at the top of the staircase, suddenly jump onto the banister and slide to the bottom, skirts whirling.

"Griphon!" she shrieked.

"*Griphon?*" Revin wondered.

Grip ran to the banister. He caught her as she reached the bottom, then twirled her around in the air while she squealed again with excitement.

"Now, now," Grip said. "What would mother say about this unseemly behavior!"

"'A young woman must always be stern'," she recited by rote, but then smiled mischievously. "But mother's not here and you are!"

Then she turned her eyes on Revin and said, "And who's this?"

From the moment Revin saw her, he was entranced. He felt like his heart stopped. She was tiny and charming and there was a vivaciousness to her every movement. Her face was lively and expressive. Her huge eyes captured his and seemed to draw him in so that he couldn't look away. His mouth opened and closed like a fish as he struggled to respond appropriately without saying anything and giving himself away.

"Ah. Momo ... No, no. Let me do this properly," Grip said. "Ahem! My dear Lady Momoire Isabelle Celandine Belthingstone of Belleriand, please allow me to introduce Squire Revin Minerson of Devishire."

Grip indicated Revin, who bowed low, if for no other reason than to conceal his utter astonishment that Grip would somehow know his full name and the obscure duchy of his origin.

"Milady, Squire Revin saved my life recently and I humbly request that you invite him into your good graces."

"I'm very pleased to make your acquaintance, Squire," Momo said as she curtsied prettily. "And I give thanks for your service to my wayward brother and our family."

Revin, remembering his orders, nodded, but said nothing.

"He doesn't talk much," Momo observed to Grip.

"No," agreed Grip. "But, come, let's retire to the Library so you can catch me up. What's this I hear about you getting married?"

Momo stuck her tongue out and then they all walked through a dizzying series of rooms — the Blue room, the Tapestry room, the Porcelain room — each more opulent than the last, until they came, at last, to the Library.

Momo and Grip walked to a quiet nook and carelessly fell into a comfortable sofa. Revin stood in the doorway gawking. He had never seen so many books in one place.

"Excuse me, Squire," said a young woman with a cart.

Revin hurriedly stepped into the room. He started toward the sofa, but got stuck again when he reached the middle of the room, where he turned around and around to take in the full panorama of the two-story, floor-to-ceiling shelves of books. The woman was pouring tea for Momo and Grip when he hurried over. He stood uncomfortably behind Grip, not sure about the dictates of propriety.

"Please, Squire," Momo said, patting the seat next to her. "Won't you sit with us?"

Grip made an encouraging gesture, so Revin sat gingerly at the edge of the sofa and accepted a cup of tea from the servant.

"Now tell me about this marriage," Grip said.

"I don't know a whole lot about it," Momo admitted. "Father called for me and said," here she adopted a gruff tone of voice to imitate his diction and cadence, "We've received a marriage proposal for you along with word that it would be in our best interests to accept it. You should ready yourself for whatever comes next."

"Stranger and stranger," Grip said. "Have you seen the contract?"

"I was told it had arrived," she said. "But you know I've no head for such things."

"Yes, well, Revin here trained as a lawyer, so this should be perfect for him."

Revin's eyes must have bugged out of his head.

Momo covered her mouth and laughed. Revin was transfixed by her laughter; it was so bright and cheerful.

"Ah! So the man of few words is a wordsmith," she said. "How interesting!"

Grip leaned back and rang a bell cord that was near to hand.

Within moments, Youngman arrived.

"You rang, Milord?"

"Youngman, I understand that the contract for Milady's wedding has arrived. Would you please show my squire the way to my office and bring the contract to him?"

"It will be as you say, Milord."

Youngman led Revin upstairs, and through another head-spinning series of rooms in the palace, and eventually to a comfortable room containing a desk, fireplace, and a window seat that overlooked a lovely courtyard with a fountain. Revin took a turn around the room waiting for Youngman to return with the contract to see what he could learn about his enigmatic companion.

Above the mantel hung a huge painting of an older man who shared certain familial traits with Grip. *His father perhaps? Or another noble ancestor?* A small puzzle box on the mantelpiece caught his attention. Revin picked it up and looked it over. He found one catch in just a few moments, another took longer. He was still looking for a third when Youngman arrived with the contract. He set it silently on the desk, bowed (slightly), and then went to depart. He paused at the door and turned to point at a cord near at hand to the desk.

"Should you require anything, Squire, please don't hesitate to ring."

Revin nodded and returned to the puzzle box, turning it over and over in his hands. Eventually, he found the third catch, cleverly concealed. Once triggered, the box popped open, and Revin inspected its contents: a lock of blond hair, bound up with a ribbon, and a lace handkerchief embroidered with the initials 'RG'. Revin blushed, and closed the puzzle box back up and carefully replaced it where it had been on the mantelpiece.

He took one last look around, then seated himself at the desk to get to work. He was just about to open the contract when he noticed a picture frame lying face down on the desk. He lifted it up and saw the portrait of a breathtakingly beautiful young woman looking at him. He wondered if this was RG — the hair color matched — but he finally put the picture down and got to work.

The contract was almost twenty pages long and written in a somewhat unfamiliar style. Much of the language was obviously standard. There were a whole series of clauses about titles and rank and property and severability. It appeared pretty watertight to Revin. He didn't see anything to specifically object to; it all seemed pretty reasonable on the face of it. But he did notice one point: a pre-wedding interview was mentioned, as the prospective bride and groom had not yet met. And if one side raised an objection, there were serious penalties for withdrawing from the arrangement — unless it was by mutual agreement. Under that circumstance alone, both parties could withdraw, and the wedding would be canceled.

Revin leaned back and stretched. He was about to get up when he heard the door creak as it opened. Momo came in carrying a tray. Revin sprang to his feet.

"Sit, sit! I just brought you something to eat. My brother," she said, rolling her eyes. "He never stops to think about other people. You must be starving."

Revin opened his mouth and then closed it again.

"And he told me the silly thing he said to you about not talking," she said. "So you can drop the fish impersonation."

"Thank you," Revin said, blushing. "Thank you very much. I was getting really hungry."

"No. Thank you!" she said. "For helping my brother. He has a hard time letting people help him. So the fact that he depends on you really tells me a lot."

"I would do anything for you," Revin said. "I mean him! I mean ..."

Revin was so embarrassed he wanted to sink into the floor, but she just laughed merrily and placed the tray in front of him. Revin took a big bite of the hearty sandwich. Layered between very sour sourdough bread were ground mustard, spinach, tomato, some kind of smoked sausage, and a strong, flavorful cheese. He made appreciative noises as he wolfed it down. He started to choke from eating too fast, but she handed him a glass of water to wash it down.

"Thanks again," he said. "What kind of cheese is this?"

"It's called 'red cheese'," she replied. "It's one of my favorites."

Revin looked at the sandwich and then looked back at Momo.

"But it's not red: It's white," he said.

"Oh! The cheese comes covered with red wax," she said. "But you take the wax off before you eat it."

"Who is RG?" Revin asked, turning up the picture frame.

"Oh, that's Rachel! She was Griphon's fiancé. He was so head-over-heels in love with her. But she broke things off when ..." Momo trailed off for a moment. "I wonder if he'll try to start things up with her again now that he's back."

"Not bloody likely," Revin muttered, forgetting himself.

"What? What! Wait. Do you ... You *know* something, don't you! Tell me! Tell me!" Momo insisted.

"I'm very sorry, Milady," Revin said, hastily. "It's not my story to tell."

She pouted at him dramatically, but then spoiled the effect by winking.

Grip arrived just as Revin had finished the last bite and was licking his fingers. He asked what Revin had learned.

"Well, the contract is pretty clear that there are serious consequences if we don't agree to the wedding," Revin said.

"I have just spoken with the Baron — our father," Grip said. "He wouldn't tell me who was pulling the strings to arrange the marriage but that, on the face of it, it was not an undesirable match."

Revin's head was spinning trying to parse the double-negative.

"But he was emphatic," Grip continued. "That the arrangement must not be terminated unilaterally by our side. We need to somehow persuade *them* to terminate the contract if we want to prevent the marriage."

They all looked at one another for a moment.

"Maybe I could pretend to be simple," Momo said, making a funny face. They all chuckled.

"Some men might actually prefer that," Grip warned.

Momo grimaced, genuinely disturbed by that thought.

"Maybe if she weren't so pretty," Revin said, suddenly blushing again.

"Or what if she wasn't even a girl?" Grip said.

Revin's heart leapt into his throat, but he swallowed hard and said nothing.

"Now, that's an idea! I could dress up like a man. And maybe use makeup to change my appearance! But would it be convincing enough?

"What do you think?" Momo said, looking at Revin with her innocent and open gaze.

"I ... um ..." Revin hesitated, unsettled, his tongue stumbling over the words. "I'm ... I'm sure you can do it."

Momo beamed with this encouragement.

"You have a tailor, don't you?" Momo asked Grip. "You must take me to him first thing tomorrow."

"We should get some sleep now," Grip said. "I'm exhausted."

Momo said goodnight and departed while Grip pulled the cord to summon a servant. Waiting for someone to arrive, he nudged Revin with his elbow.

"I think *someone* has a crush on you," he chuckled. "Should I inquire whether your intentions regarding my little sister are entirely honorable?"

"Please don't tease me," Revin pleaded.

Grip laughed, then directed the young servant who arrived to lead Revin to a guest chamber for the night and to attend to his needs.

The young man introduced himself as "Terrier, like the dog" and led Revin through the passages of the palace. Revin tried to keep track of the twists and turns they took to get there, but his head was already swimming.

They eventually arrived at a door that the servant opened and held for Revin. Again, the room was immense and luxurious at a scale that was beyond Revin's ability to comprehend; there was simply nothing to compare it with in his frame of reference.

Revin stepped in and then looked around trying to figure out what to do.

"You'll find sleeping apparel in this closet, Squire," Terrier said. "Let me assist you with your clothing."

Revin tried to decline politely, without the horror showing on his face, and the servant bowed and silently showed himself out.

Revin collapsed onto a fainting couch and took a number of deep panting breaths before calming himself down enough to take off his shoes and climb into the bed, still fully clothed — though he took time to loosen his chest binding. He was asleep in moments.

•   •   •

The next morning, Revin was awakened by Terrier, who had seemingly been assigned to him. Terrier was careful to not show any reaction, but Revin imagined he was judging him and had lowered the rating substantially upon discovering that Revin had slept in his clothes, having spurned the offer of sleeping apparel.

"You are expected to breakfast at 6 bells, Squire," Terrier said. "A tub of hot water has been brought in for you to bathe. May I assist you with bathing?"

Revin waved him away, blearily, too groggy to even maintain the pretense of being polite. Terrier left, but silently making clear that Revin's rating was now firmly in the basement.

After Terrier left, Revin checked the door, which appeared to have no lock or bolt. He opened the door and cautiously looked out in both directions. Seeing nothing, he closed the door, stripped, and stepped into the steaming water. It was glorious and he raised his eyes skyward in silent praise. He found a small bottle of shampoo on a shelf of the tub and lathered up his hair, and then washed the rest of his body, scrubbing away the last vestiges of mud and dust from their long journey. He had just reclined back into the water when the door popped open and Momo breezed in.

"Are you decent?" she sang sweetly.

Cursing, Revin shrank back into the tub, grateful for the foam that made the water mostly opaque.

Laughing, she handed him a cup of coffee.

"I thought you might want a little coffee early to clear your head, since you're going to be having breakfast with Papa," she said. "Don't let it worry you too much. He knows how to appreciate people. Ta ta!"

Momo blew in and blew out like a tropical storm leaving emotional chaos in her wake. Revin gratefully sipped the coffee and slipped deeper into the deliciously warm water.

Having completed his ablutions, Revin dressed himself and headed out to find breakfast, forewarned.

Revin was directed by the servants to a small, comfortable dining room that felt totally out of character of the rest of the palace. It was downright cozy, with a serviceable wooden table, and a homey, tattered tablecloth.

He arrived just as 6 bells were striking. Grip and Momo were already eating, and an older couple had already finished a light breakfast and were drinking coffee. Revin started to sit next to Grip, when the older man at the head of the table spoke up.

"You must be Squire Revin," he said. "Come here and let me get a look at you!"

Revin stood back up and walked up to Grip's father, the Baron.

He was an imposing figure, probably in his late 50s, clean-shaven, with some dark hair yet, but gray on the sides. He was a large man, still fit, but no longer in fighting trim. From under his chiseled brow, the Baron's penetrating gray eyes studied Revin. Then he snorted.

"You told me he was a man, Griphon!" he said.

Revin quailed inside, but stood firm.

The Baron continued, laughing. "But this is a youth. A boy! And yet you tell me he saved your life?"

"Without doubt, sir," Grip said to his father. "I would not be here today were it not for the quick thinking and bold action of this young man. And I took him for my squire with no further recommendation."

"Darling," the older woman said. "Don't keep the boy from his breakfast."

"That's right," the Baron said. "A boy like you is always hungry, like as not. Eat your fill!"

Revin smiled gratefully at Lady Belthingstone and returned to his seat, though he rather doubted he could keep anything down with this much stress. Terrier, on his best behavior before the Baron and Lady, didn't let Revin's low rating show on his face while he served him coffee and fruit and eggs and hashed-brown potatoes and bacon and toast and coffee cake. Once the food was placed before him, Revin realized he was, in fact, starving and ate his fill. He looked up at one point and the Baron caught his eye and nodded smugly to see him eating so well.

After breakfast, Momo was eager to visit the tailor's shop and dragged Grip and Revin there as quickly as she could. They arrived just as Cedric was unlocking the door.

"This may be an unusual request," Grip said. "But we're looking for a men's suit for Lady Momoire's matchmaking interview."

"What?" Cedric said, confused.

"But if we're successful, you'll be off the hook for making our vestments because there won't be a ceremony."

Grip explained the circumstances and Cedric, scratching his head, led Momo behind the screen to take her measurements. Revin amused himself looking again at the different clothes that hung around the shop. Some of the interesting costumes he assumed must be for some kind of festival or masquerade ball — he had at least heard of such things among the nobility. In one ear, he listened to Cedric explaining to Momo the kinds of adjustments they would make to help conceal her curves as they came back from around the screen.

"Oh! Squire! Why don't you show her what we did for your chest binding?" Cedric said to Revin as they rejoined Grip.

Momo looked at Revin with shock.

"You're ... Are you?" Momo sputtered at Revin, her shock changing to horror and then to anger.

Words utterly failed Revin and he stood there mute, unable to reply.

"Oh," Cedric said. "Oh, I'm sorry. Was I not supposed to say that?"

Momo turned her back on them. Grip put his hand on her shoulder to try to remonstrate with her, but she shook him off angrily.

"Since this was the plan, I'll go along with it. But I don't ever want to see *her* again," Momo snarled.

Revin felt crushed by her vehemence.

They returned to the palace in silence. Revin felt completely defeated, but followed along behind Grip, trying to maintain his role as dutiful squire. Momo set a brutal pace and, as soon as they arrived, immediately departed for her quarters.

Grip and Revin looked at one another.

"I'm sorry, Revin," Grip said. "Let's go to the Library."

They sat in the Library quietly. Grip found a book to look at, but Revin was too upset to try to read. He just sat on the sofa staring at the floor. He'd been reviled before, but it had never hurt as much as it did now. Seeing Momo's charming face twisted with disgust felt like a knife twisting in his guts. It took everything he had to not burst into tears.

Terrier arrived in the Library, walked up to Revin, and waited. Revin looked up. Terrier's face was impassive and gave no clues.

"Lady Momoire requests your presence in her chambers," Terrier said.

Revin nodded silently and stood. Terrier led him away. This time Revin was so caught up in his own misery, he didn't bother to pay attention to the twists and turns traveled to reach their destination. Terrier delivered him to a door and departed.

Revin knocked quietly.

"Enter!" Momo said.

Revin let himself in.

Lady Momoire occupied a luxurious suite of rooms on a corner of the palace, with windows looking north and west, over the ocean. Revin imagined watching the sunset through the windows and then shook the image out of his head.

Momo was seated in front of a vanity with cosmetics laid out.

"You called for me, Milady," Revin said.

"Apply the makeup like ... like you said, Squire," she said, imperiously.

"Yes, Milady."

Revin looked over what she had available, made some selections, and set the rest aside. He picked up a sponge and began to apply some foundation to Momo's face. She sat rigidly with her fists clenched.

"Why are you choosing such a dark color?" she asked. "I normally choose something lighter."

"You're very fair, Milady," Revin said. "We need to use a very light touch to just create shadows to conceal the roundness of your face. And we don't want to use much makeup because men don't generally wear cosmetics. So it needs to be subtle."

Revin worked in silence while Momo stared straight ahead. After creating the shadows, Revin used some concealer to thin her lips, and mascara to thicken and lower her eyebrows. After several minutes, he stepped back to study the results.

"Please stand, Milady," he said. He gestured for her to turn so he could see the effect of different angles of light and made a few adjustments.

"Now, about your hair," he said. "I think a ponytail could work, but men generally wear theirs a bit lower. May I?" She nodded and suffered him to pull her hair back and tie it. He looked at the nape of her neck, so close to his fingers, and swallowed hard.

"Don't forget to pay attention to your posture and body language," he said. "Men tend to stand balanced, with their feet farther apart and toes pointed out. Yes, like that. Now put your shoulders back and look at me more directly. Very good, Milady."

"You are dismissed, Squire," she said, turning her back on him.

Revin turned and walked to the door. He paused there for a moment and almost turned back to say something. But thought better of it and left quietly.

Revin wandered the halls aimlessly at first, but found he was in fact starting to get the hang of the palace and managed to make his way back to the Library where he resumed his silent vigil on the sofa.

•   •   •

The matchmaking interview took place that afternoon in the Portrait Gallery. Revin stared in wonder at the long hall with stone pillars and vaulted ceilings that featured huge paintings of the barons over the generations. He felt very small in such an immense space.

Each party was allowed to bring two representatives, besides the candidate. The Baron had directed Grip and Revin to serve in his stead. Revin stood two steps back from Grip and tried to maintain an impassive expression as the other side came in from the far door. Momo was trembling with agitation and Revin wished he could do something, but dared not. He nudged Grip and gestured at Momo, so he put a hand on her shoulder to steady her.

She needn't have been so worried, because she really looked the part, Revin thought. She was small, but Cedric had done miracles to make her look taller, with shoe inserts, and a stylish black coat and slacks with sleek lines. These were complemented by a crisp white shirt, a dark maroon cumberbund, and a sharp, narrow blue-and-white tie with the family colors that enhanced the illusion. There were also some nice details: matching gold cufflinks and a tie-tack, both featuring ravens from the Belthingstone coat-of-arms. The ensemble was topped off with a beret, worn at a rakish angle. All Momo lacked was a riding crop to go on a hunt. Moreover, despite Revin's minimal coaching, she had the body language down cold. She stood firmly, balanced, on the balls of her feet with her shoulders back, and looked at everyone directly with a serious, composed expression — in spite of her evident nerves.

A table had been set up in the middle of the hall. Both sides walked slowly toward it, trying to take the measure of the other side. Revin studied the other party, but realized that something was wrong. An older man stood with a guarded expression beside two persons wearing formal dresses. When they reached the table, Momo and the youngest of the three on the other side stepped forward.

"Welcome to Ravensbelth. Please allow me to introduce Lady Momoire Isabelle Celandine Belthingstone of Belleriand," Grip said. "I am her brother Griphon and this is my squire, Revin. We are at your service."

"Thank thee, I do, for thy invitation, Lord Belthingstone," said the older man. "Though surprised I am to not see yon lady's father. The Earl Pennick Felder Kenderback the Second, I am, and this is my … assistant, Julia. And let me introduce my son, Lord Pennick Felder Kenderback the Third."

A person stepped forward wearing elegant white gloves and a long dress.

The dress was a billowing gown of taffeta in a shade of pale pink, with a hint of lilac. The off-the-shoulder neckline plunged to a daring décolletage, embroidered with silver thread strung with tiny pearls matched by a stunning string of large pearls, doubled, and worn as a necklace. Large pink diamond earrings complemented the dress tastefully. And, although he was wearing impossibly high heels, he walked confidently, showing he must have practiced at some length. But his curtsy, though creditable, was of only middling grace. He looked down, as if shyly, until he caught sight of Momo's shoes. Then his eyes traveled up and up until they reached her face.

The younger Pennick and Momo looked at each other and locked eyes. There was a moment of utter silence. Then both of them began to laugh. And then everyone started laughing.

"I take it," Grip said. "That this match is not desired by either side."

"Evidently not," said the Earl. "We can safely tear up the contract, I think."

"Can you explain how this happened?"

"Blackmailed, we were, into announcing the wedding," the Earl said. "My son committed an … indiscretion last year and someone found out about it. We received a letter that we needed to agree to this match or certain documents would be made public. But they said it only mattered that the announcement be made and that we could cancel the wedding. But our house, though old, is not so wealthy as to pay the cost of canceling unilaterally."

"Hmm. Do you know who was blackmailing you?" Grip asked.

"No. No idea, have we."

After several minutes of pleasantries, the parties retired to their separate quarters, but with an agreement to dine together before the Pennicks returned to their remote estate.

Grip and Revin returned to the Library while Momo went back to her quarters to change. Revin leaned back on the sofa, relieved that they would be able to leave soon.

"Is there anything else you want to do here before we head back?" Revin asked.

"I think we can depart tomorrow," Grip said. "I was glad to see my sister free of this inappropriate match. But there's nothing for me here."

"We never found out who arranged the marriage, though," Revin said.

"True," Grip said. "But we stopped the wedding and that's the main thing."

Momo appeared at the doorway with a note in her hand.

"I just got a note from Pennick asking me to meet him on the roof," she said. "He said he wants to show me something about the blackmailer."

"Let's go," Grip said, rising.

Revin followed along. They traveled through a series of hallways until they reached a narrow door that led into a circular stairway that led up, up, and up. When they finally reached the top of the stairs, they emerged through a doorway onto the rooftop. The roof of this part of the palace was flat with a low, crenelated wall around its perimeter. Several gables and turrets stood along the periphery.

Then they saw the body lying out in the open: It was Pennick, the young groom to be. Grip and Momo ran to check, but Revin hung back, surveying the rooftop.

When he arrived at the body, Grip saw the fletching of a crossbow-bolt protruding from the space between the man's neck and collarbone. He had seen death often enough to know at a glance that the young man was gone. Momo tried feeling for a pulse, then pulled her hand back in horror, as his clothes were soaked with his blood.

Revin spotted a figure on a nearby turret and shouted, "Look out!"

Grip jumped back and a crossbow bolt skipped off the pavement where he had been a moment before. The bolt, though slowed, still caught him in the calf. Grip fell, rolling in pain. Momo stood paralyzed while the man calmly reloaded and cocked the crossbow. Revin gestured frantically at her to join him, but she was petrified with shock.

Revin tried to think of something he could do. He remembered where he was and he got out his signaling mirror. He scanned the horizon over the ocean searching for the *Queen*.

"Well, well, well, Griphon," the man shouted. "I knew that wedding announcement would flush you out. How does it feel now? I'm going to kill you. But not before I kill your cocktease of a sister!"

"Leave her alone, Maris," Grip responded. "Vent your anger on me alone."

"No way," he sneered. "She was leading me on. This is all her fault!"

"She was a child!" Grip yelled. "You tried to force yourself on her."

"Now she dies," Maris said, raising the crossbow. "Any last words, bitch?"

At that moment, Revin stepped into view and used his signaling mirror to reflect the sunlight so that it played across the eyes of the assassin. Maris tried to aim at Revin, but was momentarily blinded, causing the shot to go wide.

Revin darted across the roof to Momo. He grabbed her hand and dragged her forward with him. They ran until they were sheltered behind a gable, shielded from view of the tower.

Maris calmly reloaded again.

"Well, so now I'll have to kill you first, Griphon. But fear not. I will track down and kill your bitch sister yet this day."

He raised his crossbow again, drawing a bead on Grip, but a shadow suddenly fell over him. He spun to face the threat. Will, flying out of the sun with the glider, landed both his feet on the man's chest and kicked hard. Maris was flung from the turret, falling to the pavement below. Maris' broken body twitched in a growing puddle of blood and urine before finally remaining still. Momo threw herself against Revin and buried her face in his chest, sobbing. He awkwardly enfolded her in his arms and tried to comfort her.

Will descended and alighted on the roof, taking a few running steps, and coming to a stop well before the edge. He unstrapped himself from the glider and ran to Grip.

Momo watched with astonishment as he hugged his first mate and lavished kisses upon him. She turned and looked at Revin bewildered.

"Is that ..." Momo stammered. "Are they ..."

"Yeah. Pretty much," said Revin.

"But how did he even know?" she asked.

"Oh!" said Revin. "I signaled the *Queen* with my mirror first. Just 'GRIP HURT WIL FLY'. But I knew the Cap'n would know what to do."

Suddenly, a flood of men appeared on the roof. The *Queen* had come alongside the edge of the palace and set the gangplank onto the roof. One team of pirates ran to collect the glider, while another came to assist Grip.

Will, once again the stern captain of pirates, called out, "Hurry, men! Be careful with that or the Professor will have your hides! Board up! Their airships will be on us before you know it!"

"Goodbye, Milady," Revin said, with a bow. Then he turned and ran for the *Queen*.

"Revin!" Momo called after him.

He paused, then turned back. The men watching called him to hurry, but then began to laugh as they saw why he was running back.

She stood firmly, tear-stained and streaked with blood. Revin stood before her, uncertainly.

"I'm sorry for how I treated you," she said. "I was so hateful to you. But you saved my life. And my brother's life. You really are a true hero. My hero."

"I was just glad to be of service, Milady," Revin said.

She drew a handkerchief from her pocket and proffered it to him with both hands, "Squire Revin, please accept my favor and may it bring thee good fortune wherever thy travels may bear thee."

The men were silent.

"By your grace, Milady," he replied, gravely accepting her handkerchief.

Then he turned and sprinted for the airship, with the men erupting in cheers.

The *Queen of Belleriand* rose and turned back toward the sea, other airships in hot pursuit. But they had no hope of catching up with the speedy *Queen*.

Momo waved until they were out of sight and fancied she could see a white handkerchief being waved in reply.

INTERLUDE

THE *QUEEN OF BELLERIAND* RETURNED to Kapper Island and, after she was unloaded (a perfunctory gesture, as she'd captured no prizes), the hands were dismissed as usual. As Revin began to walk away, Will hailed him.

"You're still looking a bit green around the gills," he said.

"I keep seeing that man's face," he said. "I ... I've never seen anything like that."

"Well, let me be the first to thank you," Grip said. "I'd have been in trouble if he'd been able to loose another quarrel."

"Thank you," Revin said. "I wouldn't have been able to live with myself if ... if anything had happened to you. I don't ... I think ... I don't feel good." Revin covered his mouth with hand as another wave of nausea washed over him.

"Go freshen up. But I think what you need is occupation," Will said. "For the next few days, why don't you work with the

Professor. He can show you how we maintain the airship and give you something to do that will take your mind off things."

Revin nodded and several minutes later, after dropping off his things, he went looking for the Professor. He found him on scaffolding with several workmen looking at the fabric on the nose of the *Queen of Belleriand*.

"Hmph," he growled when Revin arrived. "Took you long enough."

"What can I do?" Revin asked.

"You're small," he said. "Go onto the *Queen* and find Moose. You can help with the inspection."

"Moose?"

"Get moving, Cabin Boy!" the Professor barked.

"Aye, aye!" said Revin, retreating at the quick march.

He descended the ladder from the scaffolding and then entered the *Queen* via the gangplank.

He ran from one end of the aircraft to the other, but didn't find anyone. Finally, on his second circuit, he noticed an open hatch in the ceiling of the observation deck.

"Moose?" he called up into the darkness.

Someone grunted. And Revin climbed the ladder and poked his head inside.

"The Professor said I should come help you."

The man, who was large and gawky, pointed forward where there was a narrow crawl space.

"Check the fabric for fit and wear," he said.

"For ... what?" Revin asked.

"The fabric should be taut," he said. "And where it comes in contact with the frame, make sure it's not wearing thin."

"Aye, aye," Revin said, headed to the crawlspace.

"Wait!" Moose called. when Revin turned, he continued, "Take this." And he handed Revin a knife in a sheath.

"In case you get enveloped in fabric or need to get out fast, always carry a knife."

"Aye, aye," he said, and slipped the sheath onto his belt. Then he started down the crawl way.

Revin was reminded of when he was moving through the interstitial spaces of the *Madeline*. The *Queen* was constructed somewhat differently, but the feel was the same.

Revin reached the end of the crawl way and realized he was seeing the framing and skin of the airship from the inside. He noticed a bright spot of light.

"I can see a pinhole," Revin called back.

"Just one?"

"Yeah."

"Now check all of the sections of fabric. Are any baggy or loose?"

"Oh!" Revin said. "Yeah. I can see some fabric ... billowing in one section."

"You're good at this!" Moose said. "Come back out for a minute and let me get you set."

Revin backed out through the narrow crawl way and Moose met him as he emerged.

"Two things," he said. "First, take this pot of glue and a patch kit. You can just smear some glue over the hole and then stick one of these small, round patches over the pinhole. Then smooth it for a minute or two until the glue sets.

"And also take this wrench. There are spacers holding the ribs apart. Find the bolt and then turn it to smooth out the fabric that's billowing."

"That's it?" Revin said. "It sounds easy!"

"Whoa," Moose said. "You may find that when you smooth out the fabric in one place, it starts to billow in an adjacent place."

"Yeah?" Revin said.

"So you might have to adjust adjacent panels as well."

"Okay."

"And this is just the first crawl way. There are thirty-two more."

"Oh, no!" Revin said.

Revin spent the next six hours checking all of the crawl ways. He found two more pinholes to patch and had to adjust sixteen panels to smooth the fabric evenly across the frame of the *Queen.*

"This is a lot of work," Revin said.

"Now we need to check the gasbags," Moose said.

"The what?"

"The *Queen* uses big bags that are full of lighter-than-air gas. They provide the lift that keeps the *Queen* aloft."

"Where does this gas come from?"

"That's a good question," Moose said. "After we're done here, I'll let the Professor answer that one. For the moment, we just need to top off the gas bags to ensure they're full. The gas is always leaking out all the time, so we always need to add more before the *Queen* sets out. And the leakage determines our range. As people drink the water — and then ... eliminate it — we lose weight. And those things tend to cancel each other out, so that, even though we're losing gas we don't lose so much buoyancy that we crash. But if we didn't refill just before she leaves, she might not make it back."

"How many gasbags are there?"

"The Queen has ten."

"Ten!" Revin exclaimed.

"A larger airship, like those big passenger ships, sometimes has fifteen or even twenty."

Revin was speechless.

Moose directed Revin along an interior gangway above the passenger spaces that was just below the huge gasbags that filled the upper part of the airship. At each, Revin found a tied off section that he could open and then attach a thick hose that Moose passed up to him.

"Watch the sides of the gas bag," Moose said. "You should see movement as the gas fills the gasbag. Once the movement is below the last structural element, you can tie off the gasbag and move to the next one."

Revin did as he was told, moving from one to the next until all of the gasbags had been replenished.

Finally, late in the day, Moose released him and Revin went

down and joined the rest of the pirates, already well into their cups. He grabbed a few skewers of roasted chicken and took a seat off to the side. He took a few bits, leaned back, and released a big sigh, finally able to relax.

"Ahem," said a gravelly voice at his elbow. Revin flinched as he looked over to see the Professor.

"Moose said you worked hard today," he growled.

"I tried to," Revin squeaked, defensively.

"You did well!" the Professor said quickly. "You did very well!"

"Really?" Revin asked, mollified.

"Yes. I wish half of my staff worked half as well as you."

"Oh!" Revin said. Then after a pause, he added, "Thank you."

"Tomorrow, I want to show you something," the Professor continued. "Come find me right after breakfast."

"Yessir," Revin said.

The Professor hand-walked away with his crutches and Revin took a few deep breaths to calm himself.

•　　　•　　　•

When Revin awoke, at sunrise, he remembered he was meeting the Professor and wondered what it was he wanted to show him. He washed his face, went to breakfast and, afterwards, walked over to where the *Queen* was tied up under the camouflage netting.

"There you are," the Professor growled. "Finally."

"How long have you been here?" Revin asked.

"Long enough," he barked. "Come this way."

Revin followed as he hand walked away from the *Queen* and along a forest path under the low scrub that covered most of the island.

"Where are we going?" Revin asked.

"I want to show you something," the Professor said.

They followed a level path around the side of the mountain and came to a more open area. Revin perceived that, nearby, were long tubes lying along the ground at one end, the tubes were opaque, but then there were long sections of transparent glass tubing connected together with brass rings. Inside there was greenish, pinkish … stuff.

"This is how we generate our hydrogen," the Professor said. "It serves as our lighter-than-air gas. It's the lightest gas there is," he continued. "But it's explosive. That's why we have to be so careful."

"How do you make it?"

"We have colonies of algae and bacteria inside the glass parts of the tube. They use sunlight to chemically split water into hydrogen and oxygen," he said. "And the bubbles of hydrogen are released to flow through the tube back to big bags where we collect the hydrogen until we're ready to add it to the gasbags in the *Queen*."

"Why do they do that?" Revin asked.

"To be honest," the Professor admitted. "Nobody's quite sure why they do it. But they do it and we can use it to generate the hydrogen we need."

"I guess you can't argue with that," Revin said.

"But every day we need to walk the full length of all of the glass sections to look for colony die back."

"Die back?"

"Sometimes the colonies get out of balance and start to die. If we don't catch it and correct it, it will spread and ruin the colony for the whole tube."

"What do we do when we find one?"

"We can remove the contents of a single section and then let it get recolonized from either side."

"Okay," Revin said. "What do you want me to do?"

"Start walking longshanks," the Professor snapped.

"Oh," Revin said. "How do I recognize colony die back?"

The Professor handed him a handful of little stakes with flags.

"Just look for any sections that look different. And then mark them with a stake. I'll send Moose to check them later. Now get to work."

"Aye, aye," Revin said.

After the Professor hand walked back down the path, Revin began walking the length of the first tube. They were longer than he'd imagined, stretching around the mountain. At the far end, he found a network of hoses that carried water from a dammed-up stream that fed into the tubes. Then he started walking back along a second tube.

It was boring work. His mind began to wander. He reflected on his recent terrifying adventures. He shivered to think of how close he'd come to a bad end. But then he saw a section of the tube where a section of the algae were brown and black rather than the greenish-pinkish of the healthy sections. He stuck a stake in the ground and then kept walking. Over the next two hours, he found three more sections that were showing signs of die back.

The sun was growing high and Revin was getting hot and thirsty when Moose arrived and handed him a water skin.

"Drink," he said, unceremoniously.

Revin drank deeply and then squirted some on his head.

"You're half way there!" Moose said, encouragingly. "Do you need more stakes?"

Revin shook his head and started walking again.

A half hour later, he saw Moose arriving with two other men. He waved Revin over.

"Here's how we fix the die back," he said.

They brought a big wrench and loosened the brass rings that connected the sections of glass tubing. Water began to flow out of the joints as they removed the section of tubing and extracted a section of wicker latticework.

"The algae grow on this structure. We need to clean out the bad stuff and put a fresh lattice back in, and the algae and bacteria will colonize from the adjacent sections."

With a long brush, they scrubbed out the glass tube, slipped in a new wicker latticework, then reinserted the glass tube and tightened the brass rings. Water began to fill the tube.

"Keep inspecting," Moose said. "We'll fix the rest of the sections you marked."

Revin kept at it for another hour and half until he finally reached the end of the last section. He was exhausted, drenched with sweat, and sunburned. Moose waved at him to go back to the pirate base while he continued to direct the men who were cleaning out the sections with die back.

As he returned to the base, tired and footsore, the Professor saw him and hand-walked over to meet him.

"Knocking off early, are we?" he laughed.

"Is there something else I should do?" Revin groaned.

"No, boy," he said, slapping Revin's backside. "Moose said you did a good job. If you get tired of being Cabin Boy, I can always find a spot for you on my team. But, tomorrow you can go again, and this time, take the clippers to cut back all the new woody growth."

Revin nodded, but privately, he fervently hoped that the *Queen* would be headed out on a new mission soon.

3

STORM CLOUDS GATHER

"STORM AHEAD, CAP'N," Revin called.

Will came forward to the observation deck of the *Queen of Belleriand* and looked over Revin's shoulder. A towering cumulonimbus thunderhead spread out dead ahead and above them. Flashes of lightning flickered here and there, illuminating different parts of the roiling clouds, then tracing the sky in long tongues of light.

"It's a big storm," Will said. "We're not going over that one. We'll need to tack around. Which way is it moving?"

"It's moving west by southwest, headed right for us, Cap'n."

"Grip!" Will called.

"Yes, Will?"

"Have the remmers take us north. Let's give this one a wide berth."

"Aye, aye, Will!" Grip said, and headed back to the remmer deck.

Revin waited for the *Queen* to tack toward the north, but nothing happened. A moment later, Grip ran in, breathless.

"The remmers can't find any etheric streams! They're all gone!"

Will sprinted back to the remmer deck and Revin followed. The remmers used large lenses, mounted on poles that ran from the deck to the ceiling, to locate the etheric streams and bind them with a towline to a pole. But they searched everywhere with the lenses, unable to find streams to tie to.

Will pulled out his monocle and studied the sky for streams first on one side and then on the other.

"I don't see any close by either," he said. "I can see one a long way off. Let me try for that one."

A weak towline snapped into place and the *Queen* sluggishly began to turn.

The other remmers stood awestruck that Will could see, let alone attach to, a stream so far away. Once they saw his, the other remmers on that side all tried; two of them were able to catch the stream as well. The *Queen* picked up speed, but Will felt her buffeted by the outer winds of the huge storm.

"Call attach life lines," Will said to Grip as he headed back to the cockpit.

"Attach life lines," Grip bellowed, running through the ship.

The men yanked out their life lines and snapped them to rings set through the ship.

Revin followed Will to the cockpit where they both snapped in. The *Queen* shuddered under the battering winds. Several times she suddenly dropped or climbed a dozen feet in the turbulent air. Revin held on, his stomach uneasy. Will stood firm with Revin at his shoulder as the *Queen* slipped past the huge storm and headed for the calmer air beyond. In about thirty minutes later, it was finally behind them.

"What happened?" Revin asked. "What was that?"

"I have no idea," said Will. "I've never seen anything like that before."

·   ·   ·

"Mail call!" Grip said.

Revin ignored him because he never got letters. They had returned to Kapper Island, the pirate's secret base, days earlier, but Grip had just returned from a provisioning trip to the nearby island of Candlemain, where the pirates purchased most of their food and supplies.

"Mail call!" Grip repeated, tossing Revin a letter.

Surprised, Revin caught it. It was a small letter in a fancy cream-white envelope. His name was beautifully penned on it. On its other side, the flap was sealed with wax.

"Who is this from?" he asked.

Grip grinned at him. "Open it and see!"

Revin carefully unsealed the letter and pulled out a piece of thick, matching stationery and read the letter.

My dearest hero, it said. *We had such a short time together, but there's so much I want to know about you! I beg that you might keep a journal for me, that we may exchange them when next our paths cross. You are ever in my thoughts. Truly yours,*

It was signed merely, *M.*

"A journal?" Revin mused.

Grip raised an eyebrow, so Revin passed the note to him. He read it, his grin getting wider and wider.

"I think you've been given your marching orders," Grip laughed.

"Hmm," Revin said, unconvinced.

Grip returned the letter and Revin read and re-read it again. He looked up and saw Grip, who had been evidently watching him with a grin, look away suddenly.

"There's a nice lady at the market on Candlemain who sells bound journals," he said. "Maybe you should come with us the next time we go."

"But what would I even write in a journal?" Revin asked.

"You're thinking about it too hard," Grip said. "She's living in a gilded cage and you're living a life of adventure. Anything you write about will seem amazing to her."

"How did she even send a letter to me anyway?" Revin asked.

"Two years ago, when I left Belleriand, I told her how she could contact me by writing to an address in Candlemain. And whenever I go there, I check for mail," Grip replied. "Do you know how many times she's written to me?"

"I have no idea," Revin said. "Four times?"

"Zero," he replied. "And all she said in this letter was, 'Please give this note to my hero.'"

Revin looked at the floor. He blushed, but found he couldn't stop smiling. Grip chuckled as he walked away to deliver the rest of the mail.

After Grip left, Revin sat on his bed and pulled out Momo's lace handkerchief, which he kept tucked away near his bedside. He unfolded it and felt Momo's embroidered initials. He closed his eyes and held the handkerchief up to his nose and inhaled, imagining he could still detect a note of her perfume.

●　　　●　　　●

Revin stared at the ground the next day, but not with a smile, as he ran with tiny steps up the steep trail. Everyone else had passed him, and some had already started passing him coming back down. Revin doggedly kept his pace. Two weeks ago, he could only run for a minute or two up the mountain and then had to walk. Now, he could run, albeit slowly, the entire way.

"Hurry up, boy!" Will said, slapping his backside while coming back down.

Revin growled, but lacked sufficient breath to yell the word he was thinking. He doggedly kept running at his pace all the way to the top and then back down, his legs burning with pain at the effort. But running was just the beginning.

As soon as he caught his breath, Will led the pirates in calisthenics, isometrics, and gymnastics. Grip, who was still convalescing from his injury in Belleriand, lay in a hammock in the shade and raised a cool drink to Revin, who stood sweating and cursing in the sun.

Revin had been skeptical about all the effort, but found that the training — and the gymnastics, in particular — helped with his balance, strength, and endurance. He was leaner now, and had more energy to throw himself into accomplishing demanding tasks. He grudgingly acknowledged that it wasn't that hard, once he got used to it, and it made him feel better.

On alternate days, after the daily run, Revin took weapons training. Grip was the only pirate who had any formal training in weapons, and so it fell to him. At first, he would hobble around with a crutch and critique Revin's form. And then, as his leg healed, they would increasingly spar.

When they started, Revin had been excited to look at weapons. The pirates had a large collection of swords captured over the previous months. Revin tried picking up some, but quickly became discouraged at how heavy they were. After trying out a variety of options, they settled on a smallsword as the best fit for Revin's arm.

"I hate to say it, Revin," Grip said. "But you just aren't strong enough for a cutlass or a saber. You need something light — at least until you get stronger."

Grip then sent Revin to the Professor to request he construct a practice sword with similar properties to the real sword. He looked at the sword, then looked at Revin fiercely from under his bushy eyebrows.

"You're going to get yourself killed if you play with these things," he grumbled.

"I want to be able to protect my friends," Revin said.

"Worry about yourself first," the Professor said. "You can't help anyone if you're dead."

"Please?" Revin said, sweetly.

"Ugh. It's your funeral," the Professor said. "We'll have something for you by tomorrow."

At their next practice session, Grip stalked up and down in front of Revin, expounding on theory.

"Look. So here's the thing. Normally, I would have a new student practice a parry-and-riposte cycle with the pell — that's that post over there. There's a certain rhythm to it, and it will help strengthen your arm and let us practice form. But I'm not going to do that with you, and here's why: I want you to defend yourself only and aim to defend yourself just until you can disengage and escape.

"If you're cornered and have no choice but to fight, you need to defend yourself first and foremost. But never forget that an experienced swordsman will still be able to kill you very quickly. Your best bet is to parry and try to disengage. Got that? Parry and try to disengage. Please depend on the rest of us to kill the swordsman and you just keep yourself alive. Okay? Please?" He made Revin promise.

Instead of the pell, Grip used a wooden sword to give Revin practice in parrying. Revin wore a helmet and gloves to protect his hands, but Grip showed no mercy in giving him painful bruises on his arms and thighs — and whacking him on the helmet if he failed to parry correctly.

"You're dead!" Grip would shout. "You're dead! Faster! Keep your arm up! Don't look away! Never look away!"

But afterwards, no matter how difficult the training had been, he would relent and give Revin an encouraging smile or word. And Revin would bask in the glow of praise well earned.

●   ●   ●

One day, Will unexpectedly asked Revin, "What did your test for remmer ability say?"

"My what?"

"Your test for ... Wait! Are you telling me you were never tested?"

"I don't have any idea what you're talking about," Revin said. "Nobody ever did anything like that where I grew up."

"Well, follow me," Will said, coming to his feet. "Let's go down to the shore so you can see the sky better."

They followed the trail with its switchbacks down to the narrow strip of sand that passed for a beach on the pirate's island. When they reached the shore, Will turned.

"There are three parts to the test. The first is whether or not you can see etheric streams. Some people can see them all the time — I'm like that, though some people can supposedly see them more clearly than I can. Some people can only see them with a lens. And most people can't see them at all.

"I would just ask if you can see them, but you probably wouldn't know because everything just looks the way it's always looked. So, here. Use my monocle. Does anything look different?"

Revin held the monocle up to his eye and gasped.

"Well," Will said. "I guess that answers that. Now for step two, try this: See this pebble?" He nudged a stone with his toe. "Pick an etheric stream — pick the biggest, closest one you can see. Now visualize a towline coming down to this pebble."

Revin tried for a minute with no effect and then shook his head.

"It's not working," he said. "Maybe I can't do it."

"Don't give up so easily, boy!" Will said. "Close your eyes for a minute. Take a few deep breaths. Relax. Okay. Now try again. Just let your eyes go out of focus and don't force it. Just let it happen."

Revin did as he was instructed and, after a minute with no results, he tried to visualize a hand reaching up and pulling a long fiber down from the braided etheric stream he could see. Down, down, down until it touched the pebble. Suddenly he could see it! It was very faint, but it was there: a tiny glowing towline, as fine as a thread. The pebble wobbled and then the towline seemed to evaporate.

"I did it!" he crowed, exultantly. "Did you see that?"

"That's step two," Will said. "Step three is going to take a lot longer. Now the question is how big of a towline can you make: How much can you pull? I want you to take an hour every day to come down here and practice. Let's see where we are in a week."

Revin started to hand back Will's monocle, but he waved it away and then tousled Revin's hair.

"You keep that one for the moment. I've got another. But let me show you something. Close your eyes. Now look again with your eyes shut — without the distraction of seeing the world. Can you still see them?"

Revin gasped and then nodded.

"Without the lens, you can probably only see the brightest, closest etheric streams," Will continued. "They're not much good for airships, because the closest ones are generally useless for steering anyway. But in a pinch, they're better than nothing."

Revin practiced diligently. At first, he could only make pebbles rock back and forth. Then he was able to lift one off the ground for a moment. As he gained confidence, he gained control. On the third day, he could send one into the sky and, if he was careful, he could toss the pebble out to sea or even just toss it up and (usually) catch it. But he still couldn't lift more than a small stone.

After a week, Will walked with him back to the shore and watched while Revin showed him what he could do. After going through his recitation, Will indicated another pebble and said, "Go ahead and try to lift this one."

Revin centered himself, took a deep breath, inspected the streams, and had just formed a towline, when Will casually grabbed a different pebble with a towline and popped Revin in the face with it. The towline Revin had just formed winked out.

"Ow!" Revin said. "What was that for?"

"It's all well and good to be able to settle yourself and take your time. But you should also practice making towlines under pressure. You're not always going to have the luxury of taking your time without distractions."

"What good is just lifting a pebble anyway?" Revin said, discouraged.

"Well, as you've just seen, it can be a great distraction, especially when used unexpectedly. Don't sell yourself short, lad! Who knows when it might prove handy? You might be surprised."

Will clapped him on the shoulder and the two of them returned to the pirate's base.

•   •   •

On market day, Revin took the sailboat with Will, Grip, Ham (the quartermaster), and two others to get supplies on Candlemain. They departed at sunrise in the *Little WormMaid* — the small sailboat the pirates maintained. As there was no harbor, the boat needed to be kept on land and launched each time they used it. And, as it was quite small there was only very limited room for people, since they would be fully laden with provisions on the return trip.

The trip took about two hours across the open ocean before they arrived in Candlemain harbor. They paid the docking fees willingly, given the amount of supplies they intended to take on, and then strolled through town to the plaza where the market was held.

In a brightly-painted open structure, men sold meat and fish, while women sold crafts, fruits, and vegetables. Will and two others fanned out through the market to dicker with the vendors and buy provisions for the crew. The crew had become familiar faces at the market, and everyone knew that, while they might drive a hard bargain, they would also buy large quantities. So there was fierce competition to sell to them.

"That's the lady that sells the nice, bound journals," Grip laughed, pointing to a stall on the far side.

Revin blushed again, which only made Grip laugh harder. But Revin walked through the market over to the woman's stall and looked at what she had on display. An older, heavy-set woman with a kind smile, she nodded and murmured encouragingly when he asked if he could touch the merchandise.

He looked through several of the journals. Some were bound with leather and some with cardboard; some had little straps to keep them closed. One even had a lock with tiny keys. One that caught his attention had a raven on it. Or possibly a crow. But Revin liked the look of that one which reminded him of the Belthingstone coat of arms. He was about to purchase it when he felt a sting in his arm. His head began to swim and he lost the ability to think coherently. He was not unconscious or asleep, but it was like he had become a passive observer in his own body.

"This way," a voice said in his ear and steered him away from the market.

They walked a short distance to a cart backed up to the market.

A bearded and burly man opened a large crate that was tipped on its side with the top facing toward the back.
"Get inside," he said to Revin.
Revin didn't want to, but lacked the ability to resist. They pushed him into the crate and closed it up. Revin perceived that there were air holes and sat passively, unable to react.

The cart began to roll. Revin sat, bounced over a bumpy path out of the plaza and into the town. He noticed when the pavement changed to cobblestone and then smoother pavement. Revin could smell the sea and hear the cries of sea birds.

"Revin! Revin!" he heard.

And then, quite nearby, he heard Grip and Will arguing good-naturedly, but with their anxiety causing their banter to wear thin.

"If my squire has been abducted right under my nose," said Grip. "I'll never forgive myself if anything happens to him."

"*Your* squire? He's also *our* cabin boy! And we won't find another like him. Let's keep looking. You go that way."

Revin desperately wanted to tell them that he was not ten feet away. But, under the influence of the drug, he couldn't bring himself to do anything. He cursed himself for being unable to react.

After a few minutes, the crate was loaded aboard a boat. It set sail only a few minutes later. Revin could see nothing, but could feel when the boat left the harbor and met the larger ocean swells.

Just as the drug was beginning to wear off, someone opened the crate. Revin caught a glimpse of the island vanishing in the distance before they shoved a hood over his head and bound his hands behind his back.

Minutes later, he was strapped into a basket and hoisted by rope to an airship that carried him to points unknown.

•　　　•　　　•

Revin, still hooded, was half dragged through a corridor and then into a room. He was thrust roughly onto a chair and the hood was yanked off his head. The room contained only his chair, another chair, and a small table between them. Harsh gas lights on the back wall, turned up bright, made Revin's eyes blink and water. A man sat across from him at the table, visible only as a silhouette. He opened a folder with documents and studied them silently for several long, uncomfortable minutes. Then he looked up.

"When were you first approached about working for Havelock?" the interrogator asked.

Revin digested this, but the question didn't make sense. He said nothing.

"How did you learn that Dirge was working for Belleriand?"

Revin tried to not let surprise show on his face. Was Professor Dirge not just the stodgy academic everyone believed he was? It must have been a deep cover, as Revin had worked for him for the better part of a year on a book project before traveling to Havelock. But still Revin said nothing.

"You know I'll break you, eventually," the interrogator continued. "So why not talk now?"

"I know," Revin finally said. "But since I know you'll break me eventually, why would I say anything now?"

The interrogator made a gesture and two burly men grabbed Revin's arms and held him up on his toes. A third man took a large pair of shears and proceeded to cut off all of his clothing. Revin shuddered to feel the cold metal slide along his skin.

When the man cut off the chest bindings and released Revin's breasts, he said, "Hey, look! It has tits!"

All of the men laughed.

They dragged him down a narrow hallway and into a dimly-lit room with no windows and a drain in the middle of the floor. A set of manacles dangled from the ceiling over the drain. They attached the manacles and then raised the chain until he was left standing naked on a cold stone floor, his wrists chained above his head. Then they turned out the lights and left.

On tiptoe, he could take the pressure off his wrists. But, as his calves began to fatigue and spasm, he would start to dangle and the cuffs cut into his flesh — gravity, a tormentor with endless patience.

A pair of men came back after a time. They mocked him casually, and then one slapped him suddenly, which snapped his head to the side and made his ears ring. He lost his balance and had to fight to get back to his feet. They walked away laughing.

Revin lost track of time. He was unable to sleep, yet unable to stay awake. He would nod off and then be jerked awake by the manacles cutting into his wrists. Tormented by thirst, he became light-headed from dehydration. He imagined phantom sounds and worried that he was beginning to hallucinate.

Two men, the same or different ones from earlier, entered carrying a wooden table with an inclined top, a piece of cloth, and a bucket of water. One grabbed Revin's face while the other stood back.

Revin recognized that he was growing weaker and, if he didn't take any action quickly, he would soon become too weak to do anything. But he understood that, by working in pairs, even if one were incapacitated, the other could still call for help. So he bided his time and did nothing.

"Do you know what this is for?" the man purred in Revin's ear. "You'll be begging to talk once we use this. Are you sure you don't want to save yourself the pain?"

Revin still said nothing. They eventually departed and left Revin in the dark again. Revin had managed to stay strong while the men were there, but after they left, he broke down into agonized sobs.

After another indeterminate period of time — maybe minutes, maybe hours — Revin heard steps coming down the stairs. But only a single set of footsteps this time. Revin strained to stand on his tiptoes and grasped the chains above the manacles, then slumped back into a posture of unconsciousness.

The door opened and the man with the shears from earlier— the one who had commented on his breasts — came back in alone. Revin's heart raced, but he remained in a slumped posture with his eyes closed. He heard the man approach quietly. Suddenly, the man grabbed his breasts and squeezed them hard. Revin was revolted and felt like he was going to vomit, but he pushed his chest out and up and affected a quiet moan, as though aroused. The man bent down to put his mouth on Revin's nipples.

When he could feel the man's breath, Revin put his full weight onto his hands on the chains and convulsively brought up his knees into the man's chin. All of the physical training he'd been doing paid dividends. Revin's knee connected. The man's jaw clacked shut, his head snapped back, and, after falling over backward, he cracked his head on the stone floor. The man moaned incoherently and passed out.

Revin reached desperately with his foot toward a key chain on the man's belt. He managed to get his toes on it and was pleasantly surprised he could pull it off. But then he was stumped. He had the key ring in his toes, but how to get it to his hands over his head?

He tried tossing the keys with his foot and managed to get the ring up to his knees, but it was pretty clear that this was hopeless. He was on the verge of screaming with frustration when he remembered lifting pebbles on the beach.

Revin closed his eyes, centered himself, and tried to see the etheric streams. He looked for one moving up and toward his back, then tried to form a towline to the keyring. The keyring flew up and smacked him right in the face.

"Ow!" Revin said, involuntarily. He then listened with terror that someone might have heard the noise and come to investigate, but his luck held and there was silence.

He tried a second time. This time, the keys flew up and struck the ceiling. As they dropped, he frantically tried to catch them as they went by, but they hit him on the shoulder, then slipped to the floor. He tried again and again and, finally, managed to catch them in his hand.

Flushed with elation, he stood on his tip toes and began trying keys in the barrel lock of the manacles. The first key didn't work, nor the next or the next. There weren't many keys and Revin began to panic. But, finally, a key fit, snapped, and he got one manacle off. And then the other.

He collapsed onto the floor, his arms and shoulders burning, and his legs tingling with the strain. After a few moments, he dragged himself to his feet and checked on the unconscious guard. He was still out cold. Revin resisted the temptation to kick him.

Revin went to the bucket of water. It seemed to be only clear, fresh water, so he took a deep drink until he ran out of breath. Then, once he caught his breath, he drank again with pleasure.

Much refreshed, he stripped the unconscious guard and, after he found the catch, he lowered the chain to the ground and locked the manacles on the man's wrists. He wasn't strong enough to raise the man up. So he simply left him where was on the floor.

The clothes were too big for him, but he cinched the belt, rolled up the cuffs of the pant legs, and decided it didn't look too bad. The man carried almost nothing, but he did wear a belt knife, although it was insignificant as a weapon.

He listened carefully to be sure that there was no one on the lower level, and began to quietly climb the stairs. Halfway up, he heard quiet voices and footsteps. Revin paused and considered how he could get past the guards. He wracked his brain and then seized upon an idea.

Tearing a strip from the bottom of the shirt, he used the knife to cut a small slice in his forearm, he let it bleed freely, and collected the blood in his mouth. Then, with a mouthful of blood and spit, he bound up the wound as best he could and climbed to the top of the stairs.

He opened the door, doubled over as if in terrible pain and spat the blood and saliva in his mouth out while making gagging noises like he was vomiting. The guards, who had run over to investigate, suddenly recoiled. They hustled him out the door and onto the street, shouting, "Go to the doctor!". The door slammed behind him. Revin couldn't help grinning, with blood running down his chin, while he looked at his surroundings.

He was in a city. He scanned the environment for anything recognizable. Then the clock struck seven bells and he recognized the distinctive sound of its chimes. He was in the capital of Belleriand! He ran to the nearest intersection to get a better view of the horizon and spotted one of the turrets of Ravensbelth — the Belthingstone palace — and he headed that way at a trot. Then he heard shouting behind him. The guards had evidently figured out that he'd escaped and were in pursuit.

Revin ran as fast as he could down the unfamiliar streets, panting and out of breath — but still able to run, seeking the shortest path to the palace. He heard yells, but he was yet out of the view of his pursuers. He emerged from an alleyway at full speed and was confronted with the twelve-foot wall that enclosed the grounds of Ravensbelth. Without breaking stride, Revin found a strong etheric stream going his way, appealed to the sky, and put everything into making the strongest attachment he could. A fat towline snapped into view, and he ran straight up the wall and rolled over the top.

He fell and landed in a holly bush, where he was scratched and scraped. But safe — for the moment. He heard his pursuers emerge from the alley and split up to go both left and right and to double back to find where they had lost him. Revin caught his breath, laid low, and watched. After a few minutes, a guard wearing Belthingstone colors emerged from around the palace on the right and passed through the formal garden where he was concealed under the holly.

Revin considered surrendering to the guard, but he decided against it — at least, unless he had no other choice. It could be that these guards would not turn him in. But he had insufficient confidence in that. So he simply watched until the guard passed around the far side of the palace on the left.

By now, Revin had gotten his bearings. He was on the north side of the palace and he remembered that Momo's suite was on the north-west corner. Crouching, he stayed to the shadows near the wall and made his way to opposite her windows. The curtains were closed, but he could see that lights were on.

Revin waited some little time until seemingly the same guard appeared again around the corner of the palace. He was encouraged to think there was just the one guard watching inside the walls. He waited until the guard passed from view again and then began to slink toward the palace, keeping low.

He crept toward the wall under Momo's windows and looked for another etheric stream. He found one, but this time, he could only get a thin, wobbly towline. Grimacing, Revin raised his aching arms and started to free-climb the wall. There were enough protrusions and decorations that it was possible, although he was in agony. His shoulders were already overstrained, and his arms were trembling even before he started. Halfway up, he nearly fell, but just managed to catch himself. He fully realized that, if he did fall, he'd never make it up this far again, so he gritted his teeth and powered the rest of the way up as fast as he could. He dragged himself over the railing onto her balcony, collapsed to its floor with a thump, and laid there like a dead thing, his strength utterly expended.

The curtains fluttered for a moment, as someone peeked out, and then Revin heard the door onto the balcony click. He looked up to see Momo emerge onto the balcony wearing a nightgown with her pretty, blonde hair wrapped in a towel. She ran to him, her face a picture of concern.

"My hero! What are you doing here?"

"I got caught," he said, feeling stupid. "But I escaped."

"Oh, no! Look at you!" she said. "You're all bruised! And scratched! And bleeding! Come inside!"

She crouched down to get her arm under his shoulders, and tried to take as much of his weight as she could.

Revin managed to get his feet under him and leaned on Momo as she brought him into her room. She had evidently just emerged from her bath and the tub of hot water was still here.

"Here, here, here," she stammered. "Get into the bath."

"No, no," he said. "I couldn't! I ..."

"Get. In." Momo said fiercely, emphasizing each word by tapping him on the chest.

"Yes, Milady," he said.

Momo helped him pull off the filthy stolen guard's uniform. She guided him to the bath and helped him get in and sit down. She shrugged out of her nightgown and got in with him.

"Milady!" he protested.

"Oh, Revin," she said. "Just relax and let me help you."

Momo gently laved water onto Revin's head and lathered him up with shampoo. She rinsed his head and then carefully washed his shoulders, arms, and the rest of his body, noting and paying careful attention to his many injuries. The lingering horror and terror of being tortured faded as he relaxed into Momo's tender ministrations. Her gentle attention was so sweet and precious that he could no longer control his emotions and began to sob and cry. She pulled him back against her chest and held him close as he wept.

Eventually, Revin wound down and began to nod off. Momo helped him out of the bath, dried him off, and led him over to the bed.

"I can just sleep on the floor, Milady," Revin said.

"Nonsense," she said, pulling back the covers. "Get into bed."

Revin laid on the bed and, in moments, was fast asleep.

There came a terrible noise. Revin felt himself grabbed and held by several men. He struggled, but was unable to free himself. In a flash, Will and Grip appeared from out of nowhere. Revin's heart leapt with hope! But then they were cut down before his eyes. He screamed in despair and thrashed wildly trying to escape his captors. And then he awoke, panting and drenched with sweat.

Revin panicked for a moment, trying to remember where he was. It was warm and dark. And he could hear the ticking of a clock. Then he felt Momo pressed up against his back, stroking his hair, and quietly humming a lullaby. He rolled over and she hugged him to her chest until the surge of adrenaline passed and he slipped back into a deep and dreamless sleep.

•　　•　　•

When Revin awoke again, the sun was high. He sat up, yawned, and checked himself over: he was stiff and sore, but he discovered that all of his cuts and scrapes had been treated with some kind of ointment and appeared to be healing well. He looked up and saw Momo sitting nearby watching him.

"Good morning, Milady," he said. "Thank you for your care of me."

"Good afternoon, my hero," she corrected. "It was the least I could do. Now, we should probably try to get some breakfast into you."

She brought over a tray laden with pastries and fresh fruit. Revin's eyebrows went up. And he noticed the tub of water had been taken away.

"How did you explain my presence in your bed?" he asked.

"I just threw some pillows around you and kept badgering them so they didn't look too carefully," she said with a mischievous smile. "I'm good at that."

Revin, who was starving, stuffed himself and then even wiped up the last little drops of frosting from the plate with his finger. He looked up and saw Momo watching him eat with such a fascinated expression that he colored up to his ears.

"What's next?" Revin asked, flustered.

"Well, I've been thinking that you need a disguise," Momo said with an odd light in her eyes.

Revin felt a little chill go through his body. "What kind of disguise are you thinking of?" he said, apprehensively.

"Well, no one would expect you to be wearing a dress!" she said.

"Oh, no," Revin said.

"I didn't think any of my dresses would fit you," Momo said in a rush, the words tumbling out. "But my cousin left this dress here when she was visiting last summer. Here! Try it on!"

She held up a shocking orange silk dress with frilly ribbons and lace.

"Milady," Revin pleaded. "I ... I know I look like this. But I'm really not a girl."

"You got to see me dressed up as a boy, though," Momo pouted. "And I've never gotten to see you dressed up as a girl."

"Ugh … Okay. Fine," Revin said, after a long pause.

Momo squealed with excitement. Her manifest pleasure at his agreement, albeit reluctant, offset Revin's discomfort, at least a little.

Momo helped him slip into the dress. She led him over to a corner where three mirrors were arranged to allow someone one to view themselves from multiple angles.

"Oh, but your poor wrists!" Momo said. "Here. Half a moment!"

She ran to her closet and returned with elbow-length white gloves. Revin slipped them on and then turned this way and that while they both inspected the effect.

"I'm not sure the dress is quite big enough here," Revin said, indicating his chest.

"I think I can adjust that." Momo loosened the ribbons a bit and then re-tied them. "Whoa. Most girls would kill for that kind of cleavage!"

"But I'm not a girl, Milady," Revin said. "So, that really doesn't make me happy."

"But you're so cute!" Momo gushed. "You're simply ravishing! Now, let's put on some makeup!"

Revin suffered himself to be guided over to her vanity where he had applied her makeup just weeks before. He allowed her to apply foundation to conceal the bruising and scratches. She then added blush and mascara with a light touch. Despite his discomfort, he sat fascinated watching her intent concentration and tiny changes of expression as she performed the delicate, intimate work.

"Just one more thing …" she said, using a barrette to pull his hair out of his eyes. "There!"

Revin looked at himself in the mirror. With the dress, makeup, and hair, the transformation was nothing short of astonishing. Revin considered himself plain, and had never thought of himself as attractive or pretty — as either a man, woman, or otherwise. But he had to admit that Momo had done wonders.

"You do good work, Milady," he said. "I doubt anyone would recognize me now. It would take a master physiognomist."

"Let's find out!" she said, ignoring the shocked look of horror on Revin's face. "Help me get ready too!"

In a few minutes, they were ready to leave, but Momo paused for a moment.

"Now. Do you know how to be introduced? What do you say?" Momo asked.

"Uh … How do you do?" Revin asked.

"No, no, no!" Momo said. "That's what you say if you're a man. If you're a girl, you need to say, 'I'm pleased to make your acquaintance,' and then you need to curtsy. You can curtsy, can't you?"

Revin, who'd had no formal introduction to polite society, could only shake his head. Momo sighed dramatically and showed him how to curtsy, then forced him to practice over and over again, in spite of his sore, aching muscles, and critiqued his performance until it was adequate.

"Now, let's go!" she said.

And they departed her chambers.

Revin remembered the ways of the palace, having spent several days only a few weeks ago when Grip had brought him to help investigate the particulars of Momo's proposed marriage.

Momo turned down a different hallway than he expected and headed downstairs.

"Let's start with someone you don't know. You haven't seen the garden, right?"

"Well, I kind of went through it last night, I think."

"No, no. I mean the botanical garden. Come this way!"

They emerged into a lovely courtyard with a fountain. Revin remembered seeing it from the window of Grip's office. The fountain stood surrounded by semi-circular beds of plantings with small signs indicating the different species of plants. An older woman sat under a pergola making notes in a journal.

"Aunt Cecelia!" Momo said. "I want to introduce my friend, Raveena!"

"I'm very pleased to make your acquaintance," Revin said, curtsying as he'd practiced.

"What lovely dresses you young ladies are wearing," she said with a smile. "Is there a special occasion?"

"We're on a secret mission!" Momo laughed, taking Revin's hand and pulling him away.

Cecelia chuckled and returned to her notes.

"Raveena?" Revin asked, as they wandered through the garden hand-in-hand.

"It was all I could think of," Momo said. "It's a pretty name! Now for the main event!"

They left the courtyard through a different door. Momo introduced Raveena to servants they passed until they reached Lady Belthingstone's salon. She lay reclining on a divan surrounded by a group of friends listening to a reading from a book. Momo waited quietly until they came to a stopping point and then dragged Raveena up to her mother and introduced her. Revin said his rote line and curtsied.

"I'm charmed to meet you as well, Raveena. And where are you from?" Lady Belthingstone asked.

Revin started to panic, but Momo cut in smoothly.

"She's visiting from her family's estate in Campshire," she said brightly.

"Well, I hope you enjoy your stay in the capital," Lady Belthingtone said. "And you're welcome in Ravensbelth any time."

Revin curtsied again and they departed.

"See! I told you!" Momo said. "This disguise is perfect for you! Now for the final exam!" Revin paled.

"You don't mean ..."

"Yes! Let's find Papa."

The Baron had his office near a side entrance, with guards posted, where people on business were constantly coming and going. A small army of administrative and military staff received messages from couriers and collated them for the Baron. Momo breezed past everyone, practically dragging Revin, and walked boldly into his office. He sat at a desk writing, but looked up and smiled when Momo came in.

"Papa, I want you to meet my friend Raveena who's visiting from Campshire!"

"I'm very pleased to make your acquaintance," Revin said with his most creditable curtsy thus far.

"What in the world are you doing in that dress, Squire?" the Baron asked.

Momo's mouth fell open. Revin paled and suddenly feared he was going to faint. The Baron turned to Momo.

"Momoire," he said, using her full name and bringing her snapping to attention. "Your brother is arriving momentarily. Please meet him and bring him here."

"Yes, sir," she said meekly and started to head toward the main entrance.

"No, not that way. He'll be coming from the roof. Meet him up there."

Revin started to follow her, but the Baron called him back.

"Just a moment, Squire," he said, while Momo departed.

Revin stood, sweating with tension, while the Baron finished writing something. He sealed the note and, as soon as he held it up, an attendant ran in, snatched it, and carried it away.

"While we have a moment, Squire," the Baron said. "Let me first thank you for saving the lives of my children. Further, let me congratulate you on your daring escape. You have fully earned both my gratitude and respect."

"Thank you, Milord," Revin said.

"As a father, however, I need to caution you," he said.

Revin tensed.

The Baron smiled and continued, "No, no. Nothing so dire. I just want to remind you that Momo, as infatuated as she so obviously is with you, is very young. And her life is not fully her own. So please temper whatever expectations you may have."

"You are very generous, Milord," Revin said.

"No, no. It's generous of you to indulge my daughter's eccentricities. But you really don't have to go this far," he said, waving his hand to encompass the dress, the makeup, and the whole ensemble. "Go ask for Terrier and have him take you to Griphon's chambers. I believe his tailor sent two more outfits for you — Griphon usually orders in threes — and we put them there awaiting your return. Get changed and come back as quickly as you can."

"Yes, Milord. Thank you, Milord!" Revin said, backing out of the office.

He asked the staff for Terrier, who arrived promptly and led him to Grip's elegant suite of rooms. They quickly found the package of clothes tied up in brown paper and, after Revin pushed Terrier out of the closet, he changed as fast as he could, taking one more minute to remove as much of the makeup as possible without cream, and to tie his hair back into his customary ponytail — which he had come to adopt during his stay among the pirates. He felt infinitely better to be himself again! Then he sprinted back down to the Baron's office, leaving Terrier to return the dress and other accouterments.

He arrived back at the Baron's office and was directed to a lavishly appointed conference room. In it, a huge, round, wooden table was surrounded by a dozen comfortable, upholstered leather chairs. The Baron, already seated with Lady Belthingstone, indicated a chair. Revin sat down, still out of breath. The Baron was just explaining to Lady Belthingstone that Revin had removed his disguise.

"That was really you?" Lady Belthingstone asked.

Revin nodded.

"Amazing!"

"It was a good job," the Baron said. "If I was thirty years younger, I might have been tempted to ... Ow!" Lady Belthingstone pinched him and then wagged her finger at him while he rubbed his arm. Then he stood and came over to Revin.

"Let me look at your arms, Squire," the Baron commanded.

Revin held his hands out. The Baron inspected his wounded wrists and tsked. He was standing there when Momo came in, leading Griphon and Will. They saw Revin and relief washed over their faces.

Will saw the Baron and stopped dead in his tracks.

"Well met, William," the Baron said.

"It's Curtains!" Will said.

"What?" Grip said, looking back and forth between the two of them.

"Curtains! That's what they called him back when ..." Will said, then broke off when he caught the Baron's expression. "I'll ... I'll tell you sometime later.

"Still ... It's a long way from that prisoner camp where we met," Will said to the Baron. "I always knew you were never the simple soldier you pretended to be."

"I really was," the Baron replied. "Then. Like Griphon, I was not in the line of succession, until I was. But, as you say, that's a story for another time." He turned to Momo. "Momoire, attend me: I will let you stay this time, since we're talking about your brother and his squire — to whom you've taken an obvious shine. But what we're going to discuss must remain absolutely secret and you must not share it with anyone. Is that perfectly understood?"

"Yes, Papa," she said.

While Grip and Will hugged and fussed over Revin, attendants brought coffee and refreshments for everyone, and then sealed the room.

"Two years ago," the Baron began. "We learned that Havelock was creating some kind of device that could interfere with etheric streams. So we recruited an agent to go undercover to Havelock to learn more. You knew him as Professor Dirge. Due to various, ahem, circumstances, that plan went awry.

"Now, Havelock seems to have created and tested their device, though we do not believe it is yet ready to be deployed. But we have few resources there, so we don't know how far along their development is."

"I think we may have encountered the aftereffects of the device," Will said. "It was like a dead space with no etheric streams in it."

"Was there also a large storm in the middle?" the Baron asked.

"Aye! There was!"

"We've tentatively called the device an Etheric Storm Generator, for lack of a better term," the Baron said. "I would like for you to investigate this device." Will shook his head.

"Isn't this a matter for Belleriand?" Will said. "What have we to do with this?"

"If Havelock can interfere with etheric streams, you are also in danger, are you not?"

"Doesn't Belleriand have their own intelligence service? Their own special forces?"

"Yes, but they are under the control of different factions. Without delving too deeply into the internal politics of Belleriand, let's just say that they're deeply divided. And that different nobles have more or less say over different services. I have enough influence over the airships to allow you to bring the *Queen* in safety for our conversation today. Others have more influence over the special forces — like those idiots that abducted Revin."

"You were aware that had happened?" Grip asked.

"Yes. And I was working quietly behind the scenes to get him released when, lo and behold, he got himself out."

"Ha! Well done, lad!" Will said. "I learned the hard way that you don't try to stop him."

"And, mark my words, Squire," the Baron said, grimly. "Your treatment at their hands did not pass unremarked. And there will be consequences."

Revin looked at the faces of everyone around the table, furious on his behalf, and felt warmed by their concern.

"But getting back to the issue at hand," the Baron continued. "Please also note what I did not say: I did not say that you'd be working for Belleriand. Nor that you were to bring the device here and give it to us. Of course, I would welcome those things. But knowing what I do of William, he won't work for nobles. Isn't that right?"

"The nobility are parasites. You have all this," Will said, gesturing around at the luxurious surroundings. "And yet most of your people are impoverished."

"I'm not going to have this conversation with you right now," the Baron replied without heat. "Let's return to the issue at hand. What's your reply?"

Will paused for a long moment in thought. Grip and Revin watched him carefully as he considered his response.

"You're correct in that our interests are clearly aligned in this case," Will replied. "We will investigate. But we will require a letter of marque for the *Queen*. And sufficient funds to cover the operation."

"Done and done," the Baron replied.

He handed Will a folded leather document case, clearly prepared well in advance, and a heavy pouch. But Revin noticed that the Baron surreptitiously kept back something else and wondered what it might be.

Suddenly, the door popped open and an attendant breathlessly addressed the Baron, "Guards report there are men with ropes in the garden. We believe they plan to scale the walls to capture the airship."

Everyone leapt to their feet, but the Baron, with the voice of authority, called out, "Hold! Call for guards to head to the roof. William! Take your crew and depart. Momoire! Escort your mother to the safe room. Now, move!"

Revin turned to follow the others, but felt someone grab his shirt.

"Take this!" Momo said, pressing a small, bound leather

book into his hands. "You can read what I wrote and then write back to me. And we can exchange them when next we meet."

"Thank you, Milady," Revin said.

"Please!" she said in a small voice. "Please call me Momo."

"Y...Yes ... Momo," he said.

"Please be safe, my hero!" she said and made herself smile, trying to blink away tears, her lip quivering.

Then Revin ran after the others.

By now, Revin knew the way to the rooftop. As he entered the stairway, he heard Grip halfway up cursing his injured leg.

"Let me help you, love," Will said.

"No, Will. Go to the *Queen!* She needs you!"

"I'm coming!" Revin cried. "Go on, Cap'n! I'll stay with Grip!"

By the time Revin caught up with Grip, Will had sprinted ahead and was nearly to the top. Revin stayed by Grip's side so he could lean on his shoulder. They emerged together onto the rooftop and into bloody chaos.

Revin could see a dozen men were already down, dead or with grievous wounds. Both sides continued to exchange crossbow bolts. The Baron's men had evidently charged the special forces and been repulsed. The special forces had a remmer, Revin noticed, who had evidently come up first and brought up the ropes. He stayed back and continued to bring men up, while more men were swarming up the ropes every second. The Baron's forces were regrouping for another charge. Will had already reached the airship where the pirates stood ready to cast off the lines.

Grip drew his sword and waded into the confusion heading toward the airship. Revin followed feeling terribly naked.

"Catch!" Will called.

A towline snapped into existence and bore something flying toward Revin. He caught it without thinking and found it was his scabbarded smallsword. He drew it and followed Grip closely. The special forces spotted them and sent three men to intercept. Grip engaged two, but the third circled around behind and came face-to-face with Revin.

Revin put his back to Grip and set himself *en garde*. His heart pounded with terror to be confronted with an expert swordsman, as he knew full well how inexperienced he was. He tried to remember everything Grip had taught him.

"Run, little boy," the man said. "Or I'll have to cut you down."

Revin said nothing, but he didn't move. He swore he would let himself be cut to pieces before he abandoned Grip. But he knew he needed to do something fast before the man realized the true depth of his inexperience.

The man suddenly lunged and, thanks to his training, Revin's arm moved automatically and he parried. The man's rhythm was thrown off when Revin did not follow the parry with a riposte. And, in that brief pause, Revin took a deep breath, closed his eyes, and made a towline to the tip of the man's sword. It was a tiny towline, but it was enough to pull his sword out of line for just a moment. And in that moment, Revin lunged and ran the man through the belly. The man dropped to his knees and then fell over with a look of pure astonishment on his face.

Grip, having dispatched his two opponents, turned and found Revin standing numbly, dumbfounded, with his bloodied sword.

"C'mon!" he said and pulled Revin toward the gangplank.

The pirates cast off as the special forces charged the airship — too late.

Revin watched as below them, dozens of the Baron's guardsmen emerged from other rooftop doors and the special forces men were compelled to throw down their swords and surrender. Will came up behind Revin and clapped him on the shoulder.

"Well done, lad! I told you, even a small thing at the right time can make all the difference."

Revin smiled weakly, still sick from the terror of the moment. But his heart was already at ease to be back aboard the *Queen* and among his shipmates.

"Set course for home!" Will said.

"Turn West!" Grip cried to the remmers.

Already over the ocean, the *Queen of Belleriand* turned toward the setting sun.

INTERLUDE

T HE *QUEEN OF BELLERIAND* SLIPPED almost silently through the tranquil night air. Revin heard the timekeeper quietly strike the second bell. There were some muffled thumps as the shift changed and new men came on duty while others retired to their hammocks. Most of the pirates were already asleep, but Revin was too keyed up after the day's events. In his mind's eye, he kept seeing the man's face when he was run through ... No. When Revin ran his sword through him. He'd had the shakes off and on for a while and so, to distract himself, he started to read Momo's diary.

He smiled at her descriptions of things that seemed ordinary to her, but were almost unbelievable to him.

MOMO'S JOURNAL

On Monday, Papa had the carriage brought out to take us to the country house. It was a crisp fall morning and the horses' breath was visible in the chilly air. Manny was the coachman and he handed Momma and me into the coach. He's a tall middle-aged man that Papa knew from his days in the military who got injured and Papa gave him a place in the stables.

The carriage had two handsome ponies: one Manny said was a new roan they had just brought on. The other was a reliable warmblood we had used for a long time. Once we set out, it put us in the holiday spirit to hear the bells of their harnesses as we went down the country lanes.

I wore my traveling cloak over that nice dress Momma had given me for my birthday. I was so happy when she gave me that dress. I really wanted a special someone to see me wearing it. But if they couldn't see it, it was alright to cover it up with the traveling cloak.

When we arrived at the country house, Manny handed us down and took the horses around to the carriage house. The full staff came out to the steps to welcome us to the country house. I remembered Tiffany from last time. She seemed nervous to see me. With a few words, I was able to put her heart at ease that I remembered her and was looking forward to her care again this year.

It was strange being back in the same suite of rooms that I'd been in before. It seems like a such a long time from last year when I was still a little girl. Now, with all of the experiences I've had in the past year, I feel so different.

Everywhere I look — everything I see — reminds me of that special someone. When I close my eyes … When I awake in the morning, there is only one person I'm thinking of. And when I go to sleep at night, there's only one face I see when I close my eyes.

Today Aunt Kandela arrived from Campshire with her daughter Daphnae. Daphnae is my cousin two years younger than me, but is already a bit bigger than me. She always seems ill at ease with herself and is awkward. I've tried to be a friend to her, but she doesn't want to open up. I tried to suggest that we go clothes shopping together, but she didn't seem interested. I just don't understand her at all.

The next night was the costume ball. Daphnae and I spent the whole day putting together our costumes. I decided to be a fairy princess and wore a dress with ruffles and pretty diaphanous wings that Tiffany helped me put together. Daphnae decided to be a cavalier, of all things, and wore breeches and a sword. I just can't imagine what that girl is thinking.

Aunt Cecelia came for the party. Many people commented how all of the Aspidelle girls were together for the first time in a long time. It was funny to me to see how Momma gets when her sisters are there. She's normally so elegant and reserved. But Cecelia and Kandela know how to rile her up so she gets angry and childish. It's really funny — even Papa thinks so — though no-one would ever admit it to her.

I was sad that Cecelia's Kasseh didn't come. She's so smart and funny. But Cecelia just smiles and says she's busy when I ask why she doesn't come. I suspect it's that, because she's not noble, people don't treat her right. It makes me so angry. Someday, if I'm ever able to do something about it, I'll make people sorry who do that.

There were a number of this season's eligible bachelors at the party and they kept trying to dance with me. But several of them caught the look on Papa's face and gave up. Papa's overprotective, but I didn't really mind: There's only one person I want to dance with. But I felt a little bad for Daphnae since they seemed to just overlook her. Partly it's just the look on her face. That girl scares people away. She's strange and doesn't seem to know how to relate to people. I don't know how to fix that.

By bedtime, my feet were getting sore and so I told Tiffany I wanted to find some new shoes. In the morning, she had organized a trip into town to go shoe shopping. Poor Daphnae really didn't want to go, but she got dragged along too.

Manny had hooked up the horses and took us back into town and we visited eight different cobbler's shops. When we got to the sixth one, I thought Daphnae was going to kill me. She finally wouldn't go in at all. She'd bought some horrible boots at the first place and said that was all she wanted. I saw a lot of nice shoes, but nothing that both looked and felt like what I wanted. But at the last place, I decided that some shoes I'd seen at the second place were what I wanted and so, with Daphnae tearing her hair out, we went back to the second place and I bought two pairs of the shoes I liked. By the time we got home, it was nearly bedtime. What a great day!

When I went to bed, I only thought of one person. I don't know where he is or what he's doing. Every so often, my heart races when I think of the dangers he might be facing. But then I calmed myself because I just know that I'd know if anything happened. And I ...

Revin read where the final entry trailed off in Momo's journal then snuffed out the lantern and sat with his head in his hands. He was becoming more and more confused about his own feelings. "Temper your expectations," the Baron had said. What were those, exactly? He closed his eyes and tried to still his unquiet heart.

4

CROSSING THE STREAMS

T HE *QUEEN OF BELLERIAND* returned to her berth on the steep side of Kapper Island, where the pirate's secret base was located. The men who'd been on duty went to sleep, but Will called Grip, Revin, and the Professor in for a strategy meeting.

When Revin arrived, he saw that there was an unfamiliar face there as well — a wizened, older man with thin white hair and reading spectacles. He was looking through a ledger, making notations with a pencil. He looked up as Revin came in.

"Revin," Will said. "I'd like you to meet Mr. Brill, our bursar."

"How do you do," Revin said, resisting the urge to curtsy.

Brill looked at him over his glasses and then nodded curtly.

Revin felt slightly nonplussed at the non-verbal answer, but didn't think too much about it. When Grip and the Professor arrived, Will called the meeting to order.

"Gentleman," Will said. "We have been informed of a serious threat to our operations. Havelock is developing an Etheric Storm Generator that can leave us dead in the water in the vicinity of a large storm. We will investigate this threat.

"As some of you already know, we have received a — let's call it a 'donation' — to subsidize our operations. Two hundred reggies. But ..." At this point, Will looked around the table locking eyes with each man in turn. "We are not being paid to do this work. These funds will be expended only in support of this operation. That means that any expense will need to be justified to Mr. Brill who will hold the funds and disburse them only under those circumstances.

"Do you have anything to add, Mr. Brill?" Will concluded.

Brill shook his head.

"Who is going to go, then?" asked Revin.

"Ah! You bring up a good point, lad," Will said. "First of all, I think we can all agree that the Professor should go to help ensure we collect the right information to understand the device."

There were murmurs of assent from everyone present, except Mr. Brill, who was silent.

"I understand that, after my last little visit," Will continued. "I am persona non grata in Havelock."

"There were Wanted posters on the last packet ship we took with five hundred reggies for you. And not a bad likeness either," Grip said. "They're only offering one hundred for me." He scowled as if his personal worth were up for question.

"That's right," Will said. "But Revin here was wearing a disguise."

Revin blushed, remembering how Will had convinced him to pass for a prostitute by wearing a dress and pink wig.

"So I propose that Revin and the Professor should go," Will concluded.

"Well, you'll not have me traipsing all over the countryside," the Professor thundered, pounding his fist on the table. "I'm not riding in some wagon either. If I'm to go, we're getting a coach.

A nice one. And that's a legitimate expense," he said, glaring at Mr. Brill.

Brill looked up briefly, nodded, and returned to his ledger.

"What should be the plan for once we get there?" Revin asked.

"That's your business," the Professor grumbled. "You're the leader of this little adventure. I'm just going to see this device."

"Maybe you can talk to the Duke's seneschal," Will asked. "Maybe you can still talk him into giving you a job!"

"How do I explain where I've been for the past few months?"

"I'm sure you'll think of something," Will laughed.

Revin was not reassured.

"And how are we even going to get back?" Revin asked.

"Here, Lad," Will said. "Here's a map of Havelock I found. I don't know how useful it will be because it's but a tourist map. Still, it's better than naught. See this place on the west coast?"

"Beskin Harbor?" Revin asked.

"Yes. It looks like a quiet little fishing village," Will continued. "Since the harbor is too small for anything larger than fishing boats. There's nothing there, so there shouldn't be many patrols. The *Queen* will begin to stand off-and-on every day for the hour before sunset — that should give you good light to signal with."

• • •

The next morning, just before dawn, the *Queen* dropped Revin and the Professor in a small dinghy off the coast near Beskin Harbor. Revin started rowing and, once again, thanked his training that had helped him recover so quickly from his ordeal in Belleriand. *And Momo,* he thought, remembering her in the bath with him. He was glad he was sitting with his back to the Professor while he rowed, so he couldn't see Revin's face.

"When we get ashore, how should I introduce you?" Revin said.

"Why don't we just say I'm your uncle," the Professor said. "That's vague and irrefutable."

"Ok ... Uncle," Revin said.

The waves were light in the pre-dawn and they made good time. Revin was able to row right up to the shore in town and pull the boat up onto the cobblestone beach. The Professor jumped out and struggled through the cobbles, hand walking with his arm braces. Revin pulled the boat above the high-water mark where a whole line of other small boats were stowed. Then, after grabbing their bags, he flipped it over.

They walked along the harbor to the road that ran up to the pier, where they saw several larger water craft tied up. Then they turned inland and followed the road under a low archway into a promenade that had small cafes, eateries, and other touristy businesses. Most were still closed, but one cafe was open.

Revin left the Professor in the cafe to get breakfast while he scouted around for transportation. About twenty minutes later, he returned and ordered some breakfast for himself.

"I couldn't find a coach for hire here," Revin said. "They said we'll probably have better luck in the capital. But there is a coach leaving for the capital in an hour and I've booked us seats."

"Good enough," the Professor replied. "The breakfast here is great. Be sure to try the preserves! They're homemade!"

•　　•　　•

Revin stepped off the coach in Havelock and held the door for the Professor, who hopped down with his arm braces. Revin had slept a good part of the way, but had also spent several hours studying the map, selecting locations, and concocting a story about them to explain his absence. He hoped.

Revin led the Professor back toward the University. Revin experienced a profound sense of *deja vu* returning to his familiar haunts. Revin walked up to the guards at the University gate trying to project an air of confidence.

"Do you remember me?" he asked.

"Um ... Oh! Just a minute!" one said. "You're Revin, right? You were with Professor Dirge. Where have you been?"

"Well, Dirge and I went for a research trip and he was taken ill. I stayed with him, but he kept getting sicker and finally passed away last week. So I'm back to figure out what to do next."

"You'll probably have to speak with the Provost," the man said. "He won't be in until tomorrow."

"Actually," said the other. "The Duke's seneschal came here, impounded your trunks, and secured your chambers after you didn't come back. You should probably skip the Provost and go speak directly with him."

Revin bowed and thanked the men. He stood conferring with the Professor about what to do for the night when someone said, "Professor Grexin? Is that you?"

"Eh?" the Professor said, turning toward the newcomer, a middle-aged academic wearing University garb.

"It is you!" the man continued excitedly. "You probably don't remember me: Niles Ender. I saw your talk five years ago on hydrogen generation using algae and we spoke for a bit at the reception that followed. What are you doing back here?"

"I'm just visiting my nephew," the Professor said, clapping Revin on the back.

"Wow! You must be so proud to have a famous uncle like Professor Grexin! Where are you staying?"

"Actually, we're about to look for lodging," Revin said. "Since our rooms are unavailable."

"Nonsense! We can put you up in our chambers. I'd love the chance to pick your uncle's brain! Come this way!"

•   •   •

The next morning, Revin left at first light and walked to the city center. He found the Executive Building where the government offices were located and, inside, located the office of the Seneschal. They were not open for another hour, so he went back out and found a nearby cafe to wait. He ordered a cup of coffee, and then spent the time carefully rehearsing his story.

They were opening the door just as he returned to the office.

"I'm Revin Minerson. I'm here to speak with the Seneschal," Revin announced to the receptionist.

"Do you have an appointment?" she inquired.

Revin shook his head.

"Take a seat and I'll see what I can do."

The Seneschal had a lavish set of offices adjacent to the Duke in the Executive Building. Dark wood paneling formed the basis of the décor, complemented by huge oil paintings depicting scenes of battle. A large collection of captured regimental battle flags hung from the ceiling. Revin spied one with Belthingstone colors.

Revin waited for more than an hour and grew increasingly anxious. He kept wondering if guards would appear to clap him in irons and drag him off. But he just sat quietly as others came and went. Finally, the receptionist motioned to him and he came to his feet.

"The Seneschal will see you now," she said.

Revin walked through the doorway into the Seneschal's office and then stood quietly while the Seneschal finished writing something and then looked up. Revin bowed deeply.

"Thank you very much for seeing me, sir," Revin began. "I very much appreciate you taking the time from your busy schedule."

"You've got balls to just walk in here," the Seneschal said. "Where in the ether have you been? You and Dirge just disappeared. And at a particularly suspicious point in time, I might point out. I thought about just calling the guards and letting them sort out this mess."

"Professor Dirge and I were on a research trip to the Hermitage to consult their library," Revin said. "He always had a fascination with the history of the law and there was a particular book he learned of that he wanted to consult."

"The Hermitage, eh?" the Seneschal said. "That makes sense, I guess. But why are you only coming back now?"

"On the way back," Revin continued. "Professor Dirge was taken ill at Sendia Springs."

"Well, if you're going to get ill, that's just as nice a place as any."

"We made it as far as Beskin Harbor when he took a turn for the worse. I've been there, taking care of him this whole time. But he kept getting sicker and sicker until he passed away two days ago."

"He's dead?"

"Yes, sir," Revin said. "Regrettably."

"What did he die of?" the Seneschal asked.

"The doctor said it was quinsy," Revin replied. "They tried everything they could think of, but it was no use."

"Quinsy, eh?"

"Quinsy, sir," Revin agreed.

"So you're here because you're now without a position. And you say you've just been to the Hermitage and Beskin Harbor?"

"Yes, sir. If you would be so kind, sir."

"When you both disappeared at nearly the same time as the attack on the admiralty," he said, grimacing, "There was some suspicion Dirge was involved: the description of one of the attackers sounded like it could have been him. The other wasn't you, though: It was some woman. A prostitute, by all reports."

"Thank you for your confidence, sir," Revin said.

The Seneschal paused for a moment in thought and then regarded Revin seriously.

"I'll tell you what," he said. "I need someone to run an errand. An important errand, mind you."

"I won't let you down, sir," Revin said. "You can count on me!"

"It's funny you mentioned those places. As it turns out, I need someone to escort a key scientist, who's been working on an important project, from the Hermitage to Beskin Harbor to complete his work."

"An important project, sir?"

"Yes. I'm sorry, but I can't tell you any more about it. It's top secret. But if you can take care of this errand for me, I'm sure we can find more for you to do."

"Understood. Thank you so much for this opportunity to prove myself, sir," Revin said. "You'll see whether or not I can be trusted."

"You'll need to hire a coach. Just a moment," he said, scrawling several notes on paper. "Give this note to my secretary. She'll get you a purse with 25 reggies. That should be enough to hire a coach — and a driver, if you need one. Give this other note to the Director at the Hermitage. He'll introduce you to the scientist. And be sure to show him a good time. Go ahead and stop at Sendia Springs on the way."

"You can count on me, sir," Revin said, accepting the pieces of paper. "Can I ask for one more thing, sir?"

Revin paused and the Seneschal gestured at him to continue.

"I understand that my and Professor Dirge's trunks were impounded by your office. Could those be released to me?"

"Certainly," the Seneschal said, writing a third note. "They were searched, of course, but nothing was found. Take this to the University."

After Revin collected the funds and departed the Seneschal's office, he went to the shop the office had recommended to hire a coach. The shop owner, Hirus Darkpony, a prosperous older man, showed Revin around an enclosure where they had a number of different coaches available for hire. They had a variety to choose from, and he ended up selecting a coach on the larger side which seated four comfortably and was drawn by a team of four horses.

"You know, then, how to manage horses and drive a team, Milord?" the shop owner asked.

"Well ... No. Not really, to be honest," Revin said. "Is there someone we could hire?"

"We have a list of coachmen for hire," Darkpony said. "But they're not affiliated with our shop. If you choose one from the list, we'll send a boy to get him, and he can bring the coach to you wherever you like."

"Hmm. I guess I'll just take this first one, Arthur Aaron," Revin said. "Have him bring the coach to the University at first light tomorrow."

"You'll need to pay him eight reggies," said Darkpony. "You should leave four as earnest money and pay him the rest when you get back."

Revin handed over 16 reggies for the coach, deposit and earnest money. He fingered one of the other coins and studied it. He'd seen other people with reggies before, but he'd never, himself, even held a gold coin. These were new, with crisp markings, showing the likeness of King Reginald the Arbiter who ruled on Harway over all of the island nations.

Returning to the University, Revin gave the slip of paper from the Seneschal to the guards. One of them took him to a storage room where he was able to recover the trunks.

After the dinner, he and the Professor shut themselves in their room to take a closer look inside them.

"Now watch this, Revin," the Professor said. "You said you didn't find anything inside Dirge's trunk. But you didn't know then that he was an agent. I think we should take a closer look at the trunk itself."

The Professor tapped along the trunk's edges, listening for changes in pitch. When he heard something, he began feeling carefully and found first one, and then two, rivets that could be pulled part way out. This released a long thin section of wood that could be persuaded to slide out. The slat had holes cut in it that each contained one of 25 reggies. A bit more exploring revealed a matching arrangement on the other side of the trunk that revealed 22 gold coins. He had evidently spent the others on their passage on the ill-fated *Madeline.*

"I suggest we put this money back where it was," the Professor said. "I'll start using this trunk. Let's try to use the Baron's money first and only use this in an emergency. Or if Brill tries to stiff us when we get back," he concluded with a devious chuckle.

At first light, Revin dragged their baggage out and was on hand when the coach arrived. The coachman, a tall, gangly man in his 20s, introduced himself, hat in hand, and then helped to load the trunks in the baggage compartment at the rear of the coach. Revin followed the Professor into the coach and they set off for the Hermitage.

They spent the morning rolling through an increasingly rural landscape. Unlike in Belleriand — at least in the parts Revin had recently traversed, where the farms seemed like small land-holders — here they seemed like giant agricultural enterprises, with gangs of laborers supervised by overseers. Revin found it chilling to watch the overseers menacing and bullying the workers, even as some of the workers collapsed in the heat.

By midafternoon, they had reached a vast expanse of arid grassland. Revin opened the window that communicated between the coach and the box where the driver sat.

"Hey, Art, how much farther do we intend to go today?"

"Well, Milord," Art said. "It's going to take most of the next day, so a bit more today will give us more flexibility tomorrow."

Revin closed the window and turned to the Professor.

"Why is everyone calling me 'milord'?" he wondered aloud.

"Heh," chuckled the Professor. "You're a handsome young man with a pocket full of gold. Of course, people are going to assume the worst."

Near sunset, they arrived at a large tree that stood alone in the grassland near the road. Art drew the horses to a stop and set the brake. While Revin pulled together a meal with supplies he'd brought, and the Professor busied himself with building a small fire, the coachman unhooked the horses, staked them out where they could graze, watered them, brushed them, and gave each a feedbag.

After dinner, while Art checked the horses and collected their feedbags, Revin and the Professor got ready to sleep. They were about to get into the bedrolls when Art appeared around the corner of the wagon accompanied by two other men. With their swords drawn, they charged toward Revin and the Professor.

Revin drew his sword and put himself *en garde*. Considering the Professor no threat, Art and the two men bypassed him to attack Revin. Revin began to panic, wondering how he could possibly defend himself against all three of them. Suddenly, the two other men staggered and, with their eyes rolling up in their heads, collapsed. Art looked surprised and distracted at the sudden loss of his allies. Revin lunged forward and caught him in the throat. Art fell over clutching at his neck and expired with blood spurting through his fingers.

Revin stared wild-eyed at the Professor, who stood with his arm braces raised.

"What just happened?" Revin gasped.

"I keep each of my arm braces loaded with a poisoned dart," he said. "They must have figured me for no threat. But they were wrong.

"But that coachman?" the Professor continued. "How did you end up choosing him?"

"His name was first on the list: Arthur Aaron," Revin replied.

The Professor stared at Revin, his expression unreadable.

"Revin," said the Professor. "Come over here for a moment."

Revin approached.

"Now lean over a bit," the Professor instructed him.

Revin leaned over bringing his head closer.

The professor slapped him with parental affection on the side of his head.

"Ow!"

"You bonehead!" the Professor said. "Don't ever pick the first of anything — especially with a name like 'Aaron' that was probably contrived to appear at the top of the list. Sheesh!"

Revin blushed, abashed.

"It also explains why earlier he was so eager to push on," the Professor said. "He needed to get here to carry out the ambush.

"His confederates must have gotten here ahead of us, somehow," the Professor said. "Look around, longshanks. There aren't any other trees nearby. But do you see any relief that might be enough to conceal a couple of horses? Scout around a little. But be cautious in case there are any more."

Revin was glad to be alone with his thoughts for a few minutes because he was so embarrassed about his lack of judgment. "How could I have been so stupid?" Revin thought. He shuddered to think how close they had just come to a bad end.

After a few minutes of circling around the campsite, Revin spotted a little dip of the land and, sure enough, he found two horses staked out in it. Revin pulled up the stakes and led the horses back to their campsite. Then he made a second trip to collect their saddles and tack.

The Professor had not been idle during Revin's absence. Using a rope, he had tied one end to two of the bodies in turn, hand-walked a ways into the grass, then dragged the body away. He tied Art's body last, but he left it to Revin to drag his body away.

"I'm really sorry," Revin said. "It's all my fault that ..."

"Do you want me to slap you again?" the Professor barked.

Revin paused, wild-eyed.

"It's not your fault," the Professor continued. "It's their fault for attacking us. You might have been foolish. But everyone is foolish until they learn better. And you've learned, haven't you?"

"Yes," Revin said sincerely. "I won't make that mistake again."

"Good enough. Now take this!" the Professor said, handing him two coins. "They didn't have much money. But Art had two reggies, and they each had one. So that's four: two for you and two for me."

"That must be the earnest money I had paid," Revin said.

With that, they retired to their bedrolls.

Revin watched the stars overhead for a few minutes. They looked spectacular so far from human habitation. He fell asleep to the chorus of crickets and other night insects.

•　　　•　　　•

In the morning, Revin tried to hook up the horses to the coach and discovered he had absolutely no idea what he was doing. He had never worked with horses before. There had been some ponies in the mines in his town growing up, but he had never done more than ride on one, once, as a child, at a fair.

He tried to fake his way through it and managed to get the tacking on. The horses weren't happy, though. Moreover, they seemed to be able to tell he was nervous and one gave him a painful nip. They also evidently had particular places they wanted to be in the team and were quite nasty about Revin getting it wrong.

As Revin brought the next horse to the coach, it tried to kick him. He partially dodged, but a glancing blow still caught him in the solar plexus and knocked the wind out of him.

Revin sat on the ground, gasping. He was coming to despise horses.

"Are you alright?" the Professor asked from inside the coach.

"No," Revin growled. "These horses are going to be the death of me."

The Professor chuckled as Revin got back to his feet, brushed himself off, and got back to getting the team hooked up.

Eventually, after they were all in their traces, Revin tied up the other two horses to the rear of the coach. Then he climbed onto the box, released the brake, shook the reins, and clicked his tongue as he'd heard the coachman do. The horses shuffled a bit, but did nothing. Revin growled and picked up the coach-whip and only then did the horses begin to walk and, with a bit more encouragement by snapping the reins, he got them to trot.

After perhaps an hour, Revin noticed that the horses were not in sync and kept shying to the right. He slowed down near a farm, trying to figure out what the problem was. A young woman, pulling weeds in the garden, looked up as they went by. Revin tried to guess her age, but she was skinny — almost malnourished, Revin thought — which made her age hard to ascertain. She was barefoot, wearing a grubby shift, and wore a leather collar around her neck like a dog.

"You have the harness hooked up wrong, mister," she said.

"Here, now, missy," the foreman said. "What have I told you about talking to passers-by."

"No, boss," she said, with a terrified expression. "Please don't!"

The foreman pulled out the switch he had tucked in his belt and started to thrash the girl, who lay in the dirt sobbing.

Revin set the brake, checked that he had his sword, and jumped down from the box.

"Hold on," he said.

"Mind your own business, mister," the foreman said. "Unless you want to buy this worthless thing."

"Buy?" Revin asked, aghast.

"She owes two reggies," he said. "And until she pays it off, she works for me."

Revin reached into his pocket and pulled out the 2 reggies he had gotten the night before.

"Here," he said.

"What?" the man said, stunned.

"Here. Take the money. She's mine now."

"Now, wait just a minute," the foreman said, beginning to recover his aplomb.

Revin fixed the man with a glare, started to reach for his sword, then realized he still had the coachwhip hanging from his wrist on its cord. He grasped it and menaced the foreman with one hand while still holding out the coins in the other.

"Here's your money!" he snapped. "Let her go."

"Fine!" he snarled, snatching the coins. "Good riddance. She's your problem now."

Revin crouched next to the girl and extended a hand. She cautiously accepted it and Revin helped her to her feet.

"My name is Revin," he said. "What's yours?"

"Lidja, Milord," she replied. "Are you my boss now? Are you going to use that on me?"

"What? No!" Revin said, releasing the whip so it hung again from the cord around his wrist. "No. That was for these stupid horses."

"Horses aren't stupid," she said. "You just have to know how to talk to them."

"Well, would you talk to them for us?" Revin asked simply.

She looked at him uncomprehendingly at first, then her eyes got bigger as she started to dare to hope.

"Really?" she asked.

"Really," Revin said. "Now let's get that collar off."

"But I have to wear the collar until my indenture is done," she said.

Revin loosened the collar and removed it from her neck.

"There," he said. "Done. Complete. Finished. Over."

She stood motionless, speechless. Then tears started to fall. Revin wished he had a handkerchief or something to give her.

"You're free now," Revin said. "That means, you don't have to come with us. And I will understand if you choose not to: You don't know us at all. But if you're willing to take care of our horses and drive the coach, I'll pay you the same as we were paying our previous coachman."

She nodded and walked over to the horses, still crying freely. She went up to each horse, rubbed its nose, and whispered to it too quietly for Revin to hear. Then, when she had recovered her composure, she adjusted and reconnected the harnesses and joined Revin on the box.

She lifted the reins lightly and shook them once. The horses immediately started trotting and fell into a comfortable rhythm. Revin leaned back with a smile, looked up at the sky, and then closed his eyes. Things were looking up.

Then he heard her stomach growl.

"Are you hungry?" he asked.

"I'm fine, Milord" she said. "You don't need to go to any trouble."

"Hey, Professor," he called into the window into the coach. "Pass me some of that jerky."

"Good!" he said handing it up. "You could use some more flesh on those bones."

"It's not for me!" Revin said, scandalized, over the Professor's chuckle.

He accepted the jerky and handed it over to Lidja. "Here's something to tide you over until lunch."

She accepted it and took a bite and then another and another.

Revin called down again, "Pass up that canteen too."

She took the canteen, still chewing, swallowed, and then drank deeply.

"Why are you being so nice to me, Milord?" she said. "You're scaring me that something bad is going to happen."

"First of all, you don't need to call me 'milord'," Revin said. "Just call me Revin. And you can just call my uncle back there 'Professor'.

"Second, I don't think I'm being so nice. You're performing an important service for us for which you will be compensated.

I'm sorry you've had such a rough time up until now that being treated like a regular person seems so unusual."

"I'm going to cry again, Mil... Revin," she said, snuffling.

"Well, stop the coach for a minute," Revin said.

Lidja brought the horses to a stop. Revin set the brake.

He climbed down, went to his trunk, and fished around until he found a clean handkerchief. He climbed back up and handed it to her.

"Here," he said. "Cry all you want."

She started the horses again, but then said, "Now you're making me cry and laugh at the same time and it kinda hurts."

They both laughed together.

In the mid-afternoon, they arrived at the town of Relsington, which was at the foot of the hill where the Hermitage was located. They stopped in town primarily so Lidja could purchase some things. Revin paid her the equivalent of 4 reggies as earnest money: three as gold coins and the last as 10 silver miners, so she could avoid attracting notice by spending gold.

Lidja checked the supplies for the horses. With the two additional horses, there was insufficient fodder, so she purchased more, a peck of apples, and some carrots. She gave each of the horses an apple and then went to a clothing store. When she emerged, she was wearing some kind of simple uniform with a white shirt and black trousers.

"I think these are for servants at the Hermitage," she said. "But they were inexpensive, they fit, and I thought they made me look official."

Revin nodded, pleased that she was stepping into her role so effectively.

•　　　•　　　•

They arrived at the Hermitage, a sprawling complex of buildings at the top of a large hill, in the late afternoon. The tourist map had described it as the first scholarly community in Havelock. It was created when a noble deeded his estate and expansive library to support research and advanced academic study. According to the map, the scholars claimed that the isolation fostered novel research and innovation.

A guard received Revin and the Professor and directed them to check in with the office. He also told Lidja to take the coach to the stables to bed down the horses. She could eat and bunk with the servants, he said.

"Will you be okay?" Revin asked.

"I'm sure I will be fine," she said. "This has to be easier than how I was living before."

Revin waved Lidja on and then walked with the Professor to check in at the office.

He passed the note from the Seneschal to the man at the reception desk and was soon escorted in to meet the Director. He was a tall, cadaverously thin, elderly man who spoke with an odd accent.

"Thank you for coming," he said, putting down the note and standing. "I am Director Solzen. We serve at the pleasure of the Duke."

"Thank you for assisting with my mission," Revin said. "I am Revin Minerson and this is my ... uh ... uncle."

"Professor Grexin! It's an honor to meet you again! Aren't you retired? I read your recent note on etheric wave theory. It's amazing how you keep going."

"Solzen, eh?" the Professor said. "Hmm. We must have met when I was still at the Royal Academy on Harway."

"That's right," he said. "I attended a conference there and you were the featured speaker. While you're here, let me give you both a short tour. And then I'll introduce you to Kief Senterson, the young man you'll be taking to Beskin Harbor."

The Director took them first to the library that was the pride of the institution. It was stupendous. A few weeks ago, Revin would have been awestruck. But honestly, it paled in comparison to the Belthingstone library he had just visited. Still, he was careful to express his thorough appreciation.

Afterward, the Director led them on visits to several of the labs and research spaces, including agricultural, medical, and geological research groups. At each lab, students and researchers recognized the Professor, asking him pointed and insightful questions. Finally, they headed to a newer building nearby.

"Welcome to our new Etheric Studies Building!" Director Solzen said with a flourish. "We have the leading group studying etheric phenomena of all kinds here. And let me introduce Professor Kief Senterson."

Kief, a young man in his late 20s or early 30s. Tall, slim, and bearded, with a slightly hooked nose, he gave them a warm smile.

"Senterson ..." the Professor mused. "You're not related to Baxter Senterson, are you?"

"My father," he said. "You must be Professor Grexin. My father spoke highly of you when you worked together in the Royal Academy."

"Bullshit," the Professor said. "We hated each other."

"He had a lot of respect for you, nonetheless," Kief said. "But, politically, you were far apart, I think."

After introductions, Kief walked them through the building and showed some of the work they were doing, although several of the doors were closed with signs indicating that they were off-limits to unauthorized personnel.

"Shall we dine together?" the Director said after the tour.

"May we have a few minutes to freshen up?" Revin asked. "I also want to check on our driver."

"Surely," the Director said. "We have rooms for you. My assistant can get your keys. We'll meet in the private dining room at six bells."

After getting to his room, and washing his face with the bowl and pitcher of water provided, Revin ran down to the servant's quarters to check on Lidja. He peeked in the dining room and saw her seated among a raucous crowd of cheerful people, laughing and seemingly at ease. He smiled to himself and slipped away without interrupting.

He arrived at the private dining room as the others were filing in, seating themselves around a large table with candles and elaborate place settings. A team of solemn servants stood back from the table as the Director and senior faculty arrived. After everyone was seated, the servants went around the table pouring wine. Once everyone had been served, one of the younger faculty, seated to the right of the Director, stood up.

"I would like to propose a toast," he said, raising his glass. "To our most excellent colleague, Kief Senterson, who goes now, for the confusion of our enemy, to complete his great work of science and engineering. May it tip the balance in this terrible war and rain utter destruction upon the bestial foe!"

"Hear, hear!" several of those gathered said.

Revin felt like he was going to be sick.

The Professor said nothing, but he poured his wine out on the floor. "Excuse me," he said. He slipped out of his seat, dropped to the floor, and hand-walked out of the room.

"What's his problem?" someone said.

"He's always been like that," Kief said. "At least, according to my father. He is on record saying that war is always wrong and that scientists should refuse to allow their work to be co-opted by the nobility."

"What do you think, Revin?" asked the Director.

Everyone turned and looked at Revin.

Revin cleared his throat uncomfortably. "I am here as the representative of the Duke," Revin said. "My own feelings on the matter are immaterial as I have accepted this charge and will carry it out to the best of my ability."

"Well spoken," the Director said, as others nodded. "A very diplomatic non-answer. I perceive you will have a successful career in politics."

"Hear, hear," Revin said, lifting his glass to chuckles all around.

With the toast out of the way, Revin was concerned that his lack of knowledge about polite dining would make him stand out. But he needn't have worried. The scientists couldn't care less about etiquette and appeared to use forks and spoons randomly — or not at all — which allowed Revin to relax and enjoy the meal. Watching the servants, though, he began to awaken to how easy it was to become complacent about your station in life. And to become complicit in sustaining inequalities. His respect for the Professor went up, to be willing to be true to himself and publicly demonstrate his commitment to his principles. And he began to see how the Professor and Will, a captain of pirates, had found common ground.

The meal had five courses: an appetizer of delicately seasoned quail's eggs; a salad with a light, creamy dressing; a main course with tender medallions of beef, spring vegetables, and buttered potatoes; a cheesecake for dessert, drizzled with a raspberry syrup; and, finally, some small candies served with a syrupy, highly aromatic digestif. Revin finally pushed back from the table uncomfortably full and returned to his room for the night.

Too full to sleep, Revin pulled out Momo's journal and began to write. He was careful not to put anything incriminating in writing, but instead offered a carefully redacted history of the events, lingering over the natural beauty of his trip by coach, the despicable behavior of horses, and the sumptuous repast he'd just enjoyed. He found himself avoiding any mention of Lidja and he wondered why. Was he avoiding making her worry about his fidelity? Did he have any right to expect her to feel jealous? Was he presumptuous to even imagine considering Lidja in romantic terms?

Finally, he set the journal aside and put himself — and his questions — to bed.

•　　•　　•

The next morning, the man in the office directed Revin to the cafeteria for a light breakfast, where he met with the Professor chatting with the Director. Kief arrived a few minutes later. Revin barely listened while they discussed the nature of etheric phenomena and whether they were more like one thing or another — the whole conversation was over his head.

"Your coach should be ready by now," the Director said. "I asked them to have it here by the end of breakfast. Oh! And I had them pack you a picnic lunch to enjoy enroute. Travel well!"

Revin carried their bags out to the driveway and found Lidja standing at attention next to the door to the coach. She held the door for the Professor while Revin stowed their gear in the storage compartment. A few moments later, Kief came out with a bag for Revin to stow in the back and a separate document case he kept with himself.

"Let me caution you," he said to everyone. "This case has a small incendiary charge in it that will destroy the secret documents inside if the case is tampered with. I'm telling you this, and keeping it with me, in case it goes off when we go over a bump or something, in which case one of us should endeavor to throw it out before it sets the coach on fire."

With that, Revin shut the coach door and climbed up on the box with Lidja. She gently shook the reins and the horses trotted off. Revin consulted their map and helped Lidja find the right turn in Relsington to head West toward Sendia Springs and then to Beskin Harbor.

It was a beautiful day with sun and just a few puffy, white clouds. Revin chatted amiably with Lidja, who appeared in high spirits. Revin snuck glances at her beaming with rosy cheeks. She recounted how much fun she'd had with the lively community of staff at the Hermitage.

The morning passed quickly. Around noon, they stopped to have the lunch the Director had arranged for them. Lidja watered the horses and gave them some fodder, then joined the three men for lunch.

After lunch, they were making preparations to depart and Revin considered sitting in the coach for a bit, but he found the technical conversations between the Professor and other scholars so far over his head that it tended to be extremely tedious. He shook his head and rejoined Lidja on the box as she started the horses.

In the early afternoon, they passed over a series of rolling hills. Revin manned the brake on the descents to keep the coach from rolling over the horses. On the highest hill, they paused to look out over the surrounding territory. The grassland, probably connected to where they had stayed the first night, seemed to extend to the horizons.

By mid-afternoon, Revin spotted clouds of steam rising in the distance and, a half-hour later, they arrived at Sendia Springs.

The inn was a large wooden building with a red tile roof that had a stable and several outbuildings next to a steaming river that flowed along the face of a set of low terraces — some white, some colored a brownish-yellow, and some gray. Steaming water trickled over the colored terraces and running down into a braided stream that passed in front of the hotel. Revin sat awestruck by the natural beauty. He snuck a glance at Lidja to see that she too was speechless with wonder and fascination.

Lidja forded the coach across the streams and around to the front of the hotel. A porter ran to collect their bags and show them inside. Several men from the stables came over to take charge of the coach and horses. At first, Lidja was reluctant to let the horses go without her, but Revin persuaded her to come with them into the lobby.

A woman wearing traditional dress, greeted them just inside the door.

"Greetings, honored travelers," she said bowing low. "Welcome to Sendia Springs, the premier resort on the Island of Havelock. We're very glad you are here and we hope you will let us see to your every desire. How many are you?"

"There are four of us," Revin said.

"How many rooms do you require?" the hostess asked.

"Well, um ..." Revin started.

"We can share a room, can't we, Professor?" said Kief.

"Surely," the Professor agreed.

"So ..." Revin fumbled for words.

"If you please, Revin," Lidja said. "May I share a room with you? If ... that's alright ..."

"Well ..." Revin began, reluctant to give up his privacy. But then he saw her face so full of hope, yet worried that he would say no. "Yes! Yes, of course, I'll share a room with you."

"Yay!" she said.

The hostess gave them their keys and led them to two adjoining rooms. She pointed out the features of the rooms and showed them where there were robes and towels for the bathing facilities and hot springs. Then she bowed deeply again and bade them welcome one last time.

After everyone had freshened up and changed into robes, they went to the dining room for dinner. They were seated at a low table and served by an impeccable wait staff that brought course after course of small plates for them to sample. The first plates held pickled vegetables and mushrooms that were both sour and salty. Next came fish eggs and crackers, reminding Revin of his last fateful meal aboard the *Madeline*. His eyes kept being drawn back to Lidja, who had never experienced anything like this before. Her eyes sparkled as she sampled the different dishes; she squealed with excitement when the waiter drenched a block of cheese with spirits, lit it on fire, and then extinguished the flames with the juice of a lime.

"Revin?" the Professor said. "Revin!"

"Huh?" Revin said. He noticed that Kief had stepped away from the table.

"After dinner, perhaps you can take our guest to the hot springs. I think I'll turn in early — if you know what I mean."

"Huh?" Revin said, now totally confused.

The Professor rolled his eyes.

"Revin!" the Professor said sternly. "Do you remember why we came on this little jaunt? This might be our best chance."

"Oh, right! So I just need to ..." Revin said and then realized what he was saying. "Wait! How am I going to take him to the hot spring?"

Revin, who had been walking on clouds all evening, was suddenly dragged back down to earth. He wracked his brain trying to come up with some plan or excuse or something. The springs were gendered and he fully recognized that he would be unable to pass, naked, in the men's bath. He began to sweat as he tried to think of something. Anything. He looked up uncomfortably when Kief returned to the table with another man standing behind him.

"Hey," Kief said, a little nervously, looking down. "So I ran into an ... old friend that I haven't seen for a really long time. I don't mean to cut out on you, but I want to catch up with him tonight. So, if you don't mind, I think he and I will visit the baths and then spend the evening together."

"So don't wait up for you, is what you're saying?" asked the Professor with a wink.

"Yes," Kief said, looking up with a relieved laugh. "Yes, exactly."

After dinner, Revin walked back to their rooms with the Professor and Lidja.

"Have fun, kids," the Professor said, yawning. "I'll see you in the morning."

"Good night ... Uncle," Revin said.

Revin unlocked the door and held it for Lidja.

"Are you ready to go to the hot spring?" she asked.

"Well ... Um ..." Revin said. "To be honest, that's kind of complicated for me."

"Is it because you're actually a girl?" she asked. The blood drained out of Revin's face.

"What?" Revin squeaked, backing up against the wall. "How did ..."

"I don't know," she said. "It wasn't any one thing. But I figured it out last night when you came to check on me. I saw you there at the door and something ... just clicked for me."

"I mean, I'm not a girl," Revin said. "I realized that a long time ago. But I still look like this."

"So I understand that you can't go to the men's bath," Lidja said. "But why not come to the women's side anyway. There won't be anyone you know there."

She approached Revin and took his hand in hers.

"Please," she said. "For me?"

Revin knew these feelings weren't right. There were so many things wrong with it morally and ethically — not the least of which was his relationship with her as both rescuer and employer. But he just couldn't bring himself to say no.

He removed his chest binding and undid his hair. They both took their towels and, after Revin closed the door, he let her take his hand as they walked together to the hot springs.

Inside was a steam-filled room with piping that had hot water sprinkling at many stations throughout the room. They seemed to be the only ones there.

They disrobed and Lidja pulled him to one of the showers.

"Let me wash you," she said. "Then you can wash me."

He stood under the deliciously hot spray while she shampooed his hair and the rest of his body.

After he'd rinsed, she handed him the shampoo and turned her back. He began to wash her hair. It was a strange feeling to be so intimate with another person — terrifying, yet amazingly satisfying.

"Your poor hair is so short," he said. "And so ragged."

"I had to cut it myself. It was easier, that way," she said. "Then they couldn't pull it."

Revin suddenly choked up and began fighting back tears.

"I can't believe someone did that to you," he said, hoarsely. "I can't believe people can do that to one another."

"Thank you, Revin," she said, tilting her head back and smiling up at him. "For caring."

He moved on to the rest of her body. He could feel her shoulder blades and ribs. And he could see the sharp lines of her pelvis.

"Did they starve you too?" he asked.

"We never had enough to eat," she said. "I was always hungry."

"How long were you there?" Revin asked.

"Let's see," she said. "I was sent there when I was thirteen so ... four years."

"Wait!" Revin said, shocked. "You're as old as I am! I thought you were a lot younger."

"Well, I'm not," she said, turning around, so they stood face to face. She looked up, meeting his eyes.

Revin blushed all the way to the floor.

"Let's ... Let's go into the hot spring now," he whispered.

They walked into the next room. They found a large, irregularly shaped pool filled with steaming water that gave off a strong smell of sulfur. They dipped their toes into it, looking for a place where the temperature was right, and then slipped into the pool.

Revin found a place where they could sit and look east. It was well after dark, but he could see the stars rising above the distant hills they'd traveled over earlier in the day. The braided stream below them sparkled with starlight. The rising steam looked like ghosts in the darkness. Lidja sat down next to Revin and then edged herself up against him.

"Revin," she said. "I think ... I think I love you."

"Lidja, I ... I ... "

"Is there someone else?" she asked.

"No," Revin said, nodding. "Wait! Yes? Maybe? I don't know. I'm so confused."

She wrapped her arms around him.

"Then let's not think about that tonight and just have a nice time."

Revin, initially tense, relaxed after a moment and leaned his head over onto her head and they sat contentedly together in the dark for a long while.

Eventually, they began to get too hot, so they climbed up and sat on the edge of the pool with just their legs in the water.

"How did you come to know so much about horses?" Revin asked.

"When I was a little girl, we had horses on our farm," she began. Revin was charmed, listening to her monologue about her fascination with horses. He smiled in the dark as she nattered on excitedly.

Finally, they reluctantly pulled their feet out of the pool, put their robes back on, and returned to their room.

As soon as they entered, Revin heard tapping at the adjoining door. He opened it to witness the Professor doing a double-take at seeing Revin with his hair down and without his chest binding. Then he quickly started whispering.

"Get in here," the Professor hissed. "I need your help!"

"I'll be back in a bit, Lidja," Revin said and stepped through the doorway.

"What do you need?"

"Grab a pen and start copying!" the Professor whispered.

Revin spied a thick sheaf of pages with dense writing on them. The Professor had already copied many of the pages, but there were many more to go. Revin picked up a pen and a clean sheet of paper and got to work.

Every few pages, Revin remembered Lidja in the next room. He hoped she was sleeping and wasn't worrying about him. He sighed, knuckled down, and got back to work copying.

Four hours later, in the early hours of the morning, they wrapped up. The Professor stowed their copies in his trunk and returned the pages to Kief's document case and carefully closed it.

"Get ready ... Here goes nothing," he said, and pulled a long strip of paper out through the closed and locked top. Nothing happened.

"Ha! I think I got the boobytrap re-enabled," he said. "It took me a long time to figure that out."

"I can't believe we managed to copy the whole thing," Revin said, flexing his fingers. "I haven't written so much in months."

"Off to bed with you now, young man," the Professor said. "We've got one more long day before us, but then I think we'll be on our way home."

Revin crept back through the adjoining door. He started to climb into his own bed when Lidja spoke.

"Could you come over here, Revin?" she said, quietly. "To keep me company? I keep worrying that I'll wake up and this will all have been a dream."

Revin hesitated for a moment. He recognized if he did this, he was crossing a line from which there was no return, but he couldn't bring himself to stop. He laid his robe on the other bed and then slipped into bed with her. She snuggled up against him and kissed his cheek. He turned toward her and she pressed her mouth to his. Fireworks went off in Revin's head as he slid his arms around her and desperately kissed her back.

•   •   •

In the morning, Revin awoke and was surprised to find himself alone in the bed. He got up, dressed, and then sat and wrote a couple of letters. He also counted out four reggies. He was about to go to breakfast when Lidja returned.

"Where were you?" Revin asked.

"Just checking on the horses," she said. "They're good here, but it never hurts for them to know you're watching. Oh! Someone asked about those two spare horses and whether we'd like to sell them."

"Sure," Revin said. "In a minute you can go do that, if you like. But first, I need to say something that may change your mind."

Lidja looked worried, so he took her hand.

"When we get to Beskin Harbor to drop off Kief, the Professor and I will be departing as well," Revin said. "So I want to pay you the rest of the money you're owed. And I'd like you to deliver these two letters for me. One is to Mr. Darkpony, who rented us the coach. There is a deposit on the coach and, when you return it, you can keep that as well. That should be enough money to set yourself up for a good little while. But if the horses would suit you better than money, you could keep them."

"No," she said. "A horse is a lot of expense, unless you need it for something in particular. So I think selling them is the right thing to do. But is it really okay for me to keep the money?"

"You keep it," Revin said, and then continued. "The other letter is to the Duke's seneschal. He's expecting me to come back to the capital. This letter says I've completed the task he set me, but that I have some family business to attend to and won't be back for a while. It also includes an introduction to you which perhaps might lead to something. Can you deliver these for me?"

"I will," she said. "But ... Where are you going? When will I see you again?"

"I'm ... Actually, I'm here in disguise because ... I'm a p-pirate," Revin said, stumbling over the word. "I don't know when I'll be able to come back. But! But if you write to me on Candlemain, I should be able to get it. And so you can tell me where you go so I can find you and see you again. If ... If you want to see me again."

"Oh, Revin," she said, hugging him. "Of course I want to see you again. I want to see you always. I love you so much that I can't bear we're going to be apart. But I will understand and respect whatever your heart chooses."

Revin was struck by Lidja's certainty — and courage. His feelings were such a tangle, he could barely bring himself to meet her gaze. He gave her the letters and the money. While Lidja went to sell the spare horses, Revin checked on the Professor.

After packing, the three of them went to breakfast where they found Kief already there with his "old friend".

After a hearty breakfast, the four emerged to find the bags already loaded, the coach freshly washed and shined, with the horses brushed and combed and little red ribbons tied in their manes. While Revin paid the hefty bill with the last of the Seneschal's money, The Professor and Kief seated themselves in the coach while Lidja walked to each of the horses, as she did every time, to rub their noses and whisper little words of encouragement.

Then they set out on the last leg of their journey.

•   •   •

By late afternoon, the horses were tired, but they were nearly to Beskin Harbor, so they pushed on. Revin had divided his time this day between sitting on the box with Lidja and sitting in the coach with Kief and the Professor, although he still found their dialog tedious in larger doses. The Professor was asking about the dynamics of etheric stream formation and the role atmospheric conditions played. As best as Revin could understand, Kief was arguing that atmospheric conditions played only a mediating influence — whatever that meant. But the Professor grasped the significance immediately and followed up with yet another, deeper question. Revin rolled his eyes, and leaned back to nap for a bit until they arrived.

Revin awoke when the coach came to a stop. It was now dark. Revin looked out and could see the pier at Beskin Harbor with peaceful waves lapping on the shore. He stretched, then got up and opened the door.

"I believe this is where you get off," he said to Kief.

"Yes," he said. "We're working with the boat at the end of the pier, there."

Revin climbed out and held the door. Kief stepped out onto the running board.

A bright light suddenly appeared in the sky over Beskin Harbor — some kind of firework? — and Revin could hear the sounds of yelling and screaming coming from the end of the pier.

"It's a raid," the Professor said, looking through the window. "Those are marines — probably from Belleriand. We should pull back."

"What are they doing?" Kief asked.

"We're not waiting to find out," Revin said, pushing Kief back into the coach and climbing up onto the box. "Lidja! Get us out of here!"

Lidja shook the reins and the horses started up. A party of marines racing to secure the end of the pier spotted the coach. They charged out and two of them caught hold of the coach, climbing up on the footboards at the back. Revin threw himself onto the roof of the coach and slithered on his belly toward the back.

The hands of one of the marines appeared and grabbed the bars around the top of the roof. Revin grabbed his sword and clumsily struck out at the hands. The unseen man yelled as he lost his grip and fell off the footboard. Suddenly, a towline appeared, stabbing up into the sky momentarily, and the other soldier sprang up on the towline and landed on the roof. He stamped his foot down on Revin's sword and stood over him with his own sword drawn.

"Stop the coach!" the soldier called to Lidja. "Stop! Or he dies!"

Lidja cracked the whip and the horses bolted forward. The man drew back his arm to strike, then the carriage suddenly passed under the low archway that led into the promenade and the soldier was swept off the top of the carriage.

Lidja kept the horses at a gallop until they turned the corner at the end of the promenade and entered a plaza. Then she reined in the horses to a walk.

She looked back toward Revin. "Orders?"

Revin surveyed the situation under the fading light of the pyrotechnic. A building stood between them and the harbor, but he could hear the continued sounds of combat. He could make out people running for buildings to get under cover. Another pyrotechnic went up and Revin suddenly spotted towlines and then an airship.

It was the *Queen*, Revin realized! She had come to investigate the activity.

"The Professor and I will disembark here," Revin said. "You and Kief should put as much distance between yourselves and the marines as possible. They would love nothing more than to capture or kill him. Head south to the capital."

"What are you going to do, Revin?" Lidja asked, her voice breaking with worry.

"I have a plan."

Revin pulled out his signaling mirror and began trying to get the attention of the *Queen*. Revin wasn't sure the flares were bright enough, but they were evidently watching carefully and, after several moments, he saw the countersign and the Queen began to descend into the plaza.

Revin grabbed their trunks that contained the all-important copy of the plans, and dragged them out of the carriage.

"Go!" he yelled to Lidja.

The coach rolled away.

The *Queen* touched down and the Professor hurried aboard with his arm braces while two teams of pirates ran out to collect their trunks. Revin started to run, but an inexorable force grabbed him and slammed him back against the wall of the building. The remmer marine had climbed on top of the building and had made a towline, pinning Revin to the wall.

"Go!" Revin cried to the *Queen*.

Two more airships appeared in the sky over Beskin Harbor as Revin struggled to free himself. He saw Will at the gangplank looking around and then spotting him.

"Look out!" Revin screamed. "It's a trick!"

Whatever might have happened next was preempted when a brilliant white flash illuminated the clouds from below. A ring of blue coruscating lightning bolts reached up toward the sky and began to whirl around an axis faster and faster. Revin realized the Etheric Storm Generator must have been triggered.

Suddenly, Revin felt the force holding him back vanish. All of the towlines had vanished. He sprinted for the *Queen* as she began to rise without towlines to hold her down. He leapt and caught the end of the gangplank with one hand, leaving him dangling as the craft rose higher and higher.

Will calmly walked straight out to the very end, reached down, caught Revin's hand, and pulled him up.

"Welcome home, lad," he said, with a grin, giving Revin a hug. "I somehow knew you'd be at the heart of all this."

The wind was already rising by the time they reached the cockpit. Will headed straight back to the remmer deck. The *Queen* began to vibrate and slip to the west as, without remmers to hold her on course, the wind began to drag her back into the storm.

"No streams, Will!" Grip said. "They can't see a single stream."

"Call life lines," Will said. "This is going to be a rough one."

"Attach life lines!" Grip called fore and aft. "Attach life lines!"

Will got out his monocle and began searching high and low.

A long pause followed while everyone simply watched him.

"There!" he called. "Down! Due east! Inland!"

He bound a towline no thicker than yarn. The others began trying and, after a few moments, the *Queen* stopped losing ground and began to move sluggishly east.

Revin went to the observation deck and watched as the storm grew before his eyes. The other two airships had lost all their attachments and were being pulled rapidly into the storm. In moments, they were lost to view in the nearly constant flashes of lightning one on top of another. He already couldn't see the town through the blinding sheets of rain. He could see two funnel clouds circulating around the center of the storm over the harbor. Buildings were torn apart and the air was filled with debris.

The *Queen* continued to bounce up and down with the turbulence, even as she crept away from the storm that only grew in magnitude behind her. Revin watched in horror as the town was engulfed and flattened by the storm. He couldn't imagine there would be anything left but rubble by morning.

He looked down and spotted the coach headed south toward the capital. But as they crept away from the storm and could reach more etheric streams, the *Queen of Belleriand* turned north and the coach was lost from Revin's view.

INTERLUDE

REVIN CURSED UNDER HIS BREATH while he performed calisthenics under Will's watchful eye.

"Higher, Revin!" Will called. "You can jump higher!"

Revin grumbled under his breath and tried to jump just a bit higher each time.

"I can't hear you!" Will called.

"Aye, aye, Cap'n!" Revin responded, with a sour look.

Will grinned and turned his eye toward the rest of the men.

When Revin had returned from his adventure with the Professor on Havelock, Will had asked him about how he had maintained his physical fitness and, when Revin had tried to lie through his teeth, Will had called him on it and impressed upon him the importance both of honesty and maintaining his fitness at peak levels. Hence his enhanced scrutiny for the past two weeks.

"Now that we're warmed up," Will called. "Let's go for a run!"

"Aye, aye, Cap'n!" everyone called in unison.

Will led the men toward the trail that led up the mountain.

"Revin! You set the pace!" Will said. Revin growled, but complied.

Everyone waited while Revin came to the front of the pack and then they followed him up the trail.

"Is that all the faster you can go?" Will said, passing him and then running backward in front of him. "Go! Go! Go!"

Revin picked up the pace a tiny bit. He knew his limits and knew that if he tried to go any faster, he would be out of breath once they hit the steepest parts, so he maintained his pace in spite of Will's needling.

His mind wandered as he ran. He remembered the trip across Havelock: The natural beauty and the moments of excitement. Lidja's face came unbidden before his mind's eye and, in spite of himself, he smiled to remember her face and her tiny expressions of pleasure: Her open smile, the way pink would surmount her cheeks when she blushed, and the way her eyes would crinkle up when she was truly happy. Revin nearly stumbled over a root and was brought back to the present moment and the agony of the run.

They reached the top and, without pausing, Revin turned and began the painful descent. There was no question but that it was easier at first but, after just a minute or two, the muscles on the fronts of his thighs and calves began to complain with the strain of each footfall going down. He maintained the same grueling pace all the way down.

When Revin reached the bottom, he walked around in the circle stretching and breathing deeply.

"Isometrics!" Will called. "Pair up! Do a Wall Sit!"

The pirates formed pairs and put their backs to each other to hold themselves up in a sitting position without a chair. Revin turned in circles looking for someone unmatched.

"It looks like you're working with me, Lad!" Will said cheerfully. He turned his back. Revin groaned and pressed his back up against Will.

"Now, Hold!" Will called. "One! Two! Three!" He counted slowly to thirty, by which point Revin's muscles were screaming with discomfort.

"Calf raise!" Will called. Once again they were back to back standing on their toes with their calves flexed. "One! Two! Three!" Will counted slowly to thirty again.

Will let the men through another half-dozen isometric exercises. Then he mercifully called an end.

"Well done, men!" he called. There was a ragged cheer and then men scattered, limping, to find some place to recover their strength before lunch.

Revin staggered back to his tent and collapsed onto his bunk.

Someone knocked at his tent flap. Revin groaned in reply.

"The Professor wants you," Grip said from outside.

Revin groaned again and, after he heard Grip's laughter fade into the distance, he dragged himself back out of bed and walked over to where the Professor had his "office" under the belly of the *Queen* that was moored under camouflage netting.

He found the Professor berating a group of men who had been checking the skin of the *Queen* for pinholes. Revin knew first hand what a miserable job that was.

"I made two pinholes myself and you didn't find them!" the Professor bellowed.

"What?" said one. "You made them?"

"How can I trust you if you can't find the obvious ones! Go back and look again, or I'll have your ears! Or, if that's not enough, I'll have the Captain have a word with you."

The men quailed and retreated hastily back into the *Queen* to check her epidermis again for pinholes.

"You called, Professor?" Revin said.

"Ah! I'm glad you're here," he said. "Let me show you something."

He used his crutches and hand-walked over to the other side of "office" to where there was a wooden case surmounted by a glass bell-jar.

"This is the Etheric Deflection Monitor," he said. "I've constructed it with a tiny bit of eternite."

"Eternite was that thing that was in the notes about the Etheric Storm Generator," Revin remembered.

"That's right. The Storm Generator has a shaped core of eternite. We don't have that much. I only had a tiny sliver. But by making it into a needle and mounting it on a pivot with a sensitive balance, we can collect two measurements. The first is simply a heading. When the Etheric Storm Generator is used, it consumes all of the etheric energy in an area and converts it into atmospheric energy — that's where the storm comes from. That leaves an area with low etheric energy. The needle will tend to point away from the area. So I have a dial here, where you can record the heading toward the lowest energy. That should indicate toward the dead zone left by the storm generator.

There is also a dial that records the slope of the line between the area of normal etheric energy and the dead zone. That value is recorded on this dial.

"I intend for the Queen to track down the dead zone and you need to stay as close as you can for three days. During that time, I want to record the heading and the deflection every 15 or 20 minutes. With these data, I hope to be able to evaluate whether the areas are stable, shrinking, or growing."

"How close do we need to get?" Revin asked.

The Professor glared at him from under his bushy eyebrows. "As close as you can," he growled.

"Did you hear him, Revin?" Will asked, coming up from behind.

"Aye, aye, Cap'n," Revin. "As close as we can."

"Go tell the men," he said. "We leave at first light."

"Aye, aye!" Revin said cheerfully, grateful that this meant the end of the hellish exercise regime. He sprinted off to begin informing the men to prepare for departure.

5

THE END OF HIS ROPE

R EVIN STOOD IN THE OBSERVATION DECK of the *Queen of Belleriand* as she sailed over the boundless ocean. The *Queen* rode on the trail of the monster storm that had been generated by Havelock's Etheric Storm Generator. They had been out of sight of land for two days.

"Heading!" Will called.

Revin consulted the Etheric Deflection Monitor the Professor had constructed. It stood four feet tall in a wooden case with a bell jar affixed to its top. Underneath was a dial with a needle made of eternite that aligned with the "slope of etheric flow" — or something like that, anyway. Revin was unclear on the details, but the Professor said in simplest terms that, in the absence of other disruptions, it would tend to point toward the dead etheric zone left by the Etheric Storm Generator.

"Three-hundred and forty-two degrees!" Revin called back. "Three! Four! Two!"

"Three! Four! Two!" Will confirmed.

"Aye, aye, Cap'n!"

"Two degrees to port!" Will called.

"Two degrees to port!" Grip repeated from the remmer deck.

In addition to the direction, the monitor also had a dial that indicated the magnitude of the deflection. Revin made a notation of the time, the heading, and the deflection in a small notebook. Revin felt the tiny course adjustment as the *Queen* sailed on.

Revin found himself increasingly sensitive to everything around the airship. From the sound alone, he could tell whether the sun was shining or behind the clouds. A shift in the wind or minor course correction were now enough to wake him up from a sound sleep. He felt like he was becoming a part of the airship. Or that it increasingly seemed like an extension of his own body.

At the moment, however, his body was telling him something else. He excused himself and went to the lavatory, where he replaced his sodden menstrual pad with a fresh one. He hated this particular aspect of his body, but it was simply a fact of life. He was just grateful it had waited until after he had finished on Havelock. He remembered visiting the baths with Lidja and smiled in spite of himself — it would have been a lot less convenient to visit the baths if his period had started just a few days earlier. As it was, he expected it would be done within two or three more days.

Two days earlier, they had overflown Beskin Harbor on the track of the dead zone. It had been two weeks since they had precipitously departed when the device was triggered. When they returned, Revin saw practically nothing but rubble. The stone pier was still there. And the foundations of buildings. But the buildings themselves had all been torn apart; not one was left standing. A few people below moved around with teams of horses clearing streets. Outside of town, Revin counted dozens of fresh graves. He had a hard time imagining that the quiet, picturesque, seaside village would ever recover.

Even worse were the other findings the Professor had made while studying the plans they had stolen of the Etheric Storm Generator. The first was that, until now, Havelock had been triggering the device at sea-level, which created a massive storm. But Kief Senterson, the chief scientist on Havelock, had determined that if they triggered the device at a higher altitude, the effect would be multiplied many times over — the Professor disagreed with his calculations which, he said, significantly underestimated the potential effect. The plans that Kief had been bringing suggested they were planning to launch the device with a balloon that could bring devastation not to just a small village, but to an entire city. Or island. There simply weren't enough data, the Professor said, to predict just how large the storm might be able to become. But even worse was the other discovery he had made.

Well, it was perhaps too strong to call it a discovery yet. But the Professor hypothesized that the dead zones might not be temporary. The scientists from Havelock appeared to believe that the dead zones would recover over time. When they went back to an area where it had been triggered, there were etheric streams there, after all. But the Professor proposed that the whole dead zone simply moved away from the area — a terrifying proposition. Worse, he suggested that they might never recover — that the effects might be permanent. Or nearly so. He had constructed the Etheric Deflection Device and recommended — in the strongest possible terms — that they find the dead zone associated with the storm and take measurements from as close as they could get for at least three days. With these data, he said, he could probably determine whether or not the dead zones were stable, recovering, or — an even grimmer possibility — getting worse and growing.

Revin returned to the observation deck. Recording the measurements was tedious, but it was a treat to be back aboard the *Queen* after two weeks on island. Will had worked Revin particularly hard with his physical-fitness training — running up the mountain, calisthenics, and climbing ropes — to make up for the time he'd been "slacking off" while ashore on Havelock. His period could have started then, and given him an excuse to beg off, but it had inconveniently held off until they were leaving.

Revin recorded another set of measurements. Each time, the magnitude of the deflection continued to grow. Looking ahead, illuminated by the late afternoon, he could see the towering cloud tops of a giant, cumulonimbus cloud.

"Storm, ho!" he called.

"Now, how close did the Professor say we needed to get?" Will asked.

"As close as possible," both Grip and Revin answered in unison. And then all three laughed. This had become a running gag as they had chased the storm over the past four days.

"Cap'n! Cap'n!" they heard from the remmer deck. "Our forward towlines have failed."

Will left the cockpit and went to the remmer deck. Revin sighed and continued to record his periodic measurements.

They spent three long days tagging along just behind the storm collecting measurements. Finally, Will declared their task complete and, in the early afternoon, they turned to head back home.

"Cap'n!" Revin called. "Island ho!"

Just below them, Revin had spotted a very small island that had just been lashed by the storm. All of its trees were leafless or snapped off. But on the beach, someone had arranged rocks to spell "HELP."

"The law of the sea is to always help the marooned," Will said. "Call all hands for rescue. Tell the remmers to take us down, Grip."

"All hands for rescue!" Grip called. "Remmers! Take us down!"

The *Queen* descended quickly. They set the gangplank on the beach between the E and the L. A party of pirates with weapons drawn secured the area around the *Queen*. Will, Grip, and Revin had just started walking inland. when they heard a shout of excitement.

Three men stepped out of the brush with their hands raised.

"Thank you for coming to our rescue," the first one said.

He appeared to be the oldest of the three, balding, with glasses and a grey beard. The other two men stood back. A younger man, no longer a youth wore his blond hair tucked under a bandana. The third man looked like a muscle-bound thug. He eyed them suspiciously and looked uncomfortable to be unarmed.

While the man was speaking, Revin noticed Grip tap Will on the shoulder, then lean over and whisper something in his ear. Will shot him a surprised look, then turned back to the party.

"And what are you doing here exactly?" Will asked.

"Oh, I'm sorry," the older man said. "I'm Professor Ratner from the Royal Academy on Harway. We came here by airship to conduct an archaeological dig. But a huge storm blew up out of nowhere and smashed our airship. We're very grateful to you for stopping since we lost most of our freshwater supply with the airship."

"And your companions?" Will asked.

"Right. This is Words. He's my assistant," Ratner said. The younger man waved. "And this fellow is Beck. He is our … security officer. There are another ten of us from the airship crew that were also working on the dig. A few are injured, but nothing worse than a couple of broken arms and one broken leg."

"We don't have a medical officer," Will said. "But we'll do what we can."

"That's okay," Ratner said. "Words has some medical training, so I think the men are in good shape."

"My father wanted me to study medicine," Words said. "But I always wanted to do archaeology."

"You present me with a conundrum, gentlemen," Will said. "We are on an urgent mission and so will need to take you with us back to our base. But we cannot risk disclosure of our base or operations. If you gentleman will give me your word on the matter, we will take you with us. And we will trust we can find a way to get you back to Harway in due course."

"Without a ransom?" Ratner asked.

Will looked at Grip who shook his head fractionally.

"Agreed," said Will. "No ransom."

"Done," Ratner said, raising his right hand. "I give you my word of honor that neither I nor my men will reveal any information about you, your base, or your operations."

Words and Beck did the same.

Will made a signal and the pirates followed Will and the others into the brush where they found the wreckage of an airship. The archaeology team's air crew, some in stretchers, sat in the shade.

"Revin!" Will called.

"Yes, Cap'n" Revin said, snapping to attention.

"Run and ask the cook to prepare for twice as many men."

"Aye, aye, Cap'n!" Revin said,

"Oh! Revin!" Will called after him. "Have some water cups prepared. These men are going to be thirsty."

"Yes, Cap'n!" Revin called over his shoulder.

He saw the pirates grabbing stretchers and helping the marooned airmen get to their feet and start walking toward the *Queen*.

In little more than half an hour, they brought everyone on board. The *Queen* was heavy as she lifted off and turned toward Kapper island, where the pirates made their base.

Revin was constantly busy for the next couple of hours, bringing water to the marooned men and organizing them in shifts to get food. Eventually, he went back to the observation deck. The sun had set, but there remained a reddish glow to starboard. Revin watched the light sparkle on the waves as the *Queen* sped on through the tranquil evening air.

"Excuse me," someone said behind him. "I don't think I caught your name."

Revin turned and saw Words stepping onto the observation deck, with Beck glowering behind and lingering at the entrance.

"I'm Revin," Revin said, extending his hand. "Did I hear your name is Words?"

"It's what people call me," he said. "What do you do?"

"Who, me?" Revin asked. "I'm the cabin boy. So I do a little of this and little of that. Whatever needs doing, mostly."

"Isn't it strange for a pirate ship to have a cabin boy?"

"I dunno," Revin said. "I've never been on another pirate ship. Well. Not exactly." Revin remembered stepping onto the pirate's ship when it was attached to the *Madeline*. And setting it on fire.

"Pardon me for saying so," Words continued. "But you don't sound like a pirate either."

Well, you sure don't look like an archaeologist, with that thuggish bodyguard following you around everywhere. But he said, "I studied for a while to be a lawyer. Let's just say, it didn't work out."

"I don't mean to pry," Words said. "I'm just interested in puzzles. And you, my friend, are a puzzle."

"What were you hoping to find in your archaeological dig?" Revin asked, changing the subject.

"Some of the islands out this way were inhabited during prehistory by another civilization," Words said. "Small islands, like that one, sometimes have the remains of outposts. But supposedly there was an island that had a huge eternite mine on it that everyone has been trying to rediscover. I think we were on the right track. But then this happened."

"Eternite," Revin said. "Wait. That's the metal that's sensitive to etheric energy!"

"It is," Words said. "But how do you know that? It's so rare that most people have never even heard of it."

"Oh," Revin said, not wanting to admit he had seen it while copying Kief Senterson's notes back on Havelock. "I don't know. Just something I picked up along the way, I guess."

Words just looked at Revin, so Revin just looked back. Words was a bit taller than he was and well-proportioned. His bit of blond beard stubble gave him a rakish, bad-boy look. And blue eyes, Revin noticed. In fact, he was absurdly good-looking. Even with the dirt and sweat and filthy clothes, Revin still found him very attractive.

Tired of the verbal jousting, Revin excused himself to go to the lavatory. At the entrance to the observation deck, he had to push past Beck, who had stayed there, just out of sight, keeping an eye on Words. He looked back as he left, and saw Words still looking out the observation deck windows as the stars came out.

Revin visited the lavatory and was pleased to see that his period had finally run its course and he was only spotting. After he finished in the lavatory, he slipped quietly away to his bunk.

By sailing directly back, the *Queen* was approaching Kapper Island by the end of the following day. Revin watched for the signal and flashed the countersign before they brought the *Queen* into her berth. Grip alerted the newcomers to the policy that everyone who was able was to help unload the ship before being released from duty. Since they had not captured any loot, and with the extra hands, the unloading was almost perfunctory, and everyone was anticipating being released promptly.

"One moment, everyone," Will said, coming up behind Revin, putting his hands on his shoulders, and clearing his throat. "Tonight, I would beg your kind indulgence for a few moments of your time to celebrate the newest addition to our crew, our own, our wonderful, Revin."

Revin suddenly realized what was happening and tried to slink away, but Will seized him with an iron grip.

"Revin, as you know, rescued many of you from the clutches of the Admiralty on Havelock. Moreover, were it not for his quick and ingenious thinking to stall them checking for a letter of marque, most of you'd have been hung before we even had a chance. And during our escape, he saved my life."

"He's saved my life more than once," Grip added. "And my sister's life."

"Without Revin," the Professor said, who'd appeared from behind somewhere, "the mission to Havelock would never have succeeded."

"So before we left, I arranged for us to have a little surprise party for Revin upon our return in order to recognize and promote him. No longer Cabin Boy, please welcome Revin as your new Master's Mate."

A roar of approval went up from the entire assembled population, followed by loud applause.

"Do you want to say anything?" Will asked. Revin shook his head vigorously, but people started calling "Speech! Speech!" Will pushed Revin forward.

"Thank you," Revin said, blushing. "I'm so grateful to all of you for honoring me with your trust. I … I won't let you down."

"Hear, hear!" shouted a chorus. "Hear, hear!"

"Now let's have a party!" Will shouted.

Revin discovered that a huge feast had been prepared, with tables piled high with food. To the side stood barrels, not only of ale, but also of rum. Some of the pirates struck up a tune. The archaeology crew, at first standing off to the side, was quickly embraced by the pirates who put them at their ease in the festive island party atmosphere.

"Let me buy you a drink, Master's Mate!" said a pirate to Revin.

"I've never had a drink before," Revin admitted.

"This is the time to start!" the pirate said, handing him a small glass of rum and taking one for himself. "Bottoms up!" He downed the shot in a swallow and then looked at Revin.

Revin looked dubiously at the glass of rum. But then did the same. It burned as it went down, but Revin managed to not spit it out or cough. The pirate pounded him on the back.

Another pirate came up and handed Revin another glass and Revin drank another shot. Someone handed him a third when Words came up and interposed himself.

"Hey, you should go easy on that stuff," Words said.

"But I feel great!" Revin said, raising his glass and downing it. "I've never felt like this before."

"Just be careful. It's really easy to drink too much."

"Whoo!" Revin said. "I feel great! Dance with me!"

"What?" Words said.

"Dance! With! Me!" Revin said, taking his hand.

He pulled Words out into an open space and began to dance to the folk tune the pirates were playing. The pirates cheered as Words danced with Revin, surprised at first, but relaxing after several turns. After the second tune, Revin began to stagger. Words caught him and led him off to the side.

"Master's Mate!" called a pirate, handing Revin another shot. "Drink with me!"

"Bott'm up," Revin slurred his words downing the shot before Words could stop him.

"Be careful, Revin," Words said. "You're already ..."

"Did anyone ever tell you you're really handsome?" Revin said, looking innocently at Words, who blushed. "I don't know why I said that."

"You're drunk, Revin," Words said. "You don't know what you're saying."

"I know I love you," Revin said.

Words closed his eyes, grimacing.

"Anyway," Revin continued. "I know jus' wha' I'm sayin'! You're jus' not listenin'!"

"Revin, let me take you some place quiet."

"Ooh! Yes! Someplace quiet!" Revin said, clinging to his arm, as the pirates all laughed. "Le's go to my tent!"

"No, you just need to sit down for a few minutes and sober up."

"No! I'm jus' fine! I ... I ..." Revin said, suddenly turning pale. He turned around and fell to his knees as his stomach began to systematically empty itself. Words put a hand on his shoulder and patted him gently until he was done.

• • •

The next morning, Revin awoke with a splitting headache and realized he was not alone in his bedroll. His chest binding had been removed and he was lying curled up with ... someone. Revin had just started to panic when Words rolled over and smiled at him.

"Good morning," he said. "I'm glad you're feeling better."

"Did I? Did we?" Revin stammered. "What happened?"

"I'm sorry I was too late," Words said. "They got you to drink too much before I could stop you. Then you threw up and passed out. But you were pretty cute before that though."

"Cute?" Revin squeaked, holding his head in his hands.

"Here," Words said. "Lie back down for a few minutes and I'll bring you some coffee. It will help a little."

As he departed, Revin was slightly comforted to perceive that Words was fully clothed. He wracked his brain trying to remember what had happened the night before, but there were only scattered images. He remembered laughing a lot and ... dancing with someone?

A few minutes later, Words returned with a cup of coffee and a big glass of water.

"Drink the water first," Words said. "It will help your body clear out the last of the alcohol and make your head feel better. Then you can have the coffee."

Revin sat up and chugged the water, eager for the coffee.

"Why were you sleeping with me?" Revin said, accepting the cup of coffee. "And how did my chest binding get removed?"

"You wouldn't let go of me when you were drunk. It was actually rather charming."

Revin blushed.

"But after you passed out, I brought you here and removed your chest binding, because with my medical training I know that it's dangerous to sleep with something like that on. And I stayed with you for the same reason, because sometimes when people have had too much to drink, they can stop breathing or choke. And I couldn't bear for something to happen to you."

He blushed and cleared his throat.

"You know," he amended hastily, looking away. "After your exciting promotion and all."

"Well, thank you," Revin said, coloring again. "I appreciate your care of me. But how am I going to face everyone? I feel like such a fool."

"Revin," Words said, kneeling to bring their eyes to the same level and taking his hand. "Don't worry. You're amazing and these people love you. If anything, for them to see that you're only human, is a good thing. And I think you'll find that showing this moment of weakness — showing that you're just a person — will endear you to them even more."

"Revin!" Grip called, appearing in the doorway. He pushed past Beck who was hovering outside, as usual. Then he stopped dead, perceiving the tableau of Words kneeling before Revin and holding his hand. "Your Majesty! Are you proposing to our new Master's Mate already?"

"Griphon! Don't call me that!" Words said, drawing himself up to his full height.

Revin goggled.

"Well, don't call me Griphon either!" Grip said laughing.

The two embraced slapping each other on the back.

"Your Majesty?" Revin asked, dumbfounded. "Wait! Are you ..."

"Prince Stewart," Words said, with a bow. "At your service."

"We go way back," Griphon said. "But, like me, he tries to keep a low profile when not at court."

"You have no idea, Revin, how tiring it is to have to maintain a pretense with everyone all the time," Words said.

"Actually, I think I have a pretty good idea," Revin said with a grin. "Your Majesty."

"Gah," Words said. "You must be feeling better, already. Ah, youth!"

"Let's go get breakfast," Grip said.

"I need to freshen up first," Revin said. "You both go on ahead."

"Oh. Hang on! I almost forgot: mail call!" Grip said, handing two letters to Revin.

Revin accepted the letters from Grip. One looked unfamiliar and written in a childish hand. The other was from Momo, but Revin noticed it didn't have an envelope like the previous letter she had sent. This one was cunningly folded with a strip of paper looped, then threaded through the letter, and tied in an elaborate knot. He looked quizzically at Grip.

"Ooh! It's a locked letter," Words said.

"My mother must have shown her how to do that," Grip said. "She does that when she needs to write some important secret."

Revin looked at the letter again with a mixture of worry and respect.

"Oh, my," Words said. "Is that from little Momo?"

"Not so little anymore, my friend," Grip replied.

Words gave Revin an appraising look and then followed Grip to breakfast leaving Revin with his correspondence.

He decided to open Momo's letter first.

My dearest Revin,

I expect this comes as no surprise, but you've made some people here extremely angry with your recent actions. I don't know exactly what happened, but they say you were recognized by one of the few survivors. I wanted to warn you that if you were in danger here before, it was nothing compared to now. Be very cautious about coming here because in some circles people are calling for your head. I love both you and your dear head with all my heart.

Please be safe, my hero.

Next, he opened the other letter. It was addressed only as "Revin, Candlemain." He was amazed it had reached Grip at all. As he had guessed, it was from Lidja.

Lidja wrote, in large block printing:

Dear Revin,

I don't write good. But I love you. You are hero here because you saved Kief. Boss read your letter and gave me job! I drive coach for office now. Thank you!!!! I have room and food. I am very happy. I hope you come soon. But if soon maybe I gone to Harway? Boss looking at map yesterday. Be careful. I love you!

Revin smiled to himself, imagining Lidja with her tongue out writing so carefully in her laborious block printing. He felt warm all over to be so beloved. A tiny doubt niggled at him about having two girlfriends, but he set it aside, tucked the letters away, and got dressed for breakfast.

After breakfast, Will called a meeting. Revin arrived to find the thuggish Beck standing outside. Inside, the Professor sat chatting amiably with Words and Ratner. Of course the Professor would know who they were. Words looked up and winked at Revin when he arrived. Grip and Brill arrived shortly afterward. Brill seated himself and continued working on his ledger without acknowledging the meeting in any way.

"I've analyzed the data you collected over the past several days," the Professor said. "It shows that the etheric streams do not recover quickly, on the order of days or weeks. There is some regeneration that does not appear to be just random variation. But it will take months or years before the streams are fully restored — if ever."

"So where will that dead area go?" Will asked.

"I'm not sure anyone knows how etheric streams circulate," the Professor replied. "But the spot seems to maintain its coherence and so it may return unexpectedly from some other direction in weeks or months. Without a lot more data, there's no way to predict.

"But if Havelock triggers their device at a higher altitude, as they plan to do, it will create much, much larger dead spots. If they're large enough, they might shut down etheric flows altogether."

"Will the storms keep getting bigger too?" asked Revin.

"The storms we've seen represent the energy from the disrupted etheric flow being redirected into the atmosphere. But as the scale increases, the effects may be non-linear. That is, they might change in character from just being storms to creating climatic disruption. Or worse."

"Is there anything we can do to stop them?" Grip asked.

Revin imagined the device being triggered over the capital of Belleriand and wiping Ravensbelth — and the whole city — clean off the map. He swallowed hard, worried about Momo.

"I have one thing," the Professor said. "I had some of my workmen construct this!" He held up what looked like a fishnet, but Revin realized that it was made of woven metal strands. "It's an etheric shield. I believe if this is wrapped around the device, it will block the etheric disruption. At least partially. I hope. Maybe."

"How many of these devices can they make anyway?" Will asked.

"I'm not sure how they made even the one," the Professor asked. "They contain a large, shaped core of eternite. But that's certainly more eternite than I've ever seen in one place. I had a tiny fragment from my mineral collection that I used for the needle in the Etheric Deflection Monitor. But you'd need at least a hundred ... No, a thousand times that, to make a storm generator."

"So where are they getting so much eternite?" Grip wondered.

"They must have found the island," Ratner said. "The island we've been looking for with the giant eternite mine. They've probably disturbed the whole site and ruined a vast amount of the scientific knowledge to be gained."

With difficulty, Revin managed to suppress his mirth at someone who was seemingly more concerned about the loss of archaeological data than saving his island kingdom from destruction.

"So that's one thing we need to do," Will said. "We need to find the eternite mine and shut off their access to eternite to build these devices."

"But they could already have enough stockpiled for several devices already," the Professor said. "And one will already be too many."

"But how are we going to stop them before they strike Belleriand?" Grip asked. "We have to warn them."

"Okay," said Will. "That's number two: we need to report to the Baron and warn Belleriand."

"Just a sec," Revin said. "Let me think for a minute. In Lidja's letter, she mentioned that the Seneschal was looking at a map of Harway. What's the chance Havelock might attack Harway instead?"

There was silence while everyone looked at each other.

"So we need to warn Harway — that's three things we need to do," Will said. "But the *Queen* can only go one place at a time. So, let's do this. We will take the *Queen* to Belleriand, inform the Baron, and then head to Harway, as we need to take Words and his crew back anyway. And then Harway can mount another expedition to find the mine. Any objections?"

He paused for several long moments of silence.

"With no objections, we will depart at first light tomorrow," he concluded. "I declare the meeting adjourned. Oh! Except for the Professor and Revin: you still need to sort out your expenses with Mr. Brill."

After everyone else filed out of the room, Mr. Brill extended his hand. "Receipts?"

"What are you talking about?" Revin said. "Nobody gives receipts."

"So what are your expenses?" Brill said, looking up briefly from his ledger.

"Well, let's see. There was breakfast at Beskin Harbor and ..." the Professor began.

"I'll give you each one reggie *per diem*, so we can dispense with meals and lodging."

The Professor looked pleased as though he had won a point and Revin perceived that almost all of their food and lodging had been provided by others, so this was nearly pure profit. He began to understand how this game was played.

"There was the coach trip from Beskin Harbor and then we hired a coach and a coachman" Revin said. "That's 22 reggies. No, wait. Since the first coachman stole the four reggies of earnest money, it's 26 reggies."

"I thought the Seneschal paid to hire the coach and the coachman," Brill said.

"The Seneschal gave Revin money, it's true," the Professor admitted. "But we saved that money and we used the Baron's money to hire the coach. So we should put the Seneschal's money into the General Operating Fund."

"I'll allow it," Brill said.

"Plus there was the stay at Sendia Springs," the Professor said. "You surely can't count that against our *per diem* as it was key to getting a hold of the plans to copy them."

Little by little, they wore Brill down to extract as much money as possible from the Baron's pouch and move it into the pirate's general funds. Or was Brill actually their ally in this? Revin still wasn't quite sure. But at the end of the meeting, the Professor slapped Revin's back and hand-walked out happily chuckling with their success.

Revin, still tired from the festivities the night before, headed back to his tent to nap for a few minutes before dinner, but Will intercepted him with a hand on his shoulder.

"I didn't see you on our run this morning, boy," he said.

Revin grimaced.

"I didn't feel up to it this morning after ... last night," he said.

"Well, there's nothing stopping you from doing it now," Will said, cheerfully.

Revin groaned.

"We'll go with you," Words said, coming up from behind, followed by Beck.

Revin, Words, and Beck spent a few minutes stretching, and then Revin led them up the steep mountain path. The first part was pretty gentle, but then they hit the first steep part. Revin was breathing hard when it leveled out for a bit, but he realized they had dropped Words, who had started walking up the steepest part. But Beck was right there with Revin and not even winded.

"Do you want to go ahead?" Revin asked him.

"I like the view from back here, though," Beck said.

Alarm bells went off in Revin's head. He imagined he could feel Beck's eyes on his back — and backside — as he ran.

Revin decided to pick up the pace and sprinted up the next steep part. Beck matched his pace, though breathing heavily now. They reached the summit and Revin stopped for a few moments to pant and catch his breath. Revin noticed Beck standing nearby with his arms crossed, looking him up and down. He smiled broadly when he perceived that Revin had noticed he was eyeing him. When Words arrived at the top, out of breath, Revin patted him on the back encouragingly.

"We've been doing this for months," Revin said.

"You're in great shape," Words panted. "I need to do better."

"Take a minute to catch your breath," Revin said. "Then you can set the pace for us going down."

"But going down is going to be easy," Words said.

"Oh, no, it won't," Revin laughed. "It uses different muscles so you're going to be sore in new and different ways."

"Oh, no!" Words said.

After a minute, Words headed down, followed by Beck, with Revin bringing up the rear this time. Words was going slowly, having taken what Revin said to heart. Revin was happy to have Beck in front of him. But with everyone bunched up close together, Revin didn't have a clear view of his footing and stumbled over a tree root. He tried to speed up to get his feet back under his center of gravity, but saw he wasn't going to make it and raised his arms to prepare himself to fall on his face. But he didn't. Somehow, Beck had managed to catch him. He straightened up, still holding Revin in his arms and Revin felt him run a hand along his side and cup his buttocks while setting him back on his feet. Revin looked up at his face and caught him smirking.

After dinner, Revin headed back to his tent to turn in, before their planned early morning start. He was about to lie down when there was a gentle tap at the door.

"Come ahead," Revin said.

Words entered and Revin could see Beck standing back, on guard outside.

"Have you got a moment?" Words said.

"Sure," Revin said.

Words shut the door.

"Last night," he started, then paused to consider, then started again. "Last night, you … told me some things. And I said some things. And I just wanted to follow up with you now that you're not, well, drunk."

"Oh, no," Revin said. "I … I don't remember anything."

"Well, I do," Words said. "When you and I first spoke, back on the *Queen*, I told you that you were a puzzle and that I was interested in puzzles. Well, I'm not just interested in puzzles: I'm attracted to them. But I'm also pretty much exclusively attracted to men. Griphon and I were intimate once."

Revin nodded. Words' voice started to break.

"So I was really attracted to you and I swear I wasn't going to do anything while you were drunk, but you were clinging to me and … you said you loved me."

Revin's mouth fell open and he put his hands over it.

"But then I brought you back here to put you to bed and found your chest binding," Words said, covering his face with his hands and choking up. "And I didn't know what to think. And now I still don't know what to think."

Revin thought for a moment, then rose and approached Words. He put his hand on his shoulder, but then put his arms around him and embraced him.

"I'm just me," Revin said. "I didn't mean to mislead you."

"Well, and it's all complicated now because now you know I'm a prince," Words said, wiping his eyes. "I'm not the firstborn, so it doesn't really mean anything. But I hate when people find that out because it changes how they treat me."

"It doesn't change anything for me," Revin said. "But I'm not sure how to respond to your feelings because I don't even know my own. I like you though. And I want to get to know you better. And I want for us to be able to work together. So ... Friends for now?"

"Okay," Words said. "Good. Thank you! I ... needed to get that off my chest."

Revin hugged him hard and Words hugged him back.

"Can I ... Can I ask you why ... Why you ..." Words stammered, trying to come up with the words for a question.

"Why I decided I was not a woman and chose to become a man?" Revin finished for him.

Words nodded. Revin, mindful of Beck standing just outside, led Words over to his bedroll. He invited him to sit down and then sat down himself.

"When I was growing up, I never felt like I was a girl. Or a woman," Revin began, speaking quietly. "Where I grew up, girls only had one choice: As soon as you showed signs of 'womanhood', you were married off to a man to bear his children and do his housework. And if you talked back, you got beaten."

"You got beaten?" Words said, with horror.

"I got beaten a lot," Revin said. "I got beaten for talking back. And for not acting girly enough. I even got beaten for reading books."

Words was speechless with horror.

"But I had no education and no options. I didn't even know that something like this," he gestured at himself, "was even possible. At first, I was just cross dressing to try to escape. But I met people who helped me learn to pass as a boy. Then I met Will who asked me whether I was a woman dressing as a man or a man in a woman's body. It had never occurred to me to think of it that way before. I knew something wasn't right, but I couldn't even put it into words.

"It was Will who taught me to be true to myself. I owe him so much."

"I can't begin to imagine what you've been through," Words said. "It sounds like it's been really rough."

"No," Revin smiled. "What would have been rough would have been if I hadn't been able to escape. Every day I get to live as myself, with a community that accepts me as I am, that makes it all worthwhile."

"These pirates are a special lot," Words replied. "People like me — that is to say men who are attracted to other men — are quietly tolerated among the nobility, but less among the common people. And people like you ... even less so. But you and Will and Grip can just be yourselves here. I'm so jealous!"

"That's right," Revin said, with a grin. "The pirates are something apart. They're not bound by the same practices and prejudices. They make their own rules."

Words grinned back and got back to his feet.

"Good night, Master's Mate."

"Good night, friend."

Words slipped out, collected Beck, and headed back to the tent that had been made available to the archaeologists. Revin laid down in his bedroll and spent several minutes reflecting on his realization about the rules that governed the different communities, but then, finally, rolled over and went to sleep.

•　　　•　　　•

The next morning, at first light, the *Queen* lifted off for Belleriand. Revin was dressed wearing his doublet and hat with the Belthingstone colors which made Words' eyes pop out when he saw them.

"Well, you are just full of surprises!" he said. "Please explain yourself, Master's Mate!"

"Well, I'm kinda Grip's squire as well," Revin muttered.

"Well, whose *something* are you not?" Words said, with a smirk.

Around noon, the *Queen* reached the capital of Belleriand. They stood off and on over the ocean and flashed messages to Ravensbelth. Eventually, they were given the all-clear to come ahead and they descended to the roof of the Belthingstone palace.

In deference to the Professor, for whom traversing stairs was a challenge, the Baron had directed his staff to erect a large tent on the roof, and he was waiting there.

As Revin disembarked, he saw Momo running toward him. She launched herself at him and he caught her and twirled her around in the air, much as Grip had the first time Revin had met her, while she squealed with excitement. Out of the corner of his eye, Revin saw Grip nudge Words with his elbow and point. Words rolled his eyes dramatically.

"Ah, my hero," Momo said, hugging him. "I'm so glad you're safe."

"I'm glad to see you too ... Momo," Revin said, as she hugged him even tighter. "Here. I brought you your journal to trade."

"You remembered!" she said, accepting it and handing him a different one, as they all walked together toward the tent. "I can't wait to read what you wrote." She clung to his arm as they walked.

"He's not going to blow away, Momo," Words said.

Momo looked over and suddenly realized who it was. "Your Majesty!" she said, curtsying deeply. "Please forgive me."

"Oh, get up, Momo, and give me a hug too," Words said.

She hugged him and then hugged Grip too for good measure.

Revin stepped into the tent, where the Baron acknowledged him and invited him to be seated. Momo sat next to Revin and the rest filled in around the table. The Baron's eyes widened to see the Prince.

"Thank you, your Majesty, for gracing us with your presence," he said, standing and bowing.

"We understand," Words said, in full royalty mode. "That you have been coordinating the response to this infernal device that Havelock has constructed. As usual, you are ahead of the rest of us. We will not forget your diligence."

"Thank you, your Majesty," the Baron said.

"I think the Professor can best summarize where we are," Will said.

The Professor addressed the group. He turned over the copy he and Revin had made of Kief's documents — he said he no longer needed it — and then spoke at length for nearly 40 minutes. He briefly described their trip to Havelock, the catastrophic events at Beskin Harbor, his analysis of the notes, and the results of their data regarding the persistence of the dead zones. He wrapped up with a final warning.

"We believe Havelock next means to launch an attack using a device on a balloon either here or on Harway," he said.

"Harway?" the Baron said.

"I ... know someone," Revin said. "Who told me that the Seneschal was looking at a map of Harway. It's only the flimsiest of evidence. But a surprise attack could completely alter the balance of power among the islands."

"You're starting to think strategically, Revin," the Baron said, looking at him with renewed respect. "The Prince is here, but has Harway been warned yet?"

"No," Will said. "That's where we're headed next."

"Then I will keep you no longer. But let me offer you one thing I had considered giving you last time," the Baron said, handing Revin a small, folded document case. "This is the current set of signals for our airships. Using these, you can traverse Belleriand and head directly to Harway, without going around. Please keep them safe because you understand what could happen if they fell into the wrong hands. Travel well!"

Within minutes, the *Queen* was airborne again and cutting straight across the island of Belleriand northeast toward Harway.

During the afternoon, Revin stood in the observation deck watching for patrols and observing the scenery. Belleriand was beautiful, with a mix of forest and grassland in the middle, and mountains along the eastern edge. They had to signal patrols using the Baron's codes three times before they crossed the shore and surrounding reef to reach the open ocean.

Revin spent the evening reading Momo's journal. He found that she had started — or perhaps was being gently nudged — to take an interest in politics and current events. Revin imagined the hand of the Baron in encouraging Momo to get involved and look at things with her own eyes. It was a very different set of observations that Revin read this time about meetings and conferences and correspondence. She was careful, and didn't name names or specify dates, but her characterizations of some of the people she mentioned were so spot-on that he couldn't help but smile.

As Revin went to put down Momo's journal, he felt the *Queen's* forward progress suddenly decline. He dropped the journal, rolled out of his bunk, and ran for the remmer deck. He arrived at the same time as Will.

"No etheric streams!" said the remmers. "We can't see any etheric streams anywhere!"

"Everyone look for streams!" Will said. "You too, Revin. Anywhere! Up, down, wherever — any stream you can find."

Revin got out his monocle and began searching for streams. He began systematically scanning up and down, turning through an entire circle. There was no sound but the breathing and occasional grunt when people bumped into one another. Revin felt the *Queen* drifting and turning sideways at the mercy of the wind with no attachments.

"Hey!" Revin said. He made a tiny towline and bound it to one of the poles of the remmer deck. "Is this one?"

One of the other remmers looked up, peered through his lens, and said, "That's just a steering current."

"What's a steering current?"

"Our Revin never trained as a remmer," Will said to the other remmers. "He doesn't know about steering currents."

Then to Revin, he continued, "There are two kinds of etheric streams that you could think of as being like arteries and capillaries. The big etheric streams are useful for drawing an airship. In places where very fine control is needed, like in a busy aerodrome parking airships close together, people sometimes use the tiny steering currents for very delicate maneuvering, but they're not really useful for anything else. And so one of the first things remmers learn is to ignore and avoid binding the steering currents."

"But it's a towline," Revin said. "If we made enough towlines it might be enough to keep us from drifting on the wind."

Will was drawn up short. "The Master's Mate is right!" he said. "Everyone! Look for steering currents let's see if we can at least hold us steady and maybe even make some way."

Before long, the *Queen* ceased to drift. She held steady and then, slowly, to make way.

"Do you suppose this dead area is from an Etheric Storm Generator?" Revin asked.

"Well, but there's no storm," Will said. "Maybe this an older dead zone from one of the previous tests. The Professor did say they might circulate unpredictably."

For the next three hours, Will, Revin, and the other remmers constantly made and remade attachments to the tiny steering currents, which kept the *Queen* slowly creeping forward.

Finally, in the wee hours of the morning, one of the remmers called out, "Stream, ho! Forty degrees to port!"

Revin felt a lurch as the remmers began to find and attach real etheric streams. The *Queen* quickly picked up speed and got back on course for Harway. Revin, utterly exhausted after hours of making towlines, returned to his bunk and caught a couple of hours of sleep until the light of the rising sun made the sound of air rushing past the *Queen* take on a different tone and woke him.

Revin made his way from his bunk to the observation deck as the *Queen* approached Harway from the south. The sun had just cleared the horizon and Revin saw the light gleaming off of the spires of the King's palace in the middle of the city. Words stood in the cockpit directing Will toward the aerodrome on the west side of the city.

Revin squinted, rubbed his eyes, and looked again. There was something strange ahead. He spied a peculiar shape through the early-morning mist.

"There!" Revin shouted. "Look at that!"

Will followed his finger. It was an airship up ahead, but oddly asymmetrical — like something was growing from its side.

"I see it, lad!" Will said. "What is that?"

"They're launching a balloon!" Revin said. "They must be launching a storm generator!"

"Faster!" Will said to Grip.

"Faster!" Grip called to the remmer deck.

Revin felt the *Queen* leap forward as the remmers shifted their attachments.

"How close to the storm generator do we need to get?" Revin called.

"As close as possible!" Will and Grip replied in unison with a grim chuckle.

The airship ahead separated from the odd growth. Revin could now see clearly that it was a hot-air balloon, rising up. The other airship turned and began to flee.

"Climb!" Will said.

"Climb!" Grip called to the remmer deck.

Revin felt the *Queen* begin to rise. They began to close on the balloon, but it was rising faster. Too fast!

Revin ran back, grabbed the etheric shield, jammed it into his belt, and turned the crank to lower the gangplank. Once it was level, he took a deep breath and ran out to the end. He could see a long rope depending from the balloon. But he couldn't reach it.

"One moment, lad!" Will called.

"No time," Revin yelled as he saw the end of the rope rising.

"No, Revin!" Will shouted.

But it was too late. Revin had backed up five steps, run forward, and launched himself off the gangplank into open space. With the air rushing past him, he caught the rope in his hands and just managed to get the knot at the very end between his feet before he slid off. He swung back and forth for a moment and then began to climb. With his additional weight, the balloon rose more slowly.

By the time Will reached the end of the ramp, he was still just barely able to attach a towline to the rope that pulled the rope in. Grip and several other pirates held it while Will swarmed up the rope after Revin.

Revin struggled to reach the top and then threw himself into the basket of the hot-air balloon. The basket was mostly full of the device — egg-shaped and enclosed in a perforated metal case. Revin could hear the sound of clockwork inside.

Revin found his feet, spread the etheric shield over the device, then reached down to give Will a hand up. Together, they stretched the metal net over and around the storm generator. The device was too heavy to lift, even with the two of them, so they did their best to tuck the net underneath it.

They were still finishing when the sounds from the device suddenly increased, making an odd whirring noise. The entire basket shook, vibrating, as something inside began spinning faster and faster. Blue sparks began jumping between the egg and the metal netting, giving both Revin and Will nasty shocks and burns when they touched it.

Revin found the tied-off rope that held open the lever controlling the flame of the balloon. He released it and the flame shut off.

Revin took a deep breath and looked down from the balloon. A magnificent white palace in the center of a large, bustling city lay beneath them. The balloon passed over the palace as it descended.

Revin and Will watched helplessly as airships converged on the *Queen*. She stayed with the balloon, however, and matched their course.

As the balloon started to drop toward a lake in a beautifully manicured park, Revin pulled the lever and was rewarded with a roar as the burner relit. They skimmed the surface of the water until he let the balloon touch down on the grass just beyond. A circle of curious people started to surround the balloon, but then pulled back in alarm as the huge presence of the *Queen* loomed overhead and touched down nearby. The Professor debarked and hurried over, hand walking across the grass with his arm braces as fast as he could go.

A whistle went up and answering whistles answered from farther away. A party of guardsmen charged toward the balloon with weapons drawn while three airships circled menacingly above. Words ran out and interposed himself with his arms raised between the guards and the balloon. After a few tense words, the guards saluted him smartly, returned their weapons to their scabbards, and positioned themselves around the balloon and the Queen to keep curious on-lookers away.

Will jumped out and lifted the Professor up toward the basket of the balloon. Revin reached down and helped him scramble in, warning him to not touch the net or get shocked.

The Professor extracted a long metal rod he'd tucked inside his shirt and inserted it into a hole in the top of the device. It shocked him, but he persisted.

"The plans show a rod like this keeping the device from starting — until they're ready to trigger it," he said. "But I don't know if it will work to stop it." There was a grinding noise as he forced it down, but then it found purchase, slid home, and the sound of the mechanism ceased.

In the silence that followed, Revin heard and then felt rain drops. He looked up and saw a single rain cloud moving through above them. The sun shone through the rain and produced a rainbow over the palace. Revin let out a deep breath he didn't know he'd been holding.

•   •   •

Two days later, a national holiday was called. A huge celebration was planned to honor Revin and the crew that had prevented an island-wide tragedy. Revin, Will, Grip, and the Professor were driven by coach through the central boulevard toward the plaza before the palace. The streets were jammed with people cheering and throwing confetti. In the plaza, a huge viewing stand had been constructed.

The coach rolled up to the back of the viewing stand. Revin and the rest were directed to walk up a long ramp to the top of the viewing stand. At its top, a man sat seated on a throne. Revin thought he looked familiar, until he realized that of course he looked familiar: his face was on all of the coinage. Next to his father stood Stewart, who wore a white dress uniform that day. He really looked the part of a prince out of a fairy tale.

They lined up in front of the huge crowd.

"Hear ye, hear ye, hear ye," a crier called to the crowd. "For extraordinary courage, and for saving the kingdom from grievous harm, today we recognize Revin Minerson for knighthood. Please step forward and kneel."

Revin stepped forward and the king descended from his throne and drew his sword.

The king, tall and rangy, looked much like an older version of Words, though with leathery skin and gray stubble. *But still the same rakish, bad-boy feel,* Revin thought. The King wore an impassive, serious expression, but still with a twinkle in his eye.

Revin started to kneel, but images began to flash through his mind. He remembered Will telling the Baron that the nobility are parasites. He remembered the Professor pouring out his wine when asked to toast the war. Now he was in the spotlight. Revin was seized with conviction and straightened up.

"I refuse, your Majesty" Revin said. "While this war has been going on for years, where have you been? What have you been doing? Our people fight and die and for what? So that nobles can earn more profit? Or build another country home?

"I'm grateful I was able to protect the people of Harway — and of all the islands — from the catastrophic effects of the Etheric Storm Generator. But you bear particular responsibility. Why do you not call for a cease fire? Why have you not compelled your vassals to come to the table for peace talks? Are you their king or not?"

Revin stopped, almost panting with the tension of getting the words out.

A stunned silence answered him.

Then Revin heard the Professor break out with laughter. "You tell 'em, Revin!"

"Good for you, lad!" called Will.

He saw Words initially standing with his mouth agape, but then it became a grin and he gave Revin a broad wink.

Grip remained frozen, trying to process what he was hearing.

King Reginald looked at Revin, then lifted his sword up and rested it on his shoulder.

"You've got stones. I'll give you that," he said, with a crooked smile. "Tell you what. If you let me knight you, I'll call for peace talks."

Revin considered this from all possible sides and hesitated.

"Take a knee, young man," the King said. "As unaccustomed as you may be."

Revin knelt before the King, who raised his sword and touched it to each of Revin's shoulders.

"I dub thee Sir Revin Minerson of Devishire," he intoned. "Arise, Sir Revin!"

Revin stood and faced the crowd to a huge roar of approval. He looked over the sea of faces, wondering if he was dreaming.

The King scabbarded his sword and placed his hands on Revin's shoulders. "I hereby call for immediate peace talks between Belleriand and Havelock," he said. "To be mediated by my Special Royal Envoy, Sir Revin."

INTERLUDE

R EVIN LEFT HIS ROOM in the palace and walked downstairs, through the arcade, past the fountain and the orange trees, and presented himself at the guardroom. The guards snapped to attention.

"What can we do for you, Sir Revin?" the sergeant asked.

"I would like to go to the aerodrome," Revin said.

The sergeant sent a runner to the stables and, twenty minutes later, a coach arrived at the guard post. The coachman held the door for Revin and then climbed up on the box, whipped up the horses, and drove the team to the aerodrome.

Revin arrived and, as always, felt the excitement of the place run through him. Airships were arriving and departing. Passengers were milling about. But he walked past them toward the far corner of the aerodrome where the *Queen of Belleriand* was making ready to depart.

"Trim the ballast tanks, men," Grip cried, as a truck with a water hose fed water into the *Queen*.

"Get those provisions loaded," Ham told the porters who were unloading crates from another truck.

Revin felt a pang to see his shipmates hard at work while he just stood around.

"It's nice of you to come see us off, Lad," Will said, coming forward.

"I more than half wish I was coming with you," Revin sighed.

"You don't have to stay here," Will said. "You know that these peace talks are doomed."

Revin blanched.

"Will!" Grip said. "Let it be. Revin needs to choose for himself."

"Aye, Lad," Will said. "You know I think the peace talks are bound to fail. But I understand you feel that you need to try."

"I do," Revin said. "So many have suffered. And died! I owe it to their memory to take advantage of this opportunity."

Will made a rude noise and Grip punched him in the arm.

"Aye, Lad," he said. "You have to do as you feel is right."

A voice called out from the ship. "Cap'n the rudder is not responding!"

Will swore and headed into the *Queen*. After dithering for a moment, Revin followed him.

"Where are you going?" Will said, when he saw Revin following him.

"Maybe I can help! I might be able to crawl in someplace you can't fit!"

Revin could see Will debate with himself for a moment, but then he smiled. "Aye, Lad. You'll always be one of us. Let's see what's happening."

They headed to the cockpit where a crewman was trying to turn the wheel, but it would bind on the starboard side and couldn't be turned.

"This way, Lad," Will said. He led Revin down the gangway and then opened a port in the ceiling. "In you go!"

Revin crawled into a narrow passageway, as he had so many times in the *Queen*, and headed aft.

"Turn the wheel!" Will cried. Revin could see a cable move that ran through a series of rings along the passageway. He could see when the cable moved smoothly and then when it seemed to bind. He continued along the passageway into the bowels of the airship.

About two-thirds of the way back, Revin found a splice in the cable that had partially separated and some strands of the cable were binding against a ring that the cable passed through.

"I think I found the problem," Revin called. He described the problem.

"Does the cable still appear sound?" Will called back.

"Aye, Cap'n," Revin said. "It's just that there are these ends sticking out that are catching on the ring."

"Let's try to trim them off," he called back. "Come get some wire cutters."

Revin crawled back, took a set of wire cutters and returned to the problematic spice. In just a few minutes, he'd trimmed off the stray ends and the cable could once again move smoothly through the ring without binding.

"Steering is good, Cap'n!" the crewman called.

Revin returned and handed the tool back to Will, who clapped him on the shoulder.

"Well done, Master's Mate!"

Revin grinned sheepishly.

"We're fully provisioned and leveled, Will," Grip said.

"I guess ..." Revin said, choking up. "I guess I should go back to the palace."

Will crushed him in a hug and Grip joined in.

"Watch out for yourself, Boy," Will said. "This is no less a den of snakes than Belleriand."

"Yes, Cap'n," Revin said.

Revin walked down the gangplank, stepped off, and then, with a lump in his throat, he watched as the *Queen* lifted off and headed southwest, back toward the sea. Sighing, he walked back to his coach and returned to the Palace and his new responsibilities.

6

THEN THEY FIGHT YOU

EVIN STOOD AND WATCHED as the *Queen of Belleriand* sailed off into the distance. When she had dwindled to a tiny point, he sighed and returned to his coach that carried him back from the aerodrome to the palace. He was all by himself in a strange city.

Will had warned him that he was making a mistake. He had told him that it was pointless to expect the nobles to play by the rules and act according to reason. But with lives on the line, Revin felt that he needed to play the hand he was dealt. He had a chance to end the stupid, ugly war — to stop the fighting. And he was going to take it.

The coach dropped him off in front of the gleaming white palace in the center of the capital of Harway. He was recognized by the guards, who saluted him smartly as he entered the palace. He followed a passageway to the left that eventually led him into a beautiful courtyard surrounded by arched passageways. In the center stood a lovely fountain among orange trees. Revin stood for a moment, reflecting on the vicissitudes of life before climbing the last stairway to his room. He went in, closed the door, and then sat shivering on his bed, petrified with anxiety at the trials to come.

King Reginald the Arbiter had appointed him as Special Envoy to mediate peace talks between Havelock and Belleriand. The ambassador from Havelock claimed that it was a rogue unit that had tried to attack Harway with the Etheric Storm Generator and promised to hunt down the traitors. No one seriously believed him.

Without the *Queen* and his comrades, Revin felt utterly alone. He got out Momo's journal and spent several hours writing, pouring all of his fear and uncertainty onto the pages until, finally, he was able to sleep.

•   •   •

The following morning, Revin dressed and presented himself at court. He was asked to relinquish his sword and directed to sit in an antechamber where he then waited for hours to see the King. Finally, a page came to the room and announced him.

Revin had expected to be called into a throne room with pillars and vaulted ceilings. Instead, he was shown into a comfortable study: a messy desk covered with letters and correspondence, a table piled with books and maps, and several comfortable chairs. The King sat in one and gestured at another for Revin to sit.

Revin stood and the King had to wave twice before he finally sat down.

"So," the King said. "What do you need?"

"What?" Revin asked, genuinely puzzled.

"Okay. Look," the King said, leaning forward. "I expect when I meet with someone that they'll not waste my time looking for directions. I'm not going to give you directions,

Sir Revin. That's not my role here. You have my mandate. With that, you should be able to find the resources you need to accomplish your task.

"That said, if I hear about irregular expenses, and call you here to explain, you'd better have a good explanation. But I'm not going to micromanage you or tell you what to do. When you reach an agreement, bring it to me and I will ratify or reject it. Or if you reach an impasse and decide no further progress is possible, you can bring that to me as well. But otherwise, this is your task now. Understood?

"Yes, Your Majesty," Revin said, perhaps more stiffly than he had meant to.

He started to stand up.

"Whoa, there," the King said. "Let me add a bit more. I can see that you are out of your depth. So I've arranged just a bit of help to get you started. First, let me offer you an advisor. Hannah?"

An older woman in her 40s stepped out of a corner of the room where she had been sitting unobserved. She came before Revin and curtsied.

"At your service, Sir Revin," she said, in a gravelly voice.

"Hannah served as adjutant to the royal envoy who negotiated the peace between Woodseer and Ironton during their war fifteen years ago," the King said. "I have asked her to serve you."

"Thank you, your Majesty," Revin said.

"I've also asked Hannah to recruit some staff for an office to get you going," the King continued. "She's already requested a budget — enough to start. But, as I say, you have the resources of the Kingdom at your disposal. Use them wisely."

"Yes, Your Majesty," Revin said.

The King waved his hand. Revin bowed and took his leave.

He retreated through the antechamber, where he recovered his sword, and followed Hannah out to the hallway. Outside, he turned to speak, but she cut him off.

"Look, kid," she said, in her raspy voice. "I've seen 'em come and I've seen 'em go. But the King wouldn't have appointed you if he didn't have a pretty good reason. So don't sweat about it. For things like this, there's a playbook, and most of the work is best handled by professional staff. Let me introduce you to the staff and we can get started."

"Yes, Milady," he said.

"Call me 'Milady' again and I'll bite off one of your fingers," she said. "You can call me Hannah. Or Miss. Or that fucking bitch. But I'm not a Lady."

"Yes ... Hannah."

"Come this way," she said.

She led him down many stairs into a labyrinth of dark tunnels under the palace. They arrived, finally, at an unmarked door at the end of a dim tunnel.

"It may not look like much, but it's quiet, there are no distractions, and nobody's trying to steal your space."

She opened the door and held it for him. Inside were several tables and three people were talking amongst themselves. They looked up as Hannah and Revin arrived. Revin could see two offices beyond them.

"First, let me introduce Inky," she said.

A plump, rather mousey-looking man waved, showing off ink-stained fingers.

"He's our calligrapher. We're going to need to write correspondence, reports, and — if we're very lucky — a proclamation."

"Next," she said, pointing at a small, thin man, who looked down. "This is Guntar. He's a scholar who studies the military and diplomatic history of the islands.

"And, finally," she said, indicating a grizzled old man. "This is Checkars. He's an expert in diplomatic law."

"Wow," Revin said. "You've put together a fantastic team. Why are you not the one in charge here?"

"I'll give you just one guess," she said, squaring her shoulders.

"Umm …" Revin said. "It's because you're not a man?"

"Got it in one," she said.

"But … Why?" he marveled. "You're so good at this."

"Because we don't live in a meritocracy," she said. "And anyone who tells you we do is selling something."

"What can I do?" Revin asked.

"For the moment, just stay out of our way," she said. "We'll need you eventually. We won't actually do anything without your approval."

"But I want to be useful," Revin said. "I want to help! Can you give me anything to read? To study?"

"What do you know about the history of Belleriand and Havelock?" Guntar asked. "I can point you toward a few basic books."

Revin nodded his thanks while Guntar made a few notes on a piece of paper and handed it to him.

"Here's a precis on current diplomatic law that just came out," Checkars said, handing Revin a book. "You can keep it."

"Oh. This is the book by Professor Dirge," Revin said. "I spent a year helping him write it — before his untimely demise."

"What!?" Checkars said. "You must be joking."

"No," Revin said, flipping a few pages and pointing to where his name appeared in the forward. "See?"

"Five reggies," Hannah chuckled.

Checkars reached into his pocket grumbling.

"What?" Revin said.

"I said you were totally unqualified," Checkers said. "But Hannah bet me that there must be more to you than meets the eye. I lost."

"Thanks," Revin said, with a bemused expression. "I guess."

Revin rose to leave. Hannah pointed toward the back.

"One of those offices is for you," she said. "Which would you prefer?"

"I don't care," Revin said. "Can you point me toward the library?"

"Sure. You just go down this hallway and then take ..." she started counting to herself. "One, two, — no, three turns to the right and then take the stairs and then ..."

"I'll take you," Inky said. "They're not going to need me for a while anyway."

Once they got out in the hallway, Inky pointed to some nearby stairs.

"By the way," he said. "You can take those stairs three floors up and you'll be right around the corner from your room. I heard Hannah tell them when she said she wanted these rooms."

Revin looked back at the offices with renewed appreciation for his thoughtful adjutant.

Inky led Revin through a series of featureless tunnels under the palace and emerged into a long gallery with pages, functionaries, and nobles busily hustling from one place to another. Revin followed Inky down the gallery for what seemed like an eternity before they crossed to the other side, dodging people coming from the other direction, until they reached a set of huge double doors that opened into the library.

Inky saluted Revin, then headed back while Revin entered the library. Revin looked around, but felt rather disappointed at what appeared to be a small, rather ordinary library. He introduced himself to the reference librarian and showed them the slip of paper Guntar had passed to him.

"Oh! You're Sir Revin!" she gushed. "We've heard so much about you! Do you want us to get the books for you? Or would you like to go into the stacks yourself?"

"The stacks?" Revin asked.

"Oh, yeah. That's where most of the books are. Come here and I'll show you."

She led Revin through a set of double doors and into a large room with narrow aisles between bookshelves.

"We have five floors of books," she said. "This sign shows how they're organized thematically and then by author. Enjoy!"

Revin rubbed his hands, the corners of his mouth turning up with unconcealed glee. He could tell he was going to enjoy himself here.

He spent several hours wandering through the stacks and collected an armful of books. Revin carried his prizes back to his room and then spent most of the afternoon learning about the history of Havelock and Belleriand.

• • •

Hours later, Revin heard a knock at the door that startled him out of his immersion in the history of the islands. When he answered it, he was surprised to see Words, and even more surprised when Words invited Beck in with him.

"I thought you'd already left!" Revin said.

"No," Words said. "We leave tomorrow to search for the eternite mine. But there's one thing I want to do first. I know this is kind of a surprise, but I've asked Beck to serve as your bodyguard."

"Why? Do you really think I need one?" Revin asked.

"Revin," Words said, rolling his eyes. "A man who sleeps in a bed of cobras with a blanket made of scorpions is in considerably less danger than you." Words clapped Revin on the back. "You've met Beck. He's the best. He's worked for me for two years. But I'll sleep better knowing you have him keeping you safe."

"Thank you," Revin said, touched. "I really appreciate your concern."

"The most important thing?" Words said. "Listen to him! He's going to make you change how you do everything. And it will be a pain in the ass. But he knows his business and he will save your life. And I mean that literally. I predict that when I get back, you will be alive because Beck has saved your life."

Words excused himself and Beck spent an hour detailing to Revin all of the ways in which his life was going to change. From now on, Beck would be the first one through every door. Beck would tell him when he should wait and when it was safe to go. Moreover, he would vary Revin's routine. Each day Beck would select a different route to take.

As he was talking, Beck walked through Revin's room, checked his window and door, and made some notes to call workmen to have them reinforced and hardened.

Finally, he wished Revin a good night and directed Revin to lock the door behind him.

•   •   •

The next morning, Beck met Revin and escorted him down the three flights of stairs to the offices of the special envoy. Revin's staff was already hard at work drafting letters for the call that Havelock and Belleriand come to the peace talks. Beck took up his station just outside the door. Hannah looked up as Revin walked in.

"Ah, you're just in time. Let me go over the wording we've worked out," she said in her gravelly voice.

By lunchtime, they had looked over the letters word-by-word and gone through several rounds of revisions. It seemed to Revin that they were close to being ready to let Inky draft their final versions.

"How are these letters going to be delivered?" Revin asked.

"That's a good question," Hannah said. "We could entrust them to the mail, but I think it would be better for you to carry them personally. It would make a larger impact."

"But how will I travel? Do I purchase tickets?"

"You're the King's special envoy," Hannah said. "You should request an airship for your use."

"My own airship?" Revin said, stunned.

"Not yours," she chuckled. "The King's. But you're using it to do his bidding."

"Right," Revin said, still uncertainly feeling his way forward in this new institutional world.

After lunch, rather than walking to the stables to get a coach, Beck arranged for the coach to come to the palace and stand by nearest the entrance to Revin's room. When the coach was in place, Beck preceded Revin and hustled him down the stairs and into the coach. Beck sat on the box with the driver and directed the coach to the airship factory.

•   •   •

The airship factory was the longest building Revin had ever seen with the highest ceiling he'd had ever seen. It was enormous. It made the Portrait Gallery in Ravensbelth look like a doll house.

The coach brought them to a human-scale door near the hangar's immense entrance. Beck looked around, went to the door, opened it, and only then beckoned Revin to step from the coach.

Inside was a veritable army of workmen. There were so many, Revin couldn't begin to even estimate the number. They looked tiny, like insects, inside the giant space. Near the hangar entrance rested an airship that was nearly finished. Farther back, and extending into the distance, Revin saw other airships in various stages of completion. A man came hustling over as Revin gazed in wonder at the teams of workers scurrying around working on the airships.

"I'm Director Oaklind, Milord," the man said. "We received word that you've requested an airship."

"Yes," Revin said. "We're going to need an airship to travel to Havelock and Belleriand."

"Well, you've come to the right place, Milord," Oaklind said. "We make a new airship every three weeks."

Revin felt stunned by the scale of the operation.

"The newest is just being finished today," Oaklind said proudly.

"This one here?" Revin said, indicating the one closest to the hangar door.

"Yes, Milord," Oaklind said. "That's *Pamela's Panties*. She was originally intended for someone else, but the King has made clear that you have precedence."

"*Pamela's Panties*?" Revin asked, looking askance at the Director.

"Yes, Milord. *Pamela's Panties*. The only thing left to do is complete the painting," he said. "White — with pink hearts."

"Can we skip the pink?" Revin said. "Perhaps just some simple countershading?"

Oaklind looked scandalized, but nodded reluctantly.

"As you wish, Milord. She will be ready in two days time at the aerodrome."

"Thank you, Director Oaklind," Revin said. "I will be sure to report how helpful and accommodating you've been."

"Thank you, Milord!" he said with a bow.

When they returned to the palace, Beck checked the surroundings, then gave Revin the all-clear to step from the coach. He shadowed Revin to his room, pulled out a copy of the key to Revin's room, opened the door, and checked the interior before letting Revin inside. Revin went to enter the room, but Beck, towering over him, blocked his entry.

"Are you sure you don't want to invite me in, baby?" he said with a leer.

Revin was speechless and didn't know how to react.

"Please move," he said finally, looking up at Beck.

Beck stepped out of the way with a smirk.

Revin entered, then closed and locked the door. But he realized, with a start, that since Beck had a key, he could get in any time he wanted. He looked around the room, suddenly feeling more unsafe than he had in a long while.

* * *

In the morning, Revin headed down to the task force offices. He found Inky hard at work drawing beautiful calligraphy on the second of the two formal letters. Revin watched for several minutes in silence, in awe of the beautiful script he could generate. His calligraphy made even the simplest of letters a masterpiece.

Revin waited until Inky had drawn the last letter and set his pen down.

"Uh, oh. There's a spelling mistake," he said, teasing.

Inky just grinned at him. "Can't fool me!" he laughed.

Hannah walked in and looked over the two letters.

"They're beautiful, Inky," she said. "Nice work. Now we just need Revin to sign them."

"Really?" Revin asked.

"You're the special envoy. They only need your signature and then we just need to deliver them."

"Just my regular signature?"

"Whatever you want," Hannah said. "But if you want to come up with a fancy signature, this is the time. Maybe you could get some ideas from Inky about how to make a more impressive signature. But, to be honest, it doesn't really matter."

"Let me see your signature," Inky said. "Here. Here's a regular quill. Don't try to use my calligraphy quill."

Revin signed his name and Inky studied it for a moment.

"It's fine. It's a nice signature! But here's a couple of thoughts. Try signing your name bigger. It will look more confident that way. And here and here, you might consider using bolder strokes. Like this."

Inky took the quill and signed Revin's name to show him what he meant. Revin studied the signature that was nearly indistinguishable from his own and looked at Inky with renewed respect.

"This is amazing," he said. "Let me try!"

Revin took the quill back and signed his name several times trying to achieve the same effect that Inky had effortlessly produced.

"There! You've got it!" Inky said. "Well done! Ready for the real thing?"

Revin blew on his fingers several times then carefully dipped the quill and signed his name to the first letter. Then did the second.

"Well done," Hannah said. "Now we'll just need to deliver these and see what kind of response we get. But I wouldn't hold my breath, if I were you."

"By the way," Hannah asked. "What are you planning to wear to your meetings?"

"Oh, no," Revin said. "I guess I hadn't thought about that."

"Well, it's important," Hannah said. "Do you have a tailor?"

"Um … Not on Harway, I guess."

"Well, you need something soon," Hannah said.

Revin went back to his room wondering who he could ask about finding a tailor. Words was the obvious one, but he was half a world away looking for the eternite mine. And Revin wasn't even sure there was time in any regard — not everyone was like Cedric, willing to drop everything and do whatever it takes to satisfy a favored customer. Revin sighed.

He arrived back at his room and discovered Beck standing near a large box sitting outside the door.

"What's this?" Revin asked.

"Just a bunch of clothes," Beck said. "I've checked the contents and it's safe to open."

"Clothes? Who would have sent me clothes?"

"Some guy named Cedric on Belleriand," Beck said. "But nothing pretty. You should get something a little more revealing."

Revin stared at Beck, who stared back.

"I've seen what you've got under there, sugar," he said. "You should smile more. You're pretty when you smile."

Revin turned, livid, but Beck just grinned wider, pleased to have finally elicited a reaction.

"You're cute when you're angry too," he said with a wink.

Now furious, Revin manhandled the box into his room and then locked the door.

Sure enough, the box contained very nearly a complete wardrobe: several shirts and ties, two blazers, two pairs of slacks, and, in a special bag, a black-tie evening suit. A personalized note from Cedric thanked "Sir Revin" for trusting him with such an important order.

"Grip," Revin said to himself. "It had to have been Grip who knew what I would need." He looked skyward and offered thanks to his friend and mentor.

Revin packed his trunk. In fact, after their adventure on Havelock, the Professor had prevailed on Revin to switch trunks, so he was now using the trunk that had belonged to Professor Dirge, which had the fifty reggies concealed as a backup.

After being cleared by Beck, Revin took the trunk out to the coach for the trip to the aerodrome.

When he arrived, Revin looked out to see a beautiful new airship waiting for him: lovely white and covered with pink hearts.

"Here you go!" Director Oaklind said. "*Pamela's Panties*, as requested!"

"I thought we had agreed that there weren't to be any pink hearts," Revin grumbled.

"What?" Oaklind said, stunned. "I received word that you'd reconsidered. I thought this was what you'd wanted!"

Revin looked at Beck, who did not give even the tiniest reaction or hint that he had secretly countermanded Revin's order. Although Revin couldn't imagine anyone else who might have done so.

"Well," Revin said. "It will have to do."

Revin stepped on board and met the captain, a relatively young man, who introduced himself as Keep. He gave Revin a brief tour of the airship.

Pamela's Panties was tiny, compared to the *Madeline*, and much smaller even than the *Queen*. She, seemingly, had been originally commissioned as a pleasure craft for some rich nobleman. And, as such, she had many comforts and amenities, including a VIP cabin that was turned over to Revin. As Keep took *Pamela's Panties* aloft, Revin shut himself inside his cabin, not much caring what happened to Beck. As night fell, Revin was already asleep.

• • •

Pamela's Panties arrived at the aerodrome in Havelock, escorted by two patrol airships. After landing, Beck inspected the landing field and then motioned to Revin to come out. A coach waited nearby with Lidja standing at attention near its door. When she saw Revin, she perked up, giving him a grin from ear to ear.

"Can I call you 'Milord' now?" she asked with a wink.

"Please, just call me Revin," he said, stowing his trunk in the storage compartment of the coach. Then he directed Beck to enter the coach.

"No," Beck said. "You get in the coach and I ride up top."

"Never," Revin said, putting his foot down. "I get to ride up top this time."

Beck glared at him.

"Now, now," Lidja said, climbing up on the box. "You're acting like children. Revin gets to ride up top this time and you can have a turn next time."

Beck got in the coach grumbling. Revin vaulted up onto the box after Lidja.

Riding along with Lidja on the box of the coach brought back many fond memories. She caught Revin peeking at her and grinned back.

"I'll take you to the Seneschal, but then what are you doing tonight?" she asked.

"I thought maybe you could show me where you're living," Revin said.

"Oh, I would love to!" she said.

Lidja brought the coach around to the back of the Executive Building. Revin slid down from the box and, after letting Beck secure the area, headed into the building.

Revin arrived at the office of the Seneschal. He entered, leaving Beck in the hallway, and found the Seneschal pacing, as though he'd been waiting for him.

"Come in! Come in!" he said.

"You don't seem surprised to see me," Revin said.

"Oh, well," the Seneschal said with a wink. "We have our sources of information, you know.

"It's wonderful to have our hero back again! I can't thank you enough for keeping our scientist safe during the unprovoked attack on Beskin Harbor. If he'd been killed — or captured — it would have been a disaster. I can see why the King chose you as his special envoy."

"And as the King's special envoy, I've brought you a letter," Revin said, offering him the envelope.

"Oh, that's excellent," the Seneschal said. "We'll have a reply for you to carry back. Probably tomorrow."

"Thank you," Revin said. "After my long voyage, I think I'll retire for the night."

"Perfect. We have a room reserved for you at the Hotel Royale across the plaza. Come back at nine bells tomorrow morning!"

Revin bowed and then left the Seneschal's office.

He found Lidja and Beck waiting for him in the hallway.

"I've stabled the horses and am free now, so let's walk to my apartment," Lidja said. "I would love to fix you dinner."

"I could take you out, you know," Revin said. "I have a budget for meals and lodging."

"Oh, but I want to cook for you!" Lidja said.

"Okay, okay," Revin laughed as they exited the Executive Building onto the main plaza of Havelock's capital.

Revin noticed that Beck was on high alert the whole time they were on the street. His eyes constantly scanned the windows and faces of the passersby. Lidja led them to a small market where she selected a cut of meat and a basket of vegetables. She let Revin pay, after he insisted, and then they crossed the street and entered the run-down building of her apartment.

They climbed four stories until they reached her tiny garret at the very top. The ceilings were too low for Beck, who had to crouch to get inside. Inside, were only two small rooms: the larger was the living area with a couch, a small table with two chairs, and the kitchen with a tiny gas stove.

As she started cooking, Revin explored her apartment. The view from the window might have been pretty, but the lower floors obscured the view down and other buildings hemmed in the view out over the city. The bedroom was even smaller than the other room, with barely enough space for a small bed and a dresser.

"Do you like it here?" Revin asked. "It's just like the first place of my own that I ever had, though mine was just one room and the door was so low that even I had to duck to get in. I loved it."

"I love it too — It's simply wonderful," Lidja said, starting a pot of rice. "You have no idea how happy I was to get my own place. I've never had that before, you know."

"I'm very happy for you," Revin said. "I was worried when we left and so relieved when I got your letter."

Lidja looked up from her cooking to grin at him and Revin felt his heart clench. He felt his face heat up at her smile and he couldn't help grinning back.

"While I finish making the food," she said. "Could you open the bottle of wine?"

"Uh ... I don't know how to do that," Revin admitted.

"I can show you how," Beck said, equably.

He removed the foil from the top of the bottle and showed Revin how to insert the corkscrew and extract the cork.

Lidja didn't have any wine glasses, so Revin poured the wine into some little jelly jars she was using as drinkware. When Revin went to pour a third glass for Beck, he put his hand over the top.

"Just water for me," he said. "I'm on duty."

Revin took one glass for himself and carried the second to Lidja.

"I'm only going to drink a little," Revin said. "I drank too much the first time and ... well ... it wasn't good."

They toasted one another and sipped the wine. Revin thought it tasted terrible, but he pretended to like it since Lidja had gotten it to share with him. After a few minutes, he volunteered to set the table. Lidja owned only a few mismatched plates and an eclectic mix of silverware.

"I call this 'spicy beef,'" Lidja said, setting the pot on the table along with the rice. "Please help yourself!"

There were only two chairs at the table, so Lidja and Revin sat there, while Beck took his over to the couch.

"It's really good," Revin said, sweating. "But it's super spicy."

He poured himself another glass of the wine.

"I'm so glad you like it," Lidja said. "It was the first recipe my mom taught me."

After dinner, Revin stood to leave, a little unsteadily.

"We should probably get to the hotel," Revin said.

"Are you sure?" Lidja asked. "You could just stay here."

"That does sound nice," Revin admitted, feeling slightly woozy. "What about you, Beck? Do you want to go to the hotel?"

"I stay with you," Beck said, flatly. "If I can get a blanket, I can make do on the sofa."

Lidja took her heavier blanket and a pillow and gave it to Beck, then she took Revin's hand, led him into her bedroom, and shut the door.

•   •   •

In the morning, the three of them walked back toward the center of town. Revin hadn't gotten as much sleep as he might have, but there was a new spring in his step. And Lidja had a glow that hadn't been present the day before.

As they approached the city center, they stopped at a street cafe to buy coffee and pastries.

"What's that smell?" Revin said.

"It smells like smoke," Beck said.

In fact, the whole neighborhood seemed to be suffused with the smell of smoke. They looked around, but could see no reason for the odor. They ate their pastries and drank their coffee until it was nearly nine bells, then they walked down the street and around the corner.

On the central plaza, across from the Executive Building, they saw the smoldering ruins of a building. Firemen still picked through the rubble to find hot spots and extinguish them.

"What was that building?" Revin asked.

"That was the Hotel Royale," Lidja said, turning pale. "Wasn't that where they said they had reserved a room for you?"

"Hmm," Revin said, recalling what Words had said about the level of danger that his new position entailed, and resolved then to take his security more seriously.

Revin hugged Lidja tightly then took his leave and presented himself at the Seneschal's office.

"What?" the Seneschal said, blanching as though he'd seen a ghost when he saw Revin come in. "Why, Sir Revin! I'm so … glad you're alive. We … feared the worst!"

"I hope you have a letter prepared for me," Revin said. "I need to depart immediately."

"Yes," the Seneschal said, retrieving the letter from his desk. "Yes, here is our reply. We will be sending a delegation that will arrive on Harway in two days time. The delegation will be led by Sir Tony Vandermeer, Marquis of Beskin".

Revin saluted the Seneschal, a bit brusquely, and recovered Beck outside the office. Both went to the back entrance where Lidja had the coach hooked up and awaited them for the short trip to the aerodrome.

Beck insisted that Revin sit inside the coach this time, while he took the seat on the box. Inside, Revin drummed his fingers sadly on the armrest, wishing he could see Lidja's bright smile as they traveled. But he had to admit to himself that Beck was probably … No. Undoubtedly right when it came to security.

At the aerodrome, Revin gave Lidja one last hug before he boarded *Pamela's Panties* and they lifted off for Belleriand.

•   •   •

Pamela's Panties arrived at the aerodrome near the Belleriand capital the next day around dawn. Once again, Beck allowed Revin to take no chances. He preceded Revin from the airship and checked the surroundings before hustling Revin into the coach provided by the Baron. Revin remembered his last trip from the aerodrome to the capital: hooded and in chains, although he hadn't known where he was at the time. Revin leaned back in the luxurious coach and thanked his good fortune.

The coach deposited him at a side of Ravensbelth he hadn't visited before. This was the business entrance where couriers, courtiers, and staff came and went in a constant stream. After Beck cleared him, Revin emerged from the coach and walked to the Baron's office.

"Welcome, Sir Revin," the Baron said. "We've been expecting you."

"I have a letter for you," Revin said, handing over the envelope.

The Baron accepted it. "We are putting together a delegation," he said. "As you're aware, there are … differences of opinion regarding the peace talks. For political reasons, I've had to appoint Count Cindakor to lead the delegation. He's not going to be easy to work with, I'm afraid."

"I will do my best, Milord," Revin said.

"I would expect nothing less from you," the Baron said. "But tonight, perhaps you can divert yourself a bit. I have a box at the opera and I wondered if perhaps you would care to attend and escort Momo."

"Will you not attend, Milord?"

"I think Momo will enjoy herself more if I do not," the Baron smiled. "And I will be busy coordinating Belleriand's reply to the letter. I assure you, Sir Revin, we will have a letter for you to carry back first thing tomorrow morning."

After leaving the Baron, Revin thought for a few moments and asked Beck to wait for him. Then he slipped away into Ravensbelth and found his way to the botanical garden. Lady

Cecelia was there, among the plantings, recording observations in her journal as she had been the day Revin had met her before. But then, he'd been wearing Momo's idea of a disguise. Which, Revin had to admit, had been pretty effective.

"Excuse me, Lady Cecelia," he said. "I was hoping to make a corsage for Lady Momoire as I'm escorting her to the opera tonight. Can you help me?"

Cecelia blinked and looked at Revin curiously.

"Pardon me, but have we met before?"

"Not exactly," Revin said, bowing. "I'm Sir Revin Minerson of Devishire. I'm here as the King's special envoy."

"I'm very pleased to make your acquaintance, Sir Revin," Cecelia said, curtsying. "I would be only too happy to assist you in selecting some flowers. Do you have any thoughts?"

"These yellow lilies are pretty," Revin said, remembering the yellow dress Momo wore on the first day he met her.

"Oh, no," Cecelia said. "No, no, no. In the language of flowers, they mean falsehood. No, a white lily, that would be more appropriate. Or perhaps one of these orange blossoms — those mean 'purity equaling loveliness'. Does that suit, Sir Revin?"

Revin blushed, which made Cecelia secretly smile.

"Now, you need a few filler flowers. This double-red pink might be a good choice."

"What does that mean?" Revin asked.

"Pure and ardent love."

Revin didn't trust himself to speak and couldn't look her in the eye but simply nodded silently.

"Ah, youth," Cecelia sighed. "Let me use my clippers to cut them and then follow me over to my workroom there. I have everything you need."

"Thank you very much, Milady," Revin said.

She cut the flowers and showed Revin how to tie them together and helped him stitch them to a length of red silk ribbon.

At 6 bells, Revin had the coach brought around to the grand front entrance. Beck kept watch while Revin stood by the coach in his finery and waited until Momo appeared at the top of the stairs. She wore a stunning gown of many shades of pale pink. As she turned, and with each step, the colors shifted so that the eye was dazzled and bewildered. When she arrived at the coach, Revin knelt, then took her hand to gently tie the corsage to her wrist.

"You are truly a sight to behold, Lady Momoire," he whispered, as he helped her ascend to the coach.

He followed her into the coach and Beck sat with the driver on the box. The driver started the horses and drove them to the opera house.

When they arrived, Revin got out first and offered his hand to Momo to assist her descent from the coach. Revin saw heads turn as Momo stepped from the carriage. He could feel everyone's eyes on him as they walked hand in hand into the theatre. The head usher bowed deeply and escorted them to the box reserved for the Baron. Beck stood guard just outside it.

Revin had never been to the opera before. But sitting, on display, in the Baron's box seat gave him a unique perspective. He had never experienced anything like it. When the lights went down and the music started up, he felt like he was transported to another world where anything was possible. It all seemed rather silly to him, but the audience took it so seriously.

During the lovers' duet, at the end of the first act, he felt Momo's hand secretly questing after his. He laced his fingers together with hers while they both pretended to watch the rest of the performance.

He snuck a glance at her and caught her looking at him. They both smiled at being caught. Then she cuddled up against him.

"Are you sure it's wise for you to be seen with me like this?" he whispered.

"Let them talk," she said, dismissively.

After the opera, after the applause had died down and the lights came up, Revin escorted Momo back toward the exit. But, on the way, he encountered two large men.

"You're that ... Revin, aren't you?" one spat.

"Yes, I'm Sir Revin, the King's special envoy," Revin replied, standing up straight.

"You're an enemy of Belleriand," the other snarled. "You cost us dozens of good men at Beskin Harbor."

"That had nothing to do with me," Revin said. "That was your own stupidity."

The first, provoked, lunged at Revin, but Beck somehow interposed himself between them. The man bounced off Beck like off a brick wall.

"Gentlemen," Beck said calmly. "This is neither the time nor the place. But if you don't stop, I will stop you."

With Beck running interference, Revin escorted Momo back to the coach awaiting them.

When they returned to Ravensbelth, and the coach had come to a halt, Momo turned to Revin. "Thank you for a wonderful evening, Sir Revin."

"Please just call me Revin," he said. "Lady Momoire."

She stuck her tongue out at him. But then put her hands on both sides of his face and kissed him. He put his arms around her and, for a few moments, they clung to each other desperately.

A footman opened the door to the coach and, by the time he could look in, they had chastely separated.

"Good night, Momo," Revin said, as she stepped from the coach.

"Good night, my hero!"

•　　•　　•

The next morning, Revin returned to Ravensbelth only long enough to collect the letter from the Baron's office with the official reply of Belleriand, and then headed to the aerodrome. By noon, they were aboard *Pamela's Panties* and headed back to Harway.

Revin returned to the Office of the Special Envoy and handed the two letters to Hannah. She absolutely devoured the letters with Guntar reading over her shoulder.

"The Marquis of Beskin," she said. "He's an odd, twitchy sort of fellow."

"Beskin Harbor is where the Etheric Storm Generator was set off during the raid by marines from Belleriand, destroying the town," Revin said. "He's not going to be easy to persuade to accept peace."

"Oh, no," she said, skimming the other letter. "Count Cindakor. He's not the most reasonable man either. We're going to have our work cut out for us."

For the next two days, the team worked nearly around the clock to draft a set of ground rules for the negotiations that called for a cease fire, laid out a set of principles, and established parameters for the negotiations. Revin had never worked so hard to write something before and was pleased with the contributions of the whole team. It was heady to be working on something so significant. He'd never felt like he'd been involved in anything so important before.

The delegations arrived and were conducted to suites in the palace. Revin and Hannah went over their script and plans for the peace conference. They had selected an elegant salon and arranged for a long table with enough seats for all the delegates. They went over the agenda several times and considered many potential options depending on the responses of the delegates and possible objections. They arranged catered meals and, after the first meeting, a lavish reception with music and an open bar. No expense was spared and no detail was too small for them to consider and plan for.

Revin felt excited to have his plans finally coming to fruition. He had been working for this moment for weeks. And now it was finally happening. The delegates were finally arriving at the meeting room from their suites in the palace.

"Revin!" someone called.

Revin turned and saw Lidja with the delegation from Havelock! She came running over and threw herself into Revin's arms.

"What are you doing here?" Revin asked, surprised.

"I was sent to drive a coach for the delegation, if they needed someone," she said. "I was so excited because I knew you were going to be here."

She surprised Revin by giving him a kiss on the mouth. By chance, at that moment, the delegation from Belleriand arrived and, among them, was Momo. Revin saw her face as she caught sight of him and Lidja in a position that left no doubt as to their ... relationship. She stormed over with ill-concealed jealousy.

"And who is this?" she asked.

"Um. Hi, Momo," Revin said, uncomfortably. "This is Lidja. She drove the coach for us when we were in Havelock. Lidja, this is ..."

"Lady Momoire Isabella Celandine Belthingstone of Belleriand," Momo snapped.

"Well, aren't you a little princess," Lidja said.

"Shove it, horse girl!"

Both young women turned their backs on each other and stalked away, leaving Revin crushed and devastated.

He didn't have time to brood, however, as Hannah appeared and dragged him into the salon where the delegates were arriving and taking their seats.

"Welcome honored delegates," Revin began, bowing deeply. "Welcome to Harway. Thank you for coming to discuss our differences and how we might work together to resolve them amicably."

"I object!" the Marquis of Beskin said, coming to his feet. "Belleriand is not taking these talks seriously by sending only a Count. I demand a representative of at least equal rank to myself."

"At least Belleriand didn't send any morons," Count Cindakor said, without bothering to stand.

"Gentlemen, gentlemen!" Revin said, trying to calm things before they got truly out of hand.

"But something we can all object to," the Count said. "Is having these proceedings chaired by a woman.

"That," he continued, pointing at Revin. "Is no man. And I refuse to participate in any such proceedings until we have an acceptable envoy from the king. He can appoint women to whatever positions he wants, but that doesn't mean we need to accept them. Go back to the kitchen where you belong, you cross-dressing slut!"

A shocked silence filled the air for fifteen or twenty long seconds. Revin's face turned red as everyone stared at him. His mouth opened, but no sound came out.

And before things had even gotten started, they were over. While Revin was still trying to marshal his thoughts, both sides pushed back their chairs and swept from the room. Revin just stood there, tongue-tied, wishing he could sink into the floor. He saw Momo pause at the door but, at a sharp word from another on the Belleriand delegation, she turned and departed.

"Well," said Hannah in the long silence that followed. "That could have gone better."

"I'm ... I'm sorry," Revin said.

"It's not your fault," Hannah said. "It really doesn't have anything to do with you. It just gave them a convenient out. But I don't know where we go from here."

"I think maybe I had better go talk to the King," Revin said.

No one knew what to say. They stared glumly at one another until Revin turned and walked silently away.

Revin went alone to the King's antechamber and asked for an appointment. Once again, he relinquished his sword and waited for several hours, until late in the afternoon. He was the only one left in the room when his name was finally called. Revin was, again, directed into the King's comfortable study.

Revin did not sit but, standing, briefly described the events of the morning and, bowing, offered his resignation as special envoy.

The King looked at Revin and rolled his eyes.

"What did you expect?" he said. "Did you think it would be easy? Did you think they would be reasonable? People that fight wars are not reasonable. If they could reason, they wouldn't be fighting a war in the first place.

"But that doesn't mean what you're doing is hopeless or without value," he continued. "Nothing worth doing is easy. The easy things have all been done already."

He stood, walked over to Revin, and clapped him on the back.

"You know what they say," he said leaning close and speaking in a stage whisper. "First they ignore you. Then they laugh at you. Then they fight you. And then you fucking destroy them."

"But I thought the point was not to destroy Belleriand or Havelock?"

"Not the countries. Are the countries stopping you? No!" the King said. "It's two men who are holding things up. You need to find some leverage and use it — something to grab onto and squeeze." The King put his hand in front of Revin's face and made a fist.

"In any event," he continued. "I do not accept your resignation, Sir Revin."

Then he waved his hand and dismissed Revin from the chamber.

Revin, followed by Beck, wandered back slowly through the dark, empty hallways of the palace back to his room. Finally, Revin dejectedly climbed the last staircase to his room step-by-step. It was all well and good for the King to say that, but how was he supposed to find some way to get leverage? He didn't even know where to start.

Beck opened the door and held it for him. Revin walked into his room and then turned when Beck closed the door. Beck had stayed inside. Revin backed up a step and Beck took another step toward him.

"I think you should leave," Revin said.

"What are you afraid of, honey?" Beck said. "I can see how much you're hurting. I've got just what you need to feel better, baby."

"You're mistaken," Revin said, his voice rising to a squeak while he backed up as Beck continued to advance. He reached the wall while Beck loomed over him.

"C'mon, baby," Beck said. "Loosen up a little."

"Please leave," Revin said, his voice starting to shake.

"You're such a little bitch," Beck snarled. Then he turned and left, slamming the door.

Revin collapsed onto his bed, hyperventilating with panic.

•　　•　　•

After spending the evening sulking in his room, unable to sleep or stay still, Revin decided to take a walk. He walked down the stairs, across the courtyard, and slipped out a side door into the park. It was dark, which suited his mood, and almost chilly as he walked through the carefully-tended parkland toward the pond near where the storm generator had come to rest. Infrequently spaced light poles with gas lights cast uncertain illumination on the gravel path. Revin scuffed his feet, feeling sorry for himself.

"The Duke sends his regards," a voice said.

Revin looked up to see a hooded figure standing on the path with a crossbow. He took aim at Revin. Revin just stood there, no longer much caring whether he lived or died. Beck flashed past him, charging the bowman.

The bowman instinctively fired at Beck, who took the quarrel through his chest. Revin saw the impression of the point emerge from his back against his shirt. Then Beck was upon the bowman. He knocked him to the ground and twisted his neck.

Revin ran to Beck and tried to roll him over. He gasped, bloody spittle flecking his lips.

"Don't bother, little missy," he said. "You'll find another man someday." He started to laugh at Revin's horrified expression, but then froze in a rictus of death.

"Help!" Revin called. "Help!"

He heard the answering whistles of the guards. Revin waited with Beck's body until they arrived.

He was taken into custody and spent two hours back at the guard post answering questions until he was released on his own recognizance. He sullenly returned to his room, even more depressed than before.

Revin sat on his bed staring at the floor for hours until it was nearly dawn. And, when he finally could no longer keep his eyes open, he collapsed onto the bed and slept.

A knock sounded on Revin's door. He awoke and looked at the clock: 10 minutes before 11 bells. He sighed.

The knock came again, more insistently. And again. He dragged himself to his feet and opened the door. Momo and Lidja stood there. Together.

"What were you doing?" Momo said at the same time as Lidja asked, "Were you still in bed?"

They looked at one another and shook their heads.

"Come," Momo said, imperiously.

"Where?" Revin said.

"Come!" Momo said, pointing.

Revin followed them down the hallway and down the stairs to the courtyard.

Momo pointed at a bench. "Sit! Stay!"

Revin sat glumly on the bench, by himself, in a long arcade of the courtyard. He stared at the fountain among the orange trees. The girls had walked to the far side of the fountain and animatedly argued with one another, the sound of the water making their voices impossible to hear.

Words walked up and sat down next to him, but said nothing for a moment.

"Girl trouble?" he said finally. "Or, rather, girls trouble?"

Revin just pointed, where Lidja and Momo stood toe-to-toe arguing and gesticulating at one another on the other side of the courtyard.

"They told me to 'Stay,'" he said. "'Stay!'"

"They probably meant it in a ... nice way," Words said.

Revin just sighed. Then he suddenly sat up.

"Words! When did you get back?"

"Last night," he said. "We located the eternite mine and we have dispatched a team of marines to capture it. Ratner was livid to see how disturbed the site is."

Revin looked at Words, "Did you hear about …"

"Beck?" Words said. "Yes, I heard. I told you he'd save your life."

"Everything has gone wrong, Words," Revin said, tearing up. "The delegations have rejected me, the peace talks are a failure, Beck is dead, and, worst of all, the girls hate me now. I … I don't know what to do."

"I don't know about that other stuff, but I know something about girls," Words said, sidling up to Revin on the bench with a crooked grin, so like his father. Slipping an arm around him, he said, "Maybe you just need to make them … a little jealous."

Revin looked up at Words, reached up, and touched his face. Words winked, then bent over and kissed Revin full on the lips.

"Hey, hey, hey!" Momo said, scurrying back around the fountain. "What's the idea?"

"You can't just steal our boyfriend!" Lidja said, following close behind. "Who do you think you are?"

"Well, he's Prince Stewart," Momo said.

Lidja froze and her eyes got really big.

"Ahem," Momo said. "Revin. Pay attention. We have decided that, although what you did was unforgivable, we will forgive you anyway."

"It wasn't really that unforgivable," Lidja started to say when Momo punched her in the arm.

"Hey!" Momo hissed at Lidja. "We said we weren't going to say that. We agreed! He needs to show real contrition."

Revin got to his feet and pulled Words up too.

"I'm really sorry," he said. "To all of you. I've been such a mess lately. It seems like I can't do anything right."

"It's okay, Revin," Words said, extending his arms to encompass all of them.

They came together in a huddle around Revin and all hugged him together.

"We are here for you."

"As are we, lad!" Will said, coming up from behind with Grip.

"What are you doing here?" Revin asked, astonished.

"Words stopped at Kapper island on the way back to say you might need us," Grip admitted.

Revin wiped his eyes and then clenched his fists.

"Alright," Revin said. "Let's talk strategy."

Revin started to lead them down to his offices, but then thought better of it and instead took them into his room where they turned the bed over to the girls, Revin sat in his chair, and the rest sat on the floor.

"I was going to have us use my office, but I think it would be better if we let them have plausible deniability for what might happen next.

"There are two individuals who are making it impossible for the peace talks to proceed: the Marquis of Beskin in Havelock and Count Cindakor of Belleriand. What I need is leverage to get them to drop their objections."

"Do you mean Sir Vandermeer?" Lidja asked.

"Yes," Revin said. "That's the one. He's the Marquis of Beskin."

"I don't know if it will help," Lidja said. "But he's nuts for rare coins. He's always telling everyone who will listen about the new rare coins in his collection."

"Thanks," Revin said. "Though I'm not sure how we can use that information."

"I do," Will said. "Let's just steal his coin collection. Who knows what he might do to get it back. And we can always sell it."

"Do we even know where it is?" Revin asked.

"It's probably in his country house," Words said. "He told me I should come see it sometime — purely for historical and archaeological interest, you understand."

"Okay," Revin said, rubbing his hands. "How about Count Cindakor? What does he have?"

"He has a mistress," Momo said. "Everybody knows it. It's the worst-kept secret in Belleriand. Hope Hart is her name. He keeps her in a townhouse in the capital."

"Are you saying we should abduct her?" Revin asked, astonished.

"Oh, no," Momo said, shaking her head and making big, innocent eyes. "I would never suggest something like that. But who knows what these pirates might do?"

•   •   •

The next night, the *Queen* approached the coast of Havelock just above the water, passing over Beskin Harbor. No lights were visible as she overflew the rubble of what had once been a quaint sea-side fishing village, before it had been destroyed by the Etheric Storm Generator. Revin knew just beyond, in the darkness, lay dozens of fresh graves. And beyond that, was their target: the chateau of the Marquis of Beskin.

After slipping in low, under cover of darkness, the *Queen* touched down in a field near the chateau. The comfortable country estate stood surrounded by vineyards. The house itself sat dark and silent, just a silhouette against the night sky.

Will picked the lock and let Grip and Revin in, then followed close behind them. They walked quietly, but the floor creaked as they stepped.

"Who goes there!" cried the caretaker, awakened from sleep.

Will created a fat towline to the door to his bedroom. When the man tried to open the door, he found it immobilized, and was unable to budge it.

Revin and Grip ran upstairs and found the marquis' bed chamber. Revin went through his dresser while Grip searched the closet. When they found nothing, they moved into his study through a connecting door. Here, they found display cases filled with his collection of rare coins.

Revin stuffed his pockets with what appeared to be the pride of his collection, and then they ran back, collected Will, who left the towline in place until Revin and Grip were halfway to the *Queen*, then sprinted after them. By the time the watchman was out, the *Queen* was already lifting off and headed back to the ocean.

•   •   •

The next night, using the Baron's code book, the *Queen* sailed straight across Belleriand and arrived at the capital during the early hours of the morning. Using Momo's directions, they found the townhouse and moored on the roof. Revin and Grip waited while Will picked the lock of the rooftop door, then they tiptoed quietly until they found her bedroom and slipped inside.

"Begging your pardon, Miss Hart," Will said with a flourish. "But I humbly request that you come with us quietly."

The young woman, awakened by strange men in her bedchamber, opened her mouth and drew in a large breath to scream. Grip took the opportunity to thrust a balled-up cloth into her mouth.

"Or we can do things the hard way," Will said, lifting her up so Grip could wrap a strip of cloth around her head and then used some soft cord to tie her arms behind her back as she struggled.

"Here now, Miss Hart," Will said, as Grip threw her over his shoulder. "You've only your nightgown on. And if you squirm much more you're going to lose that!"

She settled, but looked daggers at Will. Her true fury was reserved for when she caught sight of Revin going through her dresser drawers.

"Pardon me, Miss Hart," Revin said with a bow, collecting two of her lace handkerchiefs. "If you were less contrary, I could have simply asked you. And allowed you to pack some clothes, but I'm afraid we're out of time."

In a flash, the three quietly retraced their steps, with Grip carrying Miss Hart to the roof. They all boarded the waiting *Queen* for their return flight to Harway. Once aloft, Grip untied Miss Hart and removed her gag.

"How dare you!" she hissed, as soon as the gag came off. "You're going to pay for this!"

"Miss Hart," Grip replied, with a bow. "I very much hope your captivity will be a short one, but it will pass more pleasantly if you keep a civil tongue in your head and do not provoke the men. Do I make myself understood?"

"Wait," she said. "Don't I know you?"

"It's possible, Miss Hart," Grip replied. "But I suggest you sleep in the hammock provided and awaken in time to watch landfall on Harway from the observation deck. It's not a sight to be missed." Grip exited the cabin, then turned before he shut the door. "Good night, Miss Hart."

•   •   •

Revin arrived back to the palace exhausted, but exhilarated. He headed straight to the office where he found Hannah and the others in the final stages of glumly packing up.

"Hey," Revin said, with a barely-suppressed grin. "Why so depressed?"

"It's over," Hannah said. "We gave it our best shot, but these peace talks are dead."

"Oh, I think it might be worth just one more attempt to bring them to the table," Revin said, with scarcely-concealed mirth. "Let's meet with the representatives one at a time and see if we can't get them to see reason."

Hannah just looked at Revin, cynically. But Revin's light heart and excitement piqued her interest.

"What did you do?" she asked, in her most gravelly voice.

"Oh, nothing," Revin said, trying to keep the grin off his face. "Nothing much."

"This I gotta see," she said, then turning to the others. "Don't leave until we get back!"

Hannah followed Revin as he skipped to the luxurious suite of rooms assigned to the party from Havelock.

Revin knocked at the door and was admitted by reluctant aides to speak with the Marquis de Beskin.

"What do you want?" Sir Vandermeer said. "We're heading back this morning and you're wasting our time."

"I want to make you a wager," Revin said, pulling a coin out of his pocket. "Heads you win and tails I lose."

"What kind of joke is this?" he snarled.

"Call it!" Revin said, and flipped the coin.

"Tails!" Vandermeer called, unable to stop himself.

"Oops! Why look at that! It's both heads AND tails!" Revin said. "Have you ever seen that before? It's a bennie that was overstruck so both sides are both heads and tails!"

"What?" Vandermeer said, paling. "Where did you get that?"

"It's amazing what you find in your pocket change sometimes," Revin said, jingling the coins in his pocket.

Vandermeer cringed to envision precious coins being treated with such cavalier disregard for their numismatic value.

"It's too bad you're leaving today," Revin continued. "Who knows what else I might find in my pocket change."

"Wait, wait, wait," he said.

"Well, enjoy your trip home, Sir Vandermeer," Revin finished turning away.

"Wait, I said! We'll stay. We'll stay."

"Here," Revin said, flipping him the coin. "A good faith gesture on my part. We'll see you at the summit tomorrow.

"Or else," Revin said, patting his pocket.

Vandermeer just stood there, stunned.

Revin and Hannah stepped back out into the corridor. Hannah, who had maintained her equanimity throughout the exchange, broke into hysterics once they were around the corner.

"Oh, Revin," she said finally, with tears running down her face. "Remind me to never get in a quarrel with you."

"One down, one to go," Revin said with a wink then began walking briskly toward where the Belleriand delegation was staying.

They had quite a long walk, as prudence had dictated that the two parties be widely separated in the palace.

As they arrived, Revin noted that a messenger was just departing. He looked at Hannah and winked again.

"Pardon me, but may we speak with Count Cindakor?" Revin asked at the door.

"We have no time for women," the attendant said.

"I just wouldn't want the Count to lose 'Hope'," Revin said, loudly. "Some might take 'Hart' if he left without completing the task here."

"What did you say?" the Count said, charging in from the other room.

"My, but it's hot," Revin said, fanning himself. He pulled one of Miss Hart's handkerchiefs from his pocket and wiped his face. The count saw the handkerchief and flushed with anger.

"Oh, do you need one too?" Revin said, tossing him the second handkerchief, still nicely folded.

The Count, enraged, leapt at Revin with his fists raised. Hannah took a step back, but Revin stood firm and refused to budge.

At the last moment, the Count was forcibly restrained by his attendants.

"No! Stop!" they said. "That's the King's envoy! You can't touch him."

"We're having another meeting tomorrow to sign the ground-rules agreement," Revin said, with a toothy smile. "I sincerely 'Hope' you will be able to come."

•   •   •

The next morning, Revin again stood before the salon with the delegates, but this time he didn't speak or welcome them. He handed copies of the agreement to each delegation, then set the official document on the table with a pen, and simply said, "Sign."

The delegations retired to adjoining private rooms that had been set aside for caucusing. Hannah paced nervously, while Revin just leaned back in his chair and waited. He could hear raised voices on both sides, though none of the words were audible. Revin smiled.

After slightly less than an hour, both sides emerged. Revin caught Momo's eye as the Belleriand delegation came out. She gave him an almost imperceptible wink. Revin came to his feet and waited patiently as first Sir Vandermeer, and then Count Cindakor, came to the table and affixed their signatures to the document.

"Thank you, gentlemen," Revin said. "With these ground rules in place, I declare our peace talks officially open."

INTERLUDE

REVIN STAYED UP LATE into the night with Hannah in their offices. The others had long since retired, but they sat up, surrounded by their papers and notes trying to game out what the sides might do during the next day's negotiations.

"So ..." he said. "If Belleriand proposes this, what is Havelock going to say?"

"Oh, no," Hannah said. "They'll never propose that."

"But what if they do?" Revin asked.

Hannah leaned back, nonplussed.

"How many hours have we been at this?" she asked, finally.

"We need to be ready," Revin said.

"But we also need to get some sleep," she said. "You need to be fresh for tomorrow. Go get some sleep, Revin. I'll finish getting the agenda drawn up for tomorrow and drop it off to get copied by the scribes for the meeting tomorrow."

"Alright," Revin said, yawning. "I'll see you tomorrow."

As Revin left the offices, he felt a pang to feel the absence of Beck, who had always waited for him just outside the office and been his shadow for his first weeks as the royal envoy. He had hated how Beck had treated him, refusing to acknowledge him as a man and seeing him only as some kind of sex object. But he was also forced to acknowledge that Beck had saved his life and he would not even be here but for him sacrificing himself. He recognized that, in his own twisted way, Beck must have loved him — for some value of "love". But Revin couldn't deny that he still hated how Beck had made him feel. But he was horribly conflicted and felt guilty. He sighed and climbed the stairs alone to his room.

He laid awake for several hours, tossing and turning, as he spun out in his mind what positions the opposing sides might take. It was incredibly frustrating because each side insisted on taking irrational positions that were clearly not in their own interest and seemed calculated on purely frustrating the other side or precluding any kind of rational solution to their problems.

Eventually, through force of will, Revin turned his thoughts to less frustrating topics. He thought about Lidja and recalled their idyllic voyage through the heart of Havelock. He smiled to remember cuddling with her at Sendia Springs. But then, unbidden, he saw Momo in his mind's eye, wearing her stunning pink gown at the opera. And, nearly against his will, a fantasy presented itself to him of lying in bed with both Lidja and Momo, one on each side of him. His face turned bright crimson and he sat up in bed panting with the unexpected arousal that the fantasy had brought. He went to his dresser and poured himself a glass of water and drank deeply before returning to bed. And then he chose to turn his thoughts in other directions until, finally, he was able to fall asleep.

•　　　•　　　•

"Havelock will never accept that Belleriand bring their airships within sight of Havelock," Sir Vandermeer bellowed.

"Belleriand insists that Havelock keep their fishing vessels out of sight of our airships," Count Cindakor shouted in reply.

"But your airships patrol out so far, you can see our ships at port!"

"Let them stay at port!"

Revin rubbed his temples.

"Gentlemen, gentlemen!" he said. "This posturing doesn't get us anywhere."

"There's no point in even talking to these monsters,"

"Monsters! You're the ones who keep attacking our outlying islands!"

"Gentlemen, gentlemen! Let's turn to another topic!"

"Yes, let's discuss how Havelock keeps flooding the market with cotton priced at unsustainably low prices."

"What are you complaining about? Your merchants keep buying it!"

Revin looked helplessly at Hannah who just closed her eyes and shook her head slightly.

"There must be something we can all agree on," Revin said, rubbing his temples. "Can we start with territorial integrity? I have a list of the islands between Havelock and Belleriand. Which of these are contested?"

"None of them," said Cindakor at the same moment that Vandermeer said, "All of them."

"Oh, come on!" Revin said. "None of these are even occupied! They're just rocks!"

The men both glared at Revin, but he detected a hint of embarrassment and pressed forward. He took a quill, dipped it, and drew a line on the map.

"There. These are Belleriand's and these are Havelock's.

"That gives one more to Havelock," said Cindakor at the same moment that Vandermeer said, "That gives the biggest one to Belleriand."

"But it doesn't matter!" Revin said. "Nobody really cares about these islands. Nobody uses them for anything! They're just rocks with sea birds and sea lions."

"Unlike unreasonable Havelock, Belleriand accepts," Cindakor said, smirking.

"Havelock signs first," Vandermeer said, snatching the map and affixing his initials to it. Cindador initialed it second. And then Revin carefully countersigned with the elegant signature he had developed with Inky's help.

"Let's leave off there, Gentlemen," Revin said. "We made good progress today. Let's continue with this tomorrow."

7

REWRITING THE RULES

R EVIN ARRIVED PROMPTLY at 6 bells at the antechamber of the king in response to a summons. He went to surrender his sword, like usual, but they just waved him straight through. He had typically waited for hours before being admitted to the King's presence but he was ushered instantly into a dressing room where the King stood, being fitted for a fresh military uniform.

He motioned Revin to enter. Revin stood at attention.

"Do you wish a report on the peace talks, Your Majesty?" Revin asked.

"I regret, Sir Revin," the King began. "That I need to communicate something of importance to you."

Revin leaned forward, all attention.

"While you have been pursuing peace, the Kingdom has been preparing for war," the King said. "This morning, our full armies have launched an assault on Havelock."

"What?" Revin said, dumbfounded.

"It was obvious they had intended to attack Harway from the beginning. I couldn't let that pass."

"So ..." Revin said, grasping for thoughts. "So my entire effort has been a diversion? You used me to pretend to offer peace only while you gathered your forces for an attack?"

"Once we took the eternite mine," the King said. "It was a foregone conclusion we would be at war. I received word this morning that the mine has been taken and is ours. Upon that notice, I ordered our armed forces to attack in full."

Revin just stood there, mute. Then he felt his face flush as his anger began to rise.

"I'm sorry if you feel deceived, Sir Revin," the King said. "But once Havelock attacked us, there was really no path forward but war."

"Then what are your orders, Your Majesty?" Revin said, stiffly.

"Your loyalty does you credit, Sir Revin," the King replied. "The peace talks are now ended and We will make no further call upon your services. The forces are away and there is no longer any call for secrecy. You may do as you choose. You may notify your staff. And you may tell the delegates, if you so desire. Though they will undoubtedly know soon enough."

And with a wave the King dismissed Revin.

"By your grace, Your Majesty," Revin said with a bow and, turning, departed.

Revin headed straight to the offices of the Special Envoy.

Hannah was already there, hard at work preparing the agenda for the day's meetings. "Good morning, Revin," she sang out when he came in.

"You won't think so after you hear this," he said.

"What?" she said, stopping and looking up.

"The peace talks are over. The King has been using us as a diversion," Revin said. "Harway has dispatched its armies to attack Havelock."

Hannah threw her quill across the room where it splattered against the wall.

"Oh, Revin," she said. "I'm so sorry. You must be livid."

"I think I'm still in shock," Revin said. "I guess we should inform the delegations today."

"We were making progress!" Hannah grumbled angrily.

"I thought so too," Revin said. "Let's get this over with."

Two hours later, the delegates filed into the hall and Revin could immediately tell that everyone had already heard the news. He noticed one empty chair and perceived that Momo was not attending. He cleared his throat and addressed the delegates.

"As you have all seemingly heard, I have been directed by King Reginald to conclude the peace talks," Revin said. "This was not my choice, but I serve at the pleasure of the King and I fulfill my duties to the best of my abilities. Our meetings are hereby adjourned. I thank you for your contributions. May you all travel safely in these uncertain times."

"You are an utter disgrace," Count Cindakor said, rising. "You brought us here under false pretenses and wasted weeks of our time. For nothing! Although we may agree on nothing, I feel confident that the delegates from Havelock will agree with me that you deserve censure and repudiation for your abjectly dishonest performance."

Everyone stood and silently filed out of the salon.

Revin sighed and turned to Hannah. "Thank you for everything," Revin said. "If we accomplished anything, it was thanks to you. You put together a great team and did yeoman's work to keep us moving forward. Thank you."

"It was all you, Revin," Hannah said, in her gravelly rasp. "We never would have even gotten them to the table if you hadn't pulled out all the stops. I'm glad I got to work with you, even if we don't get to go all the way. Thank you."

They nodded to each other, then departed, going separate directions.

Revin was walking through the courtyard heading back to his room when someone shoved a bag over his head. He felt his arms gripped on both sides. Stumbling, he was dragged through the door into the park. He struggled and tried to yell when someone punched him in the gut. He would have doubled over, but for the grip on his arms holding him up.

The bag was pulled off his head and he was thrown onto the ground in a wooded area of the park. Count Cindakor and a handful of his associates stood over him.

"You freak," the Count sneered at him. "You monstrosity. You're going to get what's coming to you now."

Count Cindakor's men began kicking him. Revin tried to cover his head when someone stomped on his face. He tried turning over, but they kept kicking his arms and legs and ribs. He tried to focus as panic threatened to overwhelm him. He closed his eyes and tried to find an etheric stream as the blows rained on him. He managed to make an attachment to a low tree branch which pulled away and then snapped back when he released it. The men turned when the branch suddenly swung toward them.

Revin scrabbled to his feet while they were distracted and began to run. The men gave chase. Revin had never run so hard before, his sight darkening to tunnel vision as he tried desperately to get away.

After a few moments, he heard them laughing as he ran away. He found a dense thicket and curled up inside, shivering and crying with pain and fear. He found he'd wet himself in his terror. He lay there miserably for a half hour or more until he was sure they must have left.

He crept slowly back to the courtyard, watching for anyone waiting for him, then he slipped up the stairs to his room to be safe. But when he got to the top of the stairs, he found his trunk sitting out in the hallway, open, with his belongings thrown inside. He tried his key in the door, but the lock had been changed. Revin sat down on the floor and broke down into sobs.

Eventually, Revin stood and tucked everything into the trunk. He dragged it down the steps and went out the side entrance to the guards.

"Can I get a coach to the aerodrome?" he asked.

"I'm sorry, Sir Revin," the guard replied. "We've been informed your access to the coach service has been revoked."

"I can pay," Revin said.

"We don't request private coaches," the guard said. Revin must have looked devastated because the guard took pity on him. "Normally. Let me see what I can do."

Twenty minutes later, a private coach arrived. The coachman put Revin's trunk in the storage compartment and held the door for Revin to climb into the coach. Revin settled into the back, profoundly grateful for small favors.

When he arrived at the aerodrome, he was unsurprised to find that *Pamela's Panties* was no longer available for his use and had been turned over to the nobleman who had originally ordered her. He inquired about the next seat available to fly to Candlemain and was told that he could get a small compartment on a flight leaving the next day. He paid and then sat on a bench and began the long wait.

After a bit, Revin went to the bathroom and looked at himself in the mirror. He had huge bruises on his face and a black eye. His arms and ribs were also bruised. By a miracle, he didn't seem to have any broken bones. His hair was full of dirt and twigs. He cleaned himself as best as he could and changed into clean clothes.

He got out Momo's journal and, after paging through what she'd written previously, he got out his pen and began to write.

He poured out his soul: his anger, his uncertainties, and his fears. As he wrote, he realized he'd never been so angry before. He felt like he understood better why Will didn't trust the nobility. Revin still felt conflicted, but he was finally becoming willing to admit to himself how strong his feelings were for Momo and how important she was to him.

"Did you hear?" someone said, coming into the waiting room. "Prince Stewart is finally married!"

"Really?" the man behind the counter said. "Everyone's been wondering who will finally catch him. Who is it?"

"Someone I've never heard of," the other man replied. "Someone from Belleriand. Momray? Momoray? Something like that."

"Lady Momoire?" asked Revin, stunned.

"Yeah! That's it," the man said. "Their marriage will cement the alliance between Harway and Belleriand against Havelock."

Revin looked at the journal he'd been writing and wanted to scratch or tear out everything he'd just written. His throat closed up and he felt his gorge rise. He closed the journal, put away his pen, and sat on the bench staring at the ground. His mind stopped working for a while.

"Excuse me, sir," someone said, shaking his shoulder.

Revin had fallen asleep.

"Excuse me. The waiting room is closing for the night."

"Can't I wait here?" Revin asked.

"I'm sorry sir," the man said. "We'll open tomorrow morning at 6 bells."

Revin dragged his trunk out as they locked the door behind him, then he dragged it off the aerodrome and huddled in a wooded area. It already felt chilly. Revin shivered in the dark. Revin wrapped another coat from his trunk around him. The wind began to rise and rain started falling. Revin pressed his back up against the trunk and pulled the coat over his head as he broke down and wept. It was a long and sleepless night as the rain, trickling, found its way in and soaked him to the bone.

•　　　•　　　•

The next morning dawned cloudy and misty. Revin dragged his trunk back to the passenger terminal. They had coffee, for which Revin was endlessly grateful. At 7 bells, they announced boarding for the *Bellewhether* to Candlemain via

Belleriand. Revin started when he heard that he would be traveling through Belleriand and considered trying to find some other way to go. With no other options available, he dragged his trunk on board and found his cabin — the poorest cabin at the very end of the airship.

Once in his cabin, even as the airship was still rising, he stripped off his wet clothes and put something dry from his trunk. Then he collapsed and slept for many hours.

• • •

He awoke when the *Bellewhether* landed in Belleriand. Revin looked out as soldiers surrounded the airship. As passengers disembarked, they were searched and their names checked against a list. A team of soldiers came up the ramp. Revin couldn't hear what they said, but from their expressions he could see that they were demanding to search the airship and were being barred from doing so by the crew. Revin shrank back into his seat and shivered, remembering the last time he endured the tender mercies of the Belleriand intelligence service. He rubbed his wrists reflexively, ducking down when he spotted soldiers walking around the airship looking in at the windows. They were probably too low to see anything, but Revin wasn't taking any chances.

After what seemed like an eternity, but which in truth was only about a half hour, the soldiers stepped back off the ramp, and the *Bellewhether* lifted off and headed west, over the ocean, bound for Candlemain.

Revin looked out the window remembering his first trip by airship in the *Madeline*. He remembered being fascinated by the view out the window, the blue towlines of the remmers drawing them forward over the boundless ocean. He felt a moment of peace and almost smiled, But then the reality of running away with his tail between his legs brought him back to earth and he sighed deeply.

The sun had just set when the *Bellewhether* touched down on Candlemain. There was no aerodrome — just an open field at the outskirts of town. Revin dragged his trunk down the ramp and looked at the seemingly peaceful seaside village. He knew first hand that the intelligence services of both Havelock and Belleriand were present. But he didn't see any alternative but to wait until the pirates came to resupply.

Dragging his trunk, he made his way to Mama Kane's boarding house. He'd heard pirates talk about her as being honest and offering good hospitality. A big draw was that her house was close to the harbor and offered a good view of the pier. Revin dragged his trunk up and found her chatting with guests on the patio.

Mama Kane kept her white hair under a colorful bandana. An older, large and heavy-set woman with rough, pink skin, her tiny, beady eyes sat almost lost in folds of flesh, but a big, wide smile with one gold tooth shone right in front.

"Dear me, young man," she said, catching sight of Revin coming into the light. "Did you get in a fight with someone?"

"Yeah," Revin admitted. "All six of them."

"Well, if anyone tries to give you any trouble here, you let me know about it, you hear?"

"Yes, ma'am," Revin said.

"Call me Mama," she said. "Everyone does."

"Yes, Mama."

"Now, let's find you a room. Haven't I seen you here before?"

"I've never stayed, but I might have come with Grip before."

"Ah! I thought you looked familiar. I've got just the room for you. You'll be wanting to keep an eye on the pier, I'll wager. This room at the end is good. You can pull a chair out and sit right here to watch."

Revin accepted the key and listened while she pointed out the amenities of the room.

"Now if you need anything just holler, you hear?"

"Yes, Mama."

•　　　•　　　•

Revin awoke on Thursday morning and got up, still stiff and sore from his bruises, even after three days. He dragged a chair out in front of his room where he could put his feet up and watch the shore and the pier, to await the arrival of the *Little WormMaid* — the pirate's small sailboat that they used to provision themselves, although Revin wasn't certain they would come this week. He was sitting in the chilly dawn air, before the land breeze set up when Mama brought him a cup of coffee. He nodded his thanks, not wanting to disturb the morning's peace. Then he saw her.

She wore all black: an elegant black hat with a veil and a long, formal black dress that stood out among the colorful island attire. And, even at a long distance, Revin knew instantly who it was. She walked directly up to him and planted herself in front of him.

"What are you doing here?" Momo said.

"Milady," Revin said.

"Are we back to that?"

"You're the one who got married," Revin said.

"That wasn't my decision," Momo said. "I didn't have any choice! It doesn't change how I feel. Or how Stewart feels about you!"

"I'm done with the nobility," Revin said, bitterly. "I got picked up, used, and discarded."

"I'm sorry, Revin," Momo said. "I'm really sorry. But we need you."

"What do you need me for?" Revin said, brandishing his bruised arms, spectacularly purple and yellow, and pointing to his black eye. "A punching bag?"

"Are you going to let them get away with that?" Momo snapped.

"I just don't care anymore," Revin said, standing and turning to go back to his room.

"No!" Momo said, stamping her foot, tears springing from her eyes. "You can't! You're *my* hero. And ... And! And I *order* you to serve me!"

Revin stopped, hearing Momo sniffle, trying not to sob. He paused and closed his eyes. He remembered the Baron warning him to temper his expectations. But, for a long moment, his principles did battle with his heart. For what seemed an eternity, he stood there caught on the horns of the conflict between everything he believed and everything he felt. In a flash, he remembered Momo sliding down the banister. Momo laughing. Momo stroking his hair after his nightmare. Momo taking his hand at the opera. Momo kissing him. And he decided. He turned and dropped to a knee at Momo's feet. He took her hand and pressed his lips to it.

"I once told you I would do anything for you, Milady," Revin said, looking up at her. "And I'm a man of my word. What would you have me do?"

"I need you to be my chief of staff," Momo said. "I'm surrounded by people trying to tell me what to do. I need a right-hand man. I need someone I can trust. And you're the only one I trust."

"I'm yours, Milady," Revin said. "Now and forever."

Revin looked up at Momo, then looked past her and felt a chill go through him. He struggled to his feet.

"Momo," he said, quietly. "We're being watched!"

"Oh," she said. "That's my security detail. I told them to be discreet."

Revin looked farther and saw the *Little WormMaid* approaching the pier in the harbor.

"We had better go meet the *WormMaid* before your bodyguards tangle with the pirates," Revin said.

He took Momo's hand to assist her down the steps. They walked together toward the pier while the pirates tied up the *WormMaid* and began walking down the pier toward the town.

Grip's face was filled with concern when he saw Revin's bruises, but he truly blanched when he saw Momo dressed all in black.

"Who died?" he asked, in a panic. "It's not ..."

"No," Momo said. "It's the King."

"What?!?" Revin said, floored.

"But if the King is dead then who is ..." Grip said.

"It's Stewart."

"But Stewart wasn't first born ..." Grip said.

"His older brother was killed leading the invasion force."

"But if Stewart is King then ... Your Majesty!" Revin said.

Grip looked back and forth between Revin and Momo as the enormity of what Revin had just said began to sink in.

Revin's head spun while he tried to take in what was happening. He began to realize that being Momo's — No! The Queen's! — chief of staff was going to be invested with far more responsibility than he had initially imagined.

"Harway walked into a trap," Queen Momoire said. "Havelock had an Etheric Storm Generator concealed offshore that severely damaged the invasion force and their delegation left another in the palace that was triggered after they left. It flattened the palace, killed the king, and destroyed much of the city."

"What's going to happen?" Revin asked.

"It's anybody's guess at this point — there's total chaos. There will be a summit at Ravensbelth in three days' time," the Queen said. "I came here to find you and bring you to the meeting. I wasn't joking when I said we need you."

"Let me go to Will and the Professor to see if I can get them to come as well," Revin said.

"Three days," Momo said, her lip quivering. "Don't be late."

"No, Your Majesty," Revin said. "I will not fail you."

Revin wanted to hug Momo, who was obviously on the verge of tears, but he held himself back and she pulled herself back together. She headed back to the field and, a few minutes later, they saw her airship rise and head east.

Ham and the others went to provision the pirates while Grip went with Revin to collect his trunk and check out of Mama Kane's.

"You know Will isn't going to want to get involved," Grip said.

"I know what he'll say," Revin said. "But I think I know how to persuade him."

"And what happened to you?" Grip asked. "Did you get in a fight?"

"Yeah, but you should see the other six guys," Revin retorted. "Their boots are all scuffed and covered with my bodily fluids."

"Seriously?"

"Count Cindakor and his flunkies," Revin said. "Once the King was done with me, the gloves came off."

"That bastard," Grip snarled. "He has a lot to answer for."

"Well, but if it hadn't happened, I probably would have still been there and would have died. So there's that."

Grip grabbed Revin and pulled him into a hug.

"I'm sorry for what you went through," Grip said. "But I'm very glad you're with us still."

Revin hugged Grip back and they stayed like that for a long moment. Finally, they separated and Revin went to settle up with Mama Kane while Grip hoisted Revin's trunk on his shoulder like it was nothing and carried it down to the *WormMaid*.

"Thanks, Mama," Revin said, slipping her an extra reggie after paying the bill.

"Oh, you sweet boy!" she said, crushing him in a hug. "You come back again, you hear?"

While Ham and the others finished provisioning and Grip collected the mail, Revin walked through the market. Keeping his eyes open, he went to the stall where the woman sold bound journals. The one he'd liked before with a raven or crow on the cover was still there. Or possibly one just like it. Revin selected it, paid the shy woman, then headed to the pier and boarded the *WormMaid* as Ham and the rest loaded the provisions.

Two hours later, Revin stood in the bow watching the flying fish as the WormMaid approached Kapper Island. He heard a cry go up from an observer on shore and the pirates came charging down to help unload the provisions — or so he thought. They suddenly grabbed him and carried him on their shoulders up to the pirates' base cheering all the while.

"Welcome back, lad!" Will said, coming out and embracing him. "You've been as successful as usual at keeping out of trouble, I see."

"What can I say?" Revin said, blushing with all the attention. "And just wait 'til you hear what I'm doing for my next trick!"

"Oh, no!" Will cried and the crowd roared with laughter and approval. "You can tell me all about it — after the party."

Revin turned around and around, watching the whirl of activity and seeing all the friendly and familiar faces. For the first time in weeks, he felt truly at home. He made the rounds, checking in with everyone and politely declining rum when offered. Eventually, he took a couple of skewers of meat and joined Will and Grip who sat together off to the side.

"Grip won't tell me anything," Will said.

Revin just raised one eyebrow.

"Hmph. Be that way," Will said, feigning grumpiness.

Revin grinned and took another bite of meat as the party became ever more festive with music and dancing fueled by the rum.

"Alright, you pup," Will said finally. "Let's get everyone together and hear your report."

Once everyone was gathered, Revin stood and paced back and forth in front of the room.

"Four days ago, the King summoned me to tell me that he'd been using me as a diversion while he gathered his forces to attack Havelock. And, once he was done with me, he discarded me."

"This is not a surprise to me," Will said. "I'm sorry it happened to you. But I could have told you this would happen. Indeed I think I did tell you."

"You did. But, look. We became pirates because the world has been divided into two classes: the nobles and the commoners. And we fit into neither camp. We're neither noble nor commoner.

"You could argue that there's a third class: those who serve the nobility. But ..."

Revin looked at Will and both shook their heads.

"But you'll learn that if you serve the nobility, you're still a commoner. And, sooner or later, that will be brought home to you.

"Okay, boy," Will said. "So what's happened? Don't keep us in the dark."

"The King is dead," Revin said, flatly.

"And who is the new King?"

"Stewart," Revin said. "You know him as ..."

"Words," Will said. "I know."

"But did you know Words got married?" Revin asked.

Will looked puzzled.

"Prince Stewart married Lady Momoire," Revin continued. "We now have a true Queen of Belleriand. I have agreed to serve her as her chief of staff."

"So, the King threw you out to be kicked and beaten like a dog," Will said. "And you're already so eager to crawl back to the nobility and lick their feet?"

"Not a bit of it," Revin said with a wink. "What I see is a chance to rewrite the rules. Remember it's not the nobility you hate. They're just playing their part, same as you. It's the rules that divide us. That's what we need to change."

"And how do you propose to do that?" the Professor said.

"Got 'em!" Revin thought with a chuckle. Then, out loud, he said, "Well, let me tell you ..."

He pulled out the journal where he'd begun sketching out his plan and explained his idea.

•　　•　　•

Two days later, the *Queen of Belleriand* arrived at the Belleriand aerodrome. A detachment of Belthingstone guards saluted Revin smartly as he disembarked. A coach was waiting to take Revin, Will, Grip, and the Professor to Ravensbelth. Two guards took up positions on the coach while the others rode on horseback around the coach as they attracted stares through the streets of the capital.

Youngman, the aged head butler, met them at the grand entrance of Ravensbelth, welcomed them, and led them to a lively reception in the Porcelain Room. Inside were more than a hundred people from the highest echelons of both the Belleriand and Harway nobility.

"Sir Revin Minerson of Devishire," Youngman announced upon his arrival.

Conversation halted. Dead silence fell. Revin swallowed and stepped into the room with as much confidence as he could muster. He recognized few familiar faces. At the far end of the room, he saw King Stewart and Queen Momoire standing together, still wearing the black of mourning.

"Excuse me, Sir Revin," someone said in the silence.

Revin turned, but stepped back when he found himself face-to-face with Count Cindakor.

Count Cindakor bowed deeply. "I would like to publicly apologize for my shameless and unwarranted slanders of your character. They were totally uncalled for, as was my unconscionable attack on your person by my staff. I hope you will accept my sincere apology and my personal word that I will work together with you going forward."

Revin was taken aback, stunned, but recovered quickly.

"Your apology is accepted," Revin said. "Pray think of it no further."

After a moment, Revin reached out his hand and they shook hands to a round of polite applause. Count Cindakor melted back into the crowd. Revin began trying to work his way toward Momo. He bowed to Lady Cecelia along the way. Grip introduced him to his older brother, Cordwin, who looked even more like their father than Grip did. He stood slightly shorter than Grip, but was broader and even more muscular.

Eventually, he reached the end of the room where the King and Queen waited.

"We thank you for coming," Queen Momoire said. "We hope you found the Count's apology to your satisfaction."

"Yes, Your Majesty," Revin said. "I am entirely satisfied, if you are."

Momo's eyes narrowed.

"I would have had him slow roasted over a fire and basted with lemon juice," she said. "But we need his faction too much."

"Sir Revin," the King said. "On behalf of the Kingdom of Harway, We would also offer Our apology. And We are overjoyed you will yet serve Us. We are well pleased."

"Your Majesty," Revin said, bowing deeply.

Revin spent another hour circulating through the crowd, meeting as many people as he could. Finally, as he was starting to fall asleep on his feet, he found Terrier standing at his shoulder.

"Pardon me, Sir Revin," Terrier said with a bow. "Her Majesty has tasked me with leading you to your quarters."

Terrier led Revin to a different room than he had stayed in before. It was much smaller than the luxurious guest room, but felt more comfortable.

"This door communicates directly with her Majesty's quarters," Terrier said, indicating an interior door. "She asked for you to be placed here so as to have you at hand as needed. But she asked me to tell you that she will not call on you this night so that you may rest and prepare yourself for the summit tomorrow. Breakfast will be at 6 bells as usual. Good night, sir."

"Good night," Revin said. "And thank you Terrier."

"It's very good to have you back, sir," Terrier said. "And you know that if you need anything at all, it would be my pleasure to serve you."

Revin looked in the closet and found that, not only was his trunk there, but the clothes had been carefully brushed and hung up. And there was sleeping apparel which, this time, he gratefully put on and then laid down in the comfortable bed. He closed his eyes. But, after a time, he found he just couldn't sleep.

He eventually got up and, wearing pajamas and a robe, made his way through the dark and empty corridors to the botanical garden and sat, alone, near the fountain listening to the music of the water. He looked up at the cloudy night sky and watched bats flit overhead. He sighed. Someone put a hand on his shoulder. He looked up into the face of the Baron.

"Milord!" he said, struggling to stand.

The Baron gently held him in place and smiled, then came around and joined him on the bench.

"Well met, Sir Revin," he said.

"Well met, Milord!"

"I'm glad for us to have a moment to chat before the summit," the Baron said. "And so that I can thank you for standing by my little Momoire."

"You must be very proud," Revin said.

"I'm very proud of all of my children," he said. "And I'm proud of you too."

"Huh?"

The Baron paused for a moment, as though having an internal debate, and then, having resolved it, he leaned back.

"You know that Dirge became our agent. Before we hired him, we vetted him thoroughly, of course. And that means, we also vetted you thoroughly beforehand."

"So ... You knew who I was before Grip introduced me to you?"

"That's right."

"And so you know that I'm ..."

"I've always known."

"Did Dirge know?"

"Yes, he knew. I suspected at the time, he was planning to get you to Havelock where you'd have no options or support and then try to pressure you for sexual favors. He really was not a nice man."

Revin felt like the floor had fallen out from under him.

"I keenly felt for you at the time," the Baron continued. "But I didn't feel like there was anything I could do. And, in spite of everything, you ended up rescuing Griphon. I truly owe you a great debt."

For once in his life, Revin was speechless.

"Do your parents know what's happened to you? Have you been home to see your family since you left?" the Baron asked.

"No," Revin said. "They could never accept that ... that I would never be the docile little girl they wanted. That I wasn't going to let myself be married off to an older man and beaten into submission to bear his children and do his housework."

"That's so sad," the Baron said. "You'd make a good father. Maybe you will someday."

"I ... I wish you were my father," Revin said, in a tiny voice, then started crying as feelings he never knew he had welled up from somewhere deep inside of him.

The Baron tousled Revin's hair and then pulled him into a hug as Revin tried to master his emotions.

Finally, Revin pulled away, wiping his eyes, and stood. "I think I'd better try to get some sleep, Milord," Revin said.

"Good night, young man."

Revin walked back to his room and got into bed. In moments, he was asleep.

•　　•　　•

At 5 bells, Terrier awoke Revin with a tub of hot water for bathing. Revin washed gratefully and then reclined in the bath. He wistfully remembered Momo bringing him a cup of coffee last time, but acknowledged to himself that it wasn't reasonable to expect the Queen to fetch and carry for him. But suddenly the adjoining door popped open and Momo breezed in carrying a cup of coffee.

"Are you decent?" she sang out, with a wink.

"I am not," Revin said, laughing.

She handed him the cup of coffee, which he gratefully accepted and sipped.

"The Summit begins at 10 bells," she said. "After breakfast, we should plan our strategy."

"Yes, Your Majesty," Revin said. "I'll be ready."

•   •   •

At 10 bells, Revin stood in the Portrait Gallery just behind Their Majesties and to the right of Queen Momoire. The delegates filed in and took seats. Revin went through the audience, trying to remind himself of names. He had met most of them at the reception the night before, but could only remember names for half.

"Welcome Delegates," the King began. "Today, we are here to discuss how to move forward after the disastrous failure of the attack by Harway on Havelock. As you have undoubtedly heard, Havelock triggered Etheric Storm Generators that disrupted the invasion force, destroyed the capital of Harway, and killed my father — King Reginald.

"Through fortuitous chance, just before the assassination of the King, Momo and I wed to cement the alliance between our two island nations. But we find ourselves in a delicate situation with no clear plan nor leader. We come to you to solicit your input and seek consensus for a plan.

"We have asked our Chief of Staff, Sir Revin Minerson of Devishire, to lead this meeting."

Revin stood and cleared his throat.

"Welcome, honored delegates," he began. "As you know, we are facing a crisis. After the catastrophic defeat of the invasion force and the monstrous attack on Harway's capital that claimed the life of King Reginald, we need to identify a path forward."

Revin briefly introduced the Professor, who spoke for several minutes about the Etheric Storm Generator, which was still new to many. He ended with a brief warning.

"Although Harway captured the eternite mine that we believe was the source of their material for the generators," he said. "We don't know how many devices they constructed or how much eternite they recovered. Or, indeed, whether they discovered other sources on other islands — or on Havelock itself."

Revin thanked the Professor and seeing hands raised, opened the floor for comments and questions.

"Viscount Metterwin of Westland," Revin said, choosing someone whose name he remembered. "You have the floor."

"Thank you, Sir Revin," he said. "Why is there any question? We must crush Havelock. The Duke has demonstrated we have no choice but to take him down."

There was a murmur of assent from the entire body.

"But who will lead the assault?" said a man who didn't wait to be recognized. Suddenly there were raised voices and shouts, as various names were shouted out.

"Order!" Revin shouted over everyone. "I will have order!"

Voices subsided and Revin continued.

"Count Cindakor, you are recognized and have the floor."

"The only one who can lead the expeditionary force is the Baron. I believe he is the only one that can bring us together."

Murmurs of support came from the assembled body. Revin looked toward the Baron.

"Milord?" Revin said, inviting him to speak.

The Baron rose and turned to address the body.

"I am honored by your trust," he said. "But I don't believe we have a sufficient army — even when combined with forces that remain from Harway — to assure victory. And I will not commit us to a protracted invasion that we might not win."

Silence from the assembled delegates and a sense of gloom descended upon the room.

"What if I knew how to even the odds?" Revin said.

The Baron looked at him sharply. Revin stood up straight and held firm.

"Upon your word," the Baron said. "Then I will be your most humble servant."

The room erupted in cheers as Revin shook hands with the Baron.

•   •   •

The *Queen* approached the coast of Havelock in the pre-dawn hours at a high altitude and then turned to skirt the coast. Grip cranked down the ramp while Will helped Revin strap himself into the glider.

"Unassisted, you should have no problem reaching the coast," Will said. "But even a small towline will probably be enough to keep you aloft until the city."

"And you'll be ready?" Revin asked.

"As soon as the Baron launches the assault, we will watch for your signal."

With this assurance, Will gave Revin a pat on the shoulder and helped him out onto the ramp. Revin had worn two extra shirts for some extra insulation, but was still shivering, though not entirely from the cold. He was familiar with heights, having been on airships many times. But jumping off of them was something else altogether. He pulled out the monocle he had gotten from Will and fixed it over his eye. Then, taking a deep breath, he took a running start and leapt off the ramp into open air.

At first, he panicked when it felt like he was going straight down. He struggled to get his feet up into the supports, heart racing. But once he'd picked up a little speed, he felt the glider start to gain lift and the dive flattened out into a long glide.

With the monocle, he studied the etheric flows and made an attachment to a strong flow going the right direction. He felt the glider pick up speed and it actually started to climb! He grew increasingly confident as he overflew the coast.

He had chosen to approach the city from the East, to stay well clear of the aerodrome, but it meant approaching the city from an unfamiliar direction. He strained his eyes, trying to look for familiar landmarks and trying to spot Lidja's apartment building. He was practically straight above it when he finally recognized it. He panicked for a moment, feeling like he'd missed his chance. But then he just cut the towline and began turning lazy circles, dumping altitude, until he was just above the rooftops.

The mansard roof on the building with Lidja's apartment looked forbidding to land on, but the adjacent building had a large, long flat roof. Revin lined himself up, then realized, with the wind behind him, he was flying far too fast and would overshoot the building. In a panic, with the roof of Lidja's apartment rushing at him, he found another etheric stream and made the biggest towline he could. He squeezed his eyes shut as he started to climb and just barely cleared the roof.

After climbing for a few minutes, he cut the line and looped back for another try. Heading into the wind this time, he lined up well in advance of the roof and judged the height better. As he cleared Lidja's roof, he dropped his feet out of the supports and touched down at a run. He almost lost his balance and nearly tumbled, but just managed to stay on his feet and bring the glider to a stop. He had never wanted to kiss the ground more.

After unstrapping himself, he ran to the edge of the building and, looking down a few feet, identified the window of Lidja's bedroom. He pulled a few copper bits out of his pocket and threw one against her window. And then another and another, until he saw she was opening the window to look out and see what was going on. She looked up and caught sight of Revin and her face broke into a huge smile.

"Revin!" she squealed. "What are you doing here?"

"May I come in?"

"Yes, of course!"

Revin sprang across the narrow gap between the buildings and scrambled over to the window and climbed inside. Lidja seized him in a hug and pulled him down onto the bed.

"Oh! Oh! Oh!" she said, kissing his face over and over. "I've missed you so much! But, look at you! What happened to you?"

She put hands on both sides of his face and looked at his black eye and bruises that were finally starting to fade. She kissed his eyes very gently.

"I'm here," Revin said. "And that's all that matters. What's been happening here?"

"Oh, it's really bad, Revin," Lidja said. "There are soldiers everywhere now. They're stopping everyone and searching everything."

"Are you still driving the coach for the Seneschal?" Revin asked.

"No," Lidja said sadly. "They said that until the crisis is over I should stay home."

"It just means I'll have you all to myself," Revin said. Lidja hugged him even tighter and then kissed him on his mouth when he tried to say something else.

"But there is something I want to do," he said, when Lidja finally came up for air.

"Mmmmm," Lidja said, giving him little kisses on his neck and throat and working her way lower.

"And it's dangerous," he continued as she began to unbutton his shirts.

"Mm-hmm," she said, reaching around to unhook his chest binding.

"And I'll need your help," he said.

"Mm-hmm," she agreed as she kissed him on his chest and belly.

"I'm not sure you're taking this seriously," Revin said.

"Hmm," she said, loosening his trousers and working her way even lower.

Revin closed his eyes, leaned back, and gave himself over to her completely.

•　　•　　•

Later, while Lidja fixed them some sandwiches, Revin climbed back onto the other building, collapsed the glider as the Professor had shown him how to do, and, when Lidja was ready, he lowered it to her and they slipped it through the window to keep it safe and out of sight.

"Now," she said, while they munched the sandwiches. "You're going to need a disguise. They'll be watching for you."

"This sounds familiar," he said, rolling his eyes.

They looked through Lidja's closet. Lidja was only a little shorter than Revin and she had a couple of dresses that fit surprisingly well — if a little tight across the chest. He selected a light country dress decorated with little embroidered flowers. He let his hair down and Lidja found a barrette for him to keep the hair out of his eyes. After packing some food and supplies, they headed out.

The streets were nearly deserted but for soldiers patrolling. Or, rather, looking for trouble. They tried to hurry and be unobtrusive. Revin felt naked to be without his sword — let alone wearing a dress. He and Lidja ducked into a store when a party of soldiers approached on their side of the street. The owner hustled them behind the counter and encouraged them to hide when the soldiers peered through the windows. After the soldiers passed on, they thanked the owner profusely. Revin offered him money, but he refused.

Eventually, they reached the shop of Mr. Darkpony.

"Why, hello, Lidja," he said. "What can I do for you?"

"We need to rent a couple of horses," she said.

"I'm sorry, but there's an order that everything needs to be kept back in case our stock is requisitioned for the war. So I can't rent horses right now."

"But it's an emergency," Lidja pleaded. "My sister's boyfriend beats her and she needs to get away before he kills her."

She pointed at Revin's black eye and arms that were still fantastic shades of yellow and purple. Revin tried to look sad and terrified and even managed to produce a few tears.

"I'm so sorry," he said. "I really can't … They'd shut me down."

Lidja looked discouraged and Revin stared at the floor like he was devastated.

"Look," he said, finally. "I can't rent you horses from here. But I have two horses at my country house that you could borrow. They haven't been ridden much lately, so they might be a little difficult to work with, but you know what you're doing with horses."

"Oh, thank you!" Lidja said.

Revin looked up hopefully and smiled shyly. Mr. Darkpony beamed.

An hour later, Darkpony closed the shop and led Lidja and Revin through the streets. When they turned a corner, they were confronted at a guard checkpoint.

"What's your business?" asked a bored guard.

"I've hired these women to work at my country house," Darkpony said. "And I'm taking them to get them started."

"Your name?" the guard asked, picking up a clipboard.

"Hirus Darkpony."

"Lidja Relsing," Lidja said.

"Raveena Relsing," Revin said.

"R, R, R..." the guard mused, looking through the list. Then he looked at each of them carefully and flipped through a few pages at the end. Revin twitched when he saw one was a wanted poster with a fair drawing of his face. But the guard seemingly did not recognize him.

"Okay," he said, waving them through.

Darkpony led them out of town and into a gentle landscape of rolling grassland past the outskirts. After a half hour, they reached a comfortable cottage that had several outbuildings and a barn with a paddock beyond.

"Welcome!" Darkpony said, leading them around back. "Let me take you to meet the horses."

He opened the gate and led them inside the paddock.

"The sorrel is a gelding named 'Honey' and he's sweet and gentle," he said. "The black one is a warmblood named 'Bastard' and, well, you'll see."

Lidja went up to the sorrel and had him eating out of her hand in moments.

"Sugar cube," she explained.

The other horse, a stallion, was another matter. He laid his ears back at Lidja as she approached. She stopped and watched his body language. For a couple of minutes, she just stood there and waited, eyes down and her posture unthreatening.

Eventually, his ears lifted and he shuffled forward. She offered him a sugar cube, which he accepted and, then she rubbed his nose and began to whisper to him. The stallion snorted and then put his head over her shoulder and pulled her up against his chest. She patted his shoulder and back.

"I think we're going to get along just fine," Lidja said.

Revin started to walk over toward Lidja when the horse suddenly reached over her and snapped at him. He stumbled backward and Darkpony caught him and set him on his feet.

"You're okay, little Miss," he said. "Lidja can handle him and you'll be fine on the sorrel. Just keep an eye on that Bastard. Now, let's go inside and have some dinner and I'd be happy to have you stay here for the night."

Inside, they found that Darkpony's wife, Missy, had seen them arrive and had added two more place settings to the table for dinner. Revin kept quiet during dinner, letting Lidja and Hirus carry the conversation, talking about horses and horse breeding. He snuck a glance at Missy, who winked and then rolled her eyes at Hirus and Lidja oblivious to everything except horses. Revin smiled cautiously.

"Your boyfriend did that?" Missy asked in a lull in the conversation. "Men are terrible. They're all beasts."

"They're ... They're not all bad," Revin said.

"And this one is the worst," Missy said, shaking the shoulders of her husband. "Take them to the guest room, dear, while I clean up after dinner."

He led them to a tiny room that had one small bed.

"Since you're sisters, I hope this is okay."

"This is wonderful," Lidja said. "You've been more than generous."

As soon as the door was closed, Lidja grabbed Revin and pulled him onto the bed.

"Ooh! I can hardly stand it! You're so cute when you're a girl," she whispered into his ear. "You're so shy and demure. But let's see what happens when the lights go off."

"Rowr," Revin growled in her ear, slipping his hand under her shirt.

"Oh, it's true!" she groaned a little later. "Men are all beasts!"

"Ssh!" Revin whispered. "We're supposed to be sisters here!"

•   •   •

The next morning, they came out to find that Missy had fixed them a hot breakfast. Hirus was still in bed, so they had a nice quiet meal with Missy. Afterward, she took them out to find the tack for the horses.

"I thought I would want to ride Honey more," she sighed. "It was my idea to get the horses. But I don't ride him like I ought to. So I'm really glad you're going to take him out for a bit. I think he'll really like it."

"I promise I'll bring them home safe and sound," Lidja said. "Your trust means so much to me."

"And you watch that Bastard," Missy warned. "He's well named."

"Oh, he's just a big softy," Lidja said, patting his shoulder as the horse reached over and grabbed a hank of Revin's hair and yanked it hard, throwing him onto the ground.

"Oh, yeah," Revin said, as he struggled back to his feet, rubbing his head. "This is going to be great."

After saddling the horses, Missy gave them a lunch to enjoy on the road. Hirus came out in time to wave at them as they set out on the road.

Revin had never ridden on horseback before (not counting the mine pony he'd ridden as a child). Lidja helped him quickly master the basics. He was struck by how much he'd missed when he'd traveled this route by coach before. Being on horseback was amazing — to be out in the world seeing, hearing, and experiencing everything. Revin excitedly pointed at something and then jerked his hand back when Bastard snapped at his fingers — and nearly got them. After that, he kept a wary eye for when the evil horse would try to sidle up closer.

When they stopped for lunch, Revin found he could barely walk. Being unaccustomed to being on horseback and wearing a dress, his thighs were red and chafed. Lidja nearly broke down in hysterics watching Revin try to walk with his legs apart. Luckily, she had thought to pack a little skin cream and, after liberal application, Revin took the opportunity to duck into the bushes to change out of the dress and put on his regular attire. Once again, he gave thanks to Cedric for making such excellent clothes that were not only stylish and functional, but actually fit.

By mid-afternoon, they reached the lonely tree where Revin and the Professor had been ambushed. Revin took a few minutes and acted out the whole drama for Lidja — who was appropriately shocked and horrified. Then they pressed on and, shortly after nightfall, reached the farm where Lidja had been indentured.

"Do you think we can sneak in to talk to the workers without the bosses becoming aware?" Revin asked.

"Oh, we can probably get to the bunkhouses," Lidja said. "The bosses lock up and then they get drunk, usually. I don't know how we'll get a key, though."

"What kind of pirate do you take me for?" Revin said, drawing himself up. "I was taught to pick locks by a master!"

Lidja covered her mouth with her hand and tried to stifle her laughter.

They left the horses staked out across the road and then slipped under cover of darkness to the first bunkhouse. It took Revin several tries — making him start to sweat — before he succeeded in picking the lock. When they opened the door, they found someone standing with a chunk of wood ready to wallop him on the head.

"Stop! Stop!" Lidja said, darting in ahead of Revin with her hands raised.

"Lidja! Lidja!" everyone started yelling. "Lidja! Lidja!"

Everyone surrounded her hugging and crying.

"They told us you were dead!" a man said. "We were so worried! We didn't know what happened to you!"

"I'm sorry I couldn't tell you anything," she said, crying freely. "But it was Revin who rescued me! And Revin has something he wants to tell you."

"Sorry," said the man with the chunk of wood. "Sometimes they come in at night when they're drunk to try to grab girls. Thank you so much for saving Lidja."

"Listen up, everyone!" Revin yelled over the noise. "If you want to do something about the unjust system of indenture on Havelock, there is a chance right now to fight."

"Fight?" said one man. "What can we do? They'll call out the army on us and kill us all."

"The army is going to be busy fighting Belleriand and Harway," Revin said. "If we attack while the army is occupied, we can take control and then we can be in a favorable position to negotiate."

"What good will that do?" an older woman asked. "The nobles are all the same."

"There's a new king," Revin said. "King Stewart. And Queen Momoire. They have agreed to meet with your representatives and to write a constitution that ensures fair treatment for everyone."

"This is bullshit," said another man. "You're just going to get us killed."

"Weren't you also the one who said you could trust the new boss?" Lidja asked. "Didn't you also say they weren't going to lock the doors anymore?"

Everyone laughed and the man slunk off into the shadows.

"I'm not saying it will be easy," Revin said. "Or without risk. But there's a chance here. If we act fast."

"What do we need to do?"

"We need to get as many people to the capital as fast as possible," Revin explained. "The armies from Harway and Belleriand are going to be landing soon led by the Baron."

Suddenly a murmur ran through the room.

"The Butcher Baron?" someone asked.

"Once that happens," Revin continued. "We want to hit

the capital from behind and capture it before the army does. Then we'll be in the best position to negotiate favorable terms. Are you with me?"

"This is a lot to take in," a woman said. "Who are you and why should we believe you?"

"You should believe him first of all because he's my boyfriend," Lidja said. "He's the pirate who stole my heart.

"But he is also Sir Revin. He was the King's special envoy. And he's the chief of staff for Queen Momoire."

"I'm in!" said one.

"Me too!" said another.

"Us too! Us too" said more.

"Okay! Okay!" Revin said. "We need to make a plan. We need to liberate everyone on this farm first. And then divide up and hit every farm between here and the capital."

In little more than half an hour, they had broken the locks off the rest of the bunkhouses and assembled as a mob surrounding the guard house. Armed with hoes and mattocks — or in many cases, just sticks — they charged the building with Revin at the lead. The door fell and the guards were indeed mostly drunk or asleep and fell quickly to the mob. The most violent and hated bosses were dragged out and beaten to death. Others were captured and tied up. Revin felt sickened by the brutality of the aftermath, but given what he'd seen of their suffering, he felt little sympathy for the bosses that had maintained the cruel system.

Searching through the house for weapons, they found a cache of swords and spears that were quickly passed out among the most experienced of the men. Revin found a smallsword that fit his hand well enough and took it.

"Now, get the wagons out and start heading for the capital," Revin said. "And liberate every indentured worker on the way!"

An enthusiastic cheer went up from the workers, in high spirits after their easy victory. As the workers hitched up wagons and started organizing to move to the next set of farms, Revin and Lidja snuck back to the horses and struck out cross country toward where Revin understood the allied forces were landing.

They made good time by night in the grassland, but when they reached a more wooded area, they stopped and curled up together in the damp grass and slept fitfully until sunrise.

•   •   •

As Revin and Lidja approached the pickets of the Baron's invasion force, a looped rope snaked out and grabbed Lidja and dragged her off her horse. Four men sprang out of a concealed position that had been dug into the earth in the undergrowth. A man grabbed her and put an arm around her neck.

"Get down, mister," he said. "Nice and easy, or I'll break her neck. Easy now!"

Revin slipped off the back of Honey and kept his hands raised as the men approached. But they hadn't counted on Bastard. The man with his arm around Lidja's neck started screaming when Bastard bit his neck where it joined the shoulder. Hard. Then the horse reared up, trumpeting, and brained one of the other men with flying hooves. Then he landed hard, trampling the first man — Revin heard bones crunch as the man's screams were suddenly cut off. Lidja ended up on the ground with Bastard standing over her with his head down and ears pinned back. The other two men turned their backs to Revin in the face of this terrifying new enemy. Revin drew his sword and calmly ran one of them through the back. But before he could kill the last one, the man took to his heels and fled the field.

Lidja got to her feet and wrapped her arms around Bastard's neck and hugged him, whispering her quiet words of encouragement until he was calmer. Revin kept his distance until she held Bastard's reins in her hand. Then, leading Honey, Revin walked forward with Lidja until they reached the picket line and he identified them to the soldiers.

Passed by the sentries, Revin and Lidja arrived at the command tent. The Baron glanced up over his glasses as Revin entered. He finished a note and a courier carried it off. Then the Baron turned his full gaze on Revin who snapped to attention in spite of himself.

"Report!"

"We have successfully initiated a revolt of the indentured workers of Havelock," Revin said. "Whether this fizzles or becomes an avalanche remains to be seen. But we've told them to attack the capital in two day's time."

"We will attack tomorrow," the Baron said. "And hopefully that will draw their forces and attention toward us, giving the farm workers the opportunity to attack from behind."

"I think they'll need some expert leadership," Revin said.

"I disagree, Sir Revin," the Baron said. "If we had weeks to train them, they could take advantage of expertise. But as things stand, they're going to be a mob."

"Someone should still go to help them coordinate," Revin said. "I'll go by myself."

"Pardon me," Lidja said from the doorway.

Revin and the Baron looked over at her.

"And who are you, Miss?" the Baron asked, standing.

"I'm sorry," Revin said. "I should have introduced you. If you please, Milord Baron Curtis Belthingstone of Belleriand, allow me to introduce Miss Lidja Relsing of Havelock."

"How do you do, Miss?" the Baron replied.

"I'm pleased to make your acquaintance, Milord," Lidja said, curtsying.

"You were saying, Miss?"

"I want to take the horses back," she said. "We borrowed them from Mr. Darkpony, but his cottage is in the path of the advancing farm workers. He and Missy will be in danger."

"You're right, Lidja," Revin said. "We should go immediately."

"Can you indicate on this map where you're going?" the Baron asked.

Revin looked over the map with him and pointed out the area as best as he could remember.

"Good. Get a hot meal before you go," the Baron said. "And be careful."

After visiting the mess tent, they slipped back out through the lines the way they had come and started making the long trek around the city toward the Darkponys' cottage. They kept moving even after dark, at points leading the horses on foot over the rougher terrain to avoid the roads where they assumed there might be checkpoints and guards.

The sky was growing light when they arrived in the pre-dawn hours back at the Darkpony cottage. They took the horses out back. Lidja removed Honey's tack and showed Revin how to brush him. While he occupied himself doing that, she took care of Bastard. She made sure the horses were well supplied with fodder. Then Revin and Lidja went around to the front of the cottage and sat on the front porch in the early sun while the birds called from the treetops. Revin felt conflicted knowing that just a few miles away, the attack on the capital was probably commencing. Lidja leaned up against Revin and he leaned his head over onto hers.

"You two are just too cute," Missy said suddenly from the kitchen window.

"Missy!" Lidja said, jumping up. "Let me introduce my boyfriend Revin."

She looked at Revin for a moment, then smiled.

"Hi, Raveena — I mean, Revin!" she said with a wink. "You still have a black eye. Don't worry — I won't tell anyone. Won't you both join us for breakfast?"

Hirus wasn't up yet, but they joined Missy at the kitchen table for a light breakfast with coffee. In a few minutes, Hirus came out, blearily wiping the sleep out of his eyes. He perked up when he saw Lidja.

"Is your sister okay?" he asked. "Is this your brother?"

"This is my boyfriend, Revin" Lidja said, taking Revin's hand. Missy just smiled and sipped her coffee.

"We came back to warn you that the war is starting," Revin told them. "There is an army attacking the capital from Harway and Belleriand. But indentured farm workers have revolted and are moving toward the capital from this side."

"What should we do?"

"To be honest," Revin said, scratching his head. "I'm not quite sure what to do. I don't think it would be a good idea to go into the city since fighting has already started. And I don't think any other direction would necessarily be better. I'm hoping that when the farm workers get here, we can persuade them to bypass us. But I suggest you get ready and pack a bag in case we need to run."

Revin and Lidja kept watch while Hirus and Missy got packed. As they were finishing, Revin saw some farm workers appear on the road. Behind them were more and more and more. It was a veritable army advancing. They fanned out as they approached the cottage, evidently planning to search the outbuildings. Revin went out to meet them.

When he showed himself, some of the farm workers charged toward him with spears raised.

"Hold!" Revin called, raising his hands. "We're on your side. I'm here to lead you into the capital."

They continued to advance threateningly toward Revin.

"We're on your side!" Revin called again. Then Lidja joined him.

"Lidja!" someone farther back called. "That's Lidja!"

"Lidja! Lidja!" people called. The men advancing put up their spears.

"You should stay here, Lidja, to help keep Missy and Hirus safe in case more come this way," Revin said. "I'll go with this group and try to help coordinate."

•   •   •

Revin walked at the head of a long column of farm workers armed mostly with mattocks, shovels, and spears. As they advanced on the outskirts of the capital, most people went into their homes and locked the doors. But some, bringing their own weapons, came out and joined the workers advancing on the capital.

As they approached the checkpoint at the town limits, they saw only three guards. The guards took one look at the approaching mob and abandoned their post, fleeing toward the city center.

Revin and the mob reached the central plaza and found the Executive Building ringed with fortifications. At the top of the building, an airship awaited.

The mob was reluctant to charge into the fortified positions. A few crossbow bolts emphasized their trepidation and the farm workers confined themselves to yelling insults and shaking their tools outside of crossbow range. The soldiers, evidently an elite guard for the Duke, impassively held their positions with good discipline. Revin went along the line of farm workers, exhorting them to hold firm and wait until more workers arrived. As he reached the end of the line, he saw another body of workers arriving from the east road. He sprinted toward them and spoke with their leaders as they approached, telling them to wait for a signal to all charge together. Then he sprinted back as he saw yet another group arriving and he explained again.

As each group arrived, Revin tried to count as best he could and judged that there were four to five hundred farm workers. He couldn't see how many soldiers were concealed behind the fortifications, but he judged there couldn't be more than a hundred. Stepping out in front of the lines, Revin drew his sword, raised it over his head, as he'd told them he would, and then lowered it to point at the enemy and screamed, "Charge!" The line leapt forward as one.

Revin blended in with the others running toward the lines as a wave of crossbow bolts struck the line. Dozens fell, but the line swept forward and hit the lines of sandbags. Behind him, the soldiers had spears and drawn swords and the first dozen farm workers were cut down. Howls and screams filled the air.

But then the numbers of the mob began to tell. Revin saw soldier after soldier struck down with the crude weapons of the farm workers. The soldiers fell back in an orderly process at first, but as the farm workers pressed them, the soldiers broke ranks and were routed into the building.

They tried to bar the entrance, but the farm workers' mattocks made short work of the doors and pried them off their hinges. With his naked sword in hand, Revin sprinted to the stairs and started climbing. He reached the top and came out onto the roof to see the Seneschal standing on the ramp of an airship with the name *Jolly Jenny* painted across the bow.

"Please, Your Highness," the Seneschal begged. "Let me come with you!"

Two soldiers inside the airship threw him off. The Seneschal tried picking himself up off the roof, then shrank back as he saw Revin advance.

The towlines shifted and the airship began to rise. Revin grabbed his signal mirror and scanned the sky until he spotted the *Queen* standing off-and-on near the Baron's army engaged south of the city. Revin began flashing the *Queen* until he saw her turn toward him. Then he turned his full attention to the Seneschal.

"Sir Revin," the Seneschal pleaded. "Don't kill me! I was just following orders. I always tried to help you, don't you remember?"

Farm workers arrived at the top of the building. Revin had to prevent them from killing the Seneschal until the *Queen* touched down. Revin gestured toward the ramp with his sword and the man gratefully fled on board the ship until he saw Will.

"Professor Dirge!" the Seneschal whimpered. "But you're dead!"

"Keep him under guard," Revin said, following him on board. "And follow that airship! The Duke is getting away!"

"You heard him!" Will called, running to the remmer deck.

The *Queen* had barely risen when Will began personally making the biggest, fattest towlines Revin had ever seen. Men on the roof flattened themselves or were bowled over as the Queen leapt forward still only two or three feet above the building.

Revin ran to the observation deck and looked ahead to the Duke's airship, practically just a point on the horizon.

"Two points to starboard!" he called to Grip who was manning the cockpit.

"Two points to starboard!" Grip relayed to the remmer deck.

Revin felt the floor shift under his feet as the *Queen* turned slightly to the right.

For three hours, the *Queen* made steady progress closing the distance. Sensing the inevitable, the Duke's ship ducked into clouds.

"Hold!" Revin called from the observation deck.

"Hold!" Grip called to the remmer deck.

Towlines winked out and the *Queen* drifted with the wind while Revin kept watch. Five minutes. Ten minutes. Fifteen minutes.

Revin got antsy and was just about to call for them to push forward when he saw the airship emerge from the clouds, far below making a run for the south.

"Forty five degrees to port! Full speed! Descend!" Revin yelled loud enough that, even before Grip could speak, huge towlines appeared and the *Queen* sprang ahead above the clouds and stooped on the *Jenny* like a falcon.

"Clear the decks!" Grip cried. "Ready for action! Boarding parties prepare!"

The *Queen* closed on its quarry. A fat towline sparked out and grabbed their quarry and stopped it dead in its tracks. The *Queen* came alongside in moments and grapnels tied them together. The boarding parties attacked fore and aft, cutting through the sides of the airship and charging aboard.

Revin followed the pirates with his sword drawn while boarding an airship for the first time in his life. He nearly slipped on his first step where a pirate had fallen, run through the neck, his blood sprayed liberally across the walls and floor. He heard the ring of swordplay farther down the corridor. Revin opened doors into cabins as he ran along the corridor. Empty. Empty. Empty. He worked his way back through the airship. He pulled open the last door in First Class and found a man huddled among trunks and boxes.

Soft and pale with blonde hair, his plump fingers bore multiple rings. He crouched among bags and chests loaded with treasure.

"Don't kill me! Don't kill me!" he pleaded when Revin placed himself *en garde.*

"Grip!" Revin bellowed. "To me!"

In moments, Grip was at hand.

"Confine this criminal," Revin said. "He must stand trial."

"Yessir," Grip said. "I will assure that he lives to stand trial."

Grip dragged the Duke away.

Left alone in the room, Revin looked around at bags and boxes and chests filled with treasure. Treasure looted from Havelock. Revin was filled with righteous indignation, remembering the indentured workers laboring under the lash to accumulate this monster's wealth. But then he spotted something and, after a moment's battle with his conscience, he shrugged and pocketed it. Stepping back in the corridor, he felt a weight lift off him he hadn't realized was there until its absence left him feeling elated and liberated.

The sounds of combat faded as the last of the soldiers fell.

"The ship is ours, Your Excellency" Will reported, coming from amidships.

"Stuff it with your titles," Revin laughed.

Will looked in the room and whistled.

"What are your plans for the treasure?" he asked.

"I'm going to pretend I didn't see it and leave it entirely in your hands," Revin said.

"But … But I'm a pirate!" Will said, astonished.

"You know what will happen to it if it goes back to Belleriand," Revin said. "You're a pirate. But I know where your heart truly lies."

They grinned at one another and shook hands.

It took another hour to treat the wounded pirates, and get the *Jolly Jenny* ready to travel back to Havelock.

The *Queen* and *Jenny* arrived back at the Executive Building around midnight. The fighting seemed to be over. Everything was quiet. Revin went down the stairs through the empty, abandoned building and emerged into the plaza, where he found an odd tableau. People jammed the plaza. On one side, backed by ranks of well-disciplined soldiers, stood the Baron. Encircled by hundreds of unruly, ebullient farm workers, Lidja and Darkpony were speaking with him.

"What you're requesting is … extraordinary," the Baron said.

"It is not!" Lidja said, standing toe-to-toe with the Baron and fixing him with a fierce stare. "It's fundamental to what we require. There must be an equal voice for common people."

Revin walked up and put his arm around Lidja, who shrieked with relief and hugged Revin for all she was worth.

A huge cheer went up among the farm workers.

"Revin! Revin! Revin!" they chanted.

"What she said," Revin said. "We have two demands. The system of indenture must be ended. And there must co-equal representation for common people in government."

"You know Her Majesty's mind," the Baron said. "If you are able to speak for her, we can resolve this now."

"We are victorious!" Revin shouted.

And everyone cheered.

Revin reached into his pocket and brought out the ring he had taken from the Duke's hoard. He knelt down on one knee, before an astonished Lidja, and proffered it to her.

"Lidja Relsing, I love you. Will you marry me?"

A collective gasp went up from the assembled crowd and then there was silence. The Baron grinned.

"Oh, Revin!" she squealed, hugging him. "Yes! Yes! Yes!"

Revin was engulfed by a huge roar of approval from the crowd.

•   •   •

Two days later, the *Queen of Belleriand* landed at the aerodrome on Belleriand. Will gave Revin a big hug as he readied himself to assume his duties as Chief of Staff for the Queen of Belleriand. Grip snatched Revin up and twirled him around in the air like he had for Momoire. Blushing, Revin hugged him tenderly and then tried not to cry as he descended the gangplank to step onto the soil of Belleriand. He emerged to find a gauntlet of guards in Belthingstone colors awaiting him that snapped to attention and escorted him to a coach for the short drive to Ravensbelth.

Youngman welcomed him graciously to the Belthingstone palace. Revin requested an audience with the Queen at her earliest convenience, then allowed Terrier to lead him to his chamber to freshen up and change clothes to meet with the Queen. He was still naked when she walked through the adjoining door into his room.

"Your Majesty!" Revin said, scandalized.

"Oh, Revin," she said, advancing on him and giving him a hug. "I'm so glad you're back!"

"I'm glad to be back too, Your Majesty," he said, trying to pull on some clothes.

"The prisoners arrived yesterday: The Duke of Havelock and his Seneschal."

"Good!"

"They seemed to think they had absconded with the bulk of the treasury of Havelock, yet when they arrived, there was no money."

"Huh," Revin said blushing, in spite of himself. "I guess they must have been mistaken."

"Mistaken," Queen Momoire growled. "Is that what you call that?"

"What else could have happened?" Revin asked, innocently.

"Hmm," the Queen temporized. "And I hear that, in my name, you signed off on creating some kind of government on Havelock that includes commoners? Is that true?"

"You were very enthusiastic about the idea, Your Majesty," Revin assured her.

"I can see that I'm going to need to keep you on a shorter leash," she said, scowling.

"But I did want to ask …" Revin began.

"About your horse girl?" the Queen asked with a sharp glance. "Yes, of course. By all means, you can bring her along."

"Oh, she also needs to bring her horse. A wedding present from the new Prime Minister."

"I've heard rumors about this horse already. Is it really as vicious as everyone says?"

Revin blanched, remembering both his close personal calls with the diabolical horse and seeing it trample a man to death. He grimaced.

"The rumors truly don't do it justice, Your Majesty."

"And are William and Griphon really going to stay on Havelock?"

"Yes, Your Majesty," Revin said. "And the Professor. Now that there's a government of the people, they're going to go straight and help get the new government launched."

"They're really going to give up piracy?"

"Well, they aren't 'going straight' in the other way."

"Tell me about the man who's going to be the interim Prime Minister."

"That's Hirus Darkpony. He's a good choice. He's a successful businessman and has the respect of both nobles and commoners on Havelock. He'll be a good caretaker until they can get a functional government up and running."

"Once people here get wind of this idea, they're going to demand the same."

She gave him a long, hard look. Revin just grinned.

"Yes, Your Majesty."

"Well, as long as you're here to deal with it, I guess it will be alright."

"By your grace, Your Majesty," Revin said, bowing.

SIDE QUESTS

Revin's adventure is told from his perspective; we primarily see things through his eyes. But events that impact those stories happen when he is not present. Here are three of those stories I thought readers might enjoy.

"Where There's a Will" is alluded to in "For the Favor of a Lady". This is the story of how the pirate captain Will met his first mate (and lover) Grip. This story is set several years before "Revin's Heart" begins, on the island of Candlemain.

WHERE THERE'S A WILL

ON THURSDAY, Will stood in the bow of the *Little WormMaid* as Candlemain harbor hove into view. The last of the flying fish that had escorted them over the deep water skimmed off and left him alone with his thoughts. In fact, he realized he actually was a bit lonely, and he promised himself to keep his eyes open for some fresh companionship while in town.

Under clear and sunny skies, and with a light breeze, they luffed the sail and the *WormMaid* came alongside the pier. Will sprang out and tied up the bow lines while Ham — the quartermaster — and another two of the pirate crew attended to the aft lines. After briefly conferring on assignments, Ham and his assistants headed to the market to lay in provisions for the rest of the pirates back on Kapper Island. Will paid the docking fees to the harbormaster and then tagged along behind the others, enjoying the sights and sounds and smells of market day.

Just beyond the pier, there was a bulletin board with posters and ads. Will noticed the wanted posters, including the one for himself. The sketch was terrible, and he doubted anyone would recognize him in any event. But, even if someone did, they were pretty far off the beaten track and law enforcement was not a priority here, though one still needed to watch for intelligence agents that regularly prowled neutral Candlemain. And bounty hunters.

The colorful market was bustling with women selling vegetables and fruits in the middle and the men around the periphery selling fish and meat. Still, it seemed a little thin — there were fewer vendors than usual. Will wondered if there was something else taking place on island. Most of the sellers were the regulars, but Will's eyes were irresistibly drawn to someone he hadn't seen before.

A stranger was selling some large fish he'd evidently caught spearfishing. He was stripped to the waist, tall and well proportioned, with black hair, slicked back. Furthermore, he had a muscular physique. Very muscular. And Will spent several minutes just admiring the view. His eyes narrowed as he had the notion that something about the stranger seemed familiar. But he couldn't quite put his finger on it. It was like he'd seen him before, a long, long time ago. He shook his head. This young man, in his mid twenties, just wasn't that old.

Someone walked up to ask about one of the fish and Will stepped a little closer to hear the stranger speak.

"These are bonitos," he told the prospective buyer, who then looked puzzled. "Oh, people here usually call them 'boneheads'."

Will immediately identified his accent as upper-class Belleriand: A rich boy slumming on Candlemain. Will worked to keep the sneer off his face. He started to turn away, and then thought of something better. Repressing a grin, he found Ham and told him to finish provisioning, head back without him, and send the boat back the following day. Then Will returned and hung around unobtrusively near the stranger until he'd sold all of his fish.

Will watched wistfully as the stranger put his shirt back on. And then raised his eyebrows when the stranger looped a scabbarded sword of respectable length over his shoulder. As he started to walk away, the stranger bumped into Will. Will headed the other way, laughing, with the stranger's money pouch in his hand.

"Hey, you! Stop!" the stranger yelled, once he realized he'd been robbed.

Will set off at a lope through town. The stranger sprinted after him. Will led him through one street after another, changing direction suddenly whenever he got nearly close enough to grab him. With the balance of a dancer or acrobat, Will kept just out of reach. Finally, the stranger anticipated his next sudden direction change, but Will reached up, grabbed an awning, and pulled himself up and away from the stranger's sudden lunge. Will looked down and grinned at him, panting below.

"Don't give up, boy!" he called, cheerfully, then scaled a downspout up to the roof and set off in another direction. He loped easily to the other side and slid down the downspout and right into the arms of the stranger who had somehow gotten to the other side faster than Will had imagined possible. For a moment, Will thought he might need to use his remmer abilities, but he found a way to wriggle out. Just as the stranger's arms closed, Will slithered to the ground and rolled out between his legs and he took off running again, this time out of town and up the mountain. The stranger, muttering imprecations, followed, hot on his heels.

Will would slow down until the stranger thought he was catching up, then put on a burst of speed and stay just out of reach. As they climbed the mountain, and the grades grew steeper, he had to give the stranger credit. He was panting hard, but he wasn't giving up.

All of a sudden, Will realized he wasn't hearing the footfalls behind him. He turned his head to look back and perceived the stranger wasn't there. He caught a flash out of the corner of his eye and ducked, which was lucky or he'd have lost his head. The stranger had seen a switchback coming and sprinted up early, cutting it off, and getting ahead. Will skidded to a stop as the stranger stood *en garde* in the middle of the turn.

"Draw!" he snarled, panting.

"I don't carry a sword," Will said, cheerfully, only lightly winded.

"Then you're going to die," the stranger said, lunging forward. Will, with impeccable balance, sprang to the side, dodging the stranger's thrust, then rolled over the stranger's back as he was over-extended and off-balance.

"Hold!" called a voice. The stranger whirled around and realized five men with crossbows had him covered. And he discovered his antagonist was missing, as though he'd vanished into thin air.

"Where did your friend go?" asked the man who'd spoken before.

"He's not my friend," said the stranger. "He's a thief."

"Well, we're not your friends either. But you're coming with us. Carefully now. Sheathe your sword. That's right. Now come quietly."

The men were well disciplined and acted with military precision. They surrounded him, keeping their distance and clear firing angles, then marched him off the main path following a narrower trail cut into the brush that led off along the flank of the mountain. After a few hundred yards, they emerged into an open area with ruins — overgrown stone walls covered with vines and vegetation. Nearby, he could see squared off pits where a small army of local islanders were digging up soil with hand tools and then carting it off to be dumped into some kind of giant sieve.

"Colonel," the leader of the bowman called. "We saw two and caught this one."

"We're almost done here," the colonel said. He was a florid, beefy man with closely cropped hair. "Throw him in the well. That should hold him until we're done."

The bowmen gestured with their crossbows and he walked to where he could see a low, circular wall of stone. He looked in and could see only darkness. Suddenly, they pushed him from behind with long sticks. He overbalanced and fell. He put his hands out, skidding down into the well and managed to get his feet under him before he landed at the bottom in a mass of decaying leaves and vegetation. He checked himself over and, as far as he could tell, was only bruised and scraped with no broken bones.

After a few minutes, his eyes had accustomed to the darkness and he inspected his new demesne. It was a pit lined with smooth blocks of stone laid dry. It was small, though not so tight as to be claustrophobic or confining nor narrow enough to allow him to wedge himself between the sides to work his way up. Neither were there any cracks or crevices suitable as handholds. He sat down with his back against the wall and sighed. This was just not his day.

The afternoon passed slowly. He started to get thirsty. He tried calling up for water, but there was no answer. He could hear the sounds of some activity, but not enough to have any idea what was happening.

As darkness fell, he heard a sound from above.

"Psst!"

He looked up and saw a head framed against the sky.

"Hang on, stranger. I'm going to get you out," Will whispered. Instead, suddenly pushed from behind, Will fell cartwheeling into the well. The stranger reached up and tried to catch him, but they both tumbled into the leaves with Will coming to rest on top of the stranger.

They looked up.

"I've been waiting for you," the leader of the bowmen said. "Here! Just relax for a few more hours and we'll be gone. This will help you pass the time."

He dropped a wineskin down that Will caught.

"Get off!" the stranger said, pushing Will off and getting to his feet.

In the darkness they were both just silhouettes.

"Here. You take this," Will said, handing him the wineskin. "You must be thirsty. And, before you start trying to wave that sword around, here's your money."

"Thank you," the stranger said, politely. He took a deep swig of wine and then another then handed it to Will. Will took a small drink and closed the valve.

"I'm sorry I got you mixed up in this, whatever this is," Will said. "I only meant to have a bit of fun with you."

"A bit of fun? Is that what you call it?" the stranger said, exasperated. "What on earth possessed you to do that?"

"Honestly?" Will said. "At first, your sexy muscles just caught my eye. But then I heard you speak and ... Well, I can't resist teasing rich boys that come here to vacation."

"But I'm not on vacation. I've ... I've left that life behind," the stranger said, bitterly. "My life was perfect. I was engaged to the perfect woman. But then I lost my honor. And she dumped me."

"So, Mister Not-On-Vacation, what's your name anyway?"

"It's Griphon," he said. "Lord Griphon Belthingstone of Belleriand, at ... at your service."

"Gah!" Will said. "Don't tell me your *real* name! If you're leaving your life behind, you need a new name. You need to come up with an alias."

"What do you propose?"

"How about ... 'Beefcake'?" Will suggested.

"No," Griphon said.

"Hunk?"

"No."

"Dreamboat?"

"So, what's your name?" Griphon said, refusing to dignify any more of these suggestions with a response.

"Oh. I'm Will."

"Is that your real name?"

"As it turns out, it is," Will said. "But I'm not a nobleman, so I don't have some ancient lineage to protect."

"I ... I need another drink," Griphon said. Will handed him the wineskin, and he took another deep drink, then sat back down against the wall. Will sat on the other side.

"So, Will," Griphon said. "How are we going to get out of here?"

"Oh, don't worry your pretty little head about that," Will said. "We'll think of something. I'm more curious about these men. Who are they? What are they doing here?"

"I'm pretty sure they're from Havelock," Griphon said. "It looks like an archeological dig. But their behavior is suspicious."

"You know something about archeology then?"

"No. Not really," Griphon said. "But I know someone who does."

"What strikes you as suspicious?"

"Well, their security, for one. This looks like a military operation. It looks to me like they came here in secret for something specific, they found it, and now they're trying to sneak it off island before they get caught."

"I agree," Will said. "Not that I'm totally against such behavior. But they pushed me in here without asking! Now if they'd asked me if I wanted to be trapped in a well with a hunk like you for a few hours, I probably would have said yes, anyway. But that's neither here nor there."

"We're stuck in a well and yet you're still trying to hit on me," Griphon stated, rolling his eyes.

"Whatever works, honey," Will said, batting his eyes. But the effect was lost in the dark. "Am I making any progress?"

"I'm sure I've not had enough to drink for this," Griphon said, taking another deep drink of wine. And then another.

Will had been keeping an eye on the sky and noticed immediately when he saw a remmer's towline move across the sky through the opening.

"Well," he said to Griphon. "I think it's about time for us to go see what's happening up there."

"Oh! So, now you're ready!" he asked, by now more than a little drunk on the wine. "Well, just how do you propose we get out?"

"Come over here," Will said, putting on a monocle. "Put your arm around my waist. Ooh! You're a big one! I guess we should do this then."

Suddenly two towlines sparked into view, one for each of them, and Will showed Griphon how to run up the wall until the towline had drawn them up out of the well.

Griphon looked at Will with utter astonishment. Will grinned at him, well pleased.

"You're a remmer!"

"Well, yeah."

"You could have done that anytime!" Griphon said, not a little vexed.

"Duh."

"But you can make *two* towlines at the same time!" Griphon, said, still working it out.

"Yeah?"

"I didn't even think that was possible!"

Will reached up and cupped his face.

"Just wait, sweetheart."

They looked out over the archeological dig. The locals had been dismissed, the pits abandoned, and all of the tents and equipment stowed. A huge, gray, dirigible airship was just coming to rest with the military personnel standing at attention in formation waiting to board. Will began walking that way.

"Are you nuts?" Griphon asked. "They're going to see you."

"Oh, I'm not much worried about that," Will said.

Will let out a sharp whistle and suddenly there were whistles from three other sides and Candlemain guardsmen emerged from the brush on three sides.

"Where did these guards come from?" Griphon asked, amazed.

"Oh. After I saw where they put you, I figured you'd be okay for a bit and went back to town and alerted the guards to what was going on up here. But I told them to wait until I got you out before moving in."

The colonel directed his small detachment of military personnel to take positions to repel the advancing guards while the handful of archeologists hustled several crates on board the airship.

"They're going to get away, Will!" Griphon said.

"No," Will said. "They're not going anywhere."

The Colonel boarded the airship, abandoning his men, and the towlines shifted their attachments, causing the airship to begin to rise. Suddenly, big attachments appeared all across the airship pulling it down and smashing it to the ground. Griphon counted nine.

"Are you making all those?" he asked, bewildered.

"Yeah."

"But ... That's not possible!"

"Oh, really? Watch this!" Will said.

Four more huge towlines appeared, bigger than Griphon had ever seen, two at the bow and two at the aft end of the airship, that were nearly parallel to the ground. The airship seemed to elongate for a moment and then with a shriek, the fabric gave way and the airship collapsed to the ground as the envelope was torn apart and the gasbags escaped into the sky, leaving the airship a heap of wood and canvas on the ground. Griphon looked at Will, dumbfounded.

"Now you're just showing off," he said. Will raised his arms over his head and flexed his muscles, tickled to impress his crush.

"Okay. Now why don't you put on your noble hat for a minute and talk to the leader of the guards for me," Will said. "Tell him who to contact about the archeology stuff."

"But ... But I'm ... I'm not ... I'm supposed to be ..." Griphon stuttered.

"I only got them to come here because I said an important nobleman had been kidnapped. Now, just run along and play the part for a minute."

Will sat down on the low wall of a ruin while Griphon walked over to the guardsmen who were putting the surrendered guards into chains, and found their chief.

"Thank you, Commander. I'm Lord Belthingstone of Belleriand," Griphon said, assuming an air of authority. "I am very satisfied with your work this night. I will commend your efforts when I next speak with his Majesty. In the meantime, you should contact Prince Stewart on Harway to take charge of the artifacts these dogs from Havelock were trying to appropriate."

The commander was obsequious in his gratitude and bowed deeply to Griphon.

Griphon returned to Will.

"Now what?" he asked.

"Got any plans for the night?" Will said. "Let's go to Mama Kane's. C'mon!"

They strolled back toward town.

"So, why do you hate nobles so much?" Griphon asked, after a few moments silence.

"I didn't grow up fancy, like you," Will said. "When nobles discovered what I could do, they tried to profit from me. Once I realized how much wealth they had, compared to the rest of us, I decided I would no longer serve. So I went pirate."

"That all sounds very romantic," Griphon said, "But not very realistic."

"It's better than being a fisherman," Will snorted. "Believe me. I know all about that."

Will led them through the plaza toward Mama Kane's. He kept sneaking glances at Griphon as he anticipated with relish the pleasant evening to come. As they walked by the alley that went along the side of the building, two men leapt out and shoved a bag over Will's head and dragged him struggling into the shadows. Three other men confronted Griphon with their swords drawn.

"We're turning the pirate in for the money," one said. "Just keep walking and you won't get hurt."

Griphon turned, as if to walk past, then in one smooth motion drew his sword and cut down the man on the left before he could react, then set himself *en garde* for the other two. One charged him to keep him engaged while the other tried to circle around behind, but the first discovered he was overmatched and fell in seconds at the first pass. Griphon then turned and crossed swords with the last of the three who realized he was facing someone of vastly superior skill. In a twinkling, he blanched, turned tail, and fled.

Griphon walked into the alley with his sword drawn and found the other two men trying to bind Will's arms while he struggled with the sack over his head. Seeing Griphon advancing with bloodied sword and grim expression caused them to panic. They abandoned their efforts and fled into the night.

Will pulled the sack off his head and looked at Griphon with embarrassment.

"Thank you," he said. "I must be losing my grip to let them just walk up and grab me like that. I'd hate to think what would have happened if you hadn't been here."

Then Will perked up and took Griphon's arm.

"Hey! I may be losing my grip, but maybe I've found a new Grip!"

"What?"

"You! That's your new name! Grip!"

"Grip," he mused. "I guess that could work."

They walked out of the alley, where they encountered guardsmen drawn by the sounds of combat. Grip played the nobleman again and had the guards bowing and apologizing for the unsafe conditions of the streets. They quickly assured Grip he was in no way to blame for defending himself against ruffians. While Grip was occupied, Will slipped into the office and quickly whispered something to Mama Kane. Grip came in a moment later.

"Oh, my," she said, looking him up and down. "He's a big one!"

"Grip, please allow me to introduce Mama Kane," Will said.

"How do you do, ma'am," Grip said, politely.

She came out from behind her counter and gave Grip a bone-crushing hug that left him breathless.

"Just call me Mama, you hear?"

After saying goodnight, Will led Grip up three flights of stairs to the top floor of the Inn and down to the very end of the hallway, where there was a door with a big heart on it.

"The honeymoon suite?" Grip asked, rolling his eyes. "Really?"

"Come in and check it out!" Will said, opening the door and holding it for him. "I stayed here once before."

Inside was a heart shaped bed. There were red velvet curtains and a bouquet of red roses on the table. Will drew a set of curtains back revealing a door that led out to a spacious region of the roof with a pergola covered with flowering vines that overlooked the small town and the harbor. They stood together under the bower with the land breeze in their faces, looking out over the lights of the town, the dark and quiet harbor, and the vastness of the ocean beyond.

"It's beautiful," Grip said. Will put his hand on Grip's back.

"So are you," Will said. "I don't know what happened or why she left you, but she was a fool. Have you ever been with a man before?"

"Yes," Grip said. "The one who knows about archeology? We ... did things together. For a while."

There was a quiet tapping at the door and Will stepped away for a moment, returning with a bottle of sparkling wine and two glasses. He popped the cork with a flourish and poured two glasses.

"To us!" Will said, raising his glass.

"To us," Grip agreed.

They clinked glasses and sipped the rather sweet, bubbly wine. Will leaned up against Grip.

"Dinner now?" Will asked. "Or dinner later?"

"Later, I think," Grip said.

"Later it is."

After a last sip, Will took the glasses, and set them on the table. Then he took Grip's hand and led him back into the honeymoon suite. Gently kicking the door closed, he put his arms around Grip's neck and, stretching up, pressed his lips to Grip's mouth as he pulled him toward the bed.

"Curtain's Rise", described in "Storm Clouds Gather", is set twenty-five years before the events in that story, when Will is but a young man. The story describes his initial encounter with Lord Curtiss Belthingstone, the man who would become Grip's father — and the Butcher Baron of Belleriand.

CURTAINS RISE

LYING TOGETHER in a tangle of limbs, Will and Grip cuddled together in the darkness.

"Hey! Hey!" Grip said, tapping Will on the chest. "So what was that name you used with my father?"

Will groaned and turned his head to look at Grip.

"Do you really want to know?"

"Why would I not want to know?"

"Okay. If I'm gonna tell the story, I'm going to need a drink. Or maybe two. Oh! Hang on!" Will said, getting up and rummaging around in his trunk. He came up with a dusty bottle of rum. He showed it to Grip.

"Kalanova?" Grip asked.

"He gave it to me all those years ago. It's supposed to be something special. I've been carrying it around waiting for the right moment to open it. And I think the moment has come."

He cut the seal, pulled the cork out, and poured a generous shot.

"Want one?" he asked. Grip shook his head.

"Suit yourself," Will said. He took a big sip and then began to speak.

•　　•　　•

I was an ignorant, graceless 17-year old with a talent for getting into trouble. I grew up poor in a miserable fishing village. After I ran away from home, I worked in the kitchens of an inn for a while. That was where I met Balthazar, who helped me discover and begin to use my talent for being a remmer. I thought I was smartest, coolest, and bestest. I was so stupid.

Balthazar had given me a letter of introduction and got me a place as a remmer on an airship. But I didn't like being at the bottom and having to work my way up. So I'd quit that and had been working odd jobs in the capital of Ironton.

This was all before the war with Woodseer. I was born on Ironton and I hated it. But I hated Woodseer too. And I especially hated the soldiers that were everywhere during the war. I hated pretty much everyone and everything.

Then I met the Hyena — I never knew his real name — he was the guy who helped me discover that I could assassinate people using my skill as a remmer. Balthazar must have known that such a thing was possible, but he'd never taught me how to do that. All I had to do was get close. If I could get close enough to a target, I could attach a towline to them and send them up into the sky: what goes up must come down, after all. But I didn't have to see that part. It just seemed like good, clean fun to an angry teenager. Make a towline and watch an enemy sail off into the sky never to be seen again. Oh, I was so stupid!

•　　•　　•

Will, who had been speaking compulsively for a few minutes, looked pale from having to revisit these painful memories and remember the things he had done. Grip put his arms around him, pulled him into his lap, and kissed him on top of his head. Will poured himself another big shot, took another swallow, and continued.

•   •   •

Well, one day, they were ready for me. I skyhooked this guy in a downtown plaza and they closed off all the exits to the plaza, arrested everyone, and sent us to a prisoner camp. I probably could have escaped earlier, but I knew that once they'd gotten a look at me, I would probably be on the run. I thought they couldn't figure out who I was from among so many people. I was wrong.

They put hoods on everyone, marched us into the camp, and then brought people one by one into a cell and started beating the crap out of them until they confessed. Once someone confessed, they took them out to the yard and hung them. I don't know how many people they hung before they reached me. But I had pissed my pants before they even came to get me.

I had seen enough by this point to know that if they got me in that room, they would beat me until I confessed and then they'd hang me. So I had decided I was going to make a break for it.

They finally came to get me. Once they pulled the hood off me, I skyhooked the two guys that were holding my arms and then made a towline to leap to the top of the fence.

Like I said, they were ready for me. I should have been dead. There were two guys with crossbows aimed right at me when I hit the top of the wall. But this big guy — another prisoner who was in the camp — slammed into them and threw off their aim. I got over the wall and ran for it.

At first, I was ecstatic to have gotten away. Still, I figured they'd gotten a good enough look at me to identify me and so I was getting set to make a run for it. But I kept thinking about that guy. I knew they must be furious at him and he was probably suffering — and maybe dead — for my stupidity. So, after a few hours, I decided I was going to go back and try to get that guy out.

Why? I didn't ... I still don't know why. It was stupid. I had gotten away clean. What did I care what happened to him? Maybe it was me starting to grow a conscience. I'd hardly even gotten a look at the guy. He was a big guy. Military. That was almost all I'd noticed. But once I'd decided something, there was no stopping me.

I borrowed some wire cutters from a shop where I'd run some errands before. And after dark, I approached the camp. I came at it from the far side away from the town, where there was a low hill near the camp. I wriggled up through the grass and found a good viewpoint where I could look down into the camp, from nearly the same level as the watchtower.

I watched for a couple of hours to get a sense of the activities of the guards. I noticed the numbers of guards who circulated around the camp and their routes. I looked for where there were dark areas and shadows around the perimeter of the camps. And I watched the men in the watchtower too.

I still wasn't sure where they might be holding the big guy when I suddenly saw him being dragged out of the interrogation chamber. They'd been working him over for a long time. Men on either side were holding him up as he stumbled, only semiconscious. They took him over to one of the kilns they were using as punishment cells and pushed him inside.

The camp had been constructed out of this old factory that had made charcoal for the smelters and there were these rows of stone kilns that they threw people into as a kind of torture.

The one they threw him into was one of those closest to the fence, which encouraged me. And it wasn't that far from one of the places where the shadows were deepest near the fence. So I backed down off the hill and began to make my way around the hill to the right.

I crawled the last hundred yards up to the fence, pulled out the wire cutters and cut through the bottom three strands of wire, which I hoped would be enough for the big guy to get through. Then, I waited until a circulating guard went by, slipped inside, and went up to the kiln.

There was a lock on the door, but I'd learned to pick locks as a kid, so that was no obstacle. I opened the door and slipped inside. There was an unbelievable stench of burned wood, unwashed body, and human waste.

"Hey, mister," I said. "Can you move?"

"Who are you?" he said, groaning and trying to struggle to his feet.

"I'm here to get you out," I said. "Can you move?"

"Are you that kid?" he said, peering at me in the darkness.

"I'm not a kid," I said angrily.

"Whatever you say, boy," he said, on his feet and checking himself over.

"Follow me," I said, opening the door and leading him back toward the fence. We were through the fence before a shout went up from the watchtower. I started running and he followed close on my heels. I turned to the left and headed toward a little canyon I knew that was north and east of town.

"Don't go that way!" the guy warned. "It's a box canyon. We're going to get trapped."

"Don't worry," I said. "I know a way out."

I heard him snort because he didn't believe me. But he followed me anyway.

After another five minutes we reached the end of the canyon. We could hear the sounds of pursuit approaching, but they weren't in view.

"Okay, genius," he said. "Where's the exit?"

"Here," I said. "Put your arm around me."

"What?" he said.

"Do it!" I said. Then I made two towlines and showed him how to run up the cliff at the end of the canyon. Once we jumped over the top, I cut the two lines, and we looked back as our pursuers arrived at the cliff, utterly bewildered at how we could have vanished from under their noses.

"That's a good trick, boy," he said. "And you can make two towlines at once? That's a pretty rare ability."

"I had a good teacher," I said. "He could make even more."

He put his feet together and bowed to me.

"I thank thee for thy care of me," he said formally, then continued. "I mean it. I really appreciate you coming back to get me out."

The way he said it made me feel embarrassed, but also a little angry.

"We're even," I said. "You saved me and I saved you."

"We're even," he said, holding out his hand. After a moment, I took it and he crushed my hand with his handshake.

"I need to get back to my men," he said. "Unless you need something."

"I'm good," I said. "I have to go see someone too."

He started to walk away, then stopped, and turned back for a moment.

"Just one thing, boy: Be careful," he said. "I got a pretty good look at you. That means they got a good look at you too. If I were you, I wouldn't go back to my regular routine or haunts. They probably know who you are by now. If you do, they'll catch you again. And — take my word for it — it's not much fun."

He waved before I could say anything, and in a moment, had faded into the brush and vanished.

I turned the other way and headed back toward town. I decided to meet up with the man who'd been paying me to assassinate people and tell him I was done.

I arrived at his address in the early morning. He lived on an estate that was set back from the road. There was a gate at the road that was manned by several guards who took my name and then sent a runner to the main house to inquire. After a few minutes, the runner returned, they conferred for a minute then opened the gate.

"Come in. Follow me," the man said, leading me to the main house.

It was a mansion — almost a palace. I had never seen such a thing before. It had huge windows and several wings going off in different directions. He led me into an interior courtyard where the Hyena was having breakfast in a beautiful garden, by an artificial waterfall, of all things.

"Hey, William," he said. "I thought we'd agreed to not meet here."

"I got picked up yesterday," I told him. "I got away, but they got a pretty good look at me. They're going to be looking for me, so I need to leave town."

"That's too bad," he said. "I've still got a bunch more targets that I was counting on you to take out for me."

"It's not going to happen," I told him. "I barely got away this time. I'm done."

He made a gesture and I realized almost too late what he was doing. The guy who'd led me over had gotten up behind me and had quietly drawn a knife and was ready to stick me in the back. But I made a towline and smashed him into the overhang that surrounded the interior garden. Then I did the same to the Hyena when he tried to yell. Then his girlfriend came in and screamed and, without thinking, I killed her too. And then, surrounded by dead bodies, I truly panicked and started running.

•　　•　　•

Will choked up, overwhelmed by painful memories, and stopped talking for a minute to drain and refill his glass. Then he wiped his eyes and Grip held him close while he continued to unburden himself.

•　　•　　•

I ran through the mansion looking for another way out. I was just a poor kid and seeing the opulence of the mansion made me sick and angry. He had sculptures and paintings and suits of armor in the hallways. I was furious that this scumbag had all this money while kids like me grew up poor and hungry.

Eventually, I found a door out and found myself by his zoo. The bastard had his own private zoo! With big cats! And a bear! And who knows what else. I wandered through the grounds in a state of shock. Farther back, I found where he had a yacht tied up. And not far away, there was a gigantic hangar where he had his own private airship. And not some little one! It was bigger than the *Queen*!

Eventually, I found the wall around his compound. I made a towline to get over it and started walking back to town. I realized I was walking away empty handed. I debated whether I should go back and try to look for some money or something of value to take. But I couldn't bring myself to go back in there.

Without really thinking, I was walking back to the boarding house where I had a room. I was coming up toward the building, when I noticed the curtain in my window move. I stopped up short and slipped over to the edge of the sidewalk and began looking at the people around the building. I spotted at least four people who seemed like they might be loitering around just watching the entrance of the building.

I backed away, then turned, and walked briskly in the other direction. I wasn't sure where to go, so I just walked around for a bit, but finally decided to go to Bruno's.

Bruno ran a nondescript, run-down tavern that catered to … well, to men who, like me, are attracted to other men. I had worked there in the kitchens for a while when I first came to the capital. And I'd also picked up the odd trick now and then. There were a lot of older men who liked small, young men like me — and would pay good money for a night's company.

·   ·   ·

Will patted Grip's face and kissed his forehead.

"Please don't look at me that way, my love!"

"I just had no idea," Grip said, closing his mouth. "I never knew any of this about you."

Will refilled his glass yet again and continued.

•　　•　　•

I walked into Bruno's and who did I see but the big guy I'd rescued from the prisoner camp. He was sitting by himself, watching the door for people coming in. I grinned and strutted over to him.

"I didn't know you swung this way," I said, with a leer.

"Sometimes," he said. "But right now I'm waiting for someone."

I started to say something else clever, when the door opened and a rough looking man with an eye patch came in. The big man shrank back in his seat.

"What is it?" I asked.

"That's the guy who turned me in. If he sees me, it'll be bad."

Without asking permission, I straddled his legs, seated myself on his lap, and pressed my mouth to his.

•　　•　　•

"Wait, wait, wait," Grip said.

He snatched the bottle of Kalanova away and poured himself a double. He downed it in one swallow and then poured himself another.

"Okay," he said, closing his eyes and gritting his teeth. "You can go ahead now."

•　　•　　•

I kissed him for a long, long moment, then broke off and put my mouth next to his ear, keeping my head between his face and the man with the eye patch.

"Is he still there?"

"He's … He's looking this way again."

I kissed him again, and this time he returned my kiss, wrapping his arms around me, and forcing his tongue into my mouth. I felt my body respond — and could feel his body responding too. Then he pushed me away.

"Okay," he said. "He's gone."

"Are you just going to leave it at that?" I asked, with a bit of a sneer.

"How old are you, boy?" he asked.

"Old enough to know better than to answer a question like that," I said, huffily.

He grinned and tousled my hair, which infuriated me.

"Look, boy," he said. "I must be twice your age. I'm married. And I've got one kid already and another on the way."

I got my back up because my pride was offended and I was getting ready to say or do something I'm sure I would have regretted. But at that moment, the man came in that he'd been waiting for. He was another big military guy.

"Hey, Curtains!" he said, when he saw the big guy. "Bad news. Woodseer is moving into the town from the south. They're killing everything that moves. And Ironton is hanging back to the north. It's like they want them to do it."

"We need to get the fuck out of here," the big man, Curtains, said. From the deference the other man showed, Curtains was obviously the commander.

"Hey, boy," he said, looking at me.

I was still angry and sulking from his rejection of my advances and I started to say something angry and stupid, when he knelt down in front of me to bring his face close to mine.

"I'm sorry," he said, looking into my eyes with his penetrating gaze. "I'm sorry I hurt your feelings. I like you. And if things were different, I would have enjoyed letting that go farther. But I don't have the luxury of that right now. And you don't either. If you stay here, you're going to end up dead. We need to get out of here somehow. Do you want to come with us?"

My emotions warred with me and left me tongue tied. But then we heard and yells and screams from outside.

"C'mon Curtains!" the guy at the door yelled.

"What's your name, boy?" he asked.

"William," I told him.

"This is Roughneck," he said, with a grin. "C'mon."

We ran to the door, but when we looked out we saw formations of soldiers moving through the streets and a number of bodies lying in the street.

"This way," I said. I led them back through the kitchens and out the back door, which opened into a narrow alley. I led them along the alley and then down another that led away from the main street.

"Where are we trying to go?" I asked.

"My men were guarding the museum," Curtains said. "Until they got everything out."

"We've pulled back," Roughneck said. "We're currently in defilade at the east side of town. I was just making one last check for you."

"Follow me," I said. And I led them through back streets until we reached the eastern outskirts of town.

Curtains and Roughneck led the way through an open field to a line of trees planted as a windbreak between fields. As we got closer, I could see men concealed among the trees. There were twenty or twenty-five men altogether, including Curtains and Roughneck.

"How are we going to get out of here?" Roughneck asked.

"You've got me," Curtains said. "We need an airship. But I don't see how we get to the aerodrome from here."

"I know where there's an airship," I said.

"With a crew?" Roughneck asked.

"I don't know about a crew," I admitted.

"We don't need a crew," Curtains said, jerking his thumb at me. "We've got him."

The men were obviously pleased to have Curtains returned to them. He brought me over, introduced me, and asked me to describe where we were going. When I briefly described the estate, he asked me to make a sketch in the dirt to identify landmarks and develop a plan. Then the unit decamped and moved out toward the estate.

We left the men concealed just out of sight of the gate while Curtains asked me to follow him. We went a short distance away and I made towlines to get us over the wall.

We crept toward the guardhouse. Curtains, who had evidently rearmed himself when he met up with his men, brought out a wicked-looking knife, and bashed in the door of the guardhouse and sprang inside. But it was abandoned. After finding the body of the Hyena, the guards must have scarpered off. We unlocked the gate and let the rest of the company in.

The house was standing open and appeared to have been ransacked by the fleeing guards. Most of the sculptures were smashed. Drawers had been pulled out of all the cabinets and dumped out on the floor. In just a few hours, the place had gone from showpiece to disaster zone.

Curtains spotted something and went into one room, returning a moment later with an unopened bottle of rum, which he handed to me.

"This is a bottle of Kalanova — it's a famous rum," he said. "but you can't get it anymore since the distillery burned down. You should save it for something special someday."

Farther along in the house, Curtains seemed almost physically hurt to see the smashed sculptures.

"Irreplaceable," he sighed, pointing at one. "This one was famous. I took a class once that had a whole lesson about that one sculpture."

I led them on through the estate until I found the door out. When I went to exit, I found that the zoo had been opened and the animals were gone.

"Someone's let the animals out," I said. "Watch out!"

The animals knew better than to come around people, but I didn't know that then.

We walked on toward the hangar. I noticed that the yacht was also gone — the guards had probably taken that when they left. But I was relieved to discover the airship was still there.

The name painted on it was *Silique*. She was small for a rigid-hulled airship, but still massive. She was painted gray and blue with yellow lines and markings.

"Whoa. What a beauty!" Curtains said when he saw her. "She was made on Harway. I recognize the workmanship. This Hyena might have been a bastard, but he had good taste."

Curtains conducted a quick inspection of the aircraft. Afterward, he directed his men to bring their packs on-board then take positions fore and aft to release the mooring lines. He walked with me to the remmer deck.

"I never tried to do this all by myself before," I admitted, nervously.

"You'll need to help keep us down until we get clear of the building," he said. "Then hold until we get the men on board."

"I'll do my best," I said.

Curtains stepped forward to the cockpit.

"Ready!" he called. "Release the moorings!"

The *Silique* lurched as I made first one towline, then leapt over and made a second on the other side. She heeled over for a moment, then righted herself and crept forward as the moorings were released.

"Lower! Lower!" the men called, as she began to rise and then men were clinging to the ropes to try to hold her down.

"Can you bring it lower, William?" Curtains asked.

"I'll try!" I said. I had to drop the towlines to make new ones, and the *Silique* jumped even higher for a moment, lifting some of the men off the ground. They cheered with relief when the new towlines brought her back down and they pulled with a will to get her out of the hangar. And once she was clear, they boarded.

"Take us aloft!" Curtains called back.

"What heading?" I called.

"Two hundred thirty degrees," he called.

I shifted the attachments as the *Silique* rose into the sky, turned, and we began to make way toward the southwest.

"Can we go any faster?" he asked.

"I'll try," I said again. And I shifted attachments once more, making the biggest towlines I could. It's a funny thing. Even a relatively small towline is enough to kill someone. But to move an airship requires real power.

The men cheered when they could feel the *Silique* pick up speed and again when they could see the coast approaching.

"Curtains!" Roughneck called from the observation deck. "There are two airships closing on us."

"What are the bearings?" Curtains asked calmly.

"One's at 10 degrees and the other's ... 170."

"Adjust heading to 270. Full speed."

I looked for the strongest etheric streams I could find that were going that way and shifted my attachments again. The *Silique* turned and ran, now over the ocean, but still they came on.

"Curtains! They're closing in! Should we call for quarters?"

Suddenly I felt his hand on my back and he whispered in my ear.

"Have you ever tried making more attachments?"

"I did three once," I said.

"Try for four," he said.

I swallowed and keeping the two existing attachments I had, I made a third. Then I tried making the fourth and failed. The *Silique* began to turn to port. Keeping the existing attachments up, I tried again. And again. Finally, dredging down someplace deep inside myself, I tried one more time and the fourth towline snapped into existence. The *Silique* straightened out, heading due west.

"They've stopped gaining!" Roughneck called. "They're falling behind!"

There was another big round of cheers and Curtains clapped me on the shoulders.

Two hours later, with constant sustained focus to keep the four attachments up, the other airships finally gave up the pursuit and turned back. I took a deep breath and let the two other attachments drop. Curtains brought me water and food. And a chamber pot to relieve myself since, if I left the remmer deck, the *Silique* would lose her attachments and begin to drift on the wind.

"Where are we going?" I asked. "How long do I need to do this?"

"Our best bet is Belleriand," he said. "It's going to take another ten to twelve hours."

"I was already up all night," I said. "I'm not sure I can make it."

"I'll help," he said. And he did.

He got me talking. He asked me thoughtful questions. I rambled talking about growing up poor. The petty, narrow-mindedness of people in a small, isolated fishing community. The fights I got into with the other kids when I'd made the mistake of admitting I was attracted to men. The treatment I got from my father who thought he could beat it out of me. The liberation I felt when I ran away as a kid and started working in the kitchens.

He told me about himself too, though he was clearly guarded about what he revealed. When I talked about the inn, he mentioned a similar inn he'd stayed at one time for some family gathering. And when I talked about fishing, he described going spearfishing on the reef before. And he told me about the mercenary force he'd organized after his military service that took on various jobs to rescue or secure people or, like in this case, cultural treasures. He told an amusing story about rescuing a library that was in the path of a mob.

"Why do they call you 'Curtains'?" I asked.

"Oh, that's just ..."

"I'll tell you," Roughneck said, overhearing my question and coming back to the remmer deck. "In the Academy, whenever another team was matched up against his and they saw who it was, they'd groan and say, 'Oh, no! It's Curtains for us!'"

It made me laugh out loud and then I looked at Curtains and he was blushing furiously, which only made me laugh harder.

If I needed anything, he was there in a twinkling to fetch and carry. He brought me more food and water. And coffee. And a warm jacket when I started to shiver. But, little by little, I was starting to fade.

I talked until I was hoarse. I talked about my anger and my dreams and my fury at how the world worked. I talked about my revulsion at the nobles who had everything and controlled everything. And my one commitment to make sure that I never let them take advantage of me or profit from me ever again. And he listened, without judgment.

I began to nod off when all of a sudden he gave me a little slap and shocked me back awake. And that was good for another half hour. But then I started to nod off again on my feet.

I felt something warm and wet and realized he was kissing me. I felt his tongue touch mine and press inside my mouth. I woke up as I felt my body responding to his.

"You can do this," he whispered, holding my face between his hands. "We're almost there. Hang in there!"

I started to nod off again but then I felt his hand reach down inside my breeches and begin to stroke me. That woke me right up. And my eyes popped open and stayed open, as he kept me in a state of heightened stimulation and arousal.

"Land!" Roughneck called. "I can see the coast!"

"You can start to take us down, William," he said, gently.

Twenty minutes later, we descended to the aerodrome in Campshire on the north coast of Belleriand. Once the mooring lines were engaged, he scooped me up into a princess carry and that was the last thing I remembered as I collapsed, asleep in his arms.

I awoke naked and warm in a comfortable bed with crisp fresh sheets. I stretched, touched someone, and realized I wasn't alone in the bed. Curtains was asleep next to me, naked. He woke up when I touched him. He yawned, rolled over on one elbow, and looked at me.

"Good morning," he said. "Well, it's almost noon."

"Did you? Did I? Did we?" I squeaked, trying to remember what had happened.

"We didn't do anything," he said. "But if you want to, I'm here now."

He reached over and stroked my face.

"What you did was really impressive," he said. "I don't know that anyone else could have done what you just did. And so you've earned whatever I can do for you."

I reached over and ...

•   •   •

"Okay, okay," Grip said, interrupting and pouring yet another shot and downing it quick. "Okay. I think I've heard enough now."

"There's not much more to tell," Will said kindly. "But I'll skip ahead a bit."

•   •   •

"What happens now," I asked, much later.

"As much as I would love to have you join our mercenary band for your amazing skills, we work for nobles," he said. "So I don't think that would be a good fit for you. I respect your commitment. You should always be true to yourself."

"That's easy to say, but I came through this whole episode with nothing," I said bitterly.

"What are you saying?" he said. "You've got your own airship."

"What are you talking about?" I said. "It's stolen."

"Not according to this paperwork," he said, handing me a leather document case.

I sat there, stunned for several long moments.

"Okay, but how am I supposed to keep an airship running?" I said. "I don't have any money — I don't even have a change of clothes."

"Well, you're not entirely out of money. My men agreed that your service to us entitled you to a full share."

Curtains handed me a full purse that was heavy with reggies. It was more money — a lot more money — than I had ever seen in one place before. I sat there, stunned, again. This time, I had no more quick rejoinders.

"I suggest you go to Candlemain," he said. "If you want to be independent of the aristocracy, that might be a place to make a start."

"Just who are you, anyway?" I asked, eyes narrowing. "You're some kind of noble, aren't you?"

"Oh, no," he said. "I'm just a simple soldier. A second son. A nobody."

"Yeah, right," I snorted.

•　　•　　•

Will smiled to see that Grip had fallen asleep from all the rum. He took the glass from his nerveless fingers, drained it, and then stroked his hair gently.

"When I first saw you on Candlemain, I thought you looked familiar. And you do. You look so much like him."

Will bent down and kissed Grip's forehead. He stirred, but did not wake up.

"I loved him too. But I love you more."

Will set the bottle and glasses aside, then curled up with his First Mate and went to sleep.

"Riva's Escape" is Revin's origin story. When "Revin's Heart" begins, he has already left home and transitioned from female to male. This story describes the events that immediately precede those in "Revin's Heart" and how he came to be where he is when we meet him at the beginning of the book.

RIVA'S ESCAPE

"RIVA!" HER MOTHER SHOUTED when she caught sight of her clothes, covered in mud and burrs. "Those were your good clothes! Go change right now and bring those to me."

Riva's mother was a short, stout, barrel of a woman with stiff, wiry gray hair. She had worked at home for 30 years keeping house and raising children. Riva was the youngest of seven, though all but one of her siblings had now moved out.

"Yes, Mother," Riva said. She took the bread she'd been sent to the bakery for and put it in the kitchen. Then went to her alcove, where her bed was, and pulled the curtain.

She stripped off her dress and pulled on her nightshirt, figuring she was done going out for the day. And knowing what was likely to happen when her father got home.

She carried the dress to her mother, who muttered angrily while soaking the dress in a tub with the water she had been heating on the stove for dinner.

"You just don't understand," she said to Riva after a few minutes. "Your father works hard to provide for you to have nice clothes to wear and yet you act as though his work means nothing."

"That's not true," Riva protested. "It's just that ..."

"No excuses!" her mother snapped. "This was your choice. You *could* have made a different choice. You *would* have made a different choice if you cared to."

"Yes, Mother," Riva sighed.

"Now, while I'm having to do this, you can fetch more water, set the table, and mind that the stew doesn't burn on the stove."

Riva returned to the kitchen and lifted the lid of the pot. Her mother had prepared a stew with potatoes and carrots, seasoned with sausage — though there was not much actual meat in the stew. Riva stirred the stew so that it wouldn't scorch. She replaced the lid then collected 4 plates, glasses, and sets of silverware and began setting them out on the table, along with the bread she'd picked up. After the table was set, she returned to the kitchen, stirred the stew again, and then got a pitcher and kettle which she carried out to the pump by the back door to fill. She primed the pump with the bucket, then pumped until the water ran cold, refilled the bucket, and then filled the pitcher and kettle to carry back.

When she returned, she found that her father had returned and was speaking with her mother.

She put the kettle on to boil and stirred the stew while awaiting the inevitable with barely-suppressed terror.

"Riva!" he called finally. With dread, Riva walked over to her father.

He was a large man with powerful shoulders, short, cropped hair, and still covered with coal dust from the mine.

"Tell me how you got your dress dirty," he said.

"Some boys told me I was a stupid girl," Riva explained. "So I called them names and when they chased me, I led them into a thicket where I knew I could get through but they'd be too big. And then ..."

She paused, reluctant to continue.

"Tell me the rest," he prompted.

"Then I threw dirt clods on them," Riva finished.

"Yep, this is the same story I heard," he said. "At least you didn't lie to me this time. Pull your shirt up and bend over."

Riva did as she was directed.

"Pull your panties down," her father ordered.

Face burning with shame, Riva pulled her panties down and waited, trembling, until her father began to spank her. Although it was painful, the humiliation was the worst part.

After ten strokes, he said, "Now go to bed without supper and think about what you did."

Riva pulled the curtain closed and laid down on the bed — on her stomach. She could smell the food and, after she heard her older brother come home, she heard the chairs scrape in the dining room as they sat down to their meal. Riva's stomach growled and she broke down crying in the dark at the unfairness of the world.

After everyone had finished dinner, Riva was still lying in bed feeling sorry for herself when her brother quietly slid a book under the curtain while walking by.

Girls weren't allowed to go to school beyond the fifth year, but her brother had been slipping her his schoolbooks and other books that he would check out from the library for her. With her quick mind, she could read something once and understand it. In this way, she had managed to educate herself to the extent possible. But she needed to light her lamp to read and it was necessary to wait until her parents had gone to sleep before using the lamp. While she waited, she picked up the book to feel its weight, estimate the number of pages, and then dream in the dark about all of the places it might take her.

After an hour, the house became quiet and she cautiously lighted her lamp. It was a book about the history of Harway. She opened the book and began to devour it. It was fascinating to read about distant places and people. She was utterly engrossed when the curtain was suddenly yanked back and her father stood over her in his nightshirt, his face flushed with anger.

"Reading?" he said. "You're a girl. There's no call for you to waste our oil reading at night."

He snatched the book away, swatted Riva on the head with it, then grabbed her and sat down on her bed with her over his knee and began to paddle her with all his strength. She screamed and thrashed as her already sore backside was further inflamed. After more than a minute of punishment, he pushed her off of his lap and onto the floor.

"You've lost the privilege of sleeping in a bed," he snarled with fury. "You can sleep on the floor tonight. And don't think about sneaking into that bed — or next time, I'll bring my belt."

The commotion had awakened the whole house. Her brother, his face a mask of horror, stood watching.

"And you!" her father said, and threatened him with the back of his hand. "How dare you fill her head with this garbage. She's a girl! Don't give her books to read. She'll be married in a month or two and that will be the end of it. Don't encourage these outrageous ideas she has! The next book I catch her with goes in the fire and you can pay for it yourself!"

"Oh, honey," Riva heard her mother remonstrate with her father as they went into their room. "You wouldn't use your belt on our little Riva, now would you?"

"She's as contrary as any boy," he grumbled, getting back into bed.

Riva lay on the floor, sobbing, and then spent the next several hours, cold and shivering on the hard floor, bewildered by a world that thought girls weren't worth teaching. She was smart! She was smarter than they were.

Her brother knew it. Why should she be condemned to a life of ignorance and servitude just for being a girl? She clenched her fists and resolved to escape somehow.

The next morning, she got up in the predawn hour, since she wasn't asleep anyway, and went to the outhouse. When she pulled her panties down, she found that she was spotting and panicked that she would be punished again for staining her clothes. She had only just started menstruating and her cycle was still irregular and always a surprise. In terror, she carried them to the pump and pumped water into a bucket to soak them.

It was the beginning of her period that had signaled to her parents that she was now marriageable. Her father had begun making inquiries about potential husbands, however Riva's reputation for disobedience and stubbornness did not win her many suitors. Still she had overheard several conversations with men who had expressed interest in taking her on as a challenge to beat into submission.

With relief, she perceived the stains were removed by the cold water. She hung up the now clean-but-wet panties, then put a pad in a fresh pair and dressed to begin fixing breakfast.

She went back to the pump, got water, set the kettle to boil, and started to make scrambled eggs. After a few minutes, she was joined by her mother, who took over and directed Riva to set the table again and cut bread for everyone.

For breakfast, she was once more allowed to join the family. She ate in silence staring down at her plate. Riva's father spoke to Riva's mother about his plans for the day and after several minutes, he turned to Riva.

"I think I've found an older man who might be willing to take you on," he said. "You haven't made this easy with your saucy mouth and reputation for sass. But he thinks he might be up to the challenge. We'll bring him by this weekend so he can take a look at you."

Then her father gave Riva the look and alarm bells went off in her head.

"Don't screw this up," he said in a low, menacing tone. "You will be on your very best, ladylike behavior, or there will be serious consequences."

She swallowed hard and nodded silently, but clenched her fists under the table. She'd kill herself first! And then let them try to marry off a corpse.

As her father and brother were getting ready to leave for the mine, her brother surreptitiously passed her a slip of paper.

She kept the paper hidden in her fist until they left, then went back to her alcove to read it.

"You were right," it said simply. "I left a bag by my door."

For weeks, she had been pleading with her brother to help her escape. He had resisted, saying that she was exaggerating how bad things were. But, after last night, he was finally willing to admit that she had been right all along. She cast around for what to do with the scrap of paper, but finally decided to eat it so as to leave no trace behind. Then she returned to the dining room to collect and wash the dishes.

Riva's mother, having ascertained that the kitchen would be put to rights, went out to the garden to weed around the vegetables before the day grew too hot. Riva finished with the dishes, wiped off the table and the counters, then, while her mother was out, ran up to her brother's room and snatched the small satchel she found next to the door, carried it out the back door, and snuck away from the house.

When she was out of sight, in a patch of woods by the river, she went through the bag. It contained hand-me-down clothes from when her brother was younger plus a pouch with a handful of silver coins — miners, they were called. She couldn't believe he'd given her so many! It must have been nearly his whole life savings.

Looking around, she determined there was no-one in view, and she changed into the boy's clothes. The breeches felt odd to her. She hadn't been allowed to wear pants since she was a small child. The clothes didn't fit particularly well, but nobody's clothes did, in this poor community. After she was dressed, she pulled her hair back into a ponytail, but tied it lower than usual, like a boy might.

She tried to look at her reflection in the stream, but couldn't see much. Still, she thought it looked okay. It felt right, anyway. Then she started walking.

She was afraid to go through town where she might be recognized, so she headed cross country in the direction of the capital where she hoped she might be able to blend in and find work. But it was going to be a two-day walk.

The first day, she enjoyed nice weather. She bought some vegetables at a farm stand and ate them raw for a kind of dinner. Afterward, she checked her pad and it appeared that her erratic and unreliable period this time was light. Other than some spotting, it had already ended and Riva didn't need to use another one. Afterward, she slept fitfully in the tall grass at the edge of a farmer's field a short distance off the road.

Before morning, however, the weather turned cold and rainy. She didn't have a coat or any rain gear and so she got up and started walking miserably along in the rain.

After several hours, she was shivering and her feet began to feel heavy and numb, like they were coated in mud. And she felt she was getting faint. She could see her arms were becoming flushed. She realized if she didn't get out of the cold and rain soon, she was going to collapse and probably die.

She stumbled on another quarter mile until she reached a crossroads that had a tavern and, as she started to go inside the tavern, she fainted on the doorstep.

Riva awoke in a bed. She was warm. She was dry. She was naked! She started to sit up in a panic, but realized she was too weak.

"Tiny!" someone called. "Tiny! She's awake!"

Riva suddenly realized that she wasn't alone in the bed: there were two other warm, naked girls snuggled up with her under the covers. She blushed to realize what she was touching and feeling there.

Riva looked up and a ... person came into the room. They were dressed as a woman but didn't look like a woman. They ... No. She, Riva decided. She was wearing a dress with long black hair tied back. But she was broad-shouldered, muscular, and had dark beard stubble.

"I'm Tiny," she said, in a husky voice. "And this is Margaret. And those are Emma and Dexy warming you up. And you are lucky to be alive. Hypothermia is nothing to fool around with."

"Where are my clothes? Where is my ..."

"Your money? It's safe. But tell me ... What is a little girl doing out here all by herself dressed as a boy?"

Riva looked down and didn't say anything.

"Hmm. Not even name, rank, and serial number," Tiny said. "That bad, huh, kid?"

"I had to leave home," Riva finally said. "I'm not going to wait around to be married off to some older man who wants to beat me and make me have his babies and do his housework for the rest of my life."

"You tell 'em, kid!" Tiny said. "I saw your butt. You have every right to run if someone treats you like that."

Riva turned bright red and looked down again.

"What's your name?" Tiny asked.

"Riva," she replied.

"Riva?" Tiny said. "But that's a girl's name. I thought you were going to be a boy! You should pick a boy's name."

"I should?" she marveled. "Just pick one?"

"I recommend you pick a name that sounds something like your own so it will be easier for you to remember to react when people call you."

Riva thought for a bit and then said, "How about Revin?"

"Welcome to the Traveler's Inn, Revin," Tiny said, with a flourish. "Now, if you're going to do it, you can't just call yourself a boy — you need to become a boy. Are you prepared to do that?"

"Yes," Revin said. "I am. I will!"

"Now, today, you need to rest while you can, but first," she said, putting her hands on her hips and drawing herself up. "Do you know what this place is?"

"The Traveler's Inn?" Revin asked, puzzled.

"Yes," Tiny said. "I want to make sure you know so you're not surprised. This is a brothel. We are prostitutes. We bring men here who pay us to have sex with them."

Revin's eyes got bigger and bigger as his world was suddenly enlarged. This was not a topic that any book or experience had led him to expect or anticipate. Tiny noted his response and rolled her eyes.

"Yes, that's what I was expecting," Tiny said. "You should rest in bed during the day, but tonight we'll need the bed and room, so be ready to get up then."

"Is there something I can do to help?" Revin asked. "I mean, without … having sex with people?"

"I'm sure we can find something for you to do," Tiny said with a wink, and she patted Revin through the covers. "Sleep now."

Emma and Dexy, having confirmed that Revin was now warm enough, got up and sashayed naked out of the room. After the conversation, Revin was exhausted and promptly went back to sleep.

When he awoke again, it was late in the afternoon. He felt better, so he got up and found that someone had washed and dried his clothes while he was asleep. He gratefully pulled his breeches back on.

He was putting his shirt on when Margaret came in.

"Oh! Nice timing," she said. "There's something I wanted to give you."

She handed Revin a long strip of cloth.

"If you want to present as male, you should learn how to bind your breasts. You're young enough now that they barely show. But before long they may be a problem. Let me show you how it works."

Margaret shamelessly took off her own shirt and showed

Revin how to wrap the long strip round and round to flatten, compress, and ultimately conceal his breasts. Then, she pulled off the strip of cloth and offered it to him. It was still warm. While she watched, he took off his shirt, and wound the strip of cloth around himself. She helped him get it tight enough. Then he put his shirt on and looked in the mirror.

"Now you look a proper boy," she said, tousling his hair. "Though, if you want to get your hair cut while you're here, we can do that for you too."

"Oh, I would like that," he said.

"Let me get Emma. She's good at cutting hair," Margaret said.

She slipped out and a few minutes later Emma returned with a cape and a case with scissors.

"I heard there's a boy that needs a haircut," she said, in a charming alto.

"Thank you," Revin said, coloring up to his ears.

She made him sit in a chair and put the cape around him.

"Are you sure?" she said. "It's a lot of hair. It will take you years to grow it back if you want long hair again!"

"I'm sure," Revin said.

"Are you really sure?"

"I'm really, really sure!"

After waiting for one more moment, she began to cut his hair. He watched as long hanks of his light brown hair fell to the floor. She used a comb with the scissors to give him a brush cut all over. Once she was done, she led him over to the mirror to look.

He looked this way and that, running his fingers through his short hair.

"It's perfect," he said.

She ran her fingers through his soft bristles, grinned, then asked, "Hey! Would you like to learn how to use make-up to make yourself look more masculine?"

"Yeah! That would be really useful!" Revin said.

She took the cape and scissors away and returned with a few cosmetics.

"You're quite fair, Revin," Emma said, running her fingers over his face. "So, we can use a very light touch here and here to create shadows to conceal the roundness of your face. But we don't want to use much because men don't generally wear cosmetics. So it needs to be subtle."

She showed him how to apply just a bit of foundation a little darker than his skin tone to create shadows and to use mascara to thicken and lower his eyebrows.

"Here," she said when she was done, handing the cosmetics to him. "You can keep these. You probably won't need to do this every day. Once people get used to you, they probably won't notice if you stop. But it might be a good idea for when you meet people, to create the right first impression."

As she left, Tiny came back. Revin nearly fell over when he looked at her. She was now freshly shaved with make-up just applied and the difference was nothing short of incredible. This morning, he'd wondered if she were a man or a woman, but now there was no question. She was not just a woman, but a stunning, voluptuous, sexy beauty. Revin, as young as he was, felt a powerful magnetic attraction to her allure.

"Milady," he said, bowing and quoting a romance story he'd read once. "You are charm personified."

"Well, aren't you just a perfect gentleman!" she said, offering him a hand. He pressed it respectfully.

"You said I could help," he said. "What can I do?"

"First let me get you a bite to eat. My treat! Then I'll introduce you to Cook and have you work in the kitchen," she said, leading Revin downstairs. She invited him to order whatever he wanted off the menu. He looked but everything seemed frightfully expensive.

"I think this bowl of soup would be enough," he said.

"Revin!" she scolded him. "You can get *anything* on the menu. You're a growing boy. Get something big! Get a steak! Or a lobster! Or something!"

"Okay! Okay!" he squeaked. "I'll have a steak!"

"How do you want your steak?" the bartender asked.

Revin looked puzzled and Tiny rolled her eyes again.

"Let him have it medium," she told the bartender.

In ten minutes, they set a huge plate with steak and potatoes in front of Revin and he suddenly realized just how much he was starving. He cut a piece of the steak and tried it. It seemed to melt in his mouth and juice threatened to roll down his chin. The potatoes were home-fried and crispy. He stuffed himself and nearly cried because it was so good.

Tiny returned after he'd finished and led him back behind the bar and through doors into the busy kitchen. It was hot and steamy and there was a small army of cooks preparing for the evening.

"Cook!" Tiny called. "Please let Revin work back here tonight."

Cook was a battle-axe of a grey-haired matron. She reminded Revin a little of his mother, but much larger and tougher and fiercer.

"What can you do, boy?" she snapped.

"Well, um, I uh," Revin stammered.

"Dish washing. Good! Go back there."

Revin went in the back where he found a young man with his sleeves rolled up who was washing pots and pans — since the dinner rush hadn't started there weren't really dishes yet.

"Hi," Revin said. "I'm Ri...Revin."

"Butch," he grunted. "Let me show you the ropes."

Butch demonstrated to the Revin the system that heated water for two massive dish washing tubs. Revin was almost too short to work at the tubs, but he rolled his sleeves up and tried to dive in to help.

"Yow!" he yelped when he put his hands in the water and discovered how hot it was.

"Heh! You squeal like a girl," Butch said. "Seriously though, you'll get used to it. But, look, when the rush happens, I'm just gonna have you carry for me, because you'll only get in my way here. But you can try for a while until that happens, to start to get the hang of it."

Revin plunged his hands back into the water and found that he did become acclimated to the temperature. He worked hard to learn how to do a good job. By the time they were done with the pots and pans, they started getting dishes and silverware to wash. Butch started to work faster and faster.

"Okay, Revin," he said. "I want you to run out front and grab the next tub of dishes."

Revin dried his hands and made his way through the kitchen trying to dodge the other people and stay out of the way. He passed to the front side of the tavern and then stopped, spellbound. He was awestruck by a spectacle beyond anything he'd ever imagined. Tiny was on a stage singing and the other girls, Margaret, Emma, Dexy, and the others, were wearing a rainbow of colorful, provocative, and revealing outfits. And the room was packed with loud, drunken men.

The energy of the room was breathtaking. Revin stood mesmerized for a moment while Tiny finished singing and raised her arms to deafening yells, whistles, and applause. She stepped down off the stage which broke the spell that had left Revin frozen in wonder. He started toward the bussing station where he could see a tub of dishes waiting to be collected.

"Hey, boy," a drunken man said, grabbing Revin and running a caressing hand over his backside. "Now this is what I'm lookin' for tonight."

"I'm sorry," Revin said, trying to pull away. "I'm not ... I don't ..."

"Hey!" a shout from Tiny cut through over the top of the noise. "Hands off!"

"Come on," the man said, as he pulled a struggling Revin into his arms, and licked his face. "Just let me have a taste!"

Tiny threw a powerful left jab with her fist, punched him square in the nose, and knocked him out with one blow. He started to drag Revin down with him as he collapsed, but

Tiny caught Revin and put him behind her as she turned and faced down the crowd.

"You all know the rules," she said angrily. "The girls are here to work and the help is off limits."

There was a quiet chorus of "Yes'm" and after a few moments the usual hubbub picked up.

"Mike!" she called. And a big, hulking man came in from the door. "Throw out the garbage." Mike heaved up the unconscious man and carried him out.

"I'm so sorry! I'm so sorry! I'm so sorry!" Revin said, hyperventilating.

"Revin!" she said, putting a hand on his shoulder. "Calm down. It's not your fault. You're a boy now — you don't have to take responsibility for everything anymore."

Revin looked up, surprised, and she winked at him.

"Anyway, this is exactly why I told 'em to have you stay in the back," she continued. "But Butch probably sent you out here because he didn't hear that. Take the dishes on back and then stay back there until I come to get you."

"Yes'm," he said, grabbing the tub and hustling it on back before anything else could go wrong.

By the early hours of the morning, they were washing the last of the dishes when Margaret came back in a loosely-tied bathrobe with her hair in a towel.

"Tiny told me to come get you," she told Revin. Butch nudged him with his elbow and winked at him.

Revin followed her, but she didn't lead him upstairs and, instead, took him to a room on the ground floor that had a huge, steaming, tub of hot water.

"Tiny thought you might like to take a bath," she said. She handed him a towel and a bathrobe, and then excused herself.

Revin stripped off his sodden clothes and climbed into the steaming water. It took him several tries to get himself down into the water because of his bruises, but, eventually, he settled down into the water up to his neck. He found a bottle with shampoo and put some in his hand, but when he went to wash his hair, discovered that he just had bristles and needed only a tiny amount of shampoo. He dunked under a few times to rinse his hair and then laid back in the steamy water.

After a few minutes, Tiny came in.

"Nice, huh?" she said.

"Yes! Thank you! And thank you for everything," Revin said. "I really don't know how to thank you enough."

"All I want is to see you make good on your escape," she said. "But I'm just a little worried because you don't seem to know how to stay out of trouble."

"No, ma'am," Revin said. "That's one thing I don't think I'll ever learn."

"Well, this is no place for you," Tiny said. "You should set your sights higher. Are you headed to the capital?"

"Yes'm," Revin said. "I thought I'd try to look for a job."

"It's very expensive in the capital," Tiny said. "Your money won't last but a few days there. But I might be able to help, a little. I know someone who has a boarding house. Now her regular rooms would still be too expensive, but she has a little attic room that is too low for most folk, so she doesn't normally rent it out. But you're small and young — you could do okay there. Tell her I sent you and she'll probably give you a good price. It's at number 10 Market Street, just down the street from the library. Ask for Bess."

"Got it," Revin said, committing the information to memory. And his ears perked up at the word "library".

"And now, young man, it's time for you to get out of the bath. We have others that want to bathe before bed too! When you're out, go on back upstairs. We've changed the sheets on the bed and you can sleep there again tonight."

Tiny excused herself and Revin reluctantly stood up, climbed out, and, after drying himself off, put on the bathrobe. As he departed the room, Emma was there and took his clothes, soaked from dishwashing and sweat in the hot kitchen, to wash them again.

Revin climbed the stairs in the early hours of the morning, yawning. Dexy showed him into the right room and bid him goodnight as he collapsed into the bed. Before he fell asleep, he considered the unbelievable luxury of having his own room — with a door. Having only a tiny alcove behind a curtain had been miserable, but he hadn't really appreciated how bad it was until he could experience something different.

The following morning, Revin woke up at first light and got out of bed in the silent inn. He found that someone had brought his clean and dry clothes and placed them nicely folded on his satchel. He checked and all of his money was still there. He dressed and grabbed his satchel and opened the door to find all dozen girls waiting there for him. They must have heard him get up and snuck up to the door to surprise him. They gave him a cheer and made him walk through a gauntlet of them patting his shoulders and back and running their hands through his short bristly hair. He started to cry, overcome by his feelings.

"Oh, no you don't," Tiny said with a wink. "Boys don't cry."

He wiped his eyes and tried to master his emotions.

The girls filled in behind him as he went downstairs where a big breakfast had been prepared and laid out on the tables. Revin was afforded a place of honor and everyone sat down cheerfully breaking their fast and chattering happily.

After everyone was done eating, Emma stood and called for attention.

"We heard a certain young man is headed to the capital to seek his fortune. You came in and brought a bit of excitement and sunshine into our lives. And, as you go, we want to do whatever we can to support your adventure, so the girls all did a little collection and we'd like to offer you another dozen miners to help you get started."

She handed Revin a little pouch full of coins and there was a round of applause and cheers. Revin, stunned, stood and tried to speak, but was too choked up and overwhelmed with emotion. He managed to not burst into tears, but could only croak, "Thanks!" They clustered around him and hugged him as he shouldered his satchel and headed out the door. After he crossed the road, he turned back to look one last time at the Traveler's Inn and wave, before he then turned again and pressed on.

He discovered that the Traveler's Inn was actually at the outskirts of the capital. Revin had never been to a city larger than the small town near his home, so he was amazed as he walked into the city and watched it grow up around him. As he approached the city center, he asked someone to direct him to Market Street and found number 10 before noon. He knocked at the door and an elderly woman answered the door.

"I haven't seen your face before," she said. "What's your business here?"

"My name is Revin," he began simply. "Tiny told me to ask for Bess. She said you might have an attic room you could rent me cheap."

"Oh, she did, did she?" Bess replied warmly. "Well, bless her heart. She's a free spirit, that one."

She rustled around behind the door for a minute and then returned with a key.

"Take these stairs and go all the way up, right to the top," she said. "It's going to be dusty in there, mind you. If it will suit you, I can let you have it for three miners a week — you pay for the first two weeks up front."

Revin did a quick calculation and estimated, if he was careful with food, he might be able to manage a month with what he had. That seemed doable. He agreed and climbed flight after flight of stairs to the very top where there was a tiny door so low, he had to duck to get inside.

It was a small room — dusty, like she'd said — but it had a sturdy bed and a chest of drawers. There was a tiny window, which Revin opened and almost brained himself on a bar that was set near the low ceiling in front of the window — which Revin perceived was for hanging up clothes. He was pleased to see there was a gas light, although the mantle was damaged. He left his satchel and, taking seven miners from his precious hoard, he went back downstairs.

"I'll take it," he said, handing her over the six miners, retaining one against other expenses.

"Let me get you some dust cloths and if you bring that cover down you can take it out back and pound it to get the dust off," she said. "Oh! And let me show you the dining room. For the price, you get breakfast and dinner. You're on your own for lunch."

Revin redid his mental accounting and smiled to realize how much more time the free food would give him to get his feet under him.

After cleaning, dusting, replacing the mantle on his light, and beating his bedcover, he locked his — his! — room and skipped down the stairs.

"Can you tell me which way the library is?" he asked.

"You can almost see it from the door. Just turn right and it's down two blocks on the left."

Revin walked down Market Street drinking in the sights and sounds. He was awestruck by the bustle of the big city. The buildings were mostly four or five stories high. They seemed to scrape the sky to Revin who'd never seen anything like this before. He walked on the other side of the street from the library, looking at it from afar, and preparing himself mentally to go in. Girls hadn't been allowed to use the small town library where Revin grew up, so he had only the descriptions his brothers had given to him of what it was like inside.

Apprehensive, he loitered for a few minutes in a pretty little park across the street from the library. He steeled himself, and crossed the street and walked up the steps to the door. He was about to open the door, when the door opened and a woman welcomed him to the library.

"Come in, come in!" she said. Revin was astonished to see that women were allowed in this library. And, if it was to be believed, there were women working in the library!

He began to realize just how isolated and backward the community he'd grown up in really was.

"I've just come to the city," Revin said, nervously. "Could you tell me how the library works?"

"Certainly, sir!" she said, cheerfully. "First you need to get a library card, and if you step over here, we can get you set up."

She put a form in front of Revin and handed him a quill. He very carefully dipped the quill and wrote his (new) name and address. She looked at his form, filled out a library card, and handed it to him.

"You just passed a test," she said.

"Test?" Revin asked.

"Some people come here who can't read who intend to steal books. But you just demonstrated you can both read and write. Very prettily too, I might add. Your penmanship is almost as good as a girl's."

Revin blushed but said nothing.

"I'm Melody, by the way. When you want to check a book out, you present this card. We record the number of the book and the number of your card, and then you can borrow up to two books for two weeks."

"Any books?"

"Any book that's not in the reference section. Or special collections. Those books you can only read here, in the library."

"I can ... just stay in the library? And read?"

"Yes, while we're open. And we're open from 8 bells to 8 bells every day."

Revin rubbed his hands with glee and the librarian was so obviously charmed she leaned over and asked, "What are your favorite books?"

"I ... I ... love all books. But ... If I had to choose ... I guess romance stories."

The librarian looked curiously at this odd young man who liked romances. She shook her head and then came out from behind the counter. "Well, let me show you where they are."

They walked through the library, which was housed in an old mansion that had been donated to the city by a nobleman. The books were spread across a dozen rooms with shelves sometimes tightly packed. She pointed out literature, history, philosophy, nature, and science in non-fiction, then they passed into fiction and she showed him the shelves where the romance stories were. Then she walked back and left him still rubbing his hands with excitement, trying to decide which to take first. He finally selected one, more or less at random, then walked back to history and searched until he was pleased to find the same book he'd been reading when he was so rudely interrupted, and took that one to finish.

He found an open seat in the reading room and sat down with his books. He took a deep breath, opened the first page, and began to read. The room was bright, with huge floor-to-ceiling windows that let in plenty of light. It was such a pleasure to read with good light, rather than hiding in the alcove with a tiny lamp trying to read in the dark.

As he read, he took occasional breaks to look around at the other patrons and watch the activity in the library. There was a constant flow of people in and out. Some people came to read. Many just checked out a book and carried it away. Revin saw that most patrons came and looked at the shelf labeled for new books.

In the corner, he noticed an older, portly man who had a young assistant with him. He had several stacks of books around him and was constantly consulting the books and then writing something. He would periodically dispatch the assistant to go find books from the reference section, though the fellow didn't seem to know what he was doing half the time which made the old man gesticulate angrily, though quietly.

Revin was almost ready to check out, when he heard the two librarians talking quietly to each other.

"We're so far behind on re-shelving," Melody said. "Since Robert left, we keep getting farther and farther behind."

"I guess we'll need to advertise for someone, but I don't know who we'll get. It's so hard to find anyone."

Revin popped out of his seat and hurried over, breathlessly.

"Excuse me," he said. "I couldn't help overhearing, but do you need someone to help re-shelve books?"

"It's the boy who likes romance!" Melody said.

"We do. But we can't afford to pay very much," the second librarian said. "Would you like to try? If you're willing, let's do this: we'll pay you two copper bits a day. At first, until you know your way around, it will probably take you most of the day. But in a couple of weeks, you'll probably be able to do it in just a few hours. And then we can see whether we have more work for you. Or you can find another job."

"I'll do it!" Revin said. "Can I start right now?"

Revin was swimming in happiness. Although it wouldn't provide enough money to pay for his room and board, it would extend his time a lot. And he would be working with books!

Melody showed him to the sorting room, where returned books were organized onto carts. She explained the indexing system and left him to work. Revin worked diligently and, by the end of the day, he had re-shelved half of the books and was well on his way to learning his way around.

As he left the library, he saw something move overhead and looked up to see a huge gray airship just above the buildings headed for the aerodrome, glowing blue towlines radiating outward. He had only ever seen airships at a great distance and he was floored by the immense scale of the one passing overhead. He was close enough to read the name, *Madeline,* painted on the fuselage. He imagined someday traveling to other islands and other cities. But he acknowledged that even this small city was a huge adventure over his previous life. And he was in no particular hurry to move beyond this new, exciting phase of his life.

The next morning, he was there promptly at 8 bells and found that now there were still the left-over books from the day before, plus even more books to re-shelve than there had been the previous day. He worked hard and, by mid afternoon, was caught up and spent a few glorious hours just reading. He checked out his books before dinner time and carried them home.

After dinner in the boardinghouse, he carried his prizes upstairs, lit the gas light, and laid on his belly to read with good illumination. Revin stretched luxuriously and felt a huge grin spread over his face as he enjoyed his new-found freedom. His own room! Behind a locked door! Light! Books!

The next day, Revin arrived and made short work of the re-shelving. In just a couple of hours, he returned to the front desk to speak with Melody.

"All done," Revin said. "Is there anything else I can do?"

"What?" Melody said. "How did you re-shelve everything so fast?"

"I just know where everything is now, so it's easy."

"You know where everything is, do you?"

"Yes'm?"

"Where would 'H-Tso-1250' go?"

"Um ..." Revin said, closing his eyes. "Well, that's going to be fiction — historical fiction — that's that room in the back with the green wallpaper. And the Ts are in the second bookcase to the right when you go in. And 1250 is going to be near the ... middle of the third shelf from the top."

"You've got to be kidding me!" Melody said.

She let Revin lead her to the back room, which did have green wallpaper, though she'd never noticed it before. She turned to the right, found the second bookcase, counted down to the third shelf, looked in the middle — and put her finger on the book.

"Wow! You're the real deal! What an incredible memory! I've never seen anyone who could do that!"

Revin looked away shyly, but with a grin.

"I'll speak with the other librarian and see if we can't find something else for you to do."

Revin looked up hopefully and smiled.

While he waited, Revin pulled the book off the shelf, took it to the reading room, and began to read. But he was disturbed by the portly man who was arguing with his assistant again. They were quiet, but Revin couldn't help overhearing. The man had asked for a book by Tukey but the assistant insisted it wasn't there. Revin thought for a moment, wondered if the assistant had been looking for "Tookey," and slipped into the reference section. He found the correct book, pulled it off the shelf, and took it to the man.

"I'm sorry, but was this the book you needed?"

"Why, yes!" the man said. "Thank you!"

Revin returned to his seat to continue reading, but heard the portly man send the assistant back for bringing the wrong year of an archive.

"No, no. We need the year Harway invaded Ironton!"

"Wasn't that 327?" the hapless fellow said.

The portly man looked over his glasses at the man disdainfully.

"328?"

"It was 227," Revin said.

"There! There! See? Everyone knows that!" the man berated his assistant, who looked daggers at Revin. Then the assistant looked down at his employer.

"You know what? I'm done with it. And with you! I don't need this harassment! I quit!" the assistant said, stalking off and departing the library.

Revin, relieved that the noise was over, went back to reading his book for a few minutes.

"Pardon me," said the portly man, who'd come over to Revin's table. "I can't help but notice that you've got a good memory for books and dates."

"Oh, not really," Revin said, blushing. "I was just reading a history of Harway and happened to remember that."

"What year did Harway invade Woodseer?"

"Um ... 242?"

"When did King Benjamin the First abdicate?"

"That was Benjamin the Second," Revin replied. "In — What was it? — 197? No! 199!"

"You are amazing!" he said, marveling. "I'm Professor Dirge! Can I hire you to be my assistant?"

"Well, but I just started working at the library!" Revin said.

"I can pay you more than they can," he countered.

"How much more?"

"I'll pay you three miners a week."

"Hmm," Revin mused. "It's better, but at that pay, I'll still need to keep working for the library."

"I can also teach you to pass the exam to practice law."

"Really?" Revin said, now genuinely interested. "Would it be okay for me to do my re-shelving first and then assist you when I'm done?"

"It's a deal," Professor Dirge said, holding out his hand. Revin, unused to male custom, hesitated a moment, but then shook hands with Professor Dirge, who promptly gave him a list of books to fetch.

Revin headed off into the reference section and picked up book after book, then hustled back toward Professor Dirge's table. He was just emerging from the reference section when a powerful arm snaked out and grabbed his wrist.

"I've got you now, you little minx! I just knew I'd find you here," Riva's father crowed, triumphantly. "You're coming back right now. I've got a man who paid good money for you."

Revin was overwhelmed with terror and tried to pull away. Riva's father backhanded him across the face, knocking him stunned to the ground and scattering the books across the floor.

"I'm not ... I won't!" Revin sputtered.

Riva's father drew back his arm again when Professor Dirge caught hold of it. By now a small crowd of people had assembled and were watching in rapt fascination.

"Pardon me, sir, but you seem to be assaulting my Research Assistant Revin," he said.

"What are you talking about! That's my daughter Riva!"

"I'm not!" Revin exclaimed, wiping blood from his mouth. "I've never seen this man before!"

"You are mistaken, sir," Professor Dirge said. "Revin has been my Research Assistant for the better part of a year."

"I ain't givin' that money back! You can't steal my property!"

"Sir, I am a lawyer and Revin is my law student," Professor Dirge said, in a low and menacing tone. "If you don't desist in your reckless slander and unwarranted attacks, the constabulary will take you into custody and I will sue you for defamation and take every penny you own."

As if by magic, two city guards were led in from the street by Melody. She'd run out to seek them when the altercation began. They entered the library and approached the circle of onlookers. Riva's father, with a wild look of fury mixed with fear, suddenly backed away, then turned, pushed through everyone, and left the library, muttering curses under his breath.

One of the librarians brought Revin a cool compress for his face as the crowd dispersed and the library returned to normal. Revin thanked her and gingerly pressed his swollen lip with the wet cloth.

"I'll bring these books in just a moment, Professor," he said, still shaky from the trauma.

"Take your time, young Revin," he said, and returned to the table where he worked.

After a few moments, Revin collected the books, struggled to his feet, and carried them over to Professor Dirge.

"Thank you, Professor," he said. "I thought I was ... a dead man."

"I only spoke the truth: I said you'd been with me for the better part of a year," Professor Dirge confided. "And one day working with you has been better than the whole year I spent with that dolt I had before.

"You are simply irreplaceable as an assistant, my boy," the Professor continued, with a sly glance. "With you, I've still got a shot at getting this book finished on time. Here! Can you write too? Read this book for me and try to draft a concise summary of the 2nd-century relationship between Harway and Ironton."

"Yes, Professor," Revin said, taking up the book with relish.

DEVISHIRE!

PREVIEW

DEVISHIRE!

REVIN PACED WITH ANXIETY. Lidja had been closeted with the Queen for nearly forty minutes with Revin enjoined from entering. Finally, the door opened and they emerged. They looked at Revin, then looked at each other and smirked.

"Agreed," they said, shaking hands.

Revin did not like the sound of this at all.

"What did you talk about?" Revin pressed Lidja as they walked to the stables.

"Oh, stuff," Lidja said, with a little bounce in her step. "Girl stuff."

"You can tell me, can't you?" Revin persisted.

"You're not a girl, are you?" Lidja asked, archly.

Revin scowled and Lidja hugged him.

"Stop worrying!" she laughed. "She just wanted to make sure that we can talk directly so that you don't get caught between the two of us."

Revin could already tell that balancing his responsibilities among Lidja, Momo, and his duty was going to require a delicate touch and that he was in way over his head.

When they arrived in the stables, they headed directly to Bastard's stall. He was a large, black, warmblood stallion and was well named. Revin stood back when she opened the door to muck it out as she was the only one he would suffer to come so close. But first, before she did anything, she snuggled up against Bastard's chest so he could put his head over her shoulder and she could whisper whatever sweet nothings she said to him to calm him down.

After she'd mucked out his stall and made sure he had plenty of fodder and that his water was fresh, they walked back to Revin's quarters, which he was currently sharing with Lidja. They had just begun discussing the idea of purchasing a little house in the country that would be suitable for having a horse — maybe a few horses. And a garden.

They had just arrived back at Revin's quarters when he heard the sounds of a struggle coming from the Queen's adjoining chamber.

"Run for guards," he told Lidja. He drew his sword and, taking a deep breath, he charged into her chambers. The room was empty, but he heard strange sounds coming from her dressing room. He leapt into the room to find a figure wearing a dark cloak kneeling on Momo's back and tying her hands behind her back. She was already gagged.

"Unhand her!" Revin said, lunging at the assailant. The figure sprang back and drew a knife. Revin grinned and stood *en garde.* Suddenly they reversed the knife, drew back their arm, and threw it in one fluid motion. Before he realized he was reacting, Revin had instinctively twitched his sword and knocked the knife off its trajectory. But his focus was distracted for a moment and, when he looked back, the assailant had darted away and out the other door of the dressing room. Revin gave chase only in time to see them slip out onto the balcony. Hearing Momo's infuriated noises, Revin returned to the dressing room, sheathed his sword, and found the knife the attacker had thrown. He had just turned to cut her bonds when the door popped open and the King entered the Queen's dressing room to find Revin holding a knife and standing over the Queen, who was on the floor, bound and gagged, her eyes wild with rage. "Please don't get the wrong idea, Your Majesty!" Revin pleaded.

The King grinned at Revin and, once again, for just a moment, he recognized his friend, before the facade of the King returned. As guards came running in, he called, "You two: Assist the Chief of Staff with the Queen. You others: The assailant went out the window!"

The guards sprinted to the window and Revin heard them yelling to guards patrolling in the garden.

"I think he got away, Your Majesty," one said

Revin, assisted by the guards, helped Momo to her feet as she spat out the gag. She angrily shook off their hands. Revin stood back respectfully while she tried to contain her anger. After a moment, she approached and put a hand on his arm.

"Thank you, my hero," she said, quietly.

Revin put his hand on hers and smiled.

"But where were your guards?" Revin asked.

"I don't know," Momo said. "I think they got called away."

Revin went to guards who had secured the door to the balcony and were returning.

"Who called you away?"

"It was Terrier, Sir Revin."

"Terrier?" Revin said, horror-struck.

At this moment, Terrier appeared in the doorway. He took one look and then turned and ran.

"Seize him!" cried the King. The guards spun and sprinted after him.

ABOUT THE AUTHOR

Steven D. Brewer has been a fan of science fiction and fantasy stories for as long as he can remember. He still remembers getting scolded for not reading chapter books in fourth grade because he was avidly consuming *The Hobbit* late at night, by flashlight under his covers. And he probably got his copy from his older brother and most important mentor.

Steven currently teaches scientific writing at the University of Massachusetts Amherst. He lives in Amherst, Massachusetts with his extended family.

ALSO BY THE AUTHOR

BETTER ANGELS: TOUR DE FORCE
FROM THE TRUCK STOP AT THE CENTER OF THE GALAXY

by Steven D. Brewer

The Better Angels. Entertainment. Music and Dancing. And Rescues!

Available from Water Dragon Publishing in
hardcover, trade paperback, and digital editions
waterdragonpublishing.com

YOU MIGHT ALSO ENJOY

SMASH THE WORLD'S SHELL
by Daniel Fliederbaum

A fractured world. An impossible friendship.

SNAIL'S PACE
by Susan McDonough-Wachtman

Orphaned and penniless in Hong Kong in 1884 — what's a young gentlewoman to do?

WAR MAGE
by L.A. Jacob

In war here will be dragons.